ABOVE THE ASHES

ABOVE THE ASHES

SURVIVORS OF THE SMOKE

K.M. LISTER

Cover design and interior illustration by Rena Violet (coversbyviolet.com)

Edited by Cianne McKinnon (ciannemckinnon.com) and Samantha Pico (thegotheditor.com)

Proofreading by Samantha Pico (thegotheditor.com) and Susan Doumont

Character art by @amarinartist

ISBN: 979-8-9881560-4-8 (paperback), 979-8-9881560-5-5 (hardcover), 979-8-9881560-3-1 (ebook)

Library of Congress Control Number: 2025923038

For those who hide a part of themselves from others.
Remember, you are loved.
Every side, every inch—each little nook and cranny. All loved.

Author's Note

This may seem like a simple story. A typical post-apocalyptic tale where resources are low, long travel days are common, and hope seems like a thing of the past.

However, each word within *Above the Ashes*, book one of the *Survivors of the Smoke* series, is a small piece of silk woven into a spiderweb of something larger. This is not just a story of survival. It's a story of fate . . . a story of learning to love yourself, accept your past, and understand the power of community.

The bare bones idea sprouted from my deep-rooted admiration for post-apocalyptic media like *Fallout*, *I Am Legend*, *The Book of Eli*, and *The Stand*, and intertwined with two of my favorite things: epic fantasy and romance. As I wrote each new draft of this first book and planned for the others, I realized this story and these characters transformed into a mirror, reflecting pieces of myself as I navigated some of my hardest moments and entered a new chapter of my life.

<u>There are triggering topics throughout this story readers should be aware of including:</u> *gore, guns, torture, cannibalism, starvation, masturbation, mentions of sexual assault and rape, threats of sexual assault and rape, mentions of child abuse, and suicidal ideation.*

If you or anyone you know is struggling with depression, anxiety, thoughts of suicide, sexual abuse, domestic violence, or eating disorders, there are helplines available all over the world. You can find a helpline in your country at **<u>www.findahelpline.com.</u>**

Remember, you are not alone. Things will get better.

K.M.

Glossary

CHARACTERS

Eleri Fos: [*El-er-ee Fahs*] The half–Fae, half–Witch Princess of The Underworld, trapped in The Upperworld after The Darkest Day.

Kai Eogeum: [*Kai Oh-gum*] The leader of The Pack whose mission it is to eradicate The Upperworld of threats and help those in need.

Rina Yarrow: [*Ree-nuh Yar-oh*] A member of The Pack who devotes her life to The Trinity.

Jaycen Ryuk: [*Jay-sin Ree-ook*] A member of The Pack who strives to protect Kai.

The Siren: An infamous figure known for raping and killing innocent people and feeding them to The Wake.

ENTITIES

The Pack: The name given to Kai, Rina, and Jaycen who are known to help those in need in The Upperworld.

The Wake: A large faction of cannibals that emerged after The Darkest Day. Known for wreaking havoc across The Upperworld, mainly in The East.

The Trinity: The name given to the three deities who watch over the realms. Consists of The Mother, The Daughter, and The Son.

THE MOTHER: THE GODDESS OF ALL. CREATED THE SON AND THE DAUGHTER.

THE DAUGHTER: THE GODDESS OF THE UNDERWORLD.

THE SON: THE GOD OF THE UPPERWORLD.

PLACES

THE UPPERWORLD: THE REALM CREATED BY THE SON. ALSO REFERRED TO AS "ABOVE."

THE UNDERWORLD: THE REALM CREATED BY THE DAUGHTER. ALSO REFERRED TO AS "BENEATH."

WESTERN VALE: THE WESTERN REGION OF THE UPPERWORLD. KNOWN FOR ITS SMALL TOWNS, THREE LAKES, VALLEY-LIKE TERRAIN, AND HILLS. ALSO REFERRED TO AS "THE VALE" OR SIMPLY "THE WEST."

EASTERN PLAINS: THE EASTERN REGION OF THE UPPERWORLD. KNOWN FOR ITS GRASSY PLAINS, INDUSTRIALIZED TECHNOLOGY, AND THE UPPER PALACE. ALSO REFERRED TO AS "THE EAST."

SOUTHERN COAST: THE SOUTHERN REGION OF THE UPPERWORLD. KNOWN FOR ITS SEA.

NORTHERN ICECAP: THE NORTHERN REGION OF THE UPPERWORLD. KNOWN FOR ITS GLACIERS.

ARKALA: A SMALL SETTLEMENT RECENTLY BUILT ON THE OUTSKIRTS OF THE WASTELAND.

MOUNTMEND: A LARGE TOWN OVERTAKEN BY THE WAKE AFTER THE DARKEST DAY.

THE WASTELAND: THE STRETCH OF DESERT THAT REPLACED THE EASTERN PLAINS AFTER THE DARKEST DAY.

TERMINOLOGY

THE DARKEST DAY: THE NAME REFERRING TO THE DAY THE CURSE WAS CAST.

<u>**Sun Death:**</u> A deadly disease that emerged after The Darkest Day. Symptoms include rashes, scabs, foaming at the mouth, and delirium.

<u>**The Pathway:**</u> A cave-like arch tucked in the forest between the Western Vale and the Eastern Plains. The only known entrance to The Underworld.

<u>**The Purge:**</u> The confiscation of all guns in The Upperworld. Ordered by the king.

<u>**Under-dweller:**</u> A name Upperworld citizens call those in The Underworld.

<u>**Upper-dweller:**</u> A name Underworld citizens call those in The Upperworld.

<u>**The Under War:**</u> A civil war led by supporters of the last Witch Queen more than five-hundred years ago in an effort to regain the Witches' power and rule over The Underworld after the Fae took over. Lasted four-hundred years.

THE UPPER
WELCOME TO ARKALA
THE PATHWAY

WORLD
MOURTMERD
UPPER PALACE

PROLOGUE

MANIC, CRAZED LAUGHTER ECHOED against his skull, scraping down the bone and burrowing into the very fragments of his mind. The man—wrinkled and withered—twitched at the feeling. It was incessant, brutal in its lingering lilt.

Foreign yet recognizable.

His yet not.

Yes . . . The voice—that all-consuming voice—slithered against his very being. There was no reprieve, no escape from its sinister sneer. *Yes.*

In the middle of the study—grand, with its once-white walls and dull jade floors—sat a smoking, sizzling cauldron. Its scuffed black iron stood stark against its surroundings, as if it were from another time. Pops and crackles bounced off the abandoned bookshelves tucked away in the corner, and with each passing second, sweat dripped from his temple and plopped into the concoction.

"Yes . . ." He sighed. Pleasure and pain twisted around the word, making his ragged breaths more pronounced before they contorted into that sickening cackle. "It's time."

Shifting his gaze from the shimmering liquid—liquid as dark as the night sky sprinkled with starlight—to the woman in the corner, he pinned her in place with a grin. Chained to the wall, she stayed silent and observant. Stillness surrounded her. Black eyes bore into him, and her near-translucent skin tightened around her jaw as she pressed her lips together.

Five strides, and he was upon her, gazing down at her hunched-over figure. His leer focused on her . . . could *only* focus on her as she lifted her head to lock eyes with his own. A beat passed between them. No one moved. No one dared to talk. Even if he wanted to, he couldn't.

Do it.

The man's eyes glided down the expanse of the woman's face slowly, tracing the bulging veins pumping heavily in her neck. They continued their path and trailed over her black, threadbare garments before stopping at the hem of her bell-like sleeves.

There, awaiting his next move, hung her chained forearms. Bare for him. Just as promised. Gripping harshly at the woman's wrist, he yanked her right arm up toward him until the steel pulled taut.

A long sniff along the blue and purple veins beneath her skin sent a shiver across his scalp. "Perfect."

Then he struck. His head lurched forward, and his teeth sank into her thin flesh. Pebbles of blood pooled across his tongue before he applied more pressure. Iron bloomed over his taste buds as he tore his teeth away and harshly ripped open her skin, leaving a gaping gash. Gore dripped down his chin as he sauntered back toward the cauldron and spat into the liquid.

That laughter began again—echoing . . . searing . . . incessant.

Without hesitation, he repeated the process on his own arm. His teeth dug into his skin, breaking the barrier between them and his muscle. Where pain should have erupted, none was felt. He was numb, immune to the silent scream waiting at the base of his throat, wanting to break free.

Once the blood dripped into the cauldron, black opaque smoke—glittering and enthralling—slammed out of its opening and barreled through the tiled roof.

Black swallowed the clear blue sky as it hovered above the man and the chained woman. A slow snicker quickly transformed into a crazed cackle as he beheld what he created. Then, as if his laughter sent a silent order to the smoke above, it darted west. Toward its intended target.

That manic laughter rose and rose until it was all he could hear, all he could concentrate on. Echoing against his skull . . . echoing against his walls.

"It's done."

I

ELERI

FIVE YEARS LATER

SOOT AND SAND AND shit hit Eleri Fos's face.

The dry, hot wind sliced through her cracked lips, while deeper chasms tore open and blood burst across her gums. Blood, the only thing she'd tasted in two days. Sharp, metallic, bitter.

Eleri shuddered, her stomach knotting. Hating the way her tongue lapped at it as if it were drops of water, she sighed and briefly closed her eyes. From here—behind the darkness of her eyelids—she could pretend it was.

A single breath passed before her lashes fluttered open. Grunting, Eleri winced as the brightness pressed down around her and her feet moved once more. The empty canteen swaying against her hip with each step mocked her, berated her. She hadn't calculated her water rations for this journey correctly.

"Fucking impatient fool," Eleri admonished herself, harshly swiping a bead of sweat from her cheekbone.

She could've waited to find a corpse, snatched up another vessel to fill before leaving the Western Vale when the time was right. However, she'd been twitchy—fingers fidgeting and stomach fluttering—ready to leave when she overheard that couple mention the catacombs.

Momentum overtook her then, eager to begin her journey. For the first time in five years, a tendril of elation blossomed within her chest. She was heading home.

As Eleri swallowed around nothing but beads of blood, a particularly strong gust nudged her to the side, whipping her hair free from her hood and clawing at the tattered clothes covering every inch of her body despite the unforgiving heat.

Coolness brushed against the sweat forming along her temple where the wind met her skin. Giving herself a moment to relish the feel of it, Eleri relaxed her shoulders and inhaled. Quickly, though, she pulled her hood back over her head and ducked.

That was all she could afford. Sun Death always lurked. Every second without proper cover gave the deadly illness an opportunity to dig its claws into her skin and refuse to let go. But the fear of expiring from the very thing she'd craved when she was Beneath was nothing compared to the fear she had of herself.

Eleri gnawed on her lip with furrowed brows, her cheeks stinging as dust struck the only skin exposed underneath her layers. Nothing but her face was visible. It was better that way—less temptation, fewer risks.

The wide plank road—lined with loose, deteriorating wood laid out in perfect rows—creaked beneath her boots as she faltered from the thought. The sound ricocheted around her, making her flinch as a sharp inhale snagged within her throat and coughs heaved out of her lungs.

Rot abused her senses. The arid winds that rarely seemed to die swirled around her, wrapping her in the stench. A corpse was nearby. She inhaled through her mouth, hoping to relieve herself of the smell, but a gag stopped her mid-breath. She could taste it—the rot of whatever body she was near. It was pungent—musky and sickening.

Pulling the fabric of her cloak over her mouth, Eleri sucked in a shallow breath. The smell was still present but manageable. She turned her head to the side, looking for the source of the stench. All she could see were the dilapidated cars some Upperworld residents had once used for travel—stripped for parts, metal doors missing, and seats ripped out. Broken glass and a handful of bullet casings littered the ground as well, glinting against the sun.

If only she had a gun. If only she knew how to handle one. She'd feel less exposed, less vulnerable. But guns—so rare after The Purge that happened here eleven years ago—drew attention. And that was something she never wanted. It was safer in the shadows, safer around corners.

If I wanted to kill someone, she couldn't help but think, *I wouldn't even need a weapon.*

A slight stirring in her gut—the small, fiery beast inside that begged to be released—perked up at the thought, but Eleri was quicker than it. Pushing it down, she banished the nuisance with a silent growl as she walked.

With each step she took, the heat of the hazy sun suffocated her, her clothes sticking to her thin frame, her morbid inner voice dying on a choked breath. No sounds pierced her keen ears. No birds chirped as they flew by, nor did animals' hooves skid across the brush, kicking up gravel from the roadside. Nobody and nothing were around to hear at all.

So different from her home.

Home.

A decayed crack in the wooden planks caught the side of Eleri's boot. She stumbled, her ankle rolling unnaturally underneath her weight. As she toppled forward, a dull pinch traveled up her shin before settling against her knee where her ligaments and bone met. Her worn leather gloves shot out, and her hands collided with the firm wood.

Her vision blurred. Her pounding, day-old headache prodded sharply against her skull. The pain made her vision go black.

"Water." Eleri blinked rapidly and forced down a swallow despite the gritty protest of her throat.

I need water.

The unbidden urge to stay where she was—on her hands and knees in the middle of this endless nightmare of a road and let the sun cook her dry—pushed fiercely at her aching limbs. She felt sluggish, as if her body refused to move another inch.

No.

If she was to make it past The Wasteland and the Upper Palace, she needed to find water, food—so*mething* to fuel her energy—and soon. She had to escape this desolate hellhole—a remnant of The Darkest Day, when lethal smoke had ravaged the lands, obliterating all in its wake. That deadly smoke had changed the world irrevocably and had cost Eleri, the Princess of The Underworld, everything.

Eleri's eyes quivered. A familiar burn behind her lashes betrayed her will and presented itself mockingly as her heart clenched, reaching for something that didn't exist anymore. No longer was she that princess. And no longer did The Underworld, as she remembered it, exist.

She wasn't foolish enough to hope that there would be any survivors Beneath. She had yet to come across anyone who emerged alive from the rubble that had cut her off from her home. That hope she once felt—that naïve faith she'd tried to hold on to—had vanished long ago. Her home was equally desolate. It *had* to be, for when she closed her eyes and reached out to her kin, she felt nothing.

But if she could make it down there, she could at least get closure under the ever-present starry night sky that shimmered no matter the time of day. She would be alone, but she'd been alone for the last five years. That wouldn't make a difference.

Leaning back on her heels, she rubbed her thumb across the crystal tucked into the inner pocket of her cloak. It was the last thing she had from her old life—a life where fear didn't grip at her chest endlessly and isolation didn't exist. The things she'd seen, the things she'd turned her back on just to survive . . .

"In through your nose," she croaked, a cough catching in her throat. Dust clung to her esophagus and coated her teeth. Trying again, she brushed her tongue across her canines and wet her lips before the chant flowed freely, like a comforting old friend. "In through your nose. Out through your mouth."

Another burst of iron coated her taste buds, her lips splitting with each syllable. She couldn't help the way her muscles relaxed as she repeated the words and imagined her home. The Underworld, filled with a feeling so fulfilling, a feeling that was indescribable and unimaginable until one finally experienced it. The Underworld, filled with *magic*. Closing her eyes for just a second, Eleri experienced its beauty, and her heart clenched.

A burst of steam shattered the air around her, and she recoiled. Her muscles tensed, and her eyes snapped open—suddenly pulled from the false tranquility of The Underworld and thrust back into the present, into The Upperworld.

A faint chugging bounced off the dead trees in the distance and thrummed against her eardrums, shooting white-hot dread through her muscles. No one from this realm could have heard the sound due to its distance, a sound she last heard on The Darkest Day. A steam car.

Her body turned taut; her muscles twitched, and her tendons tightened.

A steam car meant people. And people meant danger.

Fight or flight . . . or simply give up . . .

Swiftly, she peeled herself off the ground and quickly stood, spinning toward the line of dead, charred trees to the left of the road.

Flight, it was. Flight, it always was.

Eleri's need to survive—that instinct simmering below the surface, no matter how tired or thirsty or hungry she was—kicked in once again. As fast as she could, she pumped her arms and forced her legs to move, running toward cover.

I can't be caught. I can't—

As if the Gods she refused to believe in reveled in her weakened state and pathetic struggle, her boot snagged on something again just as she passed the toppled over wooden poles with thick wires lining the road. Whatever she hit caved inward on contact. Stumbling, she fell forward and hit the hard black dirt. Sticks and thorns sliced against her leather-gloved palms. Her head collided with a decaying log. Gravel flew, and that same pungent smell swirled around her.

Dazed, Eleri blinked rapidly. Her blurred vision swam, and her muscles felt buoyant as she tried to get her bearings. With another slow blink, she brushed the tender spot with her fingertips.

"Fuck." A sharp hiss rushed past Eleri's clenched teeth as she searched for any sign of blood.

None. Thank Gods.

Get up! Get up!

Ignoring that frantic inner voice—that will to survive for just a breath—Eleri turned and saw what she knew to be there. Her throat closed, cutting off the air in her lungs.

The corpse. It was yellow and green, rotting in the heat of the sun. The smell was revolting; it stung her nostrils. Bile rose into the back of her throat. Water welled along her lash line as she stared at a small torso—dismembered from the rest of its body except for the head—lying in the thorny thicket. Deep, gaping craters where their eyes should've been. Mouth opened wide in terror. Teeth missing.

They couldn't have been older than ten. *Ten.* They were only a child. A child whose thread of life had been cut too soon. A child who never stood a chance against the threats of this world. Too young to know how to constantly keep their guard up. Too young to know not to trust anyone. Too young to keep their vulnerabilities hidden—vulnerabilities that would inevitably lead to an unspeakable death.

Was it cannibals? Killers? Or something worse?

The thought churned Eleri's stomach, a heavy knot weighing down her chest and sinking deep into her gut. Whoever they were was no more. Wasted away under the heat of the sun until they were nothing but bones a scavenger would soon enough seize for trade.

Her heart pounded against her eardrums as she stared at the body, unable to rip her gaze away. This poor, unfortunate child was simply a reminder that it was safer to hide, to be alone. The walls she'd carefully built for herself over the years stood securely around her most vulnerable parts. They were necessary to keep going—to survive.

But each day, she seemed to add another brick. One for the man who'd assaulted another behind a pile of trash. One for the woman who'd grasped at her bleeding neck after a stranger slashed it open while robbing her of her flask. And one for this child, their dismembered body branded into it, so she would never forget.

The deep, frantic thumps of her heart drummed harshly against her skull as she secured the newest addition to her barrier. Occasionally, it skipped a beat, shuddering as several maggots crawled from the gashes across the child's skin.

Another beat chased her own—a faint buzz against her eardrum. The sensation coursed through her, taking root in the deepest part of her bones. A focused beat. Steady in its approach. One more joined the cacophony inside her head. Determined. And another. Calm. Three different beats collided, unknowingly racing to be in sync with hers—

Eleri's head snapped to the side. What had once been too far to see over the horizon was a patched-together steam car of different shades and scraps of metal barreling down the road in the distance.

Get up!

Clawing at the dead earth beneath her, she flung her body away from the horror not even a foot away . . . the horror that revealed the state of this world—its sanity ripped from its roots completely, leaving only savages to roam these lands.

Thump. Thump. Her heart raced, spiking just as the others' did the same, while their vehicle darted down the road. All their heartbeats . . . they sounded like an ominous death drum echoing in her ears.

The muscles in Eleri's body tensed once more, and with a fierce burst of adrenaline, she scrambled to her knees. Digging her palms into the ground, she dragged one limb in front of the other and breached the line of burnt bark toward safety.

No, not safety.

Safety was a luxury this world didn't offer. Less dangerous. That was all she sought.

She didn't stop until the hot ground gave way to cool soil. Shade from the thick canopy of bare black branches overhead cooled the earth beneath it. Even then, she scooted farther into the forest toward a leafless bush off to the side.

The vibration in her eardrums was a constant drone as the three passengers moved closer toward their prey—toward her. It was a dull drumming sensation, one she'd learned to ignore all her life, pushing it to the back of her mind until she forgot it was even there.

Eleri focused on that feeling, though. She tracked the three distinct heartbeats, urging herself not to fall into complacency, not to lose each spike. Focusing. *Surviving.*

Through the bush's spiny branches, Eleri's gaze snagged on green weeds—green with life and as rare as the sounds Eleri missed so desperately. They protruded upward between the clumps of hardened, fractured soil.

"Water."

The word slipped free like a near-silent prayer.

Crawling around the bush toward the scattered blades of grass, Eleri kept an eye out for a water source. A puddle or creek perhaps. Nothing stood out to her, but she knew water was near. Life was growing here—life so rare it felt wrong to be this close.

Careful not to touch the tiny patches of plants, Eleri followed them, as if they were a trail of breadcrumbs leading her toward salvation. Finally, she spotted a slow trickle of water over several soot-covered rocks disappearing into a hole in the ground.

It was barely anything—barely enough to lick from the rock's surface—but Eleri lunged at it, desperately lapping up any drops she could.

The edges of her vision blackened slightly from the movement, oozing into her line of sight like a sinister trail of smoke as she licked and licked at the small stream. Her temples throbbed—a sharp knife battering against her skull. She must've hit her head hard.

That didn't matter. Not then. Not when the cool caress of water glided across her tongue and down her throat—

"Well, well, well . . ." a baritone voice drawled.

Her body froze, and a shudder swept beneath her skin.

Stupid, stupid girl. The dark beast in the back of her mind growled.

How could she have let the steady vibrations caressing her eardrums get lost in the frenzy of her thirst? The three new heartbeats became deafening drones after she'd focused once more, thudding harshly against her skull.

I fucked up.

Eleri's eyes stayed trained on the pathetic excuse for a stream for a moment longer before she held her breath and slowly turned her head toward the source.

A tall, lean man dressed in black and brown layers towered over her crouched body. His eyes were the only visible feature, almond-shaped and dark. A tattered bandana covered the lower half of his face. A wide-brimmed hat atop his jet-black hair cast a sliver of shadow across his brows. Two others, clad similarly, stood behind him. "What do we have here?"

Cannibals, killers, or worse?

2

KAI

KAI EOGEUM STARED AT the cloaked figure cowering below him. He had just caught the tail end of the tattered cloth disappearing into the dead treeline when he noticed her.

It had to be her.

The vile woman they'd trailed for months after hearing terrified whispers and horror stories from those in the Western Vale. Known for luring wandering men and women into her encampments and raping them, the woman known as The Siren would then kill and dismember her victims before offering the pieces to The Wake.

It had *to be her.*

"This can't be her . . ." Rina—his companion to his right—voiced, shattering the desperation Kai felt.

He shifted his gaze to the side and glanced at her. Compassion shone across her amber irises as a gust of wind rushed past them and swayed through her short blonde hair beneath her hat. A red birthmark just below her eye peeked out over the edge of her bandana and stood stark against her dirt-smeared skin.

Swiveling his head back toward the crouched woman, Kai sighed. He knew deep down Rina was right. This wasn't the one they sought. He watched as she gripped her hood tighter, securing it atop her head.

Her limbs trembled, and her breaths came in weak, shaky huffs under his stare.

She was completely covered. Brown and black clothing hung limply over her small frame. The frayed hood cast shadows across her face. However, he zeroed in on her eyes when the wind died, and she looked up at him. Big and round and piercing blue. They were alluring, pulling him in. Never had he seen eyes so blue. Eyes so full of . . . *fear*. Fear of him and his companions.

This is not her.

This was someone scared and alone in this shit-show of a world—someone who needed help, someone whose only goal was to survive.

A long exhale escaped from Kai's left.

Jaycen—his oldest friend, his *best* friend.

Letting out a deep breath of his own, Kai consciously softened his gaze. He forced his tense shoulders to relax so he wouldn't stand so tall and tower over the woman's small frame.

"We won't hurt you." His voice came out hoarse, the sediment permanently churning in the air catching in his throat.

Kai extended his hand toward her. His glove was worn; scratch marks and stains were visible against the tan leather. A peace offering, a gesture to show they meant no harm. His hand hung idle in the space between them, but the woman scrambled away. Her boots scuffed against the ground, leaving harsh marks in the dirt—as if he had burned her, as if she feared his touch.

"Are you all right?" Rina asked, her voice softening. "Have you been hurt?"

The implication was there. Kai stiffened at the possibility of what had—or could have—happened to this woman. His home was a violent cesspool. *Anything* went in the eyes of most. But not in his.

Kai refused to stand by while others felt helpless—a feeling he knew all too well. He refused to do nothing—just as all those people had done years ago when he'd screamed and cried for them to *just look at him*, only for them to run from his bruised, swollen eyes.

Fear radiated from the woman in waves so hot it seemed to penetrate his skin as he regarded her. Kai thought Rina felt it too.

She slowly knelt, resting her right knee against the hard ground and her hands atop her thigh. The distance between her and the woman never diminished. Rina merely stayed at the same level. An invitation to trust her.

Frozen, the woman's jaw clenched as she watched him, watched all three with a stillness that was almost unsettling. It made his pulse tick up slightly as he stood there under her careful, calculating gaze. For the first time since before he'd donned his face covering nearly five years ago, Kai felt truly bare.

The woman flinched once more when Rina repeated the question, her eyes instantly hardening. Kicking up another plume of dust, she backed away.

A sigh came from Jaycen. His words were hard and sharp. "Let's just go. Leave her."

Kai's neck stiffened, and his lips fell into a frown. Anger licked across his chest, sweeping against his ribs as he turned his gaze toward his friend.

How could he say such a thing?

Swiftly shooting to her feet, Rina scowled at the large body looming over them. "We aren't the type of people who turn their backs on those who are scared and might need our help. You know that."

Thick, muscular arms crossed over Jaycen's chest. From beneath the rim of his hat, Kai saw his hazel eyes harden as a dark eyebrow lifted toward his shaved head.

He sighed. "You can't help everyone."

"We can try!" Rina's voice caught slightly at the end of her words.

Jaycen tilted his head down at her. "No. We can't. Especially if they don't want help in the first place—"

"Enough."

The word rumbled low in Kai's chest, carrying enough authority to halt his friends mid-bicker as the leader in him surfaced.

Gods. His temper was frayed. They needed to find The Siren. They needed to find food. They needed a lot of things. But as he stared into those terrified blue eyes again, he knew more than anything, they needed to help her.

A massive, hot gust of wind from the south suddenly assaulted them. It rushed up from the earth in a sharp current, nearly knocking Kai into Rina and ripping his hat and bandana from their secured spots. "Shit!"

Rina grabbed Kai's shoulders for support. Her bandana followed suit, flying into the air and chasing Kai's. Even Jaycen stumbled, uncrossing his arms to regain his balance as his hat landed at his feet.

A whirlwind rushed around them, and in the chaos, Kai's gaze met hers. The woman with wide blue eyes. A moment hung in the air between them like a fragile thread, and then—

Boots scraped against the ground. Hurried footsteps pounded and echoed through the trees. Ragged breaths escaped in shattered waves. Kai's gut dropped. She was running, propelling herself through the blackened trunks and dodging thickets of thorns. A split-second decision she'd made while the gust laid out the perfect distraction. Her cloak trailed her, whipping in the air with each frantic step just as the wind died down.

Fuck.

"Catch her!" Rina shrieked. Her mouth twisted in panic, her brows raising to her hairline as she watched the woman flee. Red inched its way up from the base of her neck and settled against the bridge of her nose. "She's—she's seen . . . she's seen your face, Kai!"

Fuck!

Without a moment to think, Kai took off after the fleeing woman, his feet propelling him forward before his brain could catch up. Quick heaves tore from his lungs as he swung his arms with nearly all his energy. She was fast. *Gods, she was fast.* He should have already caught her.

Pushing himself, he picked up the pace slightly. Rina and Jaycen were right on his heels, their steps in sync like a pack of wolves chasing a rabbit.

Kai hated the thought of that. He hated seeing himself as a predator and her, his prey.

It was unnerving. It was inhumane.

"It looks like she's heading straight for the trap!" Jaycen yelled between heaving pants. "It can't . . . it can't be wasted on her!"

Dammit, he's right.

As if adrenaline that hadn't been there as she crawled into the dead forest burst through her veins the second she fled, the woman jumped, dodged, and ran straight for the hidden rope they set up weeks ago while scouting the area for The Siren before they moved west in search of her there.

Crunching dead leaves and churning dirt mixed with their exhausted gasps as they rounded a large boulder. Then, they skidded to a halt. There she was—strung high in a tree, caught in the trap they'd set for the woman they sought. Dangling from a charred branch that seemed ready to snap, her body thrashed upside down, revealing bright orange hair. A color Kai had never seen atop anyone's head before, just like her eyes. It was long and wavy; its tips nearly touched the earth below.

And so the rabbit was caught by The—no.

Ridding himself of the thought, Kai's lips curled. He squeezed his eyes shut for a split second to steady his mind before opening them once more as the woman's fight dissipated and her movements slowed to a gentle sway. Her body turned with the loss of momentum. And his heart halted; his thoughts stilled, stomach knotting as if rocks weighed it down.

"Shit . . ." Jaycen whispered.

Kai flinched as he sucked in a sharp breath and took a hesitant step back.

Rina let out a small, high-pitched gasp. Her mouth opened and closed, but no words came out.

Kai stayed silent with wide, unnerved eyes, staring at the woman before him.

It can't be . . .

The edges of his vision blurred, his pupils working to focus on what he was seeing. There it was—plain as day—yet his mind refused to believe it. Stark against those fiery long locks were her ears. Long and pointed. She was Fae.

Tension purred around them; an electric current sparked beneath Kai's fingertips. Heavy, palpable. The air stilled. No leaves rustled. If any birds were left in this graveyard of a forest, they would've gone silent, watching this play out with bated breath.

Kai's features hardened as he stepped back once more, nearly bumping into Jaycen's side. He masked his emotions as best as he could, willing them to calm and concealing the way his muscles trembled beneath. Distrust swarmed his body, his veins flaring, heartbeat pounding in alarm. His pulse hammered at his temples . . . thumping, thumping, thumping sharply as if it screamed at him to run.

Fae.

Dirt and soot covered her face; patches of ivory skin peeked through. Her pale cracked lips—coated in dried pebbles of blood—twisted together. There was that fear again. And for the first time in nearly five years, fear gripped Kai as well when he met the eyes of this creature, an anomaly in and of itself. No Under-dweller had ever been caught Above. There was no travel between the realms.

Kai stared at her swaying body—a being of The Underworld, a land of creatures said to be conniving and malicious. A land of magic. *Magic . . .*

Magic coursed through this Fae's veins. Magic had caused of all of this—the root of the curse that swept across the land.

That unfamiliar fear rose through Kai's sternum to the base of his throat, constricting him—just as it had five years ago, when the abomination had shot into the sky and tiles had crashed to the earth. Screams of Upperworld citizens—raw and clawing—pierced the air as Kai dodged falling debris, grabbed Jaycen, and ran from his home, racing ahead of the smoke without looking back.

"We can't trust her." Jaycen's voice shattered the memory. The Fae before them shifted her eyes toward him as he spoke. "We don't know her or why she's Above or . . . What is a *Fae* doing up here in the first place? She—she could be working with The Siren or The Wake."

Kai didn't think she belonged to the cannibalistic faction or helped the monster that fed them; she looked too frightened, her body too thin for the meat of The Siren's victims. But there was always a chance a sinister monster lurked beneath the skin of its vessel.

Or worse . . . maybe she was working with him.

Kai's skin tightened over his muscles at the thought of her working with the man responsible for The Darkest Day—for all of this. A man who had somehow, some way, released a dark *magic* across the land. A man Kai knew all too well.

She could be a monster, the very thing Kai tried to rid the world of.

Think, Kai. Think.

His brain was rattled. She'd seen Rina's face . . . *his* face. Their safety—the very thing that gave them a taste of security in this world—was at risk.

I . . . I don't know what to do.

He felt as if he were failing them. His hesitation was dangerous. This Fae could be dangerous.

He needed Jaycen and Rina's input. He needed their *help*. Kai jutted his head to the side, signaling for them to follow him. Turning his back on the Fae, he walked several feet away, leaving her to hang alone upside down.

Jaycen immediately followed, a huff escaping his lips as he settled next to him. Kai studied his friend, searching for any clue as to what he could be thinking. Jaycen was an impenetrable wall—a force no one could break through unless he willed it. His bandana remained secure around the base of his head, but without his hat casting a shadow over his eyes, Kai noticed how they narrowed, the skin above his brows tightening. *Judging. Calculating.*

Rina lingered near the hanging Fae, staring at the being with wide eyes. Streaks of dirt stained her cheeks, and her cracked lips quivered. Her hair swayed in sync with her heaving chest. The splotchy birthmark below her left eye darkened with the flush rising in her cheeks.

Jaycen released a sharp whistle, and Rina tore her eyes from the unknown woman. "Come on!"

Rina sent the Fae a look Kai couldn't decipher. From the way her brows furrowed together slightly, Kai doubted the Fae could either. Another swift moment of hesitation, and Rina made her way to the others. No longer was she screeching to catch the woman, face full of fear; she was quieter—somber.

Kai released a long exhale—

"What do we do, Kai?" Jaycen whispered, his teeth digging into his bottom lip. "An Under-dweller? Here? This is way beyond our grasp."

Kai pressed his thumb and forefinger against the bridge of his nose, trying to conjure *anything* that could help them. "I . . . I don't kn—"

"And she's seen your face." Jaycen ground his molars together. "In case you forgot, we're wanted by The Wake. For all we know, she's working for them and plans to use her strange Under-dweller magic the second we cut her loose. And now that she's seen more than just those vague half-assed descriptions the group's scouts post across the land? Fuck, we're in dangerous territory."

Rina blinked at Jaycen as if his words brought her back fully from wherever her thoughts had taken her. She hissed, "What do you want us to do? Kill her so she can't talk?"

Kai's gut twisted.

Jaycen's eyes widened for a breath before hardening once more. "That's not what I—"

"Exactly." Rina glared at the two men. The word was harsh; her lips curled slightly as it fell from her mouth. "That's not us. That's not who we are or what we do."

Kai stepped between the two. One hand was on Jaycen's chest, the other atop Rina's shoulder. "You're both right. We *are* in dangerous territory. And we *aren't* people who kill just because there's an inconvenience."

His words held authority yet carried a sliver of uncertainty within each syllable. An audible shake he wished wasn't there.

They didn't know who this Fae was, why she was in The Upperworld, or who she worked for . . . if she worked for anyone. She could merely be a wanderer. She could be a lion in sheep's clothing. What he *did* know, though, pulsed on the tip of his tongue . . .

Those bandanas—and their anonymity—were their lifelines. They had no idea who they were helping. They could have helped a hurt or outcasted member of the cannibalistic group in the past, but that barrier covering their faces had given them the protection to do that.

And now this Fae, who knew what he and Rina looked like, was strung before them as his companions waited for his decision. An Under-dweller, who had the very thing that destroyed this realm within her. The thought alone made him tremble just as a shard of heaviness—of *guilt*—emerged below his sternum.

He tried to run from what he knew with every decision he made. Helping people. *Saving* people. Everything he did was penance for the knowledge he held of what had happened on The Darkest Day. Yet he couldn't decide when it mattered most.

A heavy heat burned into the back of Kai's head. Slowly he looked at the creature that stirred so much uncertainty within his body. Veins bulged in her neck, the skin beneath the dirt flushing red as blood rushed upward.

But despite that, her eyes never wavered. She stared at them; her lips pressed into a thin line as she watched . . . watched . . . watched. It was as if she could hear every word they were saying. The very thought of that made Kai's blood run cold. Swiftly he turned back toward his friends.

"We'll . . ."

What will we do?

Those big blue eyes, so full of fear, flashed before his vision. He couldn't help but think about her expression when they first cornered her. It was the same look he had seen countless times before. From the emaciated people they came across hidden in thickets of wood to those running and screaming for their lives as the curse swept over them on The Darkest Day.

No matter if she was Fae . . . she was scared. Of them.

She's dangerous, a voice in the back of his head prodded against his whirling mind.

He was certain getting away from her was the safest option short term. Perhaps she'd forget about them as she went on her way doing whatever she normally did. But perhaps she wouldn't. Perhaps she'd run to her master, whether that was The Wake or worse. Perhaps she had nothing to do with the cannibals. But what would happen if someone captured her? A shadow slinking through this forest, ready to report back to their enemies. Surely, they'd torture her, and she didn't look the type to withstand something like that.

So many uncertainties. They swarmed around his skull, bumping into one another until Kai's head pounded under the pressure. She'd talk soon enough. And that was one thing he couldn't have.

"We'll keep her close."

As soon as the words breached his lips, his gut tightened.

Just . . . just until we find The Siren, Kai reassured himself. The knot in his gut worsened, as if it knew he was letting muddled thoughts drive a decision that could prove detrimental. *We'll ensure she has nothing to do with the monster we're after or the faction she serves. And if the Fae does . . . we'll take care of her, too.*

The mask Kai wore—the certain, confident leader—hid the inner turmoil he couldn't seem to get a grip on. Staring into his friends' eyes, he raised his brow and waited for any retort. There was none. Jaycen's jaw was set. Rina nibbled her bottom lip. Their silence was enough.

"Will you run back and try to find our bandanas and hats?" Kai asked, looking at Rina, his gaze softening.

Her eyes slid past him and landed on the Fae again as her throat bobbed. Something shimmered within them that he couldn't quite place. Before he could ask about it, she nodded and began her trek through the dead trees.

"Sure."

It was nothing more than a whisper.

With a grateful nod toward the woman, Kai turned; his gaze lingered on Jaycen a moment before he faced the hanging Fae again and stepped closer.

Her piercing eyes never left his as he approached. A fire burned behind the blue of her irises. It was startling. It was as if that fire was sentient, and it set him on edge.

"You'll be staying with us now. For the time being."

Kai purposefully added grit to his voice, forcing his vocal cords to rub against one another in authority. There was a low growl within each word, a hidden threat for her to heed.

Her eyes widened a fraction, and her body jerked in protest as her jaw twitched.

Kai continued, "We can't have you running off and telling our enemies—*your* enemies, if you had any sense—who we are."

"I don't," the woman ground out slowly, "have anything to do with any of that. And I don't want anything to do with *you*."

Her voice was melodic despite the bite in her words, and as she spoke, her slightly elongated canines showed. They were stark against the rest of her teeth.

"Trust me," Kai grumbled and bared his teeth for good measure. His top lip split from the harsh movement. "We don't want anything to do with you either."

3

ELERI

A LOUD THUMP BOUNCED across the small clearing, echoed by a muffled groan. Gray and brown dust clouded around Eleri. She lay on her back, all breath ripped from her lungs when her body hit the ground. The brawny, brown-skinned man with cropped hair stared down at her. A jagged knife, with threads of rope hanging off its edge, dangled from the hand at his side.

He reached for the leather sack across his chest and drew out a long coil of rope—the same rope that had captured Eleri. His large hands unrolled it, and the knife's edge sliced through, fraying the strands. Then he looked at her, and Eleri's stomach knotted, as if cement coated her gut and dragged it down.

So much animosity. The gleam in his eye stole the breath from her lungs—something threatening, something . . . empty.

He took a step forward.

"I got our things!" The blonde woman with a unique marking on her face—one that looked as if someone had gently rubbed strawberry juice across her cheekbone—breached the tree line with two hats and one bandana. "Thankfully, these flew in this direction, but I couldn't find the other bandana. And we should be okay leaving the car for the night. I hid it behind several discarded branches near a few downed power lines at the edge of the fores—is that really necessary?"

She released what was in her hold and crossed her arms, the items long forgotten as she stared at the rope clenched in the man's coarsened fist. Taking a slight sidestep toward Eleri, she almost looked concerned—protective—as if she were placing herself between her and the man.

No. Eleri narrowed her gaze, tracing the woman's body, and discarded that thought as soon as it sprang into existence. *No one in this realm cares for anyone but themselves. No one would care for her if they knew the truth.*

"Yes," the man growled. "It is. Hands. Now."

A slight nudge against Eleri's eardrum. The vibration deepened with pressure—his heartbeat, quickening as he stepped closer and prepared to bind her wrists. He was menacing in his approach, yet that was the least of her worries. He couldn't get close. She couldn't let him.

Her heartbeat increased as well, matching his beat for beat before pattering faster and leaving his pounding behind. Her fingers dug into the crumbling dirt beneath her, ready to flee.

Close enough to bend down and meet her alarmed gaze, he reached for her, fingers splayed and threatening. "Hands!"

Eleri recoiled and scrambled backward, putting distance between herself and the fuming man.

He can't touch me. He can't *. . . No one can.*

Boring into him with her own fearful eyes, Eleri couldn't help but imagine the horror that would follow if she didn't get away from him. Flashes of skin melting off muscle. Bones crumbling in the wind. Ash—*so much ash*. And screams. Burned from within.

Goosebumps bristled across her body, and a knot formed in the pit of her stomach.

"Wait . . . please," she pleaded with the man, scooting away inch by inch as she tried to stop a memory—the worst memory of her life—from crawling out of the darkest corner of her mind.

The tips of her fingers pulsed. Her nail beds ached, and her knuckles burned as the memory overtook her. Its pull trapped her beneath the weight of grief.

No. Please, no. Her voice—the present—sounded farther away.

"Just . . ." Eleri thought she'd spoken aloud. "Just give me a moment."

Everything spun. The ground beneath her feet seemed to fall away from her, launching her into a dark pit of dread. Vision blurring, stomach churning, she clung to any semblance of reality. Eleri begged silently, willing her brain to listen for once. It didn't. Harsh and unrelenting, she was thrust into the past . . . into the day she knew her life had been ruined.

No.

No . . .

N—

Eleri opened her eyes, blinking her lashes rapidly until her vision cleared and the sky above her came into focus. It was orange. And not a beautiful orange, not like the flowers in her garden nor the hair atop her head. It was muted, sickly. Smog made it seem . . . *dirty*. Smog that hadn't been there before. She could have sworn it hadn't. The sky had been blue. She knew it had been blue until . . .

"What"—coughs ripped from her chest, as if dust coated every inch of her tongue and shards of glass were lodged into her esophagus—"happened?"

No one answered. She hadn't expected anyone to, but there was something unsettling about it this time. Silence—nothing but silence—surrounded her. She couldn't hear the heartbeat of any nearby animals. She couldn't hear the wind or the whispers from the plant life.

Something had shifted. Something detrimental.

One moment she had been tending to the newest addition to her secret garden—a Sol Flower with golden petals that curved at the tips and its bronze stem that pricked ever so slightly at the touch. She had thought it a fitting flower to add. The opposite—in a way, the other half—to The Underworld's silver Moon Flower.

The next moment, everything around her dimmed. The sun no longer felt bright against her skin, and the ground beneath her feet trembled, reverberating through her bones. She could hear the panicked whispers of the plants surrounding her, urging her to run as fast and as far away as possible. Before she could heed those warnings and fully stand, a terrifying black cloud of shimmering darkness came right at her—bolting over the tips of the forest's full trees toward her garden and The Pathway, The Underworld's arched entrance, nearby.

"What"—another cough—"was that thing?"

Every muscle burned as if shredded, pain darting from her joints into her temples. As she twisted herself around, an agonizing scream lodged itself into the back of her throat. But she pushed the ache away and sat up with a muffled groan.

Sweat slicked her skin. Dust stuck to her pale limbs, and her blue sundress clung to her. It was hot, so unbearably hot. But it felt *different*. A type of hot that made it difficult to breathe. A type of hot that pressed down on every inch of her body, crushing her organs under the force of it. A type of hot that was . . . dangerous.

Eleri searched for the smoke she swore she'd seen, but it had vanished, leaving only the eerie orange sky and smog-choked air. Instead, she was met with a sight that terrified her even more. Devastation.

Gone was The Upperworld she had loved to sneak into without anyone knowing, even if it was just this section of forest and the few surrounding towns when their shades were drawn. It hadn't been much, but it had seemed like a simple world—a world without the formalities of her life Beneath, a world she had longed to explore more.

Now, it was merely a barren valley, as if Death itself had dipped its hands into its rich, nutrient soil and sucked it dry of everything valuable. The Upperworld—now nothing but a decaying carcass. No plant life could be heard, no matter how hard Eleri strained her ears. Trees that were once engulfed with vibrant green leaves were burnt, crisp and smoking. Her beloved garden—a refuge when she simply needed to get away from the sideways glances and duties at the palace—was nothing but cinders. The Laceflower and Bitterweed she grew with a simple caress of her hand were shriveled and blackened.

"Oh gods," Eleri croaked, her heart ramming against her rib cage.

Eleri rose on unsteady feet, her vision blurring as the ground swayed beneath her. Her body crumbled as her knees gave out; her limbs trembled. After a moment, she stole away the leaden feeling in her gut, took a deep breath, and gained her footing once again.

But her momentum stalled as soon as the disorientation began to dissipate and its absence finally made itself known. A hollow crater gaped in her chest where her mother and father had always been—no matter how far she was. Some magic her mother imbued within them when she was born—a spell to detect one another, to let the others know they were all right. And that airy, swirling feeling became a dark pit, cut off completely as if the string of connection had snapped in two.

"Oh Gods!" she shouted, the two words tearing through her throat without resistance.

Forcing her feet to unstick from their spot, Eleri ran toward the entrance to The Underworld. Each frantic step was a loud echo against the charred ground. She had to get home. She had to make sure they were okay. She needed to know her people were safe and her realm untouched.

"Oh, please, Mother. Please, Daughter." The prayer slipped between her heaving breaths. "Please let everyone be all right."

She ran and ran and ran until—

Eleri's feet came to a screeching halt. The cave-like arch that led to her home was completely destroyed. Large boulders and rubble blocked the entrance—caved in, as if it had been made of pebbles. Vines that surrounded the entrance were withered and limp. The rocks themselves had looked as if they had died. Blackened and scorched.

No. No, no, no. This can't be happening.

Eleri lunged forward and clawed at the debris. She needed to get down there. She was desperate to. Her family . . . her *home*. A choked sob poured from her quivering lips. The nude tips of her nails cracked and bled, snapping with the force of each desperate attempt to breach the rubble and break through. Smears of red painted the rocks' surface beside the white scratches left behind.

"Fuck!" she screeched.

"P-Princess?" a weak voice wheezed from the rubble.

Eleri whipped toward the sound, and a pained gasp slipped free. In the bottom corner of the debris lay a bloodied Gnome. His lower half was completely covered by the boulders—trapped and most likely crushed. His upper body hung limp; his arms were mangled, and deep, dark blood dripped from his mouth onto his white beard.

"Princess . . ." The Gnome coughed just as Eleri approached and crouched low enough to meet his eyes. "I was sent to look for you before the king and queen realized you were gone. I-I looked everywhere. On a whim, I decided to make the journey up here. Do your parents know you're Above? Does anyone—wait . . . w-what happened?"

Eleri saw the realization settle as the question fell from his blood-smeared lips. Craning his head as far as his small body allowed, the Gnome tried to look behind him. As he took in the boulders on top of his body, his chest heaved and his eyes watered. His heartbeat—so loud and fearful—pounded against her eardrums.

"I-I can't feel my legs. I can't . . . A-am I going to die? I-I just wanted to do well. To serve you and the Crown. What . . . happened? Why . . . wait! My locket! My daughter's locket! I don't want to die without it. I-I fed it to The Pathway, to come here. I—"

Eleri gently shushed the Gnome as her heart clenched. So much—too much—blood was lost. But she had to do something, anything for him. A sad smile pulled the corners of her lips upward.

"It's going to be okay. I will get you out of there, and we will figure out what happened together, all right?"

The Gnome pressed his lips together, tears gliding out of his fear-stricken eyes and down his reddened cheeks. "Okay," he wheezed.

"Okay," Eleri echoed, her voice distant, as if it didn't belong to her.

With shaking hands, she stood. The crack of her knees pierced the air around her. She focused her eyes behind the Gnome, studying the pile of rubble in great detail and searching for the safest, most effective way to free him. It seemed deadly, with not a loose rock in sight.

What had *happened?*

Her mind raced. Her teeth dug into her bottom lip, and her brows tugged together. She didn't know what to do. She couldn't see a way to free h—

There. A barely noticeable sliver between two boulders stuck out to her.

"Okay . . ." Eleri repeated. She turned back to the male, who was watching her with eyes full of hope.

She didn't know this Gnome. He hadn't been one who tended to her in the palace, and, usually, those who didn't kept their distance. That fire inside her stirred at the thought. She knew why that was. The part of her that made them shy away—the part of her known across The Underworld to be brutal, remarkably strong, and bloodthirsty. Her Witch heritage.

She squeezed her eyes shut, willing herself to stay focused, then opened them once more. "What's your name?"

His mouth gaped at the question. "M–Merrin. Your Grace."

Eleri's heart clenched; she waved off the formality. "Okay, Merrin. I think I'll be able to shift this boulder here"—she pointed to the one atop his lower back—"and then pull you out. Are you all right with that?"

The Gnome nodded frantically. "Thank you. Yes, thank you, Your Grace."

Sending Merrin a hesitant smile, Eleri took a deep breath, nodded, then worked at the massive rock. She slipped her fingers into the narrow gap, wiggling them deeper until she secured a grip on the boulder. After a moment of heavy breaths and strained muscles, she successfully began to lift it. It hovered no more than an inch over him, but it was enough.

"Okay, Merrin. Give me your hand, and I'll pull you out." Eleri reached her hand down toward the Gnome.

It was an uncomfortable angle—her elbow ached with each strain—but she ignored it. She had to free him.

Merrin lifted his hand, trembling and covered in blood and filth.

So close. She *would* get him out.

He placed his small hand into her palm, and a shrill shriek pierced the air around them. That sound . . . Eleri could only gape in horror as she immediately snatched her hand away when Merrin's skin burned. It started where they had barely touched and slowly—so agonizingly slowly—crept up his arm and neck, then down his chest toward his crushed legs.

"Help!" Merrin screamed, his eyes wide and panicked. "Help! Help me, Princess Eleri! Oh, Laurel! M-My daughter. My sweet baby girl, Laurel! I can't leave her! Help me! Please!"

Each shriek for his life, for his daughter, branded itself into Eleri's chest as she sat there with a trembling chin and a racing pulse. The smell of burnt meat swelled around them and stuck to the back of Eleri's throat. A hot gag shoved its way up her esophagus, harshly leaving a trail of stinging bile in its wake, and a frantic buzz in her ear pushed harder and harder until it nearly drowned out Merrin's screams. His heartbeat—erratic and gnashing through the stale air—prodded at her before it slowed as more and more of his body disintegrated.

Thump . . .

Merrin's eyes were full of tears as the skin melted off his cheekbones.

Thump . . .

A dry breeze began to blow around them, picking up pieces of ash—pieces of *him*—toward the hazy sky.

Thump . . .

His final scream breached his trembling lips. His final beat vibrated against Eleri's ears.

Only a pile of ash remained where the Gnome had been.

He . . . had burned alive. Right in front of her eyes. Merrin was there one moment and then gone the next. She—she'd done that.

Eleri's hands shook violently. Lifting them toward her, she stared at them. Her stomach clenched, and rational thought vanished as she gazed at her pale palms. They looked unchanged, yet—

"No . . . no! What happened to him? What happened to *me*?"

The words ripped free from her parted lips. She shook her head violently, and her throat clamped shut. This wasn't right. Eleri was blessed with the gift of life. Never had she taken it before. A sob bubbled up her chest.

She couldn't string her thoughts together coherently. Over and over, three words repeated, banging against her throbbing skull.

I. Killed. Him.

Another gust—this time harsh and heavy—blew around her, nearly knocking her over. It was hot and muggy, yet she just stared and stared at her hands before flitting her eyes to what was left of Merrin. As the wind picked up, the remaining pieces of ash blew away with it.

"No . . ." her voice was hoarse, shattered. "No, this can't be happening. This can't be real."

Desperately, she grabbed for the ash, clawing at the air as if doing so would bring Merrin back. She snatched several pieces before they slipped through her clenched fingers and drifted away on the breeze again . . .

Floating . . . dancing on the wind . . .

Up and up the ash went . . .

Up . . .

And up . . .

4

Eleri

Eleri blinked away the images from that day—the day that stole the life she once lived from her. No longer could she roam her realm and lie in the Moon Flower Fields. No longer could she sit in her father's study while he worked, reading smuggled books from The Upperworld—books of adventure and love and tragedy. Nor could she sneak away from her mother's spell-work lessons just to meet with whichever Fae Lord she wanted that week.

She furiously wiped at her wet lashes and the streaks cascading down her cheeks, her covered palms quivering as they harshly scrubbed away the tears and memories with them. Even that reminded her of the cursed outcome of The Darkest Day: no living thing was safe from her; anything alive would turn to ash from the lightest of touches. Even the barrier of her clothing didn't stop the destruction. No people, no plants, *nothing* . . . yet she could touch herself.

It was as if she were dead . . . as if *she* were nothing. A being destined for a lonely life in solitude. Feeling the poisoned residue of the curse traveling through her veins and burning her very being from the inside out, she held on to her wall of protection as it quivered beneath the weight of her reality.

No longer a blur behind her tears and memories, the man came back into view. He was in the same spot, as if no time passed. Perhaps no time had at all. Merely a blink in this reality as she lived that day over again.

His gaze slashed through her, glaring into her soul as he took in her tear-stained face. The bandana concealing him swayed with each heaving breath; his knuckles creaked when he furled them around the rope before thrusting it out toward her again. Adamant on tying her up.

"Please!" she screamed, dodging his touch once more and scooting away.

She didn't mean to . . . didn't want to show them how truly scared she was. She didn't realize the word had torn from her throat until it burned against her vocal cords. "Please . . ."

Eleri's plea transformed into a whisper, and the man's hand stopped mid-air. Something flashed before his hardened eyes—something Eleri didn't understand—as if that single word knocked through the barrier between them for a split second. Then, like smoke on the wind, it disappeared, and he shifted his weight as if he were going to lunge forward again.

"Stop!" Her molars ground together. "I'll do it myself."

Eleri's voice was louder, pushing away the crippling distress crawling beneath her skin and channeling the princess she once was. The princess who had been born to command an entire realm once her parents stepped down. They needed to *listen*. Their safety depended on it.

Anything to get him to come no closer.

"I promise. I'll . . . I'll make sure it's tight. I just . . . *please.*"

A long exhale sounded behind the man.

"Give her the rope."

Shifting her eyes past the looming figure, she was met with the other man. The one who found her. Kai. That was what the others called him. The name suited him. There was a rigidness to it. A strong, one-syllable name that also rolled off the tongue like a prayer. Strong and soft. Strong like the man before her. Soft like the man he was before he knew what she was . . . *part* of what she was.

His fists curled at his sides under her gaze. The tan skin of his forearms, peeking out from his rolled sleeves, tightened around lean muscle as he crossed his arms over his broad chest, and his sharp, dirt-covered jaw clenched as he eyed her. Something heavy sat behind his leer. Eleri couldn't tell what it was, but it was there nonetheless.

"What?" the man in front of her growled, never taking his eyes off her.

"You heard me." A heavy pause lingered as Kai's heartbeat quickened, its uneven rhythm jolting her ears. "Give her the rope."

The man started. "She has *magic*—"

"And a piece of rope surely won't keep her at bay, whether we tie it or she does."

Finally, Kai glided his gaze toward the other man and stepped forward with his spine straight and chest inflated. The blonde woman was still behind them, silently watching the exchange. That uneven beat of Kai's heart stuttered more, barely noticeable to Eleri, but then she focused on the pattern.

Fear. Fear roiled through him.

Kai continued.

"An Under-dweller can surely escape something as insignificant as a single rope." His leer slid back toward her. "And who says you won't? Who says you won't slip through that false binding and betray us? Or slaughter us with your unnatural powers?"

A spark of anger rumbled through Eleri's chest, twining in ribbons around her lungs. He didn't know a damn thing. Not of her, nor her once-lost power. Not of the curse that ran through her veins and betrayed everything she once was. A sudden urge to rip out his throat and pull his spine through his chest barreled into Eleri. It nearly gave her whiplash.

There it was—that little beast unfurling and tightening the rope inside her, pulling at her natural rage. It relished the heat burning through Eleri's body with its sharpened claws and sinister grin. The darkness surrounding it pulsed and writhed when provoked.

Eleri bit the inside of her cheek and, internally, stomped toward the fiery beast, banishing it within its cage seated in the farthest part of her soul . . . a cage that held it at bay more often than not.

The woman's voice bit through the air, cutting off Eleri's thoughts. "We don't know if she's like that." She stepped toward Eleri, her hands slightly held up in surrender, her eyes shining with hesitant wonder. "What's your name—"

"A magical curse destroyed this world," the other man hissed, his tone dropping. Each word was merely a rumble within his chest. "She's a magic user. We can't trust her. End of discussion." He risked a glance at Kai, whose sharpened eyes stayed trained on her.

Eleri ignored the men, shutting out the grinding of Kai's teeth and the creak of his holster as his chest expanded, her eyes narrowing on the woman. Names weren't a luxury to exchange in a world like this. Usually, no one cared enough to know the name of the one they might betray.

"Don't listen to him," the woman said with a small smile.

A smile. Aimed at her. The first in five years since . . . Merrin, when he saw it was the wandering princess who found him.

Eleri's heart picked up, ramming into her chest. Her blood immediately chilled. She couldn't reveal who she was. Surely, they'd know her name. Unless . . . perhaps those in The Upperworld were just like them. She wrung her fingers and chewed on the inside of her cheek.

Perhaps, to them, I'm merely the Under Princess. Just as there were the Upper King, the Upper Prince, and—when she was alive—the Upper Queen.

Titles like that distanced the realms—or at least that was what she was told. Not knowing the true names of those Above was a way to remind them there should be a chasm between them. The two lands thrived by staying separate.

But if I say nothing, how will they react?

They didn't trust her, and she didn't trust them.

If they didn't have the same policy with names as those in The Underworld, would they recognize hers? Would they kill her, knowing what she was? A half-Fae, half-Witch. Perhaps they'd string her up and leave her to die. Maybe they'd hand her over to the highest bidder—abandon her with clean hands and guilt-free consciences.

She had seen it before; the purchasing of Humans was common post-Darkest Day. She saw women clawing at their handsy owners before their hands would be chopped off, leaving only stumps. She witnessed children kneeling on nails for the entertainment of those who passed. The image of the child with no limbs and maggots infesting their body rammed into her skull. That could be her if she weren't careful.

She saw too much. Nearly every day, a new blood-soaked horror reminded her it was safer to be alone, even if the core of who she was still yearned for companionship despite the dangers of it all.

No. They couldn't know.

Never was she so thankful that her Witches' Marks weren't black. White and barely noticeable against her skin when it wasn't dirtied by grime. Nothing like her ancestors.

I will not reveal such deadly details to Humans I don't know.

"El," she finally said. "My name is El."

The woman stared at her, and the corners of her mouth tugged upward, a soft smile barely forming. Just enough for Eleri to see. There was a sadness laced within the gesture. But there was something kind about her. A tender heart underneath the hardened exterior that must've formed after The Darkest Day. The tense knot in Eleri's stomach loosened, and her chest collapsed with the breath she was holding. A light sense of being at ease washed over her. It was a feeling she hadn't felt in five years. And it terrified her.

This woman cannot be trusted . . .

But somehow, her kind eyes gave Eleri a taste of her old self within minutes. It was overwhelming. Tears pricked at her lash line, and her lower lip trembled.

"What's . . ." Eleri cleared the lump in her throat, banishing the sudden, dangerous thoughts. She gripped her wall and held on to it for dear life. "What's your name?"

A simple question that seemed so incredibly complex.

The woman smiled widely. Soft grumbles reverberated from Kai and the other man nearby, clearly displeased with the interaction. Eleri kept her eyes from them, drawn instead to the calm the woman radiated. "I'm Rina."

Rina. It was a nice name, a pretty name . . . a name that didn't fit this horrendous reality they were living in.

Before she could say anything, Rina's fidgeting fingers drew Eleri's gaze from those wide amber eyes. They were wrapped around a pendant hanging past the fabric of her tunic. A necklace. It was rusted and grimy, and even if it weren't, Eleri wouldn't have been able to make out what was etched atop it. It was too faded—as if a thumb rubbed over the pendant one too many times—even for her exceptional sight.

Rina's teeth dug into her bottom lip as she thought something over. She wanted to say more, Eleri realized. She was biting her tongue, trying to keep the words at bay. So quickly Eleri would have missed it if she weren't looking, Rina shifted her eyes to the side—toward the other two—then opened her mouth before thinking better of it.

Rina blurted, her arm extended toward the two men, "This is Jaycen and Kai—"

"Rina!" The burly one—Jaycen—snapped and ripped his gaze away from Eleri for the first time since cutting her out of the tree.

Rina's short blonde hair whipped around as her head swiveled to meet his scathing eyes, and she perched her hand atop her hip. Rina's cheeks heated, the mark below her eye turning a deeper shade of red. It was splotchy and uneven, yet Eleri thought it was pretty. Unique. It suited her in a way.

"What?" Rina's pitch rose. "She gave us her name. We should have the courtesy to share ours."

"There is no courtesy in these lands anymore," Jaycen growled, then faced Eleri once more before narrowing his hazel eyes at her.

She met his gaze head-on and took him in. Her stare was unbreakable—watching him carefully, trying to get a read on him . . . something she felt she was quite good at. He was angry. That was obvious, but there was something else. Something always present and impenetrable. A concrete fortress to keep him and the most vulnerable parts of himself safe.

You and me both.

Then Eleri shifted her gaze toward Kai. He was simply staring at her, taking her in just as she took him in. The pattering beat of his heart, which didn't quite reach the correct rhythm, started again every few seconds or so. Fear stirred within him as she watched him try to decipher what power ran through her veins.

Little did he know.

Kai forced his focus away from her with a swallow. Ever so slightly, his jaw loosened. His neck was slick with sweat, and his muscles twitched. He appeared on edge, unsure of what to do next. A silent minute passed. Eleri kept her eyes trained on him. Rina and Jaycen did the same. Then he turned to address his companions as the eerie sun descended and the orange sky darkened into a deep red.

"We'll set up camp here for the night. Jaycen, scout the perimeter. Rina, build our fire." Kai's voice was stern—gruff from dryness. He stared at Eleri again, nostrils flaring. "I'll take first watch."

Trickles of annoyance ran up Eleri's spine and settled against the pulse point beneath her jaw. That beastly thing inside her stirred. He was looking at her as if she were a monster—a caged animal he had to keep his eyes on, lest he wanted her to attack. A real-life personification of the anger inside her.

Little did he *fucking* know . . .

Jaycen threw the rope onto the ground by her feet with a scoff before turning and entering the dead forest beyond. Eleri studied him for a moment, then shifted her gaze to the rope. She hesitated.

"Go on. I'm curious to see what knot you choose to make me believe you're trapped."

A smirk tugged slightly at Kai's cracked lips. He rolled out his neck smugly before freezing, his gaze training on something a few feet away.

Eleri's chest clenched. She knew what it was as soon as it was in his sight. The comforting weight of it in the side pocket of her cloak felt empty as her focus shifted to where it was supposed to be. Three steps were all it took for him to reach the light-purple crystal peeking out of the dusty soil. Bending down, he picked it up. The way his large hands wrapped around one of her most prized possessions—her only prized possession—made her gut tighten. He didn't deserve to be touching it at all.

"What's thi—" Kai turned toward her, the end of the word falling silent as he took her in. "Hm, it's important, huh? You're not very good at hiding your emotions, *El*."

His eyes narrowed, the accusatory gaze cutting straight through her.

A long sigh slipped through her teeth and rolled off her tongue. "Give it back."

"I don't think so." Plopping down on the dead ground in front of her, Kai shook his head. "Collateral."

Collateral? Sure, it was the only thing left from her home, but it meant nothing if she could *actually* get back there. The arrogance radiating off this asshole was astonishing.

A whisper of a thought appeared before her as she studied the cockiness suffocating them. *Use him. Use him to get as far east as possible. That's the direction they were traveling in the first place.*

Her pulse increased. *Yes.* That was what she would do. Use this asshole to her advantage.

Eleri stole away her plan and hid it close to her heart before falsely twisting her features into one of annoyance.

"Unbelievable," Eleri huffed. She grabbed the discarded rope and tied her wrists, shaping it into intricate knots she'd learned from her old groundskeeper. "You don't need collateral. I don't work for or with whoever it is you're so desperate to catch."

Her eyes never left Kai's, her gaze an irritated, taunting challenge. The corners of his mouth ticked up into another cocky smirk.

Too easy.

Pulling the rope extra tight, she allowed herself one last look at the man before her with her left brow raised. A surveying glance from the tips of his boots, across his crossed legs and taut muscular body, along his corded arms and up to his prominent nose and straight eyebrows.

Tall. Strong. Rugged. She might have been able to outrun him if their trap hadn't ensnared her. Genuine annoyance flared at the thought.

Bear with it, Eleri, she silently gritted out. *Pretend they have the upper hand. Pretend they have all the power. Anything to get home.*

Eleri turned her back toward him and leaned against an ash-covered trunk before closing her eyes and willing her thoughts to stop replaying the moments leading up to this.

It didn't work.

5

RINA

RINA YARROW'S EYES SNAPPED open, pulled from her sleep, as if something nudged her awake.

The backs of her eyelids burned, her lashes dragging shut. She squeezed them closed and rubbed them, shaking her head and stifling the groan rising in her throat.

She was second watch tonight. The worst shift to have. Waking after finally relaxing into sleep was always harder than initially staying awake.

Shit, she silently grumbled. *I guess it's time.*

Sitting up, Rina ran her fingers through her knotted hair. The gritty texture of the dust caking each strand tugged at her knuckles. She winced with every pull until it was easier to glide her hand through. Then she reached for her canteen tucked away in her leather pack.

Her throat ached for water as she smacked her dry lips together. Her supply was still more than halfway full—she was grateful for that, but she needed to be careful. Since they'd left the Western Vale and its three lakes, water sources had been scarce—especially the farther east they went.

The Vale was hit less hard than the Eastern Plains on The Darkest Day. They were able to adapt better since that area of The Upperworld wasn't as industrialized. The lake levels were decreasing, however, which was a cause for concern, but Rina's mind was preoccupied—on their mission, on traveling east despite its harsh Wasteland and its single source of water: the river, with winding banks leading toward the Southern Coast.

Rina took another sip before screwing shut the metal cap and stuffing it back into her bag. As she stood, she swiftly grabbed the bandana and walked toward Kai and the sleeping Fae.

A real, honest-to-Gods Fae. Here in the flesh.

She—El—was like a beacon in their land. Even under the blood-like night sky—perched against one of the crumbling tree trunks in a small ball—she looked ethereal. The Fae's stillness was enthralling. A stillness that must've helped her survive all this time.

The hood of her cloak was bunched around her shoulders. Her chapped lips were slightly parted; pointed ears peeked out through the bright orange strands that framed her face. She was magnificent. It was as if her skin shone despite the dirt covering almost every inch of her and the black clothes that nearly swallowed her whole. An aura surrounded her that Rina was drawn to.

It was familiar. It was welcoming.

"Brynn . . ." she whispered under her breath, gently rubbing her forefinger and thumb across the pendant between her collarbones as if doing so would ease the pressure in her chest. "I wish you were here. She's a sight to behold."

Kai's back straightened slightly as Rina approached him. He didn't turn his head toward her, his eyes remaining on El. She wouldn't be surprised if he hadn't budged since Rina shut her eyes as the sun set hours ago. His hardened stare looked even fiercer beneath the maroon sky.

"Kai." Rina placed her hand atop his shoulder, hoping not to spook him. He hummed. "Take this."

She held out the bandana. After several silent seconds, Kai finally released his gaze from the Fae and turned his head toward it. "That's yours."

Rina nodded. "I know, but you should wear it. I'm nobody important—"

"I'm not either," Kai grumbled.

She stayed silent, offering him a faint smile before saying, "Wear the covering, Kai."

Kai's eyes locked onto hers. They wavered before he nodded and took the bandana, placing it atop his thigh.

"I'll be back," she whispered, venturing into the surrounding trunks of burnt bark.

Careful not to wander too far, Rina looked for the perfect spot to pray. Anywhere would do, but she tried to show more respect toward The Trinity. They deserved more than just *anywhere*.

After a handful of turns, Rina found a small clearing. Fewer spiny branches hung overhead, the sky in full view no matter how unnatural it looked after all this time. The forest floor lay smooth, and in the faint moonlight veiled by smog, it seemed less dead. It wasn't much, but to her, it was perfect.

Kneeling in the middle of the clearing, Rina settled on her knees, ready to give her love and devotion toward her Gods. She tried to pray every morning if she was able. It was a tradition she'd had since she was little, before her parents left for the fields on their horses and she had to go to school.

She invited Kai and Jaycen to join her on occasion, but they refused. That was okay, though. She wouldn't push them, even when they said they couldn't wrap their heads around doing something so pointless during the end of the world. End of the world or not, Rina's faith never wavered.

Rina straightened her back and placed her hands atop her thighs, taking several deep breaths. Enough to steady her, to ground her. When ready, she opened her eyes and scanned the clearing for anyone lurking nearby.

Tucked into the twining trunks and ash-covered branches, an altar caught her eye. Her heart beat rapidly as the pile of small bones sat at its edge.

"Fucking zealots," Rina muttered, twisting her body around so her back faced the blasphemous offering The Wake was known for leaving The Son. "The Son would hate every last one of you for the things you do."

After several breaths to calm the anger that began to boil, Rina focused once more on the reasons she was here. To clear her mind. To honor her Gods. To remind herself that she was doing good, that she was saving people. She had to save them. *Had* to.

Guilt wrapped itself around Rina's chest and squeezed. Like a constricting serpent, the heaviness gripped tight and wouldn't let go, twisting into something sharp. She didn't save Brynn . . . couldn't save her. And that ate Rina alive day in and day out. Brynn's eyes shone in the people they helped. Rina saw her smile when they thanked her profusely while going on their way. Brynn, her sister, was everywhere.

Water gathered in the corners of her eyes; her nose burned. Guilt tugged at her lips as if tearing her apart from within. She tried to squelch it, tried to banish it far, far away. It was hard to do. That guilt she hated so much was the one thing keeping her going.

It's okay, Rina. Sit with that feeling. No matter how much it hurts.

Thoughts she knew were wrong burrowed into her skull and nestled deep into her soul, like a knife digging itself in and twisting over and over again. Doubt. Anger. Unfaithful emotions were at war with one another.

Inhaling one deep breath, Rina held onto it. She filled her lungs to the brink, closed her eyes, and did just that. Sat with the weight of her past. When the black seeped into her consciousness, she finally released the air into the clearing.

"Dear Great Trinity," Rina said, barely a single sound breaching her lips. She had prepared a prayer for them the night before, just before her heavy eyelids closed. But the words wouldn't come to her. Instead, new ones fell from her lips. "Why? How could you—"

A whisper of a breeze stirred from nowhere. It trickled into the clearing and fluttered against Rina's cheek, her hair tickling her skin and a flush running up her neck. Her lips parted, and a small gasp slipped free. Tears quickly gathered behind her eyes.

Her soul suddenly sang. Her heart swelled to double its size.

They were here. With her. She knew it just as well as her own name. *The Trinity.*

This wasn't the first time she had felt their presence. When she was seventeen, she skipped her prayer early one morning to sneak into town to meet a boy she wanted to impress. He invited her to his house before school. When she arrived, she was met with his sparkling green eyes holding so much pride. In his hand was a small revolver. It was gray, stark against his palm.

"But," Rina had said, "The Purge. You shouldn't have that."

The boy shrugged and sent her a smirk. "The king's guard stopped by last week to confiscate it. My dad hid it well. Want to go shoot it? I saw some rabbits behind my house the other day—"

"No!" Rina shrieked and stepped back. "You need to give that to the king. It's dangerous."

"Gods, Rina. I didn't think you were so boring." The boy fiddled with the gun, running his finger down the barrel and back up toward the trigger. "You won't go telling anyone about this, will you?"

"Run . . ." a woman's voice whispered across her mind.

Rina turned, shaking her head violently, and ran away as fast as she could. She never talked to the boy again. She never mentioned what had happened either. But that voice . . . it came and went on occasion over the years, when she needed to hear it most. It was The Mother. Certainty surged through her bones every time she heard it.

And as she sat in this clearing, she knew it was her. Rina felt The Mother bend over her as if she were truly there. Her ghostly fingers ran through Rina's hair, a simple reminder to have faith. Closing her eyes, Rina focused on that feeling. It was as if The Mother were saying it was okay if Rina didn't understand why something happened.

"Everything happens for a reason." The words floated into Rina's mind, ringing across her soul, as if they were truly spoken aloud. *"You are right where you need to be, my child."*

Faith. That word crawled down her cheek and settled against her chest.

There, she felt The Daughter. Her presence was cooler than The Mother's but no less comforting. Rina shifted her focus toward the feeling of The Underworld's deity. Rina's lower lip wobbled as the Goddess pressed her palm down atop her heart where the necklace sat.

She didn't say anything. She never did, for The Daughter was not Rina's true creator. But she always showed. And Rina always basked in her presence.

Her creator—*her God*—was there too, keeping his distance as he normally did when they showed. The Son was aloof, a mystery to her despite her faithful practice all these years. He ran the hottest of the three—a fiery spirit that combated The Daughter's ice. Two ends of the spectrum. Two sides of the same coin. Both created by The Mother of All.

The Son watched her. Even off to the side, she could feel him. Knowing he was always there, nonetheless, calmed Rina. Her creator was there. Her creator cared.

Suddenly, that trickle of a breeze rushed through her in a whirlwind of ice and fire before ending in absolute peace. The Mother's combating earth settled across Rina's entire being and grounded her to the present.

"Everything happens for a reason," Rina muttered softly.

With a straight spine and closed eyes, Rina remained on her knees for several long minutes. The midnight wind whipped around her, taking her Gods' presences with it. Pure silence filled the clearing again. Only her breath echoed around her.

One minute passed, then another. After several more, it was time. She rose, glanced around the clearing, brushed past the altar, and headed for that night's campsite.

Nothing had changed since she left. Jaycen was still passed out. Kai was still intently staring at El as if she were their captive, their prisoner. Rina's heart knotted at the thought.

It seemed like that, didn't it? She sighed.

Slowly walking toward Kai, Rina was careful not to step on brittle sticks or crumbling dead leaves. She didn't want to wake the Fae or alarm Jaycen. Within arm's length, Rina noticed how Kai was barely breathing. She placed her hand atop his shoulder, and Kai flinched, turning to her.

Shining brightly, a swirling funnel of emotions circled his irises. Uncertainty. Wariness. Fear. She saw it all. Before she could say anything, though, it was gone. A mask donned to ease her. *Oh, Kai . . .*

"I'll take over from here."

Rina waited for him to stand before taking his place, keeping her gaze on him until he relaxed against a tree and closed his eyes. Then she turned to El, truly taking in the otherworldly woman before her.

Sitting unmoving in the residual grace The Trinity left behind, she felt alive in this moment—never having felt it this much in years. Since before The Darkest Day. But a Fae—a real Fae in the flesh—was here with them. Rina didn't know her story or what had happened to her. All she knew was that El was scared, and if she could help her . . . maybe she wouldn't feel the burden of her past as heavily.

Rina, full of unwavering faith and trust, took it as a sign. Just like The Mother said, everything happens for a reason.

"I couldn't save you, Brynn." El stirred at the whispered words.

Rina continued her thought silently. *But maybe . . . Maybe I can save her. I'm right where I need to be.*

6

Kᴀɪ

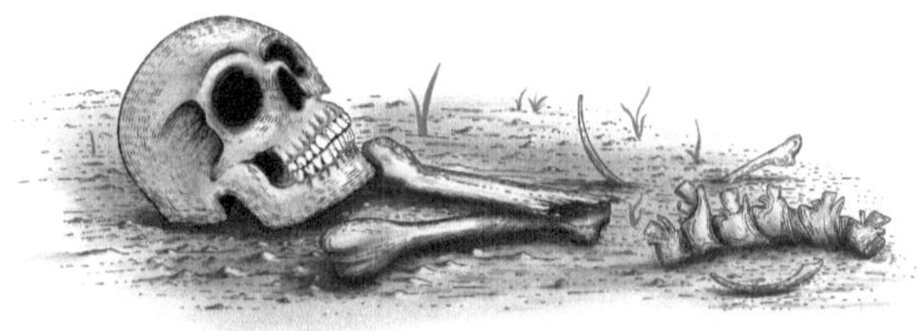

"Gᴇᴛ ᴜᴘ."

Kai towered over the Fae under his watch.

El. That was her name. His heart sped up, and his gut twisted at the thought of having a name to a face. It was one that tugged at his curiosity just enough to sound alarms in his head.

No. A name makes this tangible, makes this real. This can't *be real.*

It had been hard for him to fully surrender to sleep last night. His heart would pound sporadically at the thought of this creature—a creature he had no idea how to navigate—being so close to them. Just as it was now.

Most of those Above didn't bother learning about their neighbors Beneath. Why would they want to when they were told at young ages how deceitful Under-dwellers could be? Tricksters with their deals and potions. Monsters that kept children from leaving their beds at night.

For Kai, he never thought it was important to learn much more than that; he never imagined the two worlds would collide. When his tutors tried to give him lessons about the unfamiliar world and its inhabitants when he was younger, his mind always wandered. Jaycen tried to pay attention for both of them. He said the information was vital, but Kai distracted his friend, pulling him away from their books and into made-up, childish games and gossip. Though he wished he hadn't.

Because the line that separated the two realms was now blurred. Here she was, a Fae. Kai looked down his nose at her, studying her. She was caved in on herself. Her lower back was against the bottom of the shredded tree. Her body was hunched over, folded in half while orange strands of hair hung down across her face. The tips grazed the blackened ground near her hips with each inhale and exhale.

"Get up," he repeated.

The words were no louder than the first time he uttered them. It was as if they were stuck, not wanting to be released. Asleep, she was not as big a threat to them. He could freely study her, observe her movements and try to understand what a Fae was truly like when all inhibitions were lost.

Kai wasn't granted the time to do that.

El's limp fingers twitched, then several breaths later, she woke. Her eyes remained closed, but Kai could tell she was alert. Her breathing changed. Instead of the long, languid movements—*in and out . . . in and out*—of each breath, her inhales were shallower, and her exhales were quicker. Only slightly but enough for him to notice.

He didn't move a muscle as he waited for her to quit pretending. She was feigning slumber in what he thought was a move to find her bearings. His back remained straight, his shoulders stiff, anticipating this being to finally reveal herself. Watching . . . waiting.

Then, as if sensing he was as ready as he would ever be, she rolled up her spine—stacking one vertebra atop another—as she sat up and opened her eyes. Kai's breath caught in his throat, getting lost in her dark blue irises just as he had the day before. They were free from hazy sleep, sharp and alert, luring him in and waiting to spring a deadly trap. And he was frozen, not knowing what to do as she ensnared him with a stillness he could only guess a Fae would have.

Kai had only heard stories of those Beneath. But that was all they were, *stories*. Murmurings at revels from attendees who swore they fed The Pathway and journeyed down into The Underworld's depths to make a deal with a Witch for a hex. Tales from shopkeepers of Fae creeping Above in the middle of the night to snatch children out of their beds to keep as slaves. Stories of Vampires who fed on the blood of his people, mostly drunks . . . easy prey.

They had all simply felt like lies—fantastical and over-exaggerated. Something that would never truly happen in The Upperworld, for no one would be idiotic enough to feed The Pathway.

I guess I was wrong. I wish I wasn't.

He quite enjoyed his now shattered idea that the Upper and Underworlds were separate in all matters. The Son created The Upperworld—a land of normalcy and reasoning. The Daughter created its counterpart, The Underworld—a land of monsters and magic. And The Mother created the two deities, constructing what was supposed to be a harmonious trio that allowed this world to prosper.

Thriving as one world. Existing as two.

Existing as two.

His mother always spouted her naïve fantasy of bringing the two together to anyone who would listen. He didn't understand it. Neither did his father. But they let her dream. It was easier that way.

And as he gazed into El's eyes, noticing the glint of her elongated canines against the rapidly brightening day and the sharp points of her ears, he couldn't understand his mother at all. El was unknown to him—foreign and frightening. And the unknown was a dangerous thing . . . a thing to be wary of.

"Time to go," Kai grunted out, ripping his gaze away and turning his back on her before stalking toward Jaycen.

Beneath the bandana his friend never took off, and the hat atop his head, Kai saw the way Jaycen was eyeing him with furrowed brows. The crunch of dead brush beneath his boots drowned out his whirling thoughts, and with a shake of his head as he approached, Kai tried to reassure him that he was fine.

Don't let him see how you're truly feeling, Kai. It will make you look weak.

"Ready, boss?" Rina smiled as she approached them, her eyes glinting with . . .

Was that mirth? Her amber gaze appeared less burdened, less sad. Her knotted blonde hair looked smoother, too, as if she had run her fingers through it. She seemed to be in lighter spirits—more so than the day prior.

Not so tense. Not so distracted. She was back with them, no longer lost in her racing thoughts that seemed to overwhelm her after learning what El really was. Before, she had looked as if she traveled to the past—eyes empty and troubled, held captive by whatever thoughts she used to succumb to years ago for days at a time.

"Are you doing all right, Rina?" Kai asked, securing his—*Rina's*—bandana on before strapping his hat to his leather sack hanging down his back. "You really should wear this instead of me. Sun Death can—"

"I'm fine, Kai. Never better, actually," she smiled.

Kai couldn't help the worry that continued to seep down into his gut. He wanted to know where her head was, if her instincts to survive were sharp enough even with the orange-haired, blue-eyed distraction. He needed to know she was not falling back into the deep pit that used to call to her.

Rina scoffed and rolled her eyes before training them back on him with earnest. "I promise."

With that look, he believed her. She wasn't hiding from him. He was certain. Their friendship ran deep. Kai cared for her, and even though he thought he could do more for her and Jaycen, he tried to convey that.

"We should find something to eat soon. The farther east we go, the fewer chances we have to come across anything of substance." Jaycen buckled his knife's holster across his thigh, and his stomach growled loudly. As if on cue, Kai's stomach cramped as the reminder of hunger took over. Briefly glancing at El, Jaycen whispered, "Does her kind even eat?"

"Jaycen!" A hiss slipped beneath Rina's breath. Her eyes widened, and her mouth parted.

"I can hear you," El snapped. Kai couldn't help but straighten his spine as the words flew from her mouth and pierced the air like an electric current, the muscles below his shoulder blades twitching from the sudden movement. "And yes, Fae do, in fact, eat. *Asshole*."

A chortle—loud and unbidden—rushed past Kai's clenched teeth and hung in the air around them.

Huh. Kai pondered, staring at the Fae with a puzzled grin. *She has a bite to her.*

Jaycen shot him a warning glare, and it made Kai want to throw his head back and laugh again. Digging his teeth into his bottom lip as he took in Jaycen's twisted grimace, he reined it in before looking back at the Fae with interest.

Kai watched as something flashed across her eyes—something heavy and burdensome. Then she closed them tightly and turned her head to the side, fist clenching as she breathed in deeply.

Drawing his brows together and watching her closely, he tried to work her out. Things would be so much easier if he could. He'd navigate this entire situation better. He clawed at anything that might restore life before El came along, clinging to the sliver of normalcy left amid the barren land.

And he shouldn't have to do that. Not when they had other things to worry about.

An inconvenience, that was what she was.

El took one more deep, shaky breath, then glanced back at Kai. That boldness from earlier had vanished. In its place sat guarded intrigue. "Where are we going?"

Alarm bells rang and bounced against Kai's skull. He narrowed his eyes at the Fae. "Why do you want to know?"

A scoff breached El's downturned lips, and she shook her head. Pulling her gaze back toward him, she narrowed her eyes. "If I'm to be your prisoner, I'd like to know I'm not being led into a trap. You said you were worried I'm working for The Wake, but how do I know you aren't working with them or any other piece of shit that survived the blast and is taking it upon themselves to run wild?"

Kai's blood ran cold. "How could you have heard that? I made sure we were far enough away from you."

"Kai," Rina began, "Fae . . . have heightened senses, at least that's what I've heard. They . . . can hear farther, see farther."

The words came out slowly; her voice was lower, as if she was hesitant to explain this.

"What the fuck, Rina?" Jaycen chimed in, his voice rising. A stark contrast against hers. "Why didn't you say anything?"

Rina shot him an icy glance. "Don't start, Jaycen. I didn't know if it was fully true. You know anything regarding Beneath is unreliable up here."

"I can see she's the smarter one out of the bunch." El's soft voice pierced the air.

Kai watched El regard Rina, her eyes narrowing as curiosity sparked in them while she studied the blonde.

Rina glanced at the Fae and smirked. "Oh, they already knew that."

A breathy chortle brushed past the Fae's long canines, and a ghost of a smile graced her lips. The sound startled him, and his gut knotted. Rina's eyes widened—frozen—before settling into a watery grin.

A moment passed between Rina and El that Kai couldn't decipher. He didn't like it, though. He wanted to step between the two, blocking each other's view and putting an end to this . . . civility.

For Rina's sake. For all of theirs.

"That's enough," Kai gritted out.

Sitting up straighter and crossing her legs, El regarded Kai, running her eyes up and down his body meticulously. Nonchalance masked her features, but tension at the corners of her lips drew Kai's focus.

"I asked a question." El's voice tried to hold that same grit Kai forced against his vocal cords. A chill formed at the base of his head and ran up his scalp.

This . . . creature. "We don't answer to you."

"Kai." Rina crossed her arms. Gone was the delight she donned not even a minute ago. Her features hardened, and seriousness took over.

A standoff between him and her. Rina, so kind and understanding even to a being they couldn't trust. Relenting, Kai released a breath. His shoulders sagged. He looked away and met Jaycen's eyes. With a shake of his head, Kai silenced the questions churning there.

No one spoke. Kai didn't want to forfeit any information to the being. Jaycen barely looked at the Fae, shaking his head in disbelief, clearly appalled that they were even considering telling her anything. And Rina . . . Rina shifted from foot to foot. Heaviness surrounded her.

Fuck. He should've been more considerate. The topic of their destination was hard on her. Opening his mouth to finally answer the Fae, Kai was cut off before any sound could escape.

"A village northeast of here," Rina mumbled as she adjusted the strap of her bag and looked back at El. "That's where we're heading. It was . . . It was once called Mountmend before The Darkest Day. It's practically rubble now."

Kai's heart seized at the pain in Rina's voice, despite the way she softened her smile—a barely noticeable attempt to make their addition comfortable. *So kind, indeed.*

Nudging her shoulder, he sent her silent encouragement. She smiled back in reassurance. With a nod, accepting the blonde's explanation, El began working free of the intricate knots she had tied around her wrists.

"I wonder what its inhabitants will offer for you, Fae." Jaycen sucked on his front teeth and tilted his head toward El.

Kai's body tensed while the words lingered in the air, heartbeat spiking as a tendril of ire bubbled beneath the surface. El did the same, halting her movements over the knots. She whipped her head up toward the three of them with fearful eyes. Kai saw the uncertainty creeping in as if her previous question about leading her to a trap could be true. Her muscles twitched, fighting against the way her limbs yearned to flee.

"Jaycen!" Rina shrieked, slapping his chest with a loud thump. "You really are an asshole!"

Jaycen grunted before a chuckle slipped through his teeth, then walked toward the edge of the clearing. As he was about to breach the tree line, he turned back to look at her seriously. "I'm just joking. You know me, Rina."

"Don't listen to him, El. He's full of shit." Rina attempted to send El a reassuring smile.

El's gaze lingered on Jaycen before turning her attention back to her binding. She paused for no longer than a breath, then worked at the knots once more. Two twists, three pulls, and her hands were free.

Rina continued as she watched. "Mountmend—or what's left of it now—is not somewhere anyone would want to be. It's home to a variety of . . . characters. Dealers. Bandits. Murderers—"

"And The Siren," Kai grunted, looking up from El into the distance of dead trees, internally plotting their route.

No one said anything; the quiet between them swelled. The woman they were after . . . She was a heavy subject. One they all felt passionately about for one reason or another.

El stood, brushed off her pants, and looked at him. Her gaze seared into the side of his face. It made him want to cower. Forcing the heat on his skin away, he didn't acknowledge her and started toward Jaycen without a word.

"Don't"—Jaycen's rough voice impaled the silence—"even think about running."

Kai swiveled his head to the Fae, making sure she wasn't on the verge of fleeing. She wasn't. Instead, she squared her shoulders, ignoring the man and walking toward Rina, who gave her a friendly grin.

"Right." Rina clapped her palms together, looking at them and swiftly changing the subject. "We'd better get going. We'll keep an eye out for food on the road."

Jaycen grunted and pushed through the sharp hanging branches back toward the road. Rina followed, dodging the tip of one that swung from the momentum of the man leading the group.

El didn't move, standing eerily still as she watched them enter the forest.

"Go," Kai bit out.

El's nostrils flared as she turned to him, a fiery glint burning in her pupils as she forced out a long breath. Her fingers tightened on the coiled rope, shifting her grip to the end before reaching for him. "Here."

Her hands trembled as he stared at her outstretched palm. They wouldn't stop shaking.

She's hiding something.

Kai narrowed his eyes, and without a word, he reached for the rope. As soon as it left her palm, El stepped to the side with a curt nod, her lips pressed into a thin line, and turned to follow the path Rina and Jaycen had taken.

Kai stared after her, his mind going a mile a minute until he could barely see her beneath the shadowy, dead canopy. His leather gloves—the material straining against his skin—creaked as he gripped the rope, twisting and tugging in search of reprieve from his thoughts.

Food. Focus on finding food.

Within minutes, he caught up to the others. He walked behind the Fae, keeping his distance yet staying close enough to seize her if she tried anything. A bubble of taut silence seemed to wrap around them on the journey. Suffocating. Skepticism burned at the base of his throat. Trepidation and curiosity pulled his gaze toward the back of El's head.

Fear thumped heavily in his chest. Uncertainty prickled at the base of his neck.

"So, The Siren . . . she *lives* in Mountmend?" El's head turned back toward him, eyes locking on his over her shoulder, as if she could feel his gaze upon her.

A swift look at his chest, and she tilted her head at him. The quick glance reverberated down his bones and settled against his straining chest. Only then did he will his eyes away from her and toward the surrounding wood.

"It's where she . . . frequents. The Wake took the town over and claimed it as its own."

Kai willed his resolve to take root, but his tongue grew heavy as he spoke. The heinous things that woman had done . . .

She was a monster. She was a killer. She didn't deserve to walk free. She was dangerous.

Dangerous. Just like El.

Was she cut from the same cloth as the monster we sought? Under-dwellers wouldn't be far off, would they?

El stayed silent for far longer than he liked as they continued their journey. He harshly slashed his eyes toward her back. *Why is she so quiet?*

Prompting her to talk, attempting to get *something* out of her, Kai spoke once more. "You *have* heard of The Siren, right?"

A long pause.

"Who hasn't?" El finally answered quietly. Kai couldn't help but notice a quiver in her voice. "She's all the people out West talk about. Ghost stories. They vary, though. Sometimes she has blonde hair; other times, it's red. In some tales, her arms are littered with Sun Death spots, and sometimes she's flawless."

"Sounds about right," Rina threw over her shoulder. "Nothing—no information, no story—is reliable these days."

"They . . ." El trailed off. Nothing but their footfalls filled the silence. "The stories all had one thing in common, something that never changed no matter who was telling it."

Kai tilted his head and regarded her back. "And what's that?"

"What she does to them." El glanced back at him for no longer than a second.

It was a simple statement, yet Kai's stomach filled with lead and dropped. He knew exactly what she meant.

A cold-blooded killer, The Siren was. An evil bitch. No one knew exactly why she aided the cannibalistic faction that roamed most of these lands—except for the palace. The Wake killed with smiles on their faces and ate their prey all in the name of their sick, twisted version of survival.

The Wake—a name fitting of the vultures they were.

He had not heard any murmurs of The Siren partaking in the barbaric feast as they did, but like Rina said, information was unreliable. The only reason they knew she even existed was because of what she left after she was done: a jagged "S."

Sometimes it was carved into the dead trunks of the very wood they were in; sometimes it was smeared in her victims' blood across rocks. Always, though, it was there.

The foul woman took pride in her work.

El spoke up again. "Why are you going after her?"

"To kill her."

Kai didn't hesitate in answering as a thorny branch nearly scraped his neck. Using his palm, he pushed it away and nimbly dodged it—poised and graceful.

El took in a quick breath. She stepped over a pile of bones—deer, it looked like—and her fist curled at her side. "I heard you say you weren't like that . . . killing people—"

"Because of an inconvenience," Kai said sharply.

His tone made his stomach drop, yet he couldn't help it. He was *not* a killer. He was not like those he tried to stop. And for some reason, he had a feeling she didn't see it like that.

"Like you," Jaycen said.

"There's a difference." Kai ignored his friend's sharp jab and finished his thought with certainty.

"We are ridding this world of a monster. I'm sure a thought like that has never even crossed your mind. We can't all just hide—standing by and watching it happen," Jaycen tossed the words over his shoulder nonchalantly.

El dug her boots into the dirt below, stopping suddenly. Kai nearly slammed into her, missing her by inches. Dirt and sweat and something sweet hung in the air around her. Kai's lashes inadvertently fluttered closed as he took in the scents. As if cold water poured down upon him, his eyes snapped open and landed on the Fae.

Piercing blue eyes bored into his friend, gleaming with anger—rage simmering beneath, laced with grief. A growl—almost animalistic in nature—rumbled from El's chest.

"I don't—"

"Guys!" Rina squawked.

Kai's head whipped away from the Fae, and he saw it.

"Fuck!" Jaycen stormed forward as Kai merely stood there, taking in the sight.

His heart dropped. Their steam car had been stripped.

"How'd you even get this thing running in the first place?" El asked from her spot on the side of the wooden road, shifting from foot to foot. "I've only seen pieces of them—skeletons, really—every once in a while."

Kai dipped his head toward where the water tank and boiler should have been. Those were gone. So was the steam cylinder. Even the hood was taken from its hinges.

This thing is useless. Picked apart completely.

Irritation prickled against his skin, tightening over his bones. And the soft lilt of El's question grated against his rib cage and trickled down his muscles. He looked at her. "Why do you want to know?"

El narrowed her eyes and planted her hands on her hips. "*Kai*, was it? I'm merely curious. We don't have these in The Underworld."

The way she said his name made his spine straighten. It was sharp and sweet.

Rina ripped her gaze away from the horizon, abandoning her duty to keep watch. "Don't have what?"

"Cars." El shrugged, looking away from the steam car and taking in the others. Her eyes shuddered as she met their gawking. "Guns. That thing that used to light up your homes at night . . ."

Uncertainty twined around each word as Kai's jaw hinged open.

"Electricity?" he asked, disbelief pushing against each syllable.

El locked eyes with him just as a shallow gust of wind swept past them. A harsh reminder that they were out in the open on the side of the road. "Yes, that. None of your technology made it Beneath. We . . . lived differently than you."

A bored sigh—long and irritated—bounced across the discarded scraps of metal that once barreled them down this very road.

"Let's hurry this little conversation up," Jaycen voiced, wiping his palms against his pants and patting the husk of the vehicle before looking at the Fae. "We returned a missing child to his parents. His dad had been working on it years before The Darkest Day and offered to get it running—said it would be worth it if we could eliminate The Siren. There you have it. Now let's go; there's nothing salvageable here."

Rina walked back toward them from the other side of the road and rubbed her hand down her face. "I'm so sorry. I fucked up. I should have concealed it better."

"It's fine, Rina. When has walking ever stopped us before?" Kai sent her a kind smirk and patted her on the back. He walked past her and the Fae, Jaycen quick on his heels. Rina's brisk gait sounded behind him, her steps a familiar tune. The other pair of feet had yet to move. "Let's go, Fae!"

"I'm sorry about them." Kai picked up Rina's hushed voice just as El began to follow them.

Kai couldn't hear any reply.

7

Kai

THE SUN'S HEAT DIMMED as they traversed the deathly forest again—not enough for relief, but enough to ease the burning beneath Kai's clothes.

Not long after breaching the tree line—after filling their canteens at the small, pathetic excuse for a spring where they caught El licking at its rocks—he decided to take up the back of the group once more.

Best to keep everyone—her, *specifically—in my sights.*

Rina inched closer to the Fae as the group weaved through the trees, heading toward last night's clearing. Stolen glances were captured in mere seconds when she thought no one was looking. Each step closer pushed El to retreat, always keeping her distance.

"El," Rina finally said after the Fae stepped even farther away from her and dodged a sharp branch. "Will you tell us about The Underworld? What was it like?"

"Have her tell you." Jaycen looked over his shoulder. "I don't care what it was like."

"Prick," Rina mumbled, then spoke louder. "Fine. El, will you tell *me* about The Underworld?"

El didn't say anything at first, looking down at her boots as she stumbled over a thicket of branches and thorns before stopping. Rina, Kai, and, despite his aggravated sigh, Jaycen followed suit. Then she glanced back toward Rina. Sadness painted her profile; pinched lips and creased brows marred her features.

After what felt like ages—as if Kai, too, was curious to hear her answer—she uttered quietly, "Beneath is . . ."

A hush fell over them. Knitted together, her brows twisted as she pondered something—*anything*—to say. Her top teeth dug into her bottom lip, and a sigh slipped through. Hesitation lingered within it—reluctance.

El turned away from Rina, facing a nearby tree, and another sigh escaped. *A decision had been made*, Kai thought. He could see it in the way she straightened her spine, clenched her fists, and began walking once more.

"Have you ever loved something so much it hurts to remember it as it was?" El asked as she stepped over a small cluster of soot-stained rocks.

Kai didn't say a word. He rounded the same pile of rocks and followed the three in front of him while they began to venture farther into the forest. Rina didn't speak either, nor did Jaycen, despite claiming he didn't want to know. They merely continued their trek—passing through their previous campsite while heading east—and waited.

Her fingers twisted together. "Beneath . . . *was* . . . a sanctuary for all beings that were considered *other*. After such a bloody past, we were finally at peace—at least as much peace as one civilization could have after four hundred years at war. There were still prejudices, of course, toward those who were on the wrong side of history . . ." Her words floated into the air. Another hesitant moment of quiet hung between them before she began again. "But despite that, we were still a home for all. Brought together by the moon and the stars and a love that ran deep in our veins for the land we were blessed to be born into."

"Careful," Rina muttered, warning El to watch the dip in the ground.

El turned toward the woman, sent her a soft, unsure smile, and continued.

"The Underworld was filled with crystal-clear pools of sparkling water and fields of glowing Moon Flowers. Its air smelled sweeter than up here, like sugar and lemon with a hint of rain."

Kai saw the tips of her ears redden, and a movement in her jaw caught his attention. Her muscles flexed as if she were grinding her teeth. Kai could only see a sliver of her mouth from this angle, the corners tugging downward. There was a quiet longing there. But she still spoke like she was in a trance, memories pulling free the words he could tell she didn't want to release.

"It was home to the Fae Court on the western side of the realm and the Witch covens in the east. Pixies that rose out of the lush forests into the starry night, dancing to a song only they could hear. The sight . . . It was something remarkable, soul-healing. I used to sit on my balcony late at night and watch them.

"And the Gnomes . . ." Clearing her throat, El whispered, "Gnomes with more loyalty than any other being possessed in a single palm. They were the backbone of The Underworld. Mediators. Helpers. A force that held our individual societies together. You see, there was a harmony to the way we lived. Separate for the most part, yet still *one*."

No one spoke. No one wanted to shatter the heaviness that somehow wrapped around them. They let the words wash over them. Kai could tell she loved her home in a way that pulled at a part of him, a past he was ashamed of.

So, why was she here?

"Thank you." Rina raised her hand to her collarbone, her fingers gripping the necklace and rubbing the pendant. A loud, almost deafening crunch ricocheted against the trees as she stepped on a brittle stick. "It means so much to me."

Furrowing his brows, Kai studied Rina as she gazed to the side. A longing etched itself against her features. He made a mental note to ask her about it another time.

"Stop," Jaycen hissed, raising his hand to signal them to wait.

Immediately, goosebumps erupted across Kai's skin, and he rushed past Rina and the Fae. At the front, Jaycen stood silently, staring into a small cluster of trees. Just as he saw it, Rina and El approached.

"What is it?" El whispered.

Kai hushed her harshly.

Surveying the surrounding woods, Kai stared deep into the hidden shadows around them. Jaycen did the same, swiveling his torso to get a good look from every angle before his gaze landed back on the large trunk at the center.

Nailed to the bark, three pieces of parchment hung. Inked atop each one was a sketch. One of Rina. One of Jaycen. And one of himself. Hats sat on their heads, and bandanas covered their faces. But it was them, nonetheless.

The word "*WANTED*" was scribbled at the top, and just below were two words Kai despised: "*The Pack.*"

The name they were deemed by whoever they'd pissed off . . . or saved, perhaps. Either way, having a name for their trio felt too close to The Siren and The Wake. For them, it was prideful. The Wake gave themselves their name. Vultures were said to be resourceful and scavenged what was left.

"The Pack," however, left a bad taste in Kai's mouth. He simply wanted to be unknown, a shadow blending in with the other masked survivors and helping them when he could. Nothing more.

Unfortunately, the name stuck.

Kai studied the wanted posters he was so used to seeing, and that bad taste lingering on his tongue worsened. Something was off . . .

Is that—

El gasped, and Kai whirled his head toward her. Her hand flew up to cover her gaping mouth and began to tremble. Kai swore the skin peeking out below the dirt caked to her face had turned a slight shade of green.

With a heavy stomach and pounding heart, he focused on the wanted posters again, willing away what he knew deep down. He hoped his eyes were simply playing a trick on him. But then he saw it. Truly saw it. It confirmed the dread wrapping around his heart.

Tension rose within his body. His skin twitched and tightened.

Never had he seen a wanted poster like this.

The parchment wasn't parchment.

Pus oozed around its edges. Blood stained the bark. Freckles splattered across it. It was Human skin.

8

ELERI

BILE SHOT UP ELERI'S throat, burning everything in its path before dribbling down her chin onto the toes of her boots. Nothing more than the few sips of water she had at the spring and the acid in her stomach.

She had seen horrors nearly every day for the past five years, but something about the gruesome sight before her made her knees weak. Her body convulsed slightly, gagging. Her heart thundered, and a knot in her throat made it hard to breathe.

Who are these people? What have I gotten myself into? she silently screamed, squeezing her eyes shut and willing the ground to stop spinning. *Who exactly found me in the woods?*

Eleri hunched over, her body folding in half and shuddering around nothing. Her knees ached, the hard dead ground digging into them. Shards of twigs and rocks cut into her skin. Focusing on the pinch of pain, she tried to get a grip on the reality before her as her mind refused to slow. Thoughts spinning, spinning, spinning . . .

Fuck.

Her body jerked again. Still, nothing came up, yet tears gathered at the corners of her eyes, and snot dribbled out of her nose. Her lungs quivered, filling with dust and soot. Her leather gloves creaked as she dug her fingers into the ground, desperately wishing it would swallow her whole.

Hesitantly, Rina knelt next to her. "El . . ." She reached for Eleri's back, as if she hoped to rub away the distress. Her body heat swarmed around them, pulsing with her tentative movements.

As Eleri's instincts—instincts that only developed after The Darkest Day—took over, she dodged Rina's touch. Twisting harshly to the side and pressing her chest close to the ground, she crawled farther away from the blonde. Her heart hammered within the confines of her chest.

Rina's lips turned downward, and her brows tugged together. She looked hurt. She *was* hurt. Eleri saw it in her eyes.

A sudden fissure formed in Eleri's chest. Terror and sorrow and confusion dripped between her bones and settled across her muscles. If things were different, she would have relished the touch of others—just as she used to. Friendly pats to the back were nothing but bittersweet memories she had taken for granted long ago.

Sitting on her knees, heels digging into her ass, Rina looked at Eleri. Pity wafted off her in waves. Understanding glistened through her eyes. It made Eleri feel sick . . . broken . . . *unnatural.*

Rina's eyes flickered, and she nodded, pouring that curious kindness toward her into a smile, then silently stood. With that single gesture, Rina seemed to say, *It's okay. I may not understand, but I don't need to.*

Drops of gratitude and relief trickled within Eleri from Rina's peculiar understanding as the tension released in her body. With a long breath, she summoned what little courage she had left and stood up as well. Her legs wobbled, her knees cracking as they extended. Eleri wiped the bile from her mouth and refused to face Kai and Jaycen. She could only imagine their smug looks at seeing her so weak—and she didn't want to. She *couldn't.*

Instead, she looked back at the rotting skin nailed to the trees and studied each one. The illustrations were . . . incredible. At first glance, no one could tell they depicted the three Humans who stood next to her, looking akin to all those who wandered Above. But their eyes . . . they were menacing in black ink beneath wide-brimmed hats and bandanas.

Sharp, piercing leers shone through the sketches—the wanted posters looked just as Kai, Rina, and Jaycen had when she first encountered them the day before.

"It's a warning," Jaycen rumbled from deep within his chest. His fists clenched at his sides, a vein swelling at his neck as his brown skin darkened. Glancing at Kai, then toward Rina, he ignored Eleri altogether. The dismissal ground against Eleri's bones and stirred that fiery beast, but she chewed on her inner cheek to stop her harsh words from escaping. "They're trying to scare us off. They know we're on her trail. We're getting close."

Kai hummed as he crossed his arms, his hardened eyes drilling into the wanted posters with disdain. "We should keep moving."

However, he didn't budge, despite his order. Eyes lingering on the trunk, Kai was as still and menacing as a gargoyle. His hesitation and warring emotions clashed across his features. With a single nod, Rina and Jaycen both stepped to the side to give him space.

"Wait," Eleri whispered, eyes snapping to the left of the trees, then to the right. Kai sliced his gaze toward her. "Others are nearby—two people. I don't know if it's the ones who put these signs up or not . . ."

El felt two distinct pulses in the distance, languidly beating in sync. Calm. Unhurried. Rina and Jaycen immediately halted.

Jaycen shifted on his feet. "She could be ly—"

A snap of a twig rang out from deep in the woods.

All four froze. Rina barely breathed. Jaycen's shoulders tensed. Dread pooled at the base of Eleri's gut, wrapping around it like a noose—constricting and deadly. And although Kai's back was to her, she could see the rigidity in his spine.

Cracking his neck, Kai rolled out his wrists and crouched into a readied stance. Jaycen stepped up next to him, quietly reaching around to his thigh, where his knife hung. Menacing waves rippled off them and startled Eleri.

They . . . were going to fight *them off.*

Her heartbeat ticked up at the prospect of being caught in the middle of a brawl. The little beast within her peeked around its cage and purred at the thought of what would happen if she joined in.

Those two Humans wouldn't get far, her beast snickered.

Eleri squeezed her eyes shut and banished that type of thinking. Shame seeped into her pores. Her built-in self-defense, gifted by the curse, didn't bring her any comfort. In fact, it disgusted her. She wouldn't want to subject that burning horror on anyone, no matter who it was.

"Guys," Rina whispered, grabbing Kai and Jaycen's attention before glancing at Eleri.

The three stared at each other, different expressions twisting their faces. Worry and protectiveness glinted in Rina's eyes. Hardened refusal marred Jaycen's brows. A silent conversation echoed around Eleri; the quiet was resounding. After a few tense moments, Kai's shoulders sagged, as if he realized how burdensome she was.

"Stand down, Jayc," Kai whispered.

Jaycen slashed his gaze toward his friend and gawked, hissing, "What—"

"Protecting El needs to be our first priority." Rina kept her voice low and steady.

A hushed scoff rushed past Jaycen's lips, the bandana blowing with the force of it. "That's ridiculous. It could be The Siren."

Eleri stayed quiet, observing them as if she weren't the person they were discussing.

Rina sighed. "We're here to help others—"

"And killing the bitch," Jaycen whispered, his voice rising, "or anyone who condones her will do that."

Kai stepped closer, bracing a hand on the man's shoulder. Glancing at Eleri with a wrinkled nose, he leaned toward Jaycen—knowing she could hear every word—and murmured, "And what happens when you and I are too engrossed in the fight? A fight, need I remind you, that could include guns if we're dealing with The Wake. What happens when Rina jumps in to help? The Fae could flee. She could attack when we least expect it. This time, brother, we stand down."

The flame inside Eleri burst behind her eyes, turning a deadly deep red at the implication, the *accusation*. Kai stared sideways at her, leering into her soul. Distrust burned brightly within him, rivaling the heat in her own glare.

If I wanted you dead, Kai . . . If I wanted any of you dead, I would have done so the moment you cut me down from the tree.

Fear—unfiltered and nearly uncontained—ripped through her chest and battled for dominance over that abrupt rage. Fear of what she did to Merrin. Fear of the menacing thoughts that seemed to appear more often. Fear of never knowing the touch of another again. It swatted at the beast with mighty force until it retreated, sitting idle once more.

It was exhausting, that inner battle. Her want—no, *need*—to be good fought a part of who she inherently was. If only that weren't the case.

Another twig snapped, and Eleri strained her ears to listen. Deep breaths and rustling branches wove between each thump of their heartbeats. Whoever it was was far enough away that they had yet to be spotted.

"Hide," Kai mouthed, a silent order not meant to be broken.

Eleri glanced from Kai to the others. Rina was scanning the surrounding area. She eyed the posters, and disgust contorted her features before she turned away, leaving their faces nailed to the bark. Faster than Eleri could blink, Rina began scaling a nearby tree. Her movements were swift and silent. Not a single piece of burnt bark fell from her boots.

She perched atop a thicker branch, her body crouched—squatting with ease like an owl. The bare branches twisted and twined, creating spines of knots above and below her, keeping her hidden despite the high sun.

Jaycen bounded left into a dense cluster of broken trunks and branches. His large frame vanished, the dark cloth draping him blending into the sparse shadows.

And Kai headed for the trees behind them. He was so sure in his steps, so sure that it was the spot to hide. He took that certainty with him, leaving Eleri to fend for herself.

A twinge of panic overtook her as she searched for a hiding place. She stepped toward the tree Rina had scaled, and her boot—her damned boot—betrayed her. A decayed branch snapped beneath it, the loud crack echoing against the trunks.

Eleri's heart seemed to stop, plunging into the pit of her gut. Kai whipped his head around, glaring at her as if she had done it on purpose, his hardened eyes slightly widening with dread.

"Over there!"

A deep, gritty voice yelled in the distance. Pounding footsteps quickly followed, thumping in sync between the singed forest.

Eleri's eyes snapped toward the sound. *Fuck!*

Desperately, Eleri swiveled her head, adrenaline pumping across her muscles. Her mind went blank as if she had never run from conflict. *You're only alive because you've stayed hidden for five years. Hide, Gods damn it!*

She could hide in the brush, crouch as low as she could, just like she did the day before. But The Pack—that was what they were called, apparently—had found her. What was to say whoever was lurking around wouldn't, too? Scaling a tree, just as Rina had—just as Eleri used to do in this very forest for several months—was an option, but over four years had passed since she had last done so. Eleri didn't think she'd be quick enough.

Rigid, motionless, Eleri's world swirled on its axis. Solid footsteps pounded against the dead ground. Heavy breathing and hammering hearts pierced her ears as The Pack's enemies—*her* new enemies, she guessed—closed in.

"I think it's this way," the same man's voice huffed out before his companion grunted.

Kai was upon her, his long strides reaching her before she could even comprehend he'd moved. Eleri eyed him closely, taking a step back. Each twitch of his lip and flit of his gaze was so minute she wouldn't have noticed if he weren't so close. His jaw clenched and slackened as he surveyed her. His fingers jerked in her direction, and his eyes shuddered, as if he were thinking about something long ago. She saw the options roiling around his skull—the what-ifs, the doubts. All of it was bare for her to see. It was jarring. Unsettling.

Then resolve washed over him. He stepped forward, seeming to have come to a conclusion.

"El. Listen to me," Kai whispered, a frantic hush lacing each word. He glanced back in the direction of the rustling foliage and searching men. "Follow me. Do not fall behind. Do not look back. Just . . . follow me. Okay?"

His warm breath brushed across her nose. Then Kai ran. He bounded past Eleri, barely missing her shoulder by a hair in a movement as fluid as a stream, taking his oaky, natural scent with him.

A moment of hesitation passed. Then, turning heel, she flung her body into action. Dried sticks and small pebbles flew into the air. The loud crunch echoed behind her and alerted the men to her location.

"This way!" the second man's nasally, high-pitched voice rang out in alarm.

Eleri's boots grated the soil. Sweat dripped down her neck and settled in the fabric of her top. Her breaths came heavy—heaving in and out with each rushed step toward what she hoped was safety. Their hulking steps pounded in her skull, their coarse breaths rasping in her ears as if they were right *there*, right at her heels.

Sprinting for the trees and weaving between trunks and branches, Eleri ran blindly in the direction Kai had gone. Her lungs ached for air; her dried lips cracked and bled as she sucked in each mouthful. Several hanging branches dipped low and cut her skin; small scratches covered her flushed and dirtied cheeks and neck. She dodged one. She missed another. An endless cycle of stinging terror.

Ducking below a particularly low branch, Eleri avoided its serrated edge before her boot caught on a twisting dead vine. Her palms broke the fall, her wrists buckling under the weight of her body, and her cheek hit the ground.

"Shit . . ." Eleri quietly groaned.

Sharp, shooting pain lit up her right arm from wrist to shoulder. Dirt stuck to her bleeding lips and coated her gums as she sucked in a silent cry from the impact. The copper taste of her blood mixed with it, and she couldn't help but gag.

"We're close!" The deeper voice rang out, much closer than Eleri would like. "I heard something this way!"

Get the fuck up! her little beast roared.

Another stab of pain shot up her arm as she gripped the dirt beneath her and hauled her body into a standing position. Finding her footing, Eleri scrambled forward before veering right and hiding behind the thickest tree she saw.

Their pounding strides pierced her trembling soul before both men came to a stop on the other side of the tree, their boots skidding against the ground and creating a cloud of dust that wove its way into Eleri's lungs. A cough rolled up her throat. Stifling it—forcing it to stay down—she bit her tongue and held her breath as the rough bark of the trunk dug into her back. They smelled of rotting meat and body odor. It was pungent . . . revolting.

"Do you think it's them?" the man with the nasally voice asked.

His heartbeat skittered with excitement.

Eleri looked around for the leader of The Pack. She had eyes on him until she fell. Only burnt trees lined her vision, though. Small tremors skirted down Eleri's skin. Her veins pulsed with the beginnings of a panic attack.

What was I thinking? I should never have decided to stay with them after they strung me up in that tree.

Using them to guide her eastward? It was idiotic, and she never would have stayed if she had truly known who she was getting tangled up with.

"The Pack was spotted roaming these areas a few weeks ago. If it's them, surely, they would have begun to head back from The Vale by now." The other cracked his neck. "If it's not them, it's dinner."

The men laughed. The sound—like rusted saws grating on a tree trunk—made Eleri feel nauseous, her vision tilting slightly . . . or perhaps that was just their smell. Eleri held her breath nonetheless.

Movement caught her eye to her left. Several trees over, Kai peeked his head around the trunk he was crouched against and locked eyes with her. Eleri released a silent huff of air, and her muscles relaxed ever so slightly.

I'm not alone.

Kai stayed still, holding his breath, his heartbeat slowing a fraction as he stared at her with wide eyes. His brown irises flicked back and forth between her, the forest surrounding them, and the men behind her.

Time felt as if it were lost as his gaze locked with hers once more, letting this moment last an eternity. No longer were they in danger. No longer did the disabling fear wreak havoc on her taut muscles. It was just him and her. Eleri's breath caught in her throat, and her mind slowed. Just brown eyes luring in blue.

"Let's keep moving," one of the men sighed.

The voice shattered the air around Eleri. It was like a slap to the face, like a bucket of freezing water from the southernmost spring in The Underworld was thrown at her, drenching her and leaving her shivering without the warmth of someone's touch.

"No!" the other protested. A deep inhale penetrated the air behind Eleri. "They're here somewhere. I can smell them."

The blood pumping through her veins turned icy cold. Kai's heartbeat increased in speed.

Her shaking hands rose from their perch on her knees toward her face and pressed tightly against her trembling lips. With a stomach full of lead, she forced her palm to smother any sound that might try to escape.

Silent puffs of air left Eleri's nostrils as her breathing picked up. Her heart pounded against her rib cage so frantically it ached. The man took a step closer, another twig snapping beneath his weight, and her stomach dropped.

I'm going to die.

The realization hit her like a stampede.

She was going to die. She was going to die because she was too pathetic to lean into the blackened curse that ran through her. Because, despite everything she had seen since the start of this new horrendous world, the kind young female Eleri used to be still lingered. The Fae-Witch who would never harm even the silkworms hanging from the trees by the palace pounded against the wall she had to build around herself to survive, screaming for her to remember who she was. No matter what or whom she faced, Eleri refused to call on her darker side to end these men.

I'm going to die. I'm a coward, and I'm going to die because of it.

"If it was His will to find them right now, we would have. Be patient," the other muttered. "Let's head south. They could have snuck down toward the road."

Her widened eyes—eyes that had yet to leave Kai's since she spotted him behind the trunk—enlarged even more. They were so close. Holding her breath, she willed her body to stop. Stop breathing. Stop fidgeting. Stop everything.

Kai kept staring at her, too. His lips were pressed tightly together. A silent swallow ran down his throat.

"Let's go."

One man jogged toward the road without another word. The other, however, had yet to move. Eleri sensed the man behind her, the ragged beat of his blood pounding through his body.

Another deep inhale, like he was savoring the scent of the air around him . . . the air that smelled of her. A long growl ripped through his chest and penetrated the burning deep within her stomach. Then he ran after his companion, leaving Eleri a trembling mess.

As the retreating footsteps became fainter and fainter, Eleri could breathe more freely. Yet she was cemented to the ground, suffocating under the weight of what had just happened. She couldn't move. She didn't want to.

She was connected to wanted vigilantes. She had a target on her back despite having stayed out of sight for the past five years. She . . .

A tear fell from the tips of her lashes, leaving a streak in the dirt on her face in its wake.

More began to cascade, silently sinking toward the earth. She barely registered each tear that breached her lash line and burned the back of her eyes.

Frozen. Ashamed. Fearful.

I'm a coward, and I almost died because of it.

9

JAYCEN

"Where the fuck did he go?"

Jaycen Ryuk barreled from his hiding spot, swatting dried leaves from his top as Rina dropped from her branch, the deep thump echoing in his ears. His chest heaved as the dust his boots kicked up swirled into his mouth, and a harsh cough racked through his lungs. Blinking rapidly, he whipped his head from tree to tree.

No longer could he hear the men who stalked the woods for them. Nor could he see Kai or that Fae.

"Dumbass," Jaycen hissed. He bent down and tightened the laces of his boots, muttering under his breath. "Always running headfirst into situations for people . . . beings, *creatures*. Always feeling the need to save without any worry for his own well-being."

Jaycen rose, lifted his hat, and ran a hand over his buzzed hair, gripping what little he could before tugging it. Pacing, Jaycen swore under his breath.

"I need to get to him," he muttered, biting his inner cheek until he tasted blood. "I need to make sure he's okay."

I must. It's all I know how to do.

After several hurried steps toward the trees he thought Kai went through, Rina ran up to him, grabbing his bicep to stop him. "Jaycen."

He shrugged her off cruelly before taking another step, Kai and his safety the only things on his mind.

"Stop, Jaycen!" Rina repeated, putting forth her most commanding voice and cutting him off mid-step.

She dug the heels of her boots into the dirt right in front of him. Her normally too-soft eyes were hardened to the point they were unrecognizable, amber burning bright as she regarded him.

Jaycen's head shook, barely stopping to glance at the woman before him. "You don't understand. I need to protect him. I *vowed* to protect him!"

A crease formed between Rina's brows, her lips pulling downward. Her arms crossed, and she straightened her spine. "You vowed?"

The scrutiny in her voice was glaring, judgmental. *She doesn't understand. She never would.*

"Never mind," Jaycen growled, shaking his head once more. His eyes continued to scan the woods around him. "Don't worry about it. Just . . . just get out of my way. I'm going to find him."

Rina's hand shot forward and latched onto his bicep once more. Her grip tightened against his skin, digging her nails into the fabric of his tunic. Her palm was warm even over his clothes. Heat radiated into him.

"He's not a child, Jaycen. He's been leading us for years now. He doesn't need you to worry about him." She searched his features for any clue as to what might be going on in his head. Jaycen wouldn't allow that, hiding behind the fortress he began building long before The Darkest Day. He wouldn't let her see shit. "And you know damn well he'd hate to know that you do."

Jaycen clenched his jaw, his fists curling at his sides. "You. Don't. Understand."

A sharp brush of wind swung around them, whipping his bandana against his neck as Rina's blonde strands flew into her eyes. Finally, she released her grip on him and took a step back—just enough for her to look up into his looming leer properly with vigor.

"That's right, I don't," Rina muttered, then raised her voice just enough to make Jaycen take her seriously. "In fact, I think you're being ridiculous right now. What happens when you go after him, and he makes his way back here in search of us . . . for *you* . . . which, need I remind you, he's capable of doing."

A growl—deep and heady—vibrated against his rib cage, traveling up toward the base of his throat where it sat as though a rock was lodged there, making it hard to breathe. His entire body tingled with a near-unstoppable urge to storm past her without a single look back. He didn't care about anything—or anyone—but Kai. And yet . . .

She's right. Damn it, she's right, and I hate it.

Jaycen knew Kai was capable of anything, but he could never forget those flashes of fear, self-loathing, and uncertainty across his friend's face when that woman asked for help on The Darkest Day. Nor could he forget the pit Kai fell into after.

Jaycen would never let him sink that low again.

Five years ago, he made that promise. And in doing so, he silently found his purpose for the first time in his life. *I will keep Kai safe. I will do whatever it takes to make sure he survives whatever we come across.*

Jaycen stepped toward Rina, whose body stiffened.

"Jaycen . . ." she warned.

He looked down at her. Deep creases stood stark against her skin, and her fingers wrung around the choppy tips of her hair. Concern oozed off her. Concern for . . . *him.*

A deep sigh escaped his clenched teeth as he patted her shoulder. He knew Rina was kind, *good*—one of the best, really—but never had he felt like that warmth should be aimed at him. He didn't deserve it.

But she's right . . .

"I'm not going after him. I'm just checking the clearing's perimeter. Need to make sure no one else is lingering about while we wait for him."

He sounded defeated, even to his own ears.

Rina's shoulder relaxed, and a long exhale escaped her loosening jaw as she nodded, finally stepping aside and unblocking his path. "And El."

A grunt fell against the tip of his tongue. *I don't give two shits about that creature.*

10

Kai

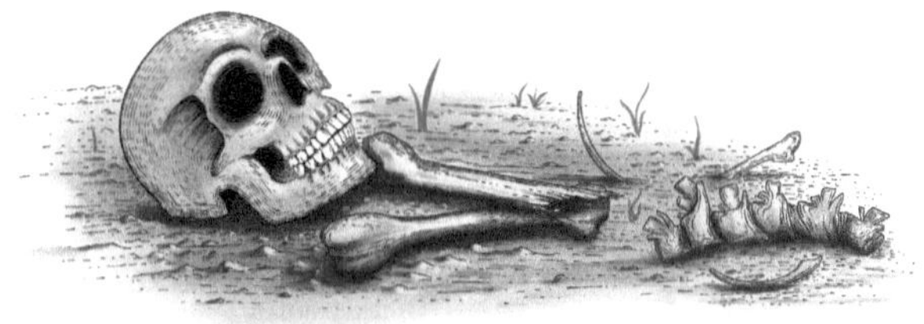

Hesitantly, Kai approached El. His heels barely grazed the earth beneath him as he tiptoed toward the rigid Fae. Her body was tucked into a ball. Her shoulders were tense, and the muscles across her face were taut.

A creature of The Underworld shouldn't look so frail, he thought. They should be terrifying—growling and biting and slashing. They should be fiery beasts, just like the flames in her eyes before.

But El's tear-filled gaze was nothing of the sort. It was vacant, hollow. Tracks smeared her cheeks and glistened against the sun's heat, revealing more ivory skin beneath the grime. Her light-pink lips were dried and cracked, wobbling under the weight of what Kai thought was the horror running through her entire being. Her eyes flitted back and forth, as if she were lost in a memory from the past . . . or the possibility of what-ifs. Bending down with a faint grunt, Kai kneeled. Eye to eye.

That empty gaze never left despite his proximity. It was as if she had yet to realize the threat was no longer present. It was as if she were staring straight through him. She was petrified, and no one—no matter if they were Human or Fae—deserved to be trapped in the unrelenting and paralyzing grip of fear.

A sharp twinge twisted in Kai's chest. He knew that feeling all too well. He had lived it nearly every day since he was fourteen. His fingers twitched at his side. A sudden urge—an itch almost too unbearable to ignore—materialized within the depths of his mind. An unknown part of him wanted to press his thumb to her bottom lip—to stop the uncontrollable quiver that wouldn't seem to cease. An unknown part of him yearned to protect her like something—a force larger than himself—was telling him to stay by her side.

Stop it. Do not trust those from Beneath. The voice in his head—the sane voice, he deemed—whispered against the edges of his mind. *They're dangerous.*

Shutting his eyes, he blocked El—stark still—from his sight and focused on the fear that had struck him when he first saw her. The same fear that rushed through him on The Darkest Day. The fear of magic.

Kai ripped that confusing urge away before it could sink into his very bones and lit it on fire. Watching it burn from behind his eyelids, Kai thrust his hand into his pocket and brushed over the crystal he'd taken from El.

Soon . . . Soon, they would find The Siren. Soon, he could rid himself of her and the only thing keeping her with them.

He allowed himself a few moments to get his head on straight. With one last deep breath in, Kai opened his eyes. The fear he was trying so hard to hold on to stared him right in the face. El's eyes were drowning in it, crushing her . . . consuming her.

"Hey." He softened his harsh tone. With a slow swivel of his head, Kai looked around at the blackened trees surrounding them. No sign of their pursuers appeared, but they couldn't be too careful. They had to move. They needed to move. He had to get back to Jaycen and Rina. Looking back at the Fae, he said, "Hey . . . El."

El blinked. It was a lazy movement, as if her eyelids shifted on their own. The fog of terror cleared from her irises slightly, but she didn't move. It was unsettling how still she was. And this, Kai realized, had nothing to do with the origins of her heritage. This was trauma-induced. This was just as he had been after seeing someone gut another for the first time . . . over a piece of bread.

Stomach knotting, Kai decided he couldn't let her fall into that hole.

Not for her. *No.* For the team. They couldn't afford delays on a mission as important as this. And they couldn't let her go. Not until it was safe for them to.

A calming caress in the storm of emotions raged in his chest. "Come back to me."

Fuck. His tongue turned dry and heavy. His heart pounded against the confines of his chest. *Where did that come from?*

Then El blinked again, clarity washing across her features. Her wide eyes focused on him before her breath caught. Recognition gripped tight—where she was, who she was with, and how close he was to her as he leaned forward, soaking in that final blink.

"Thought I lost you there for a second," he whispered.

Kai recoiled as the last word floated from his mouth. It felt like someone had control over his lips. And as if on instinct, El pressed her body away from him against the tree, digging into the bark as far as she could to put distance between them.

Distance. Yes, distance was good.

Clearing his throat and standing up, he tore his hand out of his pocket, leaving behind her stone. Kai flexed his fingers, pulled off his gloves, stuffed them in his back pocket, and wiped his sweaty palms on his pants. "Come. We need to head back."

His voice was gruffer, gritty like sandpaper. Back was the leader of The Pa—*No.* They weren't wolves . . . They weren't like The Wake. He may have led them in some decisions, but they were a team, and he refused to think of them as anything else. And with that mask he wore alongside his bandana and hat, back was his nonexistent intrigue for the magic user. "We should find the others and keep moving. We don't want The Wake on our tail."

Kai stepped away from El as she stood. She stumbled and caught herself with her right arm.

"Ah!" El winced, a hiss escaping her clenched teeth and her legs wobbling.

She was hurt.

The eyes of those who hadn't helped him all those years ago flashed before his mind. In those big, empty halls of what used to be his home, he was alone. All he wanted was someone to help him, and that instinct to right all those wrongs pushed through. A need to help her kicked in.

Kai exhaled and reached to grab her shaking hands, to steady her. In an instant, she recoiled away, swiftly dodging his touch. His chest tightened as the fearful faces of women he'd met before reflected in her gaze. Their eyes would flit from side to side. Their bodies would cave in on themselves as if that would stop the greedy hands from groping them. And El was a spitting image of that.

It didn't last, though, that compassion. Not for more than a few breaths before it transformed into frustration. Sharply looking away, Kai pinched his lips together and shook his head.

Why won't she let me help her? I can help.

Without another word, he exhaled and started his trek, weaving between the trees. At first, nothing stirred behind him. Then came rustling and frantic footsteps, as if she were stumbling, struggling to keep up.

Looking back, Kai caught the haze clouding her eyes as she followed as best she could. Terror still gripped her tight, but with each step, it cleared ever so slightly. Despite the weighted feeling in his stomach, he turned and continued his path toward his friends.

Silence lingered between them as they weaved through the trees. The scent of musk and bone-dry vegetation wafted around them with each step as they navigated the terrain. Suddenly, El stopped, her steps silent. Startled, Kai halted and turned; his full gaze was on her. El veered off to the side, slowly approaching a charred pile of rubble, half-buried under logs and cinders he wouldn't have noticed if she hadn't stopped.

Kai tilted his head to the side as he examined her from a distance. A shaking, leather-clad hand pulled out a sage-and-white book. It was dirty and frayed, yet the silver details on its spine—flowers and hearts and envelopes—glimmered underneath the orange sky. It was severely damaged, barely hanging on by a thread. A handful of pages detached from its withered spine. A corner of the book broke off and fell.

As she pulled it fully free, El's stifled breath shattered. The book fell apart. The spine split in two; the rest of its pages fell to the forest floor and caught on the breeze blowing between the branches. Dust wafted around her empty hand as she stared at the pieces of the book landing on the ground.

El's bottom lip wobbled, and her eyebrows tugged together. Kai zeroed in on her. She was upset—truly heartbroken—but just as fast as that sorrow flitted across her face, it disappeared. Masked by neutral indifference. Her crinkled forehead smoothed, and her downturned lips pulled up into an emotionless line.

A single breath passed as Kai watched El carefully. She stared blankly at where the book had once been held together by sticks and stones. Then, she stiffly stood. Her knees cracked; the sound was loud compared to the stillness of the forest. Without a word, she made her way toward him again. Raising his brow, Kai asked a silent question.

What's with the reaction? It's just a book. It's just—

Narrowing her dark blue eyes as if she felt him dissecting her, El hardened her features. "Thought I saw a can of fruit."

She wore a mask, just as he did.

Dangerous . . .

Kai let El pass. He gazed at her as she made a wide berth around a small patch of life, newly grown grass poking out beneath the dead forest floor.

Dangerous . . . and interesting.

He watched and watched her, then started his trek back once more.

II

KAI

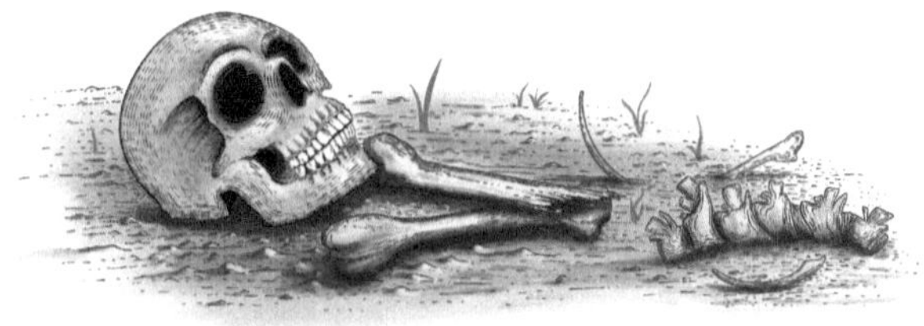

"OH, THANK GODS!" RINA gasped as Kai and El breached the tree line and drew near her and Jaycen.

The bright sun was long past its highest point, edging toward The West. The heat was still stifling; the suffocating wind picked up as it blew through the clearing.

"What took you so long?" Rina marched toward Kai and wrapped her arms around him in a firm hug before pulling away and punching him square in the shoulder. There was no true malice behind the impact. Only a slight tenderness pulsed beneath his skin as a result. "I was about to eat my words and come collect you myself before beating the shit out of you for scaring us like that."

Kai chuckled and lightly punched Rina back before rustling her windswept hair. "And I would have *let* you kick my ass if I'd ended up captured by those vile beings in the first place."

A large hand came up from behind and slapped Kai's back. It stayed there, grounding Kai like an anchor. Jaycen.

Kai glanced at his friend. His large stature obstructed Kai's view. Lean shoulders and clenched fists.

"Don't ever run off like that again." His deep voice was unwavering. Seriousness seeped through each word.

The quick retort on the tip of Kai's tongue died at the look his friend gave him. His face was hardened beneath his bandana—Kai could tell just from the rivets and lines between his brows—and sweat gathered at the bridge of his nose, wetting the fabric. Jaycen's eyes burned with simmering emotion. A shred of softness and worry Kai hadn't been allowed to see in years shone bright before it was consumed once again by the coarsened shield.

Kai clasped Jaycen's hands and squeezed. "I won't," he vowed.

As he released his friend's wrists and glanced behind him, Kai's eyes snagged on El. Standing silently off to the side near the threshold of the forest, she wasn't looking at anything in particular. She was just . . . *there*. Standing . . . Staring. Kai's gaze narrowed, turning into a leer, while he watched her.

He couldn't help but wonder what was going through her mind. *Is she thinking about the destroyed book? Is she lost in the memories of what had just happened?*

Kai winced as the sharp clap of Rina's palms echoed around them—a high-pitched crack snapping through his bones and wrenching his mind free from his silent questions.

"Let's go," she said, resuming their journey toward what used to be known as the Eastern Plains.

Kai willed his heartbeat to slow as his fingers grazed the hilt of his knife, a habit he picked up over the years, as if checking it was still there. It was a ridiculous habit, but one he couldn't seem to break. Once he was satisfied, he started for the trees, forcing the past behind him and only looking forward . . . toward The Siren.

As the day's stifling heat became slightly less suffocating and the orange sky darkened, the four navigated the forest slowly in case the two cannibals were lingering, *hunting*. No one talked. Breaths were held. Steps were silent. Not even a single twig snapped beneath their boots, nor did broken leaves rustle along the path. Deeper within the trees—all dead, all charred—they went.

Kai listened intently. His focus lay on his surroundings. Three sets of careful steps, not including his. A loud crash reverberated around them as a blackened branch plunged to the ground, the dead trunk no longer able to hold its weight. A high-pitched whistle blew through the slivers of shadow as the breeze picked up ever so slightly. And—

Rustling within the brush caught his attention. Kai suddenly came to a stop, flicking his hand in the air to halt the others. Jaycen, Rina, and El followed his command as he scanned the surrounding area. No movement to his left. None to his right. But just up ahead, camouflaged behind the dead twigs of what was once a berry bush in the distance, stood a deer. Its gray-brown coat was thin and dingy. Its spine stood out along its back as it bent over, chewing on bark and licking at the soot cemented to the ground. Just like them, this creature was trying—and failing—to find any food of substance . . . trying to survive.

Kai took a hesitant step forward. The animal paused its chewing. Head remaining bowed, the deer's eyes darted to the side. Time hung between them, the air strung taut as he waited with bated breath to see if the animal would flee. Before Kai could take in another stiff inhale, the deer relaxed and continued licking at a jagged rock. Its tongue split on the edge, blood pooling in its mouth before it lapped that up as well.

It was desperate.

Slowly, Kai reached for the knife strapped to his body. Eyes never leaving the creature, he rigidly unbuckled the holster. The click was deafening, and his heart sank. Spooked from what should have been such an insignificant sound, the deer snapped its head upward and turned toward them.

A breath caught in Kai's throat as he stared at the animal. A knot twisted in his chest, and his heart sank into the depths of his gut at the sight. The deer's skin was drooping, falling off its bones in a pus-filled mess on the left side of its face. No lips covered its chipped teeth. Shredded muscles hung limp from the gash in its neck. And the most unsettling thing of all were its eyes—glazed and milky white, like a thick fog settling over its irises.

Infected from the curse. Deformed. Spoiled.

It must have been born after The Darkest Day—arriving into this world after its mother was poisoned by the blast, the residue of the curse trickling down into its very being. It wasn't rare for that to happen. Kai had seen several children who were the same.

Fuck. Kai hesitated as he stared at the creature. *I don't want to eat that.*

Fingers jittered at his sides, hesitation imprisoning Kai. He continued to stare at the animal, his eyes locking with its milky whites. Just as the deer readied itself to flee—its muscles twitching in anticipation—another knife flew and hit its mark. Right in the center of the creature's forehead.

Kai flinched as its body collapsed with a dull thump. Whipping his head around, he caught the way Rina's hand fell to her side. A long exhale whooshed through her teeth just as she finished the killing blow. Her features were hardened, concentration tugging along the skin surrounding her eyes and furrowing her eyebrows.

Her stare shifted away from her target and slid to his, lashes shuddering and irises shifting across his features in silent understanding. A pregnant pause between them, and her shoulders slumped. "We need to eat, Kai. It's been a week."

Kai knew she did what she had to do. For all of them. Being selective when coming across any type of food in this hellish wasteland was a luxury they couldn't afford. He knew . . . He *knew.* Eat what they could get . . . or starve. Kai would always choose to eat, even if it took him a moment to accept it. But each time they dug into the ruined meat of a young animal, he couldn't help but wonder what was going into their bodies, if remnants of the magic or curse now ran in their veins.

Just as it did hers . . .

As if it had waited for the perfect moment, his body flushed and tensed, and the pull of his gaze glided toward El—

"It's not ideal . . . I know that," Rina continued, saving Kai from his eyes' betrayal. "But we won't make it long if we don't fill our stomachs with *something*."

He knew . . .

Kai placed his hand on her shoulder and sent her a warm smile. "Thank you." The words were a simple whisper—however no less heartfelt—emotion weaving through his voice. He steadied his churning gut and focused on the gratitude he held for his friend.

"Nice aim." Jaycen sent her a swift nod of approval before making his way toward the deer.

Kai bit his lip and trailed his friend, following the path his large body forged through the thicket. Rina and El followed, quietly shadowing his movements. Kneeling, Jaycen leaned toward the deer's body and studied it. Kai did the same next to him, his head tilting ever so slightly. Shoulder-to-shoulder. Brothers-in-arms.

The deer twitched as the remaining tendrils of life left its body. It looked wrong. Green pus oozed along the sides of the knife buried in its head. Its fur was moist, sickly. And its bones—ribs, shoulders, joints—protruded through its thin skin. There was barely enough muscle to feed them. Shallow gasps from its wheezing lungs escaped through the dried and cracked snout of the animal. One last exhale blew into Kai's face, then stillness.

Kai stared into the creature's ghostly eyes as they glazed over even more. So much death in this new world. So much—

Jaycen harshly yanked Rina's knife out of the deer's head. The reverberating squelch in the quiet forest as the blade dislodged from its skull caused an almost soundless inhale from behind him. Kai knew better than to think it was Rina. Glancing at the two women just as Jaycen wiped the blade clean against his pants and handed it back to its owner, Kai's eyes settled on El. Intensity sharpened her features as she stared at the creature. Something ravenous lurked behind her blue leer. She was *hungry* . . . yet that look in her eyes . . . was unsettling.

"I got it." Kai turned away from her. Determination fed his movements as he unsheathed his own knife, readying to gut and skin the deer. "We both know I'm faster."

"That's not something to brag about, brother," Jaycen quipped, a short laugh pressed against the barrier of his bandana.

Heat ran up Kai's neck and settled just below his ears.

Stealing a quick glance at El, he noticed the splotches of visible ivory skin along her face were a light shade of pink. She giggled—*fucking giggled*—and Kai couldn't help but beg The Son to open the ground and swallow him whole.

While this side of Jaycen—a side of him that rarely showed itself over the years since The Darkest Day—was refreshing to finally see once more, Kai's heartbeat picked up as he focused back on the carcass and cut into it. Each slice beneath the hide was emphasized by the pounding of Kai's pulse. Each chop was in sync with his flustered breaths.

Cut, slice, chop. Cut, slice, chop. Over and over again. Faster each time the cycle renewed.

Fucking Jaycen . . .

A SMALL FIRE CRACKLED between them. The flame flickered against the darkened sky. Light traveled a long way, even tucked into the depths of the forest, but they decided the risk of being spotted was worth it to make the meat safer to eat.

Today was close, though. Too close. Closer than Kai had ever been before to being caught by The Wake. And he knew why.

"Thank you for the food, Rina," El mumbled around a mouthful of meat.

Kai watched El in awe as she dug into the piece of thigh again without a single complaint. The greenish-gray meat didn't deter her as her canines flashed under the light of the fire and ripped into it. Frantically eating . . . Devouring.

How long has it been since she last ate? How long—

Stomach clenching, he looked away from her. He didn't want to think about that. He couldn't.

"I'm"—Rina swallowed around her last bit of rump—"happy we were able to find it. We were lucky to have found an animal at all."

Kai met Jaycen's gaze, surprise stirring at the heaviness beneath his hat. Then his attention fell to the untouched piece of backstrap in his lap.

"Jaycen," Kai started, "you need to eat."

"I'm good." Jaycen's back straightened, and his eyes darted toward El.

He was hesitant to show his face around the Fae, untrusting of her. Kai could see it in the tension he held around his eyes. And rightfully so. His bandana had been knotted securely around his head since they'd crossed paths with her. If Kai's and Rina's had been that day, they wouldn't be in this mess in the first place. But even though Kai could see him holding onto what was left of his anonymity, he needed to eat. He couldn't go much longer.

Kai leaned forward slightly, resting his elbows on his knees. "It's okay," he whispered, pouring every ounce of honesty into those two words and leaving the rest unspoken.

Jaycen's eyes flickered with an emotion Kai detected right away. Trust.

They trusted each other. Wholeheartedly. Unwaveringly.

Jaycen's shoulders sagged slightly before his uncertain eyes flicked back toward the Fae. El sucked a bit of meat off the bone held delicately in her gloved fingers before stopping. The heavy heat of her gaze warmed Kai's skin. Kai thought Rina was watching too. The campsite turned quiet and still, but his attention remained on his friend.

Trust me, Jayc.

The muscles in Jaycen's temple feathered as he turned back toward Kai. His eyes were still hardened, guarded. But a long sigh blew against the fabric covering his face. Jaycen lifted his hat from his head and slowly set it beside him, hesitating.

Eyes on me.

Jaycen's gaze locked back onto Kai, as if he had heard the words he silently spoke. Kai gave him an encouraging nod, a push to hopefully let his guard down enough to take a bite.

You need to eat.

His fingers trembled as he glided them around his head and slowly pulled free the knot of fabric. Holding the barrier against his face for a moment longer, Jaycen looked back at El, eyes hardening as a growl rumbled in his chest, before his bandana slipped to the ground.

Firelight flickered across Jaycen's features. Shadows darkened below his eyes, creating stark lines connecting his downturned lips. His coarsened leer sliced toward El. It was a look that not many could withstand. Kai's stomach churned.

"Eat, Jayc."

Once his friend reluctantly took his first bite of deer meat, Kai released a silent breath—the tension dissipating from his muscles—and reached into his back pocket to retrieve an old Upperworld map he'd grabbed when he fled his home.

It was frayed and creased and covered in dark streaks of ash and dirt. Elbows resting on his knees, he started to study it, lost in the markings across the parchment. Scribbles of information from the last five years;

safe areas, new settlements, faction territories, even places where they'd found food . . . though those places now ran dry like the rest of the land.

Jaycen circled the fire and approached from Kai's right, muffled steps and soft chewing caressing his ears before he squatted next to him. A moment later, Rina followed too; her footfalls were light. Huddling on the other side of Kai, she stared over his shoulder at the map.

"What now?" Jaycen asked, his mouth full of meat and his breath hitting the crumpled parchment.

Rina's voice, when she replied, was muffled as a pull—a force controlling his body—drew him away from the conversation. He looked up, watching El shift to the other side of the fire. She sat amid leftover chunks of meat, too fatty or spoiled for consumption. Her head tilted back, and her eyes closed. Kai observed as she took off her left glove—for a moment, it felt like he couldn't breathe.

She ran the tips of her fingers across the dead ground, lost in her thoughts as if searching for something long gone. Sadness enveloped her. He could see it pulsing off her in waves, and he lost himself in the sight before him.

So curious, this being was.

He stared and stared at the skin of her hands—smooth ivory barely covered by the dirt caked underneath her pointed fingernails. Ivory so enthralling, so—

"Kai?"

Rina's voice shattered and ricocheted around him. Snapping his eyes toward the woman, his heart raced as if he'd been caught doing something he shouldn't have.

"What?" Kai shook his head and focused back on the map and the conversation with his companions.

He needed to get a fucking grip.

"I said," Rina continued, not drawing any more attention to his obvious distraction, "we should head farther north to stay out of The Wake's trail. I don't think they'll give up their search in this area any time soon, and we need to keep moving. It'll take longer, but it's the safest option."

Kai nodded. She was right. Rina was always right. Honestly, if he and Jaycen had never found her, they'd probably be dead by now. They might have "saved" her the day they crossed paths, but she saved them in more ways than one ever since.

Glancing around the trees, Kai surveyed the area. It was clear. Nothing rustled in the brush. Nothing made the hair on the back of his neck rise. But it was better to be careful.

"We'll camp here and continue north in the morning." Pausing, he turned to look at Rina and Jaycen. "Get the ropes ready. We're climbing tonight."

Groans and grumbles echoed from either side of him. Several sighs slipped through Jaycen and Rina's lips even as they stood up and retrieved the rope from their packs. They wrapped the bindings around their thighs and waists, tying knots into each intersecting strand for the most stability.

"Do we really need to do all this, man?" Jaycen complained as he trudged toward the base of a tree, knocking his knuckles against the bark to check if the dead trunk was sturdy.

Kai chuckled over his shoulder at his friend while approaching El. "Yes."

Another huff from Jaycen fell on deaf ears as Kai stepped up to the Fae. No longer were her eyes closed. No longer was she lost in her thoughts. Big blue eyes stared up at him, waiting . . . watching. It took everything in him to not stumble over his own feet.

She's enthral—For fuck's sake, Kai. She's dangerous.

Clearing his throat, he said, "Do you know how to climb a tree?"

The words were thin, like Kai was struggling to breathe. He *was* struggling to breathe, the air vanishing from his lungs at their proximity.

El rolled her eyes while slipping on her discarded glove.

"Of course I know how to climb a tree." She stood, her tongue peeking out between her canines as she regarded him. "What do you think I did as a child?"

"I"—Kai's brain seemed to have short-circuited, rattled by the realization that he never considered the lives of those who lived Beneath—"don't know. Slink in the shadows and trick people into deals?"

A sharp scoff broke through the barrier of El's lips, and that abnormal fire blazed in her irises for no more than a split second. With a blink, it was gone, and El was left studying him. "You really do know nothing, Kai. We're not all dark-dwelling creatures void of any life, you know. We had trees to climb, just as you did here."

Her voice hitched as she spoke of The Underworld, the blue of her eyes dimming.

"I'm . . ." Kai paused. He was what? Sorry? Kai's stomach dropped. *No.* He decided to change directions. "How come you're up Above, El?" he asked, hardening his gaze just enough to protect himself and the others.

Just enough to remind him what exactly she was.

A slight inhale rushed through her teeth. A pause lingered between them.

Then El answered, emotion buried deep behind her words. "I . . . was gardening. I would sneak up here and tend to my garden when I was craving the heat of the sun. I just . . . so happened to do so on the wrong day. The curse hit, and I was trapped."

She was lucky she never got caught, Kai thought. Trial and—most likely—execution by The Trinity were what people said happened to those who were. Kai—*most sane beings*—would rather not find out if that was true.

Trying to lighten the mood—trying to do anything to banish the taut, unfamiliar air around their conversation—he quipped with a faux-playful smirk, "There's no sun in The Underworld? I thought you said you weren't dark-dwelling creatures."

Time lingered. A few seconds passed, the two staring at each other before an unexpected smile tugged at the corners of El's lips. And Kai's mind crumbled.

"You got me there," she muttered.

"El!" Rina called out, waving a coil of rope in the air.

A soft chortle danced out of El's upturned lips as she stood and made her way to Rina. Before she got too far, she stopped. Orange hair fell over her shoulder like a fiery stream cascading down a volcano as she spoke over her shoulder. "And no. There is no sun Beneath. But the thousands of sparkling stars in the night sky light up the realm just the same."

She turned her back on Kai once more.

A feeling, one that wasn't entirely unpleasant, stirred from that short conversation. It was terrifying.

Shaking his head and forcing himself to focus on their next move—on surviving—Kai stood from his spot. He groaned slightly and stretched out his tight joints before following El and retrieving the rope Jaycen had left out for him.

"It's not the best sleep," Rina told the Fae as she held out the rope, "but it's safe. Especially with The Wake out there."

"Thank you." El nodded, gingerly taking the rope from Rina and studying the way she tightened the makeshift harness around her body.

Loops and knots intertwined with one another. A skill Jaycen had taught both Rina and him how to do. Kai mirrored the movements effortlessly, as if it were second nature.

Once Rina was fully strapped in, she sent El a friendly smile.

"I can wait for you, El. That way, we can climb up together," Rina offered.

El waved her off. "I hurt my wrist back there with those two men. It's going to take me a bit longer. You go ahead."

"Are you okay?" Rina's brows pinched together.

Kai's gaze immediately landed on the hand El had been cradling on their journey back to the others as he tied several knots around his waist.

"I'm fine." El shrugged before unwinding her rope.

Rina hesitated—a long, unsure lull between them—before nodding shallowly and climbing a tree to the left. Jaycen was tucked in the branches adjacent to her.

Fastening the last bit of rope securely and ensuring nothing would come loose, Kai noticed how intently El watched Rina scale the tree before tying the rope twined around her thighs and stomach to the bark. Then she settled in with her arms folded across her chest. Kai turned to face El; he noticed her mouth move silently on its own, likely reciting Rina's movements and knots mentally.

Just as Kai took a step forward to ask if she needed help, the Fae ascended, picking a tree next to Rina's. She flinched as her right hand—her injured hand—gripped onto the bark. Digging her leather-clad nails into it, El fumbled, nearly falling. Kai stopped his body from jolting toward her. Instead, he curled his fists and kept an eye on her.

She climbed and slipped, climbed and slipped. The creak of her gloves scraped against the bark as sweat slid down her temple.

After a few minutes, she settled in on a branch, securing the ropes around her and massaging her wrist with a grimace contorting her features. Feeling like he could breathe easier, he made his way over to the tree next to Jaycen's and quickly climbed with ease. Once he was as comfortable as he could be with a branch digging into his ass, he looked up and noticed he was facing El . . .

Any trace of fatigue or weariness that settled into his bones disappeared immediately. He was fully alert as he studied the Fae across from him.

Unsettlingly still, she observed him as well—two different beings trying to figure the other out.

Time no longer touched him under her gaze. It was as if they analyzed one another for hours underneath the blood-red night sky, until El's eyelids finally grew heavy and her head slumped against her shoulder.

Kai, on the other hand, didn't get much sleep.

12

Eleri

Eleri dreamt of blood and rotting meat and ash.

Eleri dreamt of death—death surrounding her, death at the hands of others, death within her veins.

Then something shifted . . .

In her red-painted slumber, everything blurred. Crimson blended into black. Notes of ivory, brown, and amber swirled until the picture—a new, unfamiliar picture—emerged.

Eleri dreamt of blonde hair and kind smiles. She dreamt of burly muscles and hardened features. She dreamt of brown eyes and suspicious stares.

Eleri's lashes snapped open just as she tilted. A gust of wind—short and strong and full of sand—knocked her heavy, sleep-addled body to the side. She flung out her palms and gripped the soot-covered branch beneath her. The bark bit through the thin leather, the pain sharp enough to jolt her fully awake.

With a ferociously pounding heart—beating against the confines of her rib cage—Eleri steadied herself. Her nails dug into the creaking bark as she adjusted her position and found her balance once more. Deep breaths rushed between her clenched teeth, and she leaned her head back against the trunk.

It was still dark outside—as dark as the maroon sky would allow. And it didn't look to be lightening anytime soon. Staring up into the haze above, Eleri let loose a silent sigh. The events of the day before blinked into existence as she sat there. Her heartbeat pounded, quickening as the fear she'd felt crouched behind that tree trickled back into her body, as if she were reliving it.

Those two men . . . Those wanted posters . . . The Pack scribbled across oozing flesh. Eleri swallowed around nothing and bit the inside of her cheek as the realization sank in: the three Humans she'd so stupidly gotten involved with were in the center of something bigger.

They were deemed something like predators. A pack of wolves.

I need to get out of here. Away from these people, and this world of outlaws I never asked to be a part of. I just wanted to go home. I need to go home.

Eleri's gaze darted from Rina to Jaycen and Kai across the way, then toward the ground beneath her. Her vision zeroed in on it, focusing sharply on the drop. She could do it. She just needed to be quiet . . .

She'd figure out her own way east. She wanted nothing to do with this. It would be slow . . . but she'd be safe. She just needed to stay hidden.

Cautiously, she worked at the knots securing her to the tree, her fingers twisting and tugging at the rope. Keeping a keen eye on her surroundings, she flitted between Rina and Jaycen, then back to Rina, then to Kai. The bones in her chest felt as if they were about to snap from the strength of her frantically pounding heart.

The tension across her limbs lessened as she broke through the last knot. Shifting atop the branch, she readied herself for the slow descent along the tree. As quietly as she could, Eleri swung her leg to the side and gripped the bark. A wince contorted her face as pain reverberated up her arm, her wrist aching under the small amount of pressure.

But it wasn't enough to slow her down. She could withstand greater amounts of physical damage due to her Witch heritage. At times like this, she was thankful for that. Swiftly pulling off her glove, she checked her wrist. A bruise painted her skin; it was a deep purple as if she had it for days. Accelerated healing—thanks to her Fae lineage.

Securing her glove back in place, Eleri readied herself to descend the tree once more. She gripped tightly onto the trunk and slowly—one foot after another—shimmied her way down. She kept her grunts nearly silent and gritted her teeth together to stop the hisses that sat on the tip of her tongue.

To her right, Rina stirred. Halting halfway down the trunk and twisting her head to the side, Eleri held her breath. She watched; she waited. Long, deep breaths moved Rina's chest, her short bob swaying with the motion. Unruly strands stuck up, caught on the uneven pieces of burnt bark; her lips softly smacked together as she dreamed.

Eleri's muscles burned beneath her skin, and her wrist ached. After a few tense moments passed, her trembling limbs hesitantly moved once more as she continued to train her gaze toward the woman.

So close. Fuck, I'm almost there. The sweat beading at her temple dripped down her cheek and neck before plummeting toward the earth below. Her shaking boot nearly missed the trunk, scraping off several pieces of bark.

"Fuck."

The hushed word slipped free.

A shift in another tree made her heart stop. She snapped her head toward it. Jaycen let out a sleepy grumble and adjusted himself before falling still once more. He looked softer; the skin around his temples wasn't so tight, and the permanent scowl no longer marred his features.

When he took off his bandana yesterday, Eleri swore her gut sank. He looked so angry, so coarsened. A man as impassable as a canyon that overlooked a dark, never-ending abyss. She couldn't help but think she needed to steer clear of him.

Eleri stayed as still as she could. A moment passed, and with what felt like her heart lodged in the back of her throat, she bit her lip and continued her journey down the trunk. Nearly there, she held her breath until solid ground met the sole of her boot.

Thank Gods.

Securing her canteen across her hip, she slowly stepped away from the dead, withered roots of the tree toward the hole where the fire had crackled with life in merely hours ago. The cinders were still warm despite the absence of flames.

Eleri reached for a piece of deer thigh from the spit, then shut her eyes, homing in on the three Humans above her. Their heartbeats filled her focus. She needed to be certain they weren't feigning sleep. Intently listening, three distinct vibrations rubbed across her ears and buzzed around her skull. Each one was steady. Three strong beats that made up a melody of slumber.

"Okay then," she whispered.

She slid the meat off the sharp stick and stuffed it into her cloak pocket—the same one where she normally kept her crystal. The weight of it was gone; her heart seized, but she couldn't stop to grab it even if she wanted to. She needed to leave. Immediately.

With one last glance up at the sleeping figures in the trees, Eleri set off into the forest. Swift, silent steps guided her away from them. She wasn't sure she was heading east, but that didn't matter. She just needed to get as far away as possible.

Eleri's eyes darted from side to side as she weaved through the wood. Her pace was erratic; her heartbeat jumped. Yet she trekked onward—through the trees, around bare bushes, and farther away from The Pack.

She didn't slow her pace for another hour, and even then, her steps were quick. It was still dark out as she ventured farther away, the maroon sky blanketing over her eerily. But its edges lightened; maroon turned into red. Soon, the sky would brighten to that disgusting orange, and she could figure out what direction she was headed—and correct her course if needed.

As the distance between her and the three Humans she left behind widened, Eleri felt comfortable enough to stop. *For just a few minutes,* she told herself.

Standing near a large boulder tucked into woven roots, she unclipped her canteen and took a sip. The water was warm. Still, it glided down her throat and spread across her entire body just the same.

Just one sip, though. She couldn't afford any more.

A handful of minutes passed before Eleri began to walk once more, keeping an eye on the ground and looking for sprouts of life in case she ran out. So far, nothing. Rationing was her best bet. Being so close to that fresh new life put her on edge anyway.

However, she also craved it. The life that used to live within this forest. One she knew all too well. What was once lush with life was charred to its core, dead. Hares and mice that once bounded across the forest floor in games of chase were nowhere to be seen. Instead, small bones were left in eerie piles. Not even a single green leaf grew along the branches surrounding her. Its emptiness was palpable. It flooded her very soul.

And tucked in the far northeastern side of the forest, just beyond the once beautiful Pathway, lay what was left of her secret garden. She could almost smell the churned earth that once rose around her as she dug into the soil and lost herself in the fading happiness it had given her.

Her garden was just as much her home as her parents' palace Beneath. It was a section of forest she refused to return to, though. It . . . hurt too much. She hoped she wasn't blindly heading in that direction.

A huff ripped from her lungs as Eleri tripped over something, lost in the painful memories of her past. Glancing down, she gasped. A dismembered arm covered in dirt lay just behind her. Snapping her head up, she shook. As the sky lightened—the red seeping into a rusted hue that illuminated the area around her—she gaped at the sight.

Deep red painted the trunks surrounding her. Blood, so much blood. It was a massacre, the scene in front of her. She should've paid more attention. She should've smelled the iron wafting around the air that barreled into her in harsh slaps. A gag blocked her throat, and she choked on it.

It was ghastly. Suffocating.

Eleri stepped around a thick puddle of blood and moved through the trees, avoiding the gore seeping into the earth. But something snagged her attention. Something that shouldn't be there. Slowly turning her head, Eleri felt her stomach drop.

Carved into a dead, black tree was an eerie "*S*." The silence around her felt heavy. The Siren had been here. Not long ago, Eleri assumed. The light of the day, the smell of the blood, and the glaring, gut-wrenching signature displayed in front of her forced Eleri to truly face her decisions. She was alone again.

Another brick added.

"This is for the best," she mumbled, trying to convince herself of its truth. Turning her back on the horror before her, Eleri stepped into the wood untouched by The Siren and took a long breath in as she banished what she had just witnessed into the back of her mind until nothing but silence surrounded her.

Her steps were the only sound that penetrated the air.

One step. Two steps. Three . . .

Eleri didn't mind the silence, not really . . . not normally. It carried a melancholy feel, like a Moon Flower petal dancing in the wind or a drizzle fluttering from the night sky. The sensation ran up her skin and settled in her joints. However, this time felt different.

The Pack should've been long gone. But the thought of Rina and her kindness burrowed deep into Eleri's skull like a rodent searching for warmth. She couldn't help but think she'd miss her now that they parted. Rina was soft and patient with Eleri without reason.

The others, though? Eleri would be happy if she never crossed paths with them again. Jaycen was rough and so closed off that even she couldn't compete. It was unbearable to be near him. The walls she erected around her most vulnerable soft parts seemed minuscule compared to his. His was a fortress. Impenetrable.

Does he even have any soft parts to protect at all?

Her tiny beast unfurled slightly, cracking a single eye open with a satisfied smirk. It was ugly, that type of thinking. Unfair. Eleri shot a dagger-like stare at the witchy thing and added more bars to its cage. It hissed, hating being locked in when it fought to be free.

Eleri would *not* free it.

No matter how bad a small part of her wanted to when she was with The Pack—with Jaycen's pinched brows and Kai's flaring nostrils—she wouldn't dare. Kai looked at her as if she was an untamed, wild animal foaming at the mouth all because of what she was.

You should have let me free, the little beast purred. *You could have proven him right, all while basking in the rush of who you truly are as you finally released what shouldn't be stifled.*

No. Eleri flung her head to the side and skidded to a halt. She squeezed her eyes shut. *Do not think of that. You are good, Eleri. You have the light within you. You are* Fae. *You have fought to be good, so be it.*

Merrin's small white beard and watery eyes flashed before her eyelids. His screams pounded against her skull and thrashed around her eardrums. Eleri dug the tips of her fingers into her palms. Her chest caved in, and her head slumped forward as she bit her bottom lip.

I am good. *They just didn't get the chance—*

A sudden pulse—weighted and warm—nudged her temples before it traveled to the base of her throat and settled into her chest, spreading wider and wider until it enveloped her completely. She blinked hard; her body heat climbed until the water inside her seemed to boil.

"What the fuck?" Never had she felt something like this before.

Eleri glanced toward the direction from which she had come. The urge to turn washed over her, cooling her insides and wrapping around each organ. Goosebumps erupted across her chest, down her back, and over her fingers and toes.

What the fuck . . .

With a firm shake of her head, she bit her lip even harder until she tasted her blood and lapped it up before starting on her journey farther into the forest—hopefully east—again.

13

KAI

"WHY WOULD SHE LEAVE?" Rina muttered to no one in particular as she rubbed her necklace, but Kai clenched his jaw just the same.

He tried to ignore her incessant questions since they woke and found the Fae missing along with one of their leftover pieces of meat. He tried and tried because if he acknowledged it, the pounding in his ears would worsen.

He shouldn't have fallen asleep. Guilt wedged its way between his ribs. Kai hadn't meant to fall victim to slumber, wanting to give Jaycen and Rina more rest than usual.

Fuck. I should have pushed through.

Rina was slowly coiling up her rope, readying her pack before they continued their journey. Another sigh escaped through her teeth. She wouldn't let it go. "Did we do something wrong?"

The broken syllables woven throughout her words made Kai finally tear his gaze away from his own pack. His chest caved in at the sight of her, with hollowed eyes and a consistently wobbling bottom lip. He had no idea why, but the Fae had brought a lot of hope to Rina, and . . . he could see it disappearing with each passing second as the reality sank in. She would never see the Under-dweller again.

"It doesn't matter," Jaycen grumbled, tying his bag stringently before standing and bounding toward the fire pit to retrieve a leftover piece of meat. "And we're better off for it. I just can't believe that *creature* had the audacity to steal some food before she left."

Kai grumbled. "She would have had some this morning if she had stayed. It's fine."

With a firm pat to his bag, Kai stood and trudged toward Jaycen. He ripped his own piece of meat off the spit and sat next to his friend. Neither talked. Jaycen's chewing and Rina's muttering filled the campsite. It was nothing, less than nothing, but it felt like his eardrums were thumping as a sinking feeling weighed his gut; his temple pounded in sync with his pulse.

She just up and left. After I saved her ass from those cannibals.

Kai dug his teeth into the deer meat and ripped a chunk free. It tasted like cardboard—bland and rough—as he forced his teeth to knead it enough to swallow. His jaw was stiff, the tough meat doing nothing to alleviate that.

She could run into trouble and reveal what she knows. After I tried to ensure she stayed by taking her stupid rock.

Kai ripped off another chunk of meat, his fingers tightening over the greenish-gray thigh. His muscles loosened, and he cracked his neck as the weight of her strange purple crystal revealed itself, pulling the fabric toward the earth.

She's gone. Thank the Gods.

So many conflicting emotions warred against one another, banging into his skull and leaving a mess behind. Kai swallowed his last bite of contaminated deer and took a generous gulp of water from his canteen. He knew he'd regret it later if they didn't find another water source, but he couldn't be bothered. Ensuring all his supplies—some bartered for, some stolen off corpses—were in his pack, he stood with a firm roll of his shoulders.

"Ready?"

His voice was too loud compared to the quiet they were just sitting in. He needed to get moving, to help clear his mind.

One less thing to worry about. One less mouth to feed. One less person to watch over throughout the night. One less—

He didn't wait for Jaycen and Rina to reply, knowing they were ready to go. Kai knew they'd follow him into the trees, trailing along the path he decided to forge. Northward.

With each stride, El's crystal swayed in Kai's pocket, and as he ventured deeper into the deathly trunks, the sweet scent beneath her sweat and dirt faded.

"Help . . ." a muffled voice lilted through the air on the mid-morning breeze like a faint and faded ribbon. Barely breaching the trees. Barely audible.

Kai came to a halt, looking around at the empty forest beyond. It was so faint, but he knew he heard it.

Swiveling his head, he strained his ears and searched for the source.

"What is it?" Jaycen asked, taking a step closer while surveying the area.

Kai looked back at his companions. "Someone. Not too far—"

"A threat?" Jaycen's shoulders tensed, and he sucked in a readying breath.

"No."

Kai's jaw was set beneath the bandana, his molars grinding against one another as he tried to focus.

"Help . . ."

This time, all three of their heads snapped in the direction the voice came from. Northwest.

Kai, Rina, and Jaycen jumped into action. No words were said. No plan was made. They'd done this before; they knew what to do. They were an unstoppable force propelled toward the weak voice as if they couldn't help it.

They dodged protruding roots and piles of bones before coming to a stop. An old, beaten woman with no layers of clothing to protect her from the sun's brutal heat leaned against an ashy trunk. Her skin was loose and wrinkled, leather-like in a way Kai saw too often. Dark red rashes littered her arms and legs—the beginning of Sun Death, stained by the sun. The smog hovering over her was useless compared to its violent rays.

Several streaks of dirt covered her exposed arms and chest; she was marred with bruises. Painted in purple, green, and yellow. A chunk of hair was missing from the side of her head, and as she opened her mouth to suck in a deep, ragged breath, she revealed missing teeth.

Kneeling so he was at eye level with the woman, Kai spoke in a soft tone. One he reserved for all those who were hurt or tired or simply needed their help. "We aren't here to hurt you," he promised with an outstretched arm. So similar to the way he talked to El at first.

The woman was hesitant, but soon enough, she relented with a sag in her shoulders as if she didn't truly want to. She grasped Kai's hand, and he pulled her up before giving her a once over and assessing the damage. Jaycen took a step toward the woman to assist him, roaming his eyes over her frame and inspecting her frail limbs. Rina set her bag down and rummaged through it, then pulled out the last chunk of meat from the deer.

"Here," she said kindly, extending the food toward her. "You need to eat. It looks like you haven't in days, and this will help build your strength to continue on."

"I"—the woman choked on a sob lodged at the base of her throat—"I don't think I *want* to continue on."

Something flashed in the depths of Jaycen's eyes before he stepped around to her front. With a delicate hand atop her shoulder, the corners of Jaycen's eyes crinkled as if he was sending her a soft smile beneath the cloth covering his face. He held a hundred deeper meanings in that single gaze Kai couldn't understand. When did his friend become so unreadable, even to him?

"Sometimes we're dealt horrible situations that we can't even comprehend getting through. Sometimes like you said, you don't even want to get through them in the first place," Jaycen mumbled. "But you survived The Darkest Day. You survived whoever did this to you. You're obviously strong. So, you should give yourself another chance, even if it's going against everything you know."

The woman's chin wobbled before a wail pushed through, moved by his words. The sound was high-pitched and broken as tears cascaded down her cheeks, leaving wet trails between the soot. Lunging toward Jaycen, she wrapped her arms around his neck and pulled his large body against her. He stiffened under her warmth, and after a moment of taut silence, he hugged her back. It was not a swift movement. Instead, it was jagged and unnatural. His actions carried hesitation that Kai could see he tried to push past for the woman's sake.

A weak sniff, then she stepped away, sheepishly rubbing the back of her hand against her cheeks before turning toward Rina and timidly reaching for the piece of cooked deer. Slowly, she took a bite and chewed.

"That's better," Rina cooed with a soft smile.

The woman eyed them. After a swallow that seemed to take a lot of effort—her lips smacking and brows pinching—she cleared her throat. "You're them, aren't you? The Pack?"

Kai blinked. His spine straightened, and his shoulders tensed. None spoke.

"I thought so. No one would help someone in these lands without bargaining for something in return." She looked at Rina. "You're very pretty. You have a kind face."

Kai's gut dropped. He had forgotten she no longer donned her protection, too caught up in his hunger to help. Rina quickly turned away and brought her palms toward her face, shielding herself from the woman.

The woman continued after taking another hesitant bite. "Why do you want to stay anonymous when all you're doing is bringing good into the world?"

Shriveled like dehydrated fruit, Kai's throat dried up. Rina had given him her own bandana to protect him and his identity without a second thought about her own safety. Instead of pulling the cowl of her cloak over her mouth, Rina turned back toward the woman with a hesitant smile and spoke.

"It's for our protection. Bad people are after us—"

"The Wake"—the woman shuddered—"I know. Vile creatures."

Rina's eyes softened as she nodded. "Yes. Well, we blend in better with everyone when we're covered. Most people shield themselves from the sun." Her gaze pulled down toward the Sun Death littering the woman's skin. "We choose to hide in plain sight."

"But your covering . . ."

"Is lost. I didn't tie the knot tight enough. A simple mistake on my part, but I'd rather my companions keep that protection and anonymity than myself."

Rina slid her gaze toward Kai, who swallowed around nothing. Guilt ate away at him. The hysteria that took over her when El first ran from them wasn't for herself nor Jaycen. But for him. Always for him despite his protests. She had even said it then, didn't she?

"She's seen your face, Kai!"

The panic lacing her words stung as it seeped into Kai's memory. He would never forget it so long as he lived. They needed to find a replacement covering for her soon. She needed to slip back into the cocoon of safety it provided. From their enemies and the sun.

"Honorable indeed," the woman croaked before taking another bite. "I am proud to have met you. All of you."

The woman looked at Rina, then trailed her eyes toward Jaycen before landing on Kai.

"You are doing The Son's work. You are *good*. We need more people like you in this world. And do not fret, dear," she said as she turned back toward Rina, gripping the woman's hands in hers. "I will not speak of this to a soul. If I had the means, I'd rip my tunic off my body just to shield you once more so you could continue your work. For now, I never saw you. Thank you all for your kindness."

Kai sensed her sincerity leaking into the very marrow of his bones. The woman's eyes watered, and she slowly turned and wobbled away. Kai believed her, yet not El. For she had seen *him*. Despite his desperate plea for Rina to stop risking herself for him, he knew she had her reasons and couldn't deny them.

As the decrepit woman slowly hobbled and faded into the forest, a morbid thought swam into Kai's mind. It didn't matter anyway. She'd been betrayed by the sun. Unfortunately, it wouldn't be long before she was dead.

14

RINA

FOUR DAYS HAD PASSED since El escaped in the night. Four days had passed, and Rina couldn't stop thinking about her, *worrying* about her.

There was a fear within El that Rina noticed almost at once, pulsing in waves from her crouched body. A fear deeper than most, one that could consume someone and never let go.

And she was alone.

Perhaps she wanted to be alone, though. El flinched from anyone who got too close, scrambling away as if they burned her. Rina didn't know the details of her circumstances. She didn't know really anything about the Fae who instilled so much hope in her without even knowing. So whether she wanted to be alone or not, Rina hoped with all her might that El was safe . . . and happy.

"You still with us, Rin?" Kai spoke up under his breath to her right.

She twisted her neck toward him. They were walking shoulder-to-shoulder while Jaycen stayed at their back. Kai's eyes remained trained ahead, but she knew he was attuned to her reaction.

Rina nodded. "Yes," she whispered. She almost missed it—that sideways glance he shot at her—but he didn't push. He never did. And for that, she was thankful. "I hope she'll be all right," Rina mumbled, her knuckles knotting together in worry.

"We did everything we could, Rin," Kai replied as he stepped over what was once a rusted, abandoned wheel that might have belonged to a bike long ago and lightly bumped his shoulder into hers. "It'll be up to her now how she continues on."

Rina realized, he thought she was referring to the old woman. And she guessed, in a way, she was. But truthfully, she was talking about El. Rina knew she could entrust Kai with anything. But for some reason, she decided to keep El—and how important she felt—to herself. She wasn't sure why. And while Rina's mind ventured toward the missing Fae, if it had been urgent—life-threatening or life-changing—she would have shared it with him. For now, she kept it close to her heart.

It isn't important anyway. Not in the grand scheme of things.

Chewing on her inner cheek, she tried to let it go. Dried leaves crunched beneath her boots as Kai led them through a sharp bend northward, trying to steer clear from any lingering Wake members before they continued their journey east. East to Mountmend. East to her home.

She hadn't been back since she decided to join Kai and Jaycen on their journey.

She didn't want to go back.

Before The Darkest Day, Rina didn't even live *in* Mountmend. Not truly. She and her family lived on the outskirts, only going into town—littered with steam cars and twinkling lights—to trade. She would help her parents in the fields when she wasn't at school, often collecting produce she could barter for some butter. When harvest season left them little reward for their hard work, she would hunt.

The amount of things she could get with a squirrel carcass and a few frogs' feet . . . Things were simpler back then. She couldn't thank the town butcher enough for teaching her the skills of a knife during one cold winter when she was fifteen. Too young for a rifle, he had said. Without that knowledge, though, she would have perished long before Kai and Jaycen found her.

Just as they rounded a condensed cluster of black bark and rigid branches, a void replaced the memories of Rina's home when *it* came into view.

"Holy Gods." Rina marveled at the arch protruding from the ground with its soot-stained stone and shriveled vegetation.

Before them stood the only known entrance to The Underworld. Boulders—rubble—blocked the cave opening. Withered and dead vines hung limply around its edges. Vines she didn't recognize. She couldn't help but think they were plants from Beneath. A desolate aura pulsed around it. Yet it was . . .

Beautiful.

Rina had never seen The Pathway. They had barely strayed from the Western Vale or the road since she was picked up in Mountmend. But she had heard all about it from her sister. It wasn't as grand as Brynn made it out to be—she herself never having seen it before—but it was just as awe-inspiring.

Kai stopped his approach first. A quick glance back, and she saw him tilting his head as he studied the structure. Jaycen passed him, moving closer to the arch—nearly upon Rina—as she inched closer to the mouth of the cave. They both halted right before the blocked opening.

Wonder and awe glinted across her eyes as she slowly traced a single finger along the lip of the arch. Jaycen glided his palm across jagged pieces of rock, examining what was left.

"Scratch marks," he pointed out.

Frantic white lines stained the boulders. Faded red streaks did, too.

"Do you . . ." Rina whispered, the words making it hard to breathe. "Do you think . . ."

The screaming, thrashing silence between them didn't go unnoticed by her. *We're all thinking the same*, she thought. Those were *her* scratch marks . . . *her* blood.

Kai shifted, pulling Rina's attention away from the gut-wrenching sight and back to him. His body was stiff; his spine was straight. "Let's keep moving."

15

ELERI

"YOU CAN'T RUN, LITTLE lamb!"

A feminine, raspy voice penetrated the slumber that wrapped Eleri in its embrace.

Wrenched from a restless stint of sleep, Eleri's eyes snapped open, and a sharp inhale slid past her teeth. Her body tensed before her bleary brain could catch up. Several heartbeats tickled her ear as she willed her heart to slow and her mind to clear. They were rapid, racing against one another like clashing instruments.

Hidden beneath a pile of leaves and twigs she had strategically placed on top of her the night before, Eleri dared not move. Her body refused to, even if she wanted. Frantic footfalls sounded off to her right. Sliding her gaze slowly toward the approaching sound, she waited until whatever threat made itself known.

One minute passed. Then two.

A boy with blond hair and gray eyes rushed through the bare trees. He couldn't have been more than sixteen. Heaving breaths tore out of him as he spun, searching for something. A route to take, no doubt.

Laughter in the distance—howls and cackles fit for foxes—bounced off each trunk and ricocheted around the boy. His skin paled; his lashes fluttered atop his cheekbones as he blinked rapidly. Eleri lay there, watching . . . unmoving.

I should help him.

But it felt as if her body was seized, as if a layer of cement held her down and trapped her beneath the leaves. She remained motionless; she merely watched him as he took a step closer, stumbling over his clumsy feet. His eyes were panicked; his heartbeat battered harshly in Eleri's ears.

"Told you." A woman breached the tree line.

Her hair was matted, with beads or rocks—Eleri couldn't tell—dangling from a few strands. Sun-bleached bones—some large, some small—hung from her waist like a horrific belt. Around her crazed eyes, soot stained her skin in jagged, intentional designs. A tell that she was with The Wake.

The Siren, perhaps? Eleri silently inhaled, the breath catching in her throat as she observed the woman. *Or just another vulture?*

A compact black revolver sat delicately in her dirtied palm as she pulled it from a tattered pocket and aimed it at the boy. "You were fun, though."

She pulled the trigger, and the boy fell to the ground with a loud thud. His limp body landed near Eleri. A smoking bullet hole sat between his eyes. Eyes that stared right at her, as if he knew she was hiding there. Eyes that penetrated her soul. Eyes with no life left in them.

Eleri's heart rammed against her chest. The rhythm was fractured and unsteady. She bit her tongue to stop the whimper that yearned to escape. And another brick silently slid into place.

Not The Siren, then. In all the stories she had heard out West, none said she used a gun.

A group of about five others barged through the trunks and gathered around the body. All donned their black markings. Some were like masks, surrounding their eyes. Others were merely lines across their noses and down their cheekbones.

They reminded Eleri of her own Witches' Marks.

A man wearing a muzzle of finger bones unsheathed an ax and bent beside the boy. He traced a finger down his face, dipping it into the oozing blood and tucking his unruly blond hair behind his ear while licking his lips. Eleri's flesh prickled and crawled as she watched.

"Not here, Hamish," the woman said, looking down at the boy before tucking her gun away and scanning the area. "We'll clean him back at camp. Then we'll feast."

With a grunt, the man—Hamish—nodded and hauled the boy's body over his shoulder before stepping back into the woods, followed by the others.

Eleri couldn't look away, even when the boy's blood dripped from his skull and landed on the dirt beneath him.

ELERI BEGAN HER TRUDGE across the land once she had recovered enough to move. It was a slow process—an hours-long process. It started with a single twitch of her finger, then a jerk of her arm. It was as if she was thawing out, warming up after her fear had frozen her solid until she emerged from the sticks and leaves.

Brushing off a stray thorn that had stuck to her cloak, Eleri ran her tongue along the top of her mouth. It was rough and sticky, the muscle clinging to her palate. She tried to gather enough saliva from the back of her throat to relieve the uncomfortable feeling of thirst. It didn't work.

The sun beat down upon her brutally as it rose into the orange smoggy sky. Heat pulsed around her; sweat slid swiftly down her neck and spine. Her water intake couldn't keep up with the amount she was losing, an on-and-off headache pulsing behind her eyes and scraping down her skull ever since she left The Pack six days ago . . . or was it seven?

Gods, everything is blending together.

She stopped, grabbed her canteen for a small sip, and then bent to tighten her bootlaces in case she needed to run. From cannibals. From The Pack. From anyone she came across, truthfully.

"Alone is better . . ." she tried to tell herself—*convince* herself—just as she'd done over the last few days.

But the quiet she usually enjoyed carried a heaviness—a bitterness souring her tongue. Walking through these woods, Eleri *truly* felt alone . . . more so than she did when The Darkest Day first happened, and she had wandered around this very forest, fearful and starving yet still with a bit of hope blooming in her chest.

Even when she had journeyed toward the Western Vale after those first few terrifying months, and she had been surrounded by people, she never yearned to be near them. She never allowed herself to get close. But as she stumbled through this death-shrouded wood and blindly let her feet carry her east, a deep longing flared inside her.

Being near The Pack—even for the short amount of time she was—and seeing their camaraderie and care for one another ignited something deep within herself. It wasn't her witchy beast, either. No, it simply raised its head in curiosity before curling back up in its cage. This was a deep-rooted ache within her bones. A profound need to be part of something—something real, something bigger.

The Pack left an imprint on Eleri, and her nostrils flared at the thought. Her fists clenched, the leather of her gloves creaking under the strain.

I don't need them. I survived on my own . . . I will continue to do so.

An emptiness—like a hollow crater in her chest—spread over her body, just as the smoke of the curse had five years ago; her steps faltered. An unwanted voice echoed across her mind.

No one would want you around anyway. You're unlovable, cursed from within.

She tried to shove the words aside, to lock them in the cage at the back of her mind, but it wasn't her sleeping beast who had spoken. It was simply . . . her.

Unspoken thoughts—her true feelings—warred inside her without her even realizing it. Tears pricked at the corners of her eyes, and her chin quivered.

Stupid girl. You cannot mourn the life you lived and the home you no longer have when you didn't appreciate them in the first place. You snuck Above because you didn't want to be Beneath. You are the only one at fault for your deadly touch.

Wiping away a stray tear as it rolled over her lashes and skidded across her cheek, Eleri shook her head. She was so . . . alone. And her self-disparaging storm of insults wouldn't stop, even if she wanted.

You belong here now . . . You are nothing but a vessel as desolate as this realm. Like calls to like. You do not deserve to be anywhere else—

"Stop it," she growled from the depths of her chest, and ruthlessly slapped herself across the cheek. One more strike, then another, until her skin was stinging, prickles bursting over the warm flesh. "Stop it right the fuck now, Eleri. If you don't, you'll never make it home."

With each determined stomp in the dry brush, the vile voice faded, and one single word replaced it: *home.*

"Keep going," she whispered.

Home. Home. Home . . .

The trees grew more and more sparse as she went—the dead trunks few and far between—leaving large patches of earth before her. Surveying her surroundings without stopping, she looked to her left, then to her right.

Against a chopped stump was a shrine. A Human head sat atop it, blood dripping down the bark. It was fresh—a type of shrine she'd never seen in person but had heard all about. Terrified whispers out West when they thought no one was nearby.

The Wake and their fucked-up, ritualistic bullshit for a God that didn't even exist. Eleri shook her head, glaring at the sight. She wondered whose head that was, wondered how they had killed them, and if it was the same small group of monsters from that very morning.

Another brick slid into place.

Psychotic assholes.

Eleri felt her fiery beast finally stir after staying silent during the internal berating she had endured. It always relished the sweet taste of fury when Eleri thought about the Gods. This fueled it the most. It would sharpen its claws and roll out its neck when any of The Trinity was mentioned.

Gods she once believed in. Gods who had abandoned her.

The beast tiptoed out of its cage and ran its spiny finger along the walls of Eleri's entire being, its claw leaving a small indentation behind as it sauntered forward with lit eyes and an excited smile.

Harshly, Eleri bit down on her tongue and bared her teeth at the beast. "Back. In. Your. Cage. I don't want you."

The beast hissed at her, sulking slowly into the darkness once again. It never got far. Eleri knew it was itching to get out. But she refused to let the leash go.

At times, Eleri wondered if her mother had struggled as she did to tame the fire within. Eleri thought not. Her mother had been proud of where she came from. Her mother had been the exception when it came to the wary glances and wide berths in hallways. She had been beloved, a beacon of light, despite being a Witch.

She had altered their land's course one hundred and five years ago when she married Eleri's father, the Fae Prince of The Underworld, bridging the divide between Fae and Witch. Her mother had seemingly ended the animosity between the two after the Under War four hundred years prior. All it had taken was unnecessary death and the love of two beings on different sides.

Like a whip, Eleri slashed at the beast to hurry it along. She was not a beacon of light like her mother. She was not proud of where she came from.

Each step became harder and harder as Eleri continued on, with one grip on the present and the other on taming her beast and the relentless thoughts. Her legs felt frail. She slowed, her boots dragging against the forest floor and churning the dried dirt below, until she completely stilled.

No longer moving. No longer thinking.

16

Jaycen

Kai's footfalls sped up relentlessly as he wound through the dwindling trees of the forest. They were on the outskirts of the wood; soon, they'd have to face The Wasteland.

Jaycen had been dreading that part of the journey as soon as it was decided they'd travel to Mountmend. The Wasteland was just dunes of sand, an endless stretch of desert that covered much of the eastern side of The Upperworld. It had once been beautiful fields of tall grass and wildflowers. But nothing grew there now. And there wasn't even evidence that anything lived there in the first place, unlike this forest.

Kai veered sharply to the right. No warning was given—just an urgent motion that propelled him in a new direction. Jaycen followed—of course he did—barely missing a cluster of boulders with the toe of his boot.

"What the hell is up with you, man?" Jaycen grunted.

Kai had been like this for the last few days—twitchy, uneasy. He'd blink rapidly before twisting his face into a pained expression. He'd move, then stop, then move again. The usually collected man who led them through this world was nowhere to be found.

Kai shook his head. "I . . . I just know we need to go this way."

"Yeah," Rina piped up from the back of the group, a grunt slipping free from her lips as she also barely missed the boulders. "East—"

"No, not just east. I . . . don't know how to explain it. There's this pull. It's . . . I don't know what it is. Like a force deep within me, controlling me. It's telling me we need to go this way."

Rina nodded as if Kai didn't sound insane. Perhaps with her spiritual crap that had died within him long ago, it didn't sound so strange to her. But Jaycen didn't buy it.

He picked up his pace, his heavy steps pounding into the dirt. Once he was ahead of Kai, Jaycen stopped him in his tracks. Bending slightly, he forced Kai's gaze onto him. "Look at me."

Kai's eyes were slightly reddened; his brows tugged together. He seemed alert—too alert. Jaycen hadn't seen him this bad since day one of their hellish new world.

"Sit down, Kai," he ordered.

He hesitated at first, merely standing there, swaying as if in a trance, as Jaycen sighed and leaned against a tree before sliding into a sitting position. "Kai."

His friend winced as if he just now heard him. Nodding, Kai shrugged off his pack, slowly sat atop a boulder opposite him, and pulled his bandana down from around his face, inhaling deeply. Rina plopped onto the forest floor between them, taking out her canteen.

She wrapped her lips around the opening and took a careful sip, then extended her arm toward Jaycen. Jaycen's eyes stayed trained on Kai as he shook his head.

He didn't need water . . . he needed to figure out what the hell was going on with his friend.

From the corner of his eye, Jaycen saw Rina glide her outstretched hand toward Kai, who took it without a word. Guzzling it down in one gulp, Kai sighed. He wiped his lips with the back of his hand and passed the canteen to her.

"Thanks, Rin," he muttered. "Sorry. I think I'm just exhausted. The heat's been brutal the last few days."

Jaycen finally tore his gaze away from Kai as Rina sent him a warm smile. "There's no need to apologize, Kai. Don't worry about it."

Ire bubbled in Jaycen's gut. No, they most definitely *should* worry about it. It was so unlike him, so . . . abnormal it scared him.

After packing away her canteen in her own bag, Rina looked up at the quickly darkening sky. "Nightfall is going to come soon. We should set up camp for the night."

Kai nodded, not saying anything, not moving. His eyes were still distant as he looked toward The East.

What was going on in that head of his?

Standing, Jaycen's knees creaked. Rina followed suit while Kai stayed sitting. Jaycen reluctantly removed his gaze from his friend and observed their surroundings. With the trees thinning, there wasn't enough cover for him to feel safe sleeping on the ground.

"Get your ropes."

Dark smog swirled against the maroon night sky above Jaycen's head as he sat strapped to a tree on first watch, his mind churning like the plumes. He'd never get used to the sight of what his world had become. He never wanted to get used to it.

He wanted—no, *needed*—the constant reminder of the life he had been ripped away from . . . the life he was forced to live. An endless loop of wandering, scouting, saving. It should have been fulfilling work—what he and his companions did—and yet a small part of him still felt empty even when a stranger they helped walked away.

It was a shit way to live, Jaycen knew that. Deep, *deep* down he truly did, and he wished he wasn't like this. If he could change, things would be much better. But being stuck in a shithole would do that to a person.

Everything was different, worse. Even the bark he sat atop on this flimsy branch felt different. It was brittle, charred. And he couldn't help but wish The Son, The Mother, *whoever* would wipe it all out—the land, the people, *him*—because his home was no more. And although his home had stopped feeling like home long before The Darkest Day, this new altered reality was no way to live. Yet here he was, facing the death suffocating this realm day in and day out. Not for himself. But for *him*.

Jaycen's eyes fell from the eerie sky to his right, landing on his oldest friend . . . his best friend. The most important person in his life. Kai.

He was tossing and turning, his head moving side to side and his eyes flicking behind his closed eyelids. Jaycen's heart lurched when whatever dream occupying Kai's mind knocked him too far to the left, despite the ropes securing him high above.

Jaycen wanted so desperately to wake Kai, to comfort him as he always seemed to do when Jaycen needed it most. Just as he had their last night with El. Jaycen needed to eat. His stomach was clenching, hunger pains growing as the seconds passed, but he couldn't do it. Fear snaked around him so deeply he felt paralyzed at the prospect of an Under-dweller seeing him.

It felt like he couldn't release the barrier—the safety net—his bandana provided. He had leaned on that insignificant fabric for nearly five years, using it as a shield . . . a deterrent for all except Kai and Rina. And now that shield was shattered. The stray Fae they had picked up had seen him. He felt bare and weak. The thick, deep thud of his heart rammed against his rib cage. A reminder that those feelings weren't anything new.

I'm scared.

Those two words mocked him. He was scared . . . had always been scared. And he hated it. Jaycen wished he could be brave like Kai. He wished he could stay positive like Rina. But he couldn't. Instead, he had been born like this—chicken shit and too scared to even show it. So he walked around with a hardened mask that felt as if it didn't fit.

I'm scared . . . His inner voice transformed from his deep timbre to something higher in pitch. Childlike and naïve.

Jaycen's vision went out of focus, the silhouette of Kai seeping into a dark blur before him and transforming into a time long ago. The sky no longer looked sick. It was bright blue, and the sun wasn't so intense. Instead, it was like a gentle caress on his soft skin, not yet scarred and roughened by the life he lived.

It felt as if he was a kid again, reliving a memory from long ago.

"Jaycen!"

A boisterous voice rang out behind him. Turning his head, he found himself in a clearing. The charred and brittle tree he was strapped to shifted into a healthy, sturdy trunk surrounded by tall grass. A creek ran through the field, and flowers bloomed in patches alongside it.

Before him was a young teen with black hair and brown eyes. He was on the other side of the creek, waving his hands above his head. Kai.

Jaycen knew this memory. It was a pivotal moment—one of the most important in all his life. They had been merely twelve. Kai's hair had been long and messy. Mud had been smeared across his cheek.

"C'mon, Jaycen!" Kai yelled out. "It's fun! I promise!"

Jaycen stepped to the edge of the creek, moving on his own as if his body recognized the scene in front of him just as clearly as his mind. Water streamed down the narrow creek. Rushing faster than Jaycen had ever seen at that age. Already, his head was shaking back and forth.

No. The jump is too far. I can't do it.

"Jayc. It's okay. It's not bad!" Kai beckoned.

Jaycen refused once more, his head swinging. "I-I can't!"

Terror wrapped around Jaycen's thin body as he stepped back, trembling, then stepped back again. Just a few more, and he'd be back at the log he had claimed as his bench. Just a few more, and he'd be back to safety.

Kai mirrored him, stepping back again and again, widening the distance between them.

Wait, no. Where is he going? I don't want to be alone.

In the blink of an eye, Kai charged forward. His wiry arms swung back and forth; a loud grunt ripped free from his tightly pressed lips as he jumped across the creek and landed on the swaying grass closest to Jaycen.

Heaving, Kai's chest rose and fell. His breath rushed out in fast intervals as he approached him. "See, Jayc. It's not bad!"

Jaycen shook his head, staring down at his boots. Shame crawled up his spine and settled at his neck, heat flooding his cheeks as tears burned his eyes. "I can't, Kai," he whispered. "I'm scared."

Defeat inflated his words. He *was* defeated. *How could someone like Kai be friends with someone like me?*

"It's okay." Kai placed his hand atop Jaycen's shoulder and dipped his head in an attempt to look into his eyes.

Jaycen didn't meet his gaze, *couldn't* meet his gaze.

"Hey . . ." Kai said more firmly this time. "Eyes on me."

His tone pulled Jaycen's eyes upward and locked onto his. Kai squeezed his shoulder, and a smile pricked at his lips. "It's okay to be afraid, Jayc. And when you are, you won't ever have to worry. I'll always be right by your side."

Blinking, Jaycen sucked in a sharp inhale. Darkness crept back into the green, beautiful field outside Kai's old home. The grass withered, and the log blackened. His heart strained, seizing slightly as the memory faded, and Jaycen was left with an empty feeling. Wrapped around his thighs and chest, the pull from the ropes grounded him to the branch.

A stifling breeze traveled up the hem of his tunic, just as a shiver echoed across his entire body.

"N-No. No."

Jaycen's head whipped to the side, his gaze falling on Kai's sleeping form. Muscles twitched beneath Kai's ropes as his head jerked toward him. With furrowed brows and downturned lips, Kai muttered sleepily, "No. Please . . . stop. Da—"

"Kai," Jaycen barked.

Quiet enough not to wake Rina yet sharp enough to halt the nightmare—the same horrid one Kai had endured since he was fourteen, the one Jaycen could recognize from a mile away.

Just the thought of it made his blood boil.

Slowly, Kai's lashes fluttered open. A slight sheen glazed his eyes. Jaycen ground his teeth together at the sight. "Huh . . ." Kai mumbled.

"You were having a nightmare." Jaycen clenched his fist against his thigh. "You were talking in your sleep."

Two deep rivets formed on either side of Kai's downturned lips. Jaycen watched him try to recall the horrors that had entered his mind. Jaycen wished he wouldn't.

"Oh . . ." Kai breathed out. "It was that one again."

Sending him a soft smile, Jaycen tried to send comfort across the suspended air between them just as Kai always did. But as Kai's eyes slid away from him with that frantic, crazed look he had worn for the last few days, Jaycen realized his efforts went unnoticed. He didn't think he was any good at it anyway.

Jaycen's stare stayed trained on his best friend. Kai's rumpled bandana had bunched around his neck after thrashing in his sleep. His jaw feathered, and his fingers flexed atop his thighs. Something was off with him—something Jaycen couldn't help but think had to do with El. The way Kai kept looking around—toward The East—distracted unlike anything Jaycen had ever seen, worried him. His movements were erratic. His eyes were wild.

This isn't because he's eager to get to Mountmend. It's . . . It's like he's looking for her.

That creature had its claws inches deep in Kai's mind without her even being here. Jaycen's gut turned to stone.

"I hope," Jaycen muttered so low only he could hear, "we never run into that Fae again . . . for Kai's sake."

17

KAI

"Look." Jaycen pointed just ahead as they passed the last tree at the edge of the dead forest, and the earth beneath their feet transformed from dry, gritty soil to sand.

Tin shacks covered in rust and grime reflected the shining sun's rays. Cloth tents billowed in the breeze with harsh snaps. And poorly erected structures built out of the burnt trunks of trees were scattered across the horizon.

A new town.

The momentary relief Kai had found outside the looming forest, free from the suffocating force propelling him forward, vanished.

"Secure your bandana," Kai muttered to Jaycen, deep lines twisting against the smooth tan skin around his eyes. Jaycen checked the knotted cloth and squared his shoulders. "Rina, cowl over your nose. Keep your guard up."

With a nod, she complied before they both flanked either side of him. A uniformed force. Sinister. Intimidating. Beneath their hats, their eyes glowered; their stances hardened. No one in their right mind would want to cross them.

"This settlement wasn't here when we passed through a year ago." Rina's voice was a whisper.

Jaycen grunted and balled his fists at his sides. "If it's those cannibal fucks . . ."

This time, Kai huffed. "If The Wake is here"—he glanced toward Jaycen first and then Rina, determination furrowing his brows—"we'll take care of them."

Jaycen chuckled, the bandana swaying. "Good. I'm itching for a fight . . . smashing their heads in will be fun."

A short, loud laugh slipped through Kai's gritted teeth. He couldn't help but agree.

"Welcome . . . to . . . Arkala . . ." Rina said, reading the words scribbled in what looked like soot across the rotting hide of a small animal as they approached the edge of the town.

The edges were shredded, as if whoever killed it hadn't taken care when cutting its meat free. Its fur was stained red. *A hare*, Kai thought.

To their right, a woman dragged a screaming child—covered in grime and mud and missing several teeth—around the corner of a tin shack, harshly hushing him and mumbling about what might happen when his father got back from his journey.

To their left, a marketplace entrance lay tucked between two scraps of cloth hanging from rotted posts, whipping in the arid wind. Several people milled about, weaving through broken carts and buckets.

"Hides! Get your hides! One pelt for a scrap of metal!" one vendor near the entrance yelled out.

He grabbed a woman by the arm and dug his nails into her skin, her face contorting in pain. "I saw that strip of brass you got the other day, Helen. C'mon . . . don't you want something to keep you warm at night?"

The woman—Helen—reared her head back and slammed it forward into the merchant's forehead. With blood running down her face and into her eye, Helen spat, "Piss off, Alden. Or I'll tell your wife what you've been up to on your hunting trips."

The man's features contorted, and he licked his lips, growing silent. His glistening mouth pressed into a thin line, and he released his hold on the woman. "Fucking bitch," he mumbled as she walked past, bumping her shoulder into his.

The woman weaved through the settlement until she rounded a corner, as vendors continued their verbal assaults on passersby. Kai exhaled while his eyes scanned the area. With a brief pause, his nostrils flared.

Then he gritted out, "Okay. Let's go."

Kai, Rina, and Jaycen stepped into what seemed to be the borders of the town. All in unison. All a single unit.

A jagged piece of wood attached to the entryway of a log structure—a makeshift door, Kai realized—swung outward. One black boot stepped forward, dust clouding around it from the impact, before a worn brown boot followed. A round man with spotted skin and a rotting toothpick in his mouth emerged from the charred building.

"Welcome to Arkala, friends!" he bellowed out, arms out wide with a lopsided smile.

His voice was low and loud . . . raspy and sharp. It scratched at Kai's eardrums the closer he got to them. That smile never faltered, though, and the wrinkles at the corners of his eyes deepened.

Kai greeted the man with a firm handshake. "Your welcome is appreciated."

A glint at the man's hip caught Kai's eye, the high sun reflecting off metal. Holstered at his side was a revolver. Kai's muscles tensed at the sight; the hairs atop his arms and legs stood up.

Guns were confiscated by the king six years before The Darkest Day. The Purge, he had called it. Many didn't hand them over willingly. Some hid their weapons in floorboards or buried them behind their houses when word got around that the royal guards were beginning to knock on doors and search residences.

No one knew why the king decided to do it. But soon after, it was said he melted down each and every rifle and revolver confiscated. It sent a tremor across the land. Many were appalled at the decision. Others didn't mind a gunless realm. Kai was the latter.

And seeing this man proudly display the weapon for all to see above his tucked-in tunic, a sour taste spread across Kai's tongue and down his throat. The Wake mostly carried these days, somehow getting their greasy hands on the firearms hidden over the years. But this man donned no markings, no tells that he was one of them.

"Sheriff Nells, at your service." The man smiled and revealed yellow and brown teeth. "What brings you here?"

Jaycen stiffened slightly at Kai's side. He risked a glance and saw his friend crossing his muscular arms and looking down his nose at the man before them. He grunted, "Sheriff?"

Sheriff Nells nodded superciliously and smacked his lips together. "That's right. We're rebuilding, and somebody has to steer us in the *right* direction. A new world is on the horizon, friends. And we're the start of it."

A sheriff in a world with no laws. Ironic.

Kai fought hard not to scoff in the man's face. He knew it would cause more problems for them if he did.

"She with you?" this so-called sheriff muttered, head jutting forward.

His eyes were trained past them.

The three turned, and Kai's breath was stolen from his very lungs. Trudging across the sandy landscape toward the makeshift settlement was El.

Rina huffed, a small smile tugging at the corners of her lips as she pulled down the cowl of her top. "We're right where we need to be . . ."

The words were nothing more than a whisper, and Kai didn't have the slightest clue what she was on about.

"Fuck . . ." Jaycen cursed under his breath.

El was hunched over slightly, and her feet were dragging across the shifting sands. As her orange hair whipped through the wind beneath her hood, one word rang against Kai's skull: *beautiful.*

It rushed in unbidden, like a viper striking its unsuspecting prey or a towering wave slamming into the Southern Coast. And then a release of tension within his muscles seeped out instantaneously. He felt lighter, better than he had in days. Like his body was having an actual physical reaction now that El was near.

"Yes." The simple—yet so, so complicated—word left Kai's mouth, answering the sheriff's question, without him realizing it until it was too late. "She's with us."

At his side, Jaycen choked on a cough and seared Kai with a glare that burned against his covered skin.

Sheriff Nells hummed. "You better keep her close, boys . . . if you know what I mean."

Kai's toes curled inside his boots; his stomach heaved as the sleazy tone of Nells's voice ran over his skin. Red bled through his vision. Slowly, turning toward the man, he pinned him down with a dangerous leer. Kai mumbled, so only Nells could hear, "I'll rip your arm out of its socket if you touch her."

A scoff from the sordid man was all the response Kai got before Rina rang out, "El!"

The Fae skidded to a halt, looking up from her stumbling feet with wide eyes and parted lips. She was frozen between the forest and the outskirts of Arkala, but Kai couldn't help but think he saw her shoulders relax ever so slightly as she rubbed her chest.

After a moment of nothing but the taut air pulsing around them, she cautiously walked toward them. When she was close enough to Kai, he noticed she didn't look at anyone except Rina. A small, barely there smile was all she gave her.

"We were worried about you," Rina said.

El sucked in a shallow breath, her eyes round as she looked at her. "Me?"

Rina nodded, but Kai's eyes stayed trained on the Fae. Her lips were cracked; dried blood was crusted within each little crease. More dirt was caked across her face and neck. Her cheeks were hollowed out, a sharp difference from the last time he saw her sleeping across from him in the trees.

"Stay with her . . ." A distinct voice rang through his entire body. It wasn't his inner voice, nor a memory of anyone else's. A woman spoke those words. *"Protect her . . ."*

Something stirred within him. A force wrapped around him, squeezing so tightly it was frightening. It was the same feeling that propelled him through the forest, making his friends frantically follow him through all the twists and turns.

Kai felt out of control. His body no longer his; voices pressed in on him.

I'm going crazy.

No. He wasn't—*couldn't* be. He was simply dehydrated. His stomach growled, as if it, too, wanted to remind him he needed food. That was all it was. It had to be.

Without a word or another glance at the Fae, Kai turned toward the sheriff. He was studying them, eyes squinting as he looked from Kai to El and then back to him. Finally, he spoke.

"Come. We can talk inside."

18

KAI

THE WOOD PANELS BENEATH Kai's feet creaked—piercing the air of the small, shadowy room—with every step. Each piece stitched together to make the structure was decayed to its core. Black and rotted. Sparse slices of sunlight slipped through the cracks between each board and barely brightened the room.

Under his bandana, Kai's nostrils flared at the smell. Burnt wood, dirt, sweat, and mold. His throat constricted as the scent lingered. It wasn't the worst smell he had come across over the years. The crater of dismembered body parts they found two years ago came to mind. That . . . *That* was repulsive—sickening—a stench and sight that sent him to his knees as tears poured from his eyes. The thought of it alone made him lightheaded, on the verge of passing out.

This, on the other hand, was subtle. It didn't slam into his face like a wall of death. It slowly wrapped around him in a deceiving caress, seeping into his pores and strangling him from the inside out. It was a smell that would turn anyone sick as time slowly moved on, without them being the wiser. A shiver ran up his spine.

"It's okay, El. C'mon," Rina whispered, her voice traveling toward him on a gentle breeze. Kai looked behind him as Jaycen walked past. Rina stopped at the door's threshold, looking at El. Hesitation marred the Fae's features. She glanced to each side as if she wanted to run before landing back on the blonde. "It's okay."

"Sit," Sheriff Nells called out from the wooden desk at the center of the room and gestured at rickety chairs held together by dead, thin vines and spare rope. "I apologize for the state of this place. You can only do so much with what little resources this world has now."

Turning back around, Kai approached Nells and Jaycen, who decided to stay standing. His arms were crossed, chin held high, and his temples ticked under the pressure. Kai heard two sets of steps follow—Rina and El. His shoulders loosened.

Stepping to the side, Kai allowed El and Rina to sit. Rina plopped down next to him, her legs spread wide and her calculating gaze trained on the man before them. El stayed as quiet as she could be, slowly—hesitantly—sitting in the seat closest to Jaycen and burying her palms in her lap. Kai glared at the man beneath the shadow of his hat, resting his hand against the back of Rina's chair—studying this sheriff . . . analyzing him. He barely took in the dingy office they were led into.

The tension was thick, heavy. It sat at the base of Kai's throat, making it hard for him to swallow.

With a click of his tongue, the sheriff leaned against the edge of the moldy makeshift desk. "What can I do you for? It's not often we get stragglers coming to Arkala."

Nells crossed his arms, mirroring Jaycen, and glanced from him to Kai—skipping over Rina—before landing on El. Rina shifted, the chair squeaking under her weight and her face twisting in annoyance.

Kai could practically hear her now.

How dare he dismiss me so swiftly? she'd growl under her breath as soon as they walked out of this shithole. *If* they walked out of here.

"Just passing through," Kai said curtly, keeping his eye on the man. Unease seeped into the depths of Kai's being. The gun . . . His comment about El. It made Kai's skin crawl. "Making our way east."

Sheriff Nells sucked on a yellow tooth. He didn't recoil from Kai's hardened leer. Instead, he met it, their eyes clashing. "What for?"

Keeping his face and stance neutral, Kai masked the way his guard went up even more. He wouldn't put his companions in danger or in any other unknown circumstances. This Sheriff Nells wanted details . . . on them, on their plans. That was something he refused to give freely. But perhaps Kai could glean information for himself with the right questions.

"You know The Wake?"

Kai kept his voice neutral, watching for any reaction. If a member of the faction was setting up camp here, he needed to know. And then, he'd take care of the problem.

Sheriff Nells shifted, tension rippling over his muscles and his spine straightening at the mention of the group. As if on instinct, he palmed the weapon strapped at his hip, his pointer finger slowly running across the barrel. "I know them. You don't come across as a Wake member. They don't have the courtesy of conversation."

So, not a threat . . . of the cannibalistic kind.

"We aren't," Jaycen growled from Kai's left.

His friend's body straightened, and his arms fell to his sides, inching closer to his blade.

A movement right next to Jaycen caught Kai's attention for a split second. El shifted her gaze to the muscular man beside her, then quickly back to the sheriff.

"Then what business do you got with The Wake?" Sheriff Nells moved his right hand an inch closer to the holster's opening. His hackles rose—an expression of caution in his eyes.

Kai took a single step forward, bringing the sheriff's attention back to him. "We're hunting a prominent supplier for them—"

"Gods damn," Sheriff Nells huffed in disbelief. His body immediately relaxed, the tension disappearing as fast as it had come. No longer did his fingers twitch near the trigger of his gun. The sheriff slumped back against the desk and rested his palms on the edge. "You're going for The Siren, aren't you?"

Kai didn't say anything, didn't give the man an inch.

Laughter bubbled up the sheriff's throat and slipped through his rotting teeth. Nodding and catching his breath, he wheezed, "That's brave of you. I commend that. Wait"—his eyes widened, and the palm of his hand slapped against his thigh—"don't tell me The Pack is in my presence."

The room turned deathly silent. Kai's chest tightened, and small tremors traveled up his arms. No one spoke. No one breathed too loudly.

Sheriff Nells chuckled to himself as he shook his head and walked around his desk. Sitting atop the stool on the opposite side, the seat croaked in protest under his weight. He rested his elbows on the splintered wood, lacing his fingers together in thought. "I couldn't care less who you are. I want that bitch gone. She ran through here five months ago. Not long after we started rebuilding. She tore apart families. Left a trail of blood, and that revolting "S" behind before moving on . . ."

Kai watched for any sign of a lie, concentrated on every minute twitch that could reveal something more sinister. The man's brows furrowed, causing a deep crevice between them. His eyes were downcast, sorrow so strong it seemed to pulse off him in waves.

Something inside Kai relaxed—only slightly.

"Any idea where she went? Or where she could be?" Kai asked.

Shaking his head, Sheriff Nells looked back up at Kai. The wrinkles under his eyes were prominent, haunted. "By now, she's probably been everywhere and back. The woman never stops. A few of the men in town—husbands, brothers, fathers—went looking for her as some sort of act of revenge. I told them not to, to stay with their families and focus on rebuilding. They . . . didn't listen and haven't turned up yet."

"Do you think they're still out there? Alive, I mean?" El asked.

Her voice was soft and coarse at the same time, as if her normal satiny lilt was stained by the sand and soot—and most likely thirst. Her eyes were round with worry as she stared at the sheriff.

Sheriff Nells twisted his head. His teeth clenched ever so slightly as he took in her hooded form for longer than was necessary, and he hesitated before sighing.

"Gods, I hope so." He closed his eyes, then looked to Kai, Jaycen, and Rina for the first time before settling back on El. A soft flicker glinted in his gaze that Kai hadn't seen yet. "You need to be careful if you're headed toward Mountmend. She's sly and cunning. And on top of that, if she just so happens to be there, she has the rest of The Wake and its leadership there backing her up."

"Any insight on who leads The Wake? We've been searching for any clues or murmurings . . . and nothing," Rina said when the man before her finally acknowledged her. She shifted in her seat, leaning forward to rest her elbows on her knees.

She was intent on getting any information she could. Just as she always was.

Sheriff Nells paused. A trickle of distrust seemed to seep back in from the prodding questions, Kai could tell. But thankfully he stored it away and answered.

"A former royal guard who defected not long after The Darkest Day. That's . . . what I've been told."

All four of them—Kai, Jaycen, Rina, and El—stiffened at this information. Kai forced his face to remain neutral despite the racing thoughts pounding against his head and tugging at his tongue, itching to escape.

A former royal guard? A fucking guard? It couldn't be.

Information, however, wasn't reliable these days. It could just be a rumor, a tactic to scare others away. But an unsure itch prodded at him—a sliver of doubt. If it really was a former royal guard . . .

Gods. We're screwed.

"There's a reason Mountmend became their stronghold . . ." Nells continued, with a glance out the rickety door, before training his gaze back on them. "Protected by the river and The Wasteland and not far from the palace where that greedy motherfucker who still calls himself king lives."

Another pause hung between them.

Kai's skin tightened.

"Not a fan of the royals, I see." Jaycen huffed out a small chuckle, a fearless glint in his eye.

Sheriff Nells scoffed. "'Course not. He could be helping . . . condemning The Wake and rebuilding this world. Instead, the king is sitting pretty in his throne room and hogging resources just so he can have a nice meal. That fucker. Every day . . ." A long sigh slipped through his tightened lips. "Every day I pray to The Son that it will finally rain for the first time in five years. Imagine that—a torrential downpour straight into the gaping hole where the palace's roof once was, left behind by whatever spy or traitor set off that curse, and drowning the king as he sleeps. That no-good piece of shit can rot, soggy and wet, preferably."

A bark of a laugh slipped through Kai's tightening lips. From the corner of his eye, he caught El looking at him with furrowed brows. He couldn't help it though. That was one imaginative way to rid this land of its ruler. "I'd pay all my molars and half my hair to see that happen."

"The king's alive?" El asked the sheriff.

The toothy grin Sheriff Nells wore at Kai's comment lowered as he studied El with pinched lips. "You been living under a rock, girl? 'Course he's alive."

"I—" El's eyes widened, and Kai noticed the small patches of visible skin across her cheeks redden. "I've kept to myself the last five years."

El's shoulders slumped slightly as she settled back into her chair. She twisted her fingers with downcast eyes as Jaycen sent Kai an indecipherable look. Kai tried to ignore it. He also tried to ignore his knotted gut courtesy of her dejection.

Nells's features softened, as if he saw it, too. "You're just trying to survive. I get it. We all are—and keeping to yourself is a good way to do that." A small smile tugged at the sheriff's lips as he nudged his head toward the others. "I take it you being with this lot is new?"

El gulped, swallowing around nothing, as she quickly glanced at the three of them before looking back at the man behind the desk and nodding.

"Well, they seem like good people. Something about them . . . it's a gut feeling, you know?" Sheriff Nells stood from his stool and made his way back around toward the front of the desk. His eyes—dull and yellowing and slightly glossy, as if he was sick—never left her while the corner of his mouth ticked up. "If you ever want to settle down—have a place of your own—you're more than welcome to stay in Arkala."

The sheriff's smooth voice made Kai's gut twist, knotting and aching as if oil was seeping into his body and poisoning his organs. Just the thought of his offer made him flex his fingers at his sides.

El staying . . . El *not staying* with him—*them*, he meant . . . *them*. The thought of it made him uneasy. The feminine voice dug deep and reverberated across his body once more. "*Stay with her . . . Protect her . . .*"

He bit into his tongue, tasting the coppery blood pooling along his gums, and could feel the way Jaycen's eyes slid to him. His gaze was torrid against Kai's skin, with a promise to discuss his subtle reaction later. Only Jaycen would pick up on the slightest shift in him.

A breath later, Rina glanced at him as well. Kai's scalp prickled under her gaze. She must have been able to read him better than he thought. His jaw tightened further while the sheriff remained unaware. Rina tore her gaze back to the sheriff, nodded once, and said, "Thank you for taking the time to speak with us, Sheriff Nells. We should probably get going to set up camp—"

"Don't be ridiculous." He straightened his spine and stood from the lip of the desk. "Y'all will stay here. There's an empty place on the eastern side of town. You'll know it when you see it."

"Oh," Kai started. "There's no need."

Sheriff Nells simply dismissed him, his hand waving limply in the air as he made his way back to the door that led outside. "And on your way, be sure to pick up some rabbit jerky from Euan in the market. Tell him Sheriff Nells said to not give you any problems."

Kai didn't want to stay here; he wanted to leave with Jaycen and Rina . . . and El. He would rather camp in the open, risking everything, than take this gun-toting man's help. But his friends needed rest, *proper* rest.

One night. For them, he could do that.

"We appreciate it. We won't stay long, just a night to get our bearings, and we'll be on our way." Kai turned and walked toward the door with Jaycen on his tail; he heard Rina and El slowly stand from their chairs and follow.

Sheriff Nells waited for the four of them by the door, and once they approached, he walked them out. Stepping across the rickety threshold, Nells sucked in the fresh, smoggy air. Kai couldn't help but do the same. A headache had begun to form from the moldy air inside.

"Thank you for the hospitality," Rina said, gripping the rim of her hat before bowing her head in farewell. "We appreciate—Is that what I think it is?"

They all turned their heads toward the center of the town. A black iron cylinder protruded from the ground. A curved handle was attached to the top of it, and a short spout stuck out the other side.

Kai's mouth fell open. "A water pump?"

The sheriff's chest puffed out, his chin tilting up ever so slightly as he turned around to look at what Kai could only assume was the town's pride and joy. A smirk pulled at his lips. "That's right. We found a groundwater source a little less than a year ago and began to build around it. We here in Arkala have yet to go thirsty since!"

Nells turned with a spark in his eye, ignoring Rina, Jaycen, and Kai. His glossy gaze fixed instead on El. Something had shifted now that they were no longer cramped inside the small, shitty office, and the sun shone down on them. The man's smile grew, revealing his yellowing teeth, and his spine straightened even more. Arrogance wafted off him.

"You wouldn't have to be thirsty." Nells's eyes traced the expanse of El's body leisurely. Appreciation lit up his gaze, and he bit his bottom lip. "Feel free to stay as long as you need. I'll be more than happy to . . . have you."

The words were a purr scraping down Kai's spine, and his heart sank. His stomach churned; something deep within him tugged harshly as he deciphered the look in the man's eyes.

Fuck. He wants *her. Actually wants her.*

Kai didn't say anything as he tuned out any response El might have given. He didn't say anything as he let Jaycen and Rina lead them away from the seedy sheriff toward the market and through its cramped pathways between carts and stalls.

He was vaguely aware of merchants yelling all around them. It was as if he were floating, a ghost trailing the scent of life. But he couldn't seem to get a grasp on this feeling wreaking havoc inside him. It was a feeling he knew but hadn't felt since before The Darkest Day.

Kai didn't want to acknowledge it; he couldn't—*refused to*—acknowledge it. But he knew what it was, and he didn't understand why he suddenly felt this way.

Jealous. He was jealous of even the thought of that man looking at her the way he had with his forbidden weapon and rancid stench. Then, he remembered the single word that came to mind when he saw her.

Beautiful.

"Fuck," Kai breathed out, nearly no sound attaching to the air released from his lungs.

Clearing his throat, Kai said louder, "I . . ."

The others stopped their descent through the market and turned to him expectantly.

Get your shit together, Kai.

He blinked and cleared his vision after a short breath. "I'm going to scout the town's perimeter. Get a feel for this place before we settle in for the night."

Kai thanked the Gods that his voice sounded normal. Rina, thankfully, was scanning the area, making sure all was well before they proceeded, so she couldn't see what he so desperately wanted to conceal. Jaycen, however, had his eyes trained on him. And from the look he was giving him alone, Kai knew he saw right through him.

"I'll go with you," Jaycen said.

Kai turned.

Shaking his head, dismissing Jaycen's voice that hung in the stagnant air, Kai looked over his shoulder swiftly. "No, it's fine, Jaycen. Stay with them. Watch for any shady merchants."

Jaycen stepped forward. "Rina can keep an eye out."

"Jaycen. Not this time."

Kai forced out a harder tone—the tone he used when dealing with threats . . . the tone he used as their leader. That stopped Jaycen from pushing, and a small flare of guilt sprang in Kai's gut that he would have to confront later.

Roughly pushing through the bustling market, Kai exited the swaying cloths that marked its entrance and rounded a corner of a nearby tin-and-wood structure. He took a few more steps before halting and leaning against its side. He slid down the wall, arms hanging at his sides limply and eyes squeezing shut. Ragged breaths passed through his nostrils.

Why am I feeling like this? Why did I feel such relief when I saw her? Why did that word emerge at the same time? Why did that female's voice ring through my head? Why . . .

Ripping his hat off and his bandana down, he ran his fingers through his hair and sucked in as much air as his lungs could bear.

"It's nothing," Kai whispered under his breath, his fists falling at his sides and tightening into balls as he blankly stared. "I'm simply curious.

She's unknown to me. She's Fae. Thinking she's beautiful was simply a moment of weakness . . . I can't think straight because I desperately need sustenance. That's it. I do not care for her. I do not want her. I do not mind if another looks at her . . . touches her . . . fucks—"

Molars rubbing against one another, Kai clenched his jaw and shook his head. Shifting, he stood. On trembling legs, he walked toward a cluster of structures. Once he was at the farthest one, he knew he had reached the edge of town. Then he began his perimeter check.

Eyes open, Kai. Push it down. Bury it. Do your job. Make sure they're safe. That's all.

19

ELERI

IN THROUGH YOUR NOSE. Out through your mouth.

The normally steady mantra did nothing to calm Eleri's nerves. How could she have run into them again? The Upperworld was—*should have been*—big enough to never cross paths with someone twice. She expected them to be long gone. And yet, here they were in the very place she felt compelled to go.

It had been a gut feeling, her feet wandering astray and taking her slightly north. Eleri thought it was her intuition telling her to change course. Perhaps The Wake was nearby . . . or The Pack. That was what she told herself.

Turns out her intuition was a backstabbing bitch and led her straight to them.

Jaycen hastily wove through the market; his head was on a swivel, analyzing each person they passed. Eleri followed, leaving wide berths between her and others . . . never getting too close.

Merchants and salesmen shouted at anyone passing by, squawking like a flock of birds. Meat for locks of hair. Cloth for animal bones. Herbs for teeth. She couldn't help but wonder what each item was used for. She was never around any other survivors enough to learn. And a part of her—a big part—never wanted to.

Eleri blinked, her tongue prodding at the hole in the back of her mouth. A gaping and empty crater within her gum. The memory of blood filling her mouth flitted across her vision. She thought she was at her lowest that day, when she plucked a pair of rusted pliers from the railing of a crumbling bridge and yanked out her farthest molar to barter for the gloves she wore.

The seller had snatched them off the corpse of a woman only a day prior and sold her clothes on the side of the road. What he wanted to do with the teeth he acquired, Eleri had no idea. She didn't ask, didn't care. Her thoughts were solely on concealing her deadly touch.

No temptation . . . no death.

And being in this market, surrounded by so many people milling about, put Eleri on edge. A crunch broke through the noise. An insignificant sound that shouldn't have vibrated up her spine. Looking down, she saw a handful of glass bulbs that used to carry what she now knew was called electricity, half buried in the sand. Useless these days.

Why was she here in the first place? Why was she following this man who clearly wanted nothing to do with her? Eleri's vision swam; her foot kicked over a small, discarded sack filled to the brim with rusted bolts.

I could leave again . . . I could make an excuse and part ways with Rina now before we're reunited with Kai. I could sneak off in the night just as I had done befor—

"El?" Rina leaned over, blocking Eleri's unfocused sight.

Blinking, Eleri stepped back. "Sorry . . . What?"

"I asked if you're all right." Rina's lips twitched into a frown. "You seem out of it . . . and you were all alone for over a week."

Eleri huffed. "I'm used to being alone, Rina."

"That doesn't mean you have to be."

It was a simple statement. Simple in every way to anyone else but not to Eleri. She was better off alone. It was safer for others. But . . . but when she left The Pack and wandered through the forest, she couldn't help but miss the presence of having someone—anyone—by her side.

And it seemed like she was called here, toward The Pack once more, as if they were a beacon and she, a lost ship. It was as if Fate had something else in mind for her, like she shouldn't be alone even if it went against everything she told herself since The Darkest Day.

She wasn't one to believe in that stuff, *in Fate* . . . so why did she change directions instead of staying on her initial path east?

"Let's go," Jaycen grumbled as he headed straight for a cart with the word "*jerky*" painted on its side with . . . Eleri didn't want to know. "The quicker we get the food and some water, the quicker we can move on. And then you'll be on your own once again, Fae."

The little beast within Eleri growled and stretched its paws.

Fuck Fate. And fuck Jaycen. She narrowed her eyes at the back of his head as he approached the merchant. *Neither can tell me what to do.*

For the first time, Eleri allowed the beast to linger for longer than a split second. She sat with the feeling, ruminated in it as Jaycen retrieved a cloth bag from the merchant. She let the witchy monster run its claws down the edges of her mind as he turned back around and approached Rina without ever looking at her.

"Got the jerky," Jaycen said, walking right past her. "To the water pump."

Eleri's dark beast hissed at him as a shiver ran up her spine, and she almost let the leash go.

"C'mon, El!" Rina smiled at her widely.

The expression she wore tore through Eleri's very being. It was light and unrestrained . . . and *true*. Her blood ran cold, and her heart felt like it had stopped beating altogether.

Back in your cage, Eleri all but whispered. Her Witch-self pushed its luck, ignoring the command, and bared its teeth back at her. Eleri did the same and screamed at it silently. *In your cage! Now!*

As she followed Rina back through the market, dodging passersby paying no attention to their surroundings, she felt the beast sulk back into its cage just as Eleri slammed its door shut.

Reckless. So, so reckless. She squeezed her eyes shut for a single breath. Rina's expression burned behind her eyelids. She was so kind and caring . . . *Do not ever do that again.*

"Oh, sweet Trinity!" Rina exclaimed, and Eleri whipped open her eyes once more. "It's glorious!"

Before them was that strange-looking tube protruding out of the ground. Eleri had never seen anything like it before. She stood back as the people gathered around the contraption moved the handle up and down until a stream of water fell out of the open mouth of the spout.

"Isn't the ground dead?" she asked herself, hiding her awe beneath the muttered words.

Someone, however, heard. A woman with missing teeth and light green eyes turned toward her as she secured the cap onto a canteen.

"The top layers, yes, but if you dig deep enough and are lucky, you can hit the perfect spot. We're grateful Sheriff Nells found this."

Pride laced the woman's voice. Eleri guessed not going thirsty would do that.

Rina looked at the woman, who gave them a kind smile. "Is he really a sheriff?"

The woman chuckled as she secured her canteen to her belt. "Now he is. To us at least, but he wasn't always. Like all of us, he has a past. One he isn't proud of, however, but he looks after us, trying his best to keep us safe like a sheriff would have before The Darkest Day. It's like he's trying to atone. Even though he can be a real sleazeball at times to pretty girls like you, overall, he's harmless and means well. Enjoy your stay."

Eleri didn't know how to respond. She didn't think she needed to, as the woman sent them another smile and walked away with a nod, allowing Jaycen his turn at the water pump. He filled two can-teens—one for him and one for Kai, Eleri guessed.

"Nice to meet you," Rina called back to the woman before she filled hers up as well. She guzzled down a mouthful before replenishing it once more.

Next, it was Eleri's turn. Rina stepped to the side and made space for her. Eleri approached the iron faucet. She stared at it, tilting her head to the side.

"How strange . . ." she mumbled.

Then, she wrapped her gloved hand over the handle and began to push it toward the earth. Water shot out of the spout and into her canteen. The somewhat foggy water made her mouth ache for it. It looked delicious.

She brought the canteen to her chapped lips and took a few gulps before placing it back against the spout and pumping more water. *Glorious, indeed.*

Once full, she stepped toward a waiting Rina. With a grimace, the blonde said, "Jaycen already headed toward the structures on the eastern part of town. He didn't want to wait for you . . ."

"It's fine, Rina." Eleri secured her canteen to her waist. "I wouldn't have waited for him either."

Eleri and Rina arrived at a structure where Jaycen was waiting. Hung on a post near the front door was Kai's hat. It swayed in the breeze, teetering around and nearly falling every so often.

Jaycen was sitting cross-legged in the sand near the flapping cloth that covered the doorway. He ran his finger through the sand with methodical strokes.

"A structure. A real structure. It's been too long!" Rina sighed, her shoulders relaxing. She walked past Jaycen and grabbed Kai's hat from the post before briefly peeking through the billowing fabric and turning back toward Eleri.

Rina sat in the sand, and after a moment of hesitation, Eleri followed suit, leaving plenty of space between them. Enough to feel at ease with the woman who made her believe she didn't *have* to be alone.

"I'm so happy we crossed paths again, El," Rina said softly, placing Kai's hat atop her lap and leaning back on her palms.

Eleri's heart clenched as she peered up from her intertwined fingers toward Rina with large, widened eyes. "You . . . are?"

Rina stared at Eleri as if she could see past her giant walls. It was jarring. "Of course."

No sound broke free from Eleri's open lips. Her eyebrows rose; she didn't know what to say or how to react. For the first time in a long time, Eleri felt . . . *wanted.*

Rina, despite it all, seemed to understand. The woman before Eleri offered the most genuine smile she'd seen in years, then tilted her head toward the sky and closed her eyes. The smile promised she'd be a force in Eleri's life, whether she stayed or slipped away in the night. Even then, she'd never forget the stranger who had shown her such kindness. Not truly.

A light, airy sigh slipped through Eleri's teeth as she studied Rina. She chewed on her bottom lip, her stomach tightening while they sat in new, comfortable silence. Eleri didn't want to admit it, but being close with someone—talking, no longer living a life of solitude alone in the forest—felt . . . nice. Easy, when it was with the blonde.

I just can't . . . get too close.

There was nothing more to say, so Eleri sat with her thoughts. The blowing breeze tickled her neck and drowned out the merchants' yells in the distance. Looking around, she glanced over the shack she'd be staying in that night until her eyes snagged on Jaycen. He was still running his finger through the sand before him, brows pinching together in concentration.

Eleri leaned forward just enough to see what he was doing. To her surprise, Jaycen—the big, stocky asshole—was doodling, and the portrait in the sand oddly resembled Kai.

20

KAI

IT DIDN'T TAKE LONG for Kai to walk the entirety of the town. It was one of the bigger settlements he had seen on his travels but still small. On his second lap, he noticed two men with hunting rifles strapped across their backs and weapons dealers—mostly axes, knives, and the occasional whip—at the back of the market. He memorized each of their features as he grazed the hilt of his knife, deliberately hardened his eyes, and stared them down, as well as any other merchant trying to lure him in and scam him into something he didn't need.

This second pass also gave him time to clear his head. No one survived in this world with a racing mind. He needed to be sharp, focused on his goals. First, survival. Second, ridding this world of disgusting beings like The Siren and those in The Wake.

If what the sheriff said about the leader of the faction was true, they were in deeper shit than he thought. The royal guards were highly trained. Ruthlessness seeped through the cracks in their duty. And if this guard abandoned that very service, Kai couldn't even begin to imagine what pent-up anger or resentment or perhaps deranged emotions their malice was clinging on to.

A chill ran up Kai's spine and settled at the base of his skull.

Gods, they needed to regroup.

Another ten minutes passed, and Kai approached the beginning of his scouting path once more. Releasing a deep sigh from his clenched teeth, he quickly closed his eyes. He gave himself a second—one single second—to ground his thoughts . . . something his second pass around the town should have done to no avail. It was as if his mind stretched in several directions.

One . . .

That second ended too quickly, but it was all he could afford.

"Okay," Kai muttered.

Rolling his shoulders and straightening his back, he began to walk toward where their accommodation was for the night. It was about two dozen shacks away. Kai's steps slowed when he spotted Jaycen, Rina, and . . . El? His gait stuttered, kicking up sand. He had expected her to flee.

She seemed eager to leave that night in the trees while they slept, and he could tell she wasn't happy to see them here in Arkala. He couldn't help but wonder why she stayed.

He had so much to do, so much to finish, before entering The Wasteland's heart—and all of it was muddled by the Fae's return. Yet relief flooded through him at the sight of her. When she spoke earlier . . . hearing her voice for the first time in days . . . it soothed something in him. Something he wouldn't—*couldn't*—bring himself to examine too closely.

The three sat on the ground near the empty tin structure he had marked as theirs on his first pass around the town. And just as Sheriff Nells said, they would know their accommodation when they saw it.

"Took you long enough." Rina stood and stretched her arms high, a groan leaving her parted mouth.

Jaycen ran his hand over a drawing he created in the sand and stood as well, chuckling to himself and joining in on the jests made at his expense. "You get lost, buddy?"

Rolling his eyes, Kai sent them a vulgar gesture as he came to a stop next to them. "I was thorough. No one's going to bother us tonight."

Jaycen huffed out a laugh before turning a bit more serious. His brows furrowed, and he stared at Kai, wanting to make sure he was truly okay. But he didn't say a word. Kai wouldn't have wanted to talk about earlier anyway. Instead, he asked, "The inside?"

"Just took a quick glance." Kai patted Jaycen on the back in as much reassurance as he could muster before making his way toward the gaping entrance and the thin fabric covering it. "Nothing but some mats to sleep on and a stack of what looks like some canned food I assume is left for travelers in the corner since Nells sent us here in the first place."

"Cozy . . ." Rina mumbled, then winked at El, who giggled softly as she rose and wiped her hands on her thighs. Rina handed Kai his hat back with a grin and entered the shack.

Kai and the others quickly followed.

Dust coated every inch of the ramshackle structure. It was merely four large tin sheets nailed together with posts to keep them from falling down. Yet it was one of the better places they had slept since The Darkest Day.

"Beans!" El gasped, more to herself than anyone else.

The pure joy enveloping that single word made Kai's heart stutter as he whipped around to stare at her. She turned toward Kai, Rina, and Jaycen, her eyes widening. A hint of awe lit up her features at the sight of such a simple thing. A food many would have thrown away before it turned into a luxury. Kai's lips fought against his cheek muscles and lifted on their own as if they weren't connected to his body, sending the Fae a barely-there soft smile beneath his bandana.

At least she couldn't see.

"I used to hate beans growing up," Rina said as she knelt on the ground and began wiping the dust off a mat along the far side of the shack. "Now, I'm salivating at just the thought."

"Me too," El chuckled, setting down the rusty can back where she got it and claiming one of the other mats near the table, closer toward the middle of the room. She crouched next to it and wiped it clean.

The mat she chose . . . its position . . . it would be hard to run off in the night from there.

Kai bit the inside of his cheek and shook his head. Taking their lead, Kai walked toward a mat opposite El, next to Rina. But Jaycen beat him to it. He eyed the Fae. It seemed like he wanted to be as far away from her as possible. So instead, Kai claimed the mat closest to the door. It was for the best, he thought, just in case someone tried to sneak in and ambush them. It was the mat that just so happened to be nearest El. Kai didn't want to think about that or the nerves that burst within his gut.

Silence fell upon them as they used their gloved hands and any spare cloth they could muster to wipe their mats clean. The occasional cough echoed across the walls as the dust churning in the air stuck to their throats.

Kai stole glances at El, his thoughts colliding as his heart pounded and sweat pooled in his palms, grime clinging to his skin. As she wiped away the last streak of soot, she smiled at her bed for the night before looking up. Her eyes immediately met his. Her gaze was searing, as if it was drawn to him specifically.

Kai's breath caught in his throat as her eyes shuddered and brows pulled together. Before he could let that very breath free, she swiftly forced her gaze away and looked to the stacked cans of beans.

"Go ahead," Kai whispered with a swift nod toward the corner, urging her to get up as he took in the way her canines dug into her lower lip while she eyed the food. Her eyes held a layer of ravenous yearning within them. "It's okay."

Kai could see how much she wanted to break open a can and dig in. Like a child's pure anticipation during Yule before unwrapping gifts. But she hid it well and hesitated.

Had she eaten at all in the time we were apart?

The journey here was hard for Kai, Rina, and Jaycen . . . he didn't want to imagine what it had been like on her own—

Stop it, Kai. He admonished himself. *It doesn't matter. She is not my priority. Rina and Jaycen are. She is* not *one of us.*

El turned to him, lips parted. And his inner voice went mute. They stared at each other in silence. The moment didn't last long, not even half a breath. But in that short amount of time, it felt like an eternity hovered over them.

Beaut—

An unsure chuckle slipped through her lips. Blinking, Kai tried not to flinch from the sound. It felt like whiplash, slashing through a placid moment into an endless whirlwind he didn't quite understand.

When she finally stood and stepped toward the food, Kai bit his bottom lip, forcing his responding smile down.

"Oh, El! Grab me one too, please!" Rina called out, removing her hat and running her fingers through her short hair. Then she hissed out a quiet curse as the dust she had just wiped away floated down and settled back onto her mat.

Kai was reminded to finish wiping his own bed clean. A few more strokes of his palm, and he deemed it was as good as it was going to get. He settled onto the threadbare cushion and took off his bandana before bringing his knees toward his chest and resting his elbows atop them. A deep breath flowed out through his nostrils.

They survived another day.

Relief relaxed his muscles.

"Kai." Jaycen threw him the sack of jerky they received from the market at Sheriff Nells's request.

Kai caught it with one hand before stripping his leather gloves and reaching into the cloth bag. He pulled out a handful of strips, then nodded and tossed it back to his friend.

"Here, Rina." El slowly wove her way through the scattered mats toward the blonde, taking wide berths where needed.

Reaching forward, she held the can of beans near the edge of the rim. The farthest possible part of the rusted tin. Once Rina grabbed the other end, El swiftly made her way back to her mat before sitting and using a shard of scrapped metal discarded off to the side to open the can.

"Cheers," Rina said, smiling brightly at the Fae with her arm held toward her and her can tilted forward.

El paused. Then she hesitantly reached toward Rina and tapped the edge of their cans together with a quiet *tink*. "Cheers," El whispered while sending Rina a smile that lightened the shadows along her face and showed her canines.

The two dug in, slurping and gulping as much into their mouths as they could. Rina's muffled voice worked through a mouthful of beans and shattered the quiet settling across the shack. "El, I know you briefly told us about The Underworld when we first met . . . the Pixies, Gnomes, Witches, and of course, the Fae. But what about the Vampires?"

El choked on her mouthful of beans, coughing loudly as she hit her chest to clear her pipes. Kai ripped off a piece of jerky with his teeth and turned to look at the Fae next to him. He was curious about what she'd say.

"I'm sorry." A crease formed between El's eyebrows while she swallowed the last of her food. "What?"

Jaycen tipped a can into his mouth and ground his teeth before swallowing and saying, "You know, Vampires. Bloodsuckers. We've all heard the horror stories. Those creatures slinking in the dark and attacking us Humans in The Upperworld."

El chortled—loud and uncontained—as if she couldn't help it. The sound was arresting, captivating. It was the first time Kai had heard a sound like that come out of her mouth. "Vampires aren't real. And if they were, they wouldn't be of The Underworld. Humans turned immortal. *Humans*. They'd be from your realm."

"There really aren't Vampires Beneath?" Rina asked, eyes wide, full of questions.

"No." El giggled quietly and shrugged once more. "I've read plenty of books about handsome Vampires falling in love with Human women, though. Sorry to disappoint."

"You didn't." Rina didn't miss a beat. Her amber eyes sparkled as she gazed at the Fae. Water lined her lashes. "Disappoint, that is. Everything you say—every little tidbit I learn about your home and its people—is incredible. It sounds like a stunning place."

El opened her mouth—surprise contorting her features—but she said nothing. After a moment, she merely sent Rina a lopsided smile and then took another bite of beans.

Despite it all, as Kai finished his first can and reached for another, he couldn't help but silently agree with Rina. The fear rooted deep below, twining around his entire being—for The Underworld and its inhabitants and magic—thrashed against this relief he felt when the Fae was near and this curiosity about where she came from.

And although fear still sat deep in his gut—stagnant and ever-present with no end in sight—a single word bounced around his head. A word he tried to dismiss earlier.

Beautiful.

BEAUTIFUL.

Kai's gaze slid to the side. Orange hair was sprawled out across the end of El's mat, its wavy tips dusting the sand-covered ground. Her chest rose and fell in a steady rhythmic song. Up for three beats. Down for three. A silent, breathy waltz he couldn't help but get lost in as he watched.

Rina and Jaycen slept soundly on their mats, feet away. After stuffing their faces with beans and jerky, his two companions fell asleep with smiles on their faces and stomachs finally full. It took El longer to succumb to slumber, tossing and turning, sighs of frustration leaving her lips on occasion.

And Kai . . . he didn't even close his eyes. Lost in thought as he gazed up at the maroon sky above. He remembered when it used to turn black and fill with stars once the sun went down. On occasion, stars still peeked their way through the smog permanently churning in the air. When they did, they were not as bright as they used to be before the curse. Even then, he pretended to count them, conjuring up their existence as he ended each day. A way to calm himself, a way to *ground* himself.

Hours—or what felt like hours—passed. Remnants of that reoccurring nightmare—*his past*—flitted into existence occasionally before he pushed it away. Possible escape routes if needed flashed behind his eyes before disappearing. Kai's mind never slowed, never even allowing him to process what he was thinking about and where it was going next. Until she fluttered across his thoughts. Then it was as if everything had slowed.

She was captivating, intriguing . . . *terrifying*. A being that looked as soft as the grass outside his home long ago, yet as sharp as the thorns on the occasional weed that would cut his fingertips. Contradictory. Confusing. The unknown—the risk—luring him in like a moth to a flame.

Beautiful.

Kai's fingers twitched atop his stomach, itching to tuck one of those unruly strands of hair behind her pointed ear and wipe clean the dirt permanently staining her skin—

"Hmm . . ." El hummed, sleep lacing the sound.

Shifting, El turned onto her side and faced Kai. No lines or crevasses twisted her features. Her eyebrows were relaxed, and her parted lips subtly twitched as if a dream invaded her senses.

A moment later, she inhaled, then her eyes fluttered open.

Blue met brown, and time stopped. Just as it had done earlier that night. Kai lost all sense as if he was peering into the depths of her soul. Before he could get a single breath in, El blinked, and he was pulled from the tranquility falsely wrapping around him.

Ripping his eyes away from hers and feigning a cough, Kai shifted his body. His broad back rubbed against the threadbare mat roughly. What . . . was wrong with him? He needed to distance himself from her. Seeing her again muddled his thoughts, yet he swore the same relief he felt shone in her eyes under The Upperworld sun when Rina called her name and she saw them. Saw him.

"Having trouble sleeping, Kai?" El's voice was nothing more than a croak, a breathy whisper heavy with sleep. It—his name—sounded otherworldly on her lips.

Kai's gut seized as if he had been caught. He *had* been caught. Turning his head to the side—cheek smushed and hair disheveled—he looked at her once more. He couldn't help the chuckle that quietly slipped free as he felt his neck heat up. "Yeah, you can say that."

El adjusted her body, propping her arm under her head and pulling her knees closer to her chest. A hint of hesitation stifled her as if she was being careful not to wake the others. "I can't seem to either tonight. I think it's the mat. My body isn't used to anything soft beneath it."

A sad laugh—mostly air—hung between them. How shitty of a life they lived.

"This . . ." He realized this was the most they had spoken to one another. A normal conversation for a situation that felt anything but. That realization sent small, terrifying tremors down his skin. "This is definitely better than what we're used to, too. One can only handle so many branches up their ass."

El giggled and nodded. Kai tore his eyes away from her, glancing over at Rina and Jaycen, and smiled.

"Although they don't seem to mind. The fact that we even have walls around us feels like a luxury."

El nodded again, the movement scratching against the mat. "It's fucked, isn't it?"

This time, Kai laughed. It fell from his parted lips before they stretched into a wide grin.

"What?" El asked with large eyes.

"It's nothing. It's just. . ." Kai chuckled again as he really looked at her beneath the foggy moonlight. "You're interesting. You have these quick moments where you don't hold back. It's as if your true thoughts slip through before your brain can catch up. Like just now."

El's lips formed a tight line, and her neck reddened slightly. "That's why I try to keep my mouth shut most of the time. It's easier to just observe."

Kai propped himself up on his elbow and shook his head. "You shouldn't have to do that. You're fiery, I can tell. And sometimes, it's good to let that blaze burn."

A huff released from El's lungs. "Maybe . . ."

As the quiet surrounded them, Kai lay back down and closed his eyes for a moment. Perhaps he could sleep now. Perhaps he could wake Jaycen or Rina up to watch over them for just a few hours while he rested. After having a moment alone with El, he felt in lighter spirits about having her with them.

"Kai?" El's voice penetrated him down to his core.

Opening his eyes, he focused back on the Fae, who was already gazing at him. "Yes, El?"

Hesitation flickered across her eyes. "Why didn't you leave me when those men were pursuing us in the woods?"

"I—" Kai hesitated.

A choice needed to be made. He could hide behind his hardened mask and simply say it was a lapse of judgment, a moment of weakness that wouldn't happen again. If he said that, the rift between him and the Fae would only deepen, one he knew should exist. Though something in him whispered it was wrong.

Instead, he told her the truth.

"I waited because you were scared." *And I can't leave those who are because I've been left before . . .* "Even if I didn't fully trust you."

"Didn't?" El asked, her voice weak.

Kai's throat clamped shut. "*Don't.* I don't trust you."

Keeping her eyes trained on him, El nodded. As he stared at her curled-up body, he imagined her staying in a place like this . . . protected from the elements by these tin walls, having a mat to sleep on and a community of people around her, so she never had to wander by herself ever again.

This place—Arkala—could give that to her.

With a slight inhale, Kai opened his mouth. He wanted to ask her . . . needed to know. It was like some unknown craving had taken over. But the words stuck to the back of his throat. His tongue felt like ash as he let them die with the thought.

"Yes, Kai?" she questioned, round eyes looking at him expectantly.

Caught once again.

Kai cleared his throat, easing its tightness at the sound of his name, then met her eyes, hoping to glimpse her true thoughts. "What . . . What did you think about the sheriff's offer? To stay, I mean."

"Oh, that?" El chuckled and then blew away a strand of hair from her face. "I don't think he'd truly want me to stay if he knew what I was."

Her leather-clad hand reached up and pointed to her ear before she cast her gaze downward, a hint of shame . . . or was that self-deprecation? Kai couldn't figure out what she was feeling despite his astute attention on her.

She was a mystery. She was *dangerous.*

"I doubt that," Kai mumbled, not taking his eyes off her.

"Why's that?" she whispered, still looking down. Then she lifted her eyes again, gaze locking onto his. Before she could fully fall into those burdening feelings, he watched as she forced herself to wipe any hint of them away completely, replacing it with a smirk. "That's how *you* reacted."

It was a taunt to lighten the unexpectedly heavy mood. Kai knew that, yet his heart seized, and his stomach dropped as if weighed down by iron chains.

Because he knew she was right.

21

ELERI

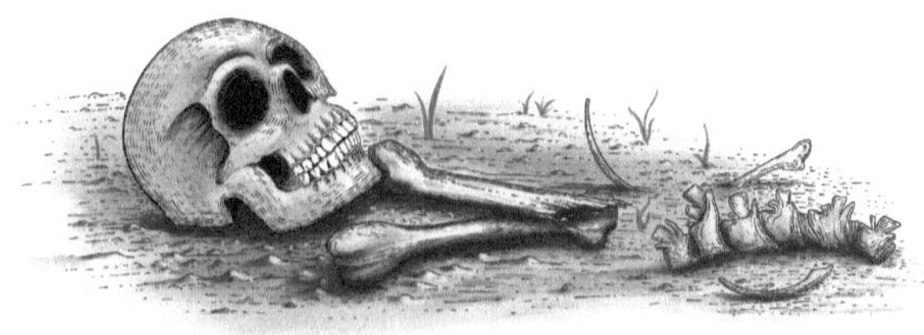

SLURPS FILLED THE TIN shack they slept in. Jaycen and Kai were sitting on their mats and devouring their third can of beans. Rina was finishing her first. Eleri, however, couldn't seem to stomach even a bite. Unused to the absent feeling of hunger, her gut clenched, and nausea overcame her senses at even the thought of food.

"Are you all right, El?" Rina questioned, having just swallowed her last bite.

With a nod, Eleri sent the woman a smile. "I'm just not hungry. I don't think my body is used to eating as much as we did last night."

From the corner of her eye, she saw Kai glance at her. Eleri pretended she didn't notice. She couldn't—*didn't want to*—acknowledge the way he seemed so different from the masked man she had met over a week ago. It was confusing, and her head couldn't seem to wrap around him.

She and Kai . . . distrust wove its way through the very fibers of their acquaintanceship. So why did it feel like something changed in the time they were apart?

Her stomach coiled, a knot forming where her food should have been as she pondered their conversation from the night before. It was simple, nothing spectacular, yet it sat with her, eating away at the deepest part of her being. And her sad attempt at a joke left a sour taste in her mouth.

Kai *had* reacted badly when he realized she was Fae as she'd hung in their trap. And the sheriff would have, too, if he had the chance to find out. She probably would as well if she were in their shoes.

It was meant to be a jab at herself, something she thought he'd appreciate . . . something she thought could bring back the dynamic between them before she fled. For it was easier to know where she stood with him when he made it known he disliked and distrusted her.

But with the way Kai's eyes furrowed and the way his chapped lips turned downward into a limp crescent moon, she wished she could take back the words. Another jolt within her gut knocked her breath away; her stomach clenched.

No.

Eleri couldn't eat solely because she was not used to it. *That was it. The only reason.*

It was not because guilt slowly inched its way up her nerves for affecting Kai the way she had. And it was definitely not because of that incessant lure she felt drawing toward him.

Rina hummed. The creak of her second can being cracked open mixed with the feminine lilt of the sound. "I understand. I feel it, too. My stomach clenches with each bite I take, but I know I have to eat something while we have it. When there's food, eat it. We don't know when we'll get another chance again."

She was right. Eleri knew she was right. As Rina's small bony fingers shoveled another bite past her teeth, Eleri clenched her jaw, squeezed her eyes shut, and inhaled. She held the air in her lungs for three seconds before releasing it into the air around her.

One . . . two . . . three . . .

A slight tremble rattled her movements as she lifted the can toward her face. Eleri's arm shook; her knuckles ached as she squeezed the tin tightly. She willed gravity to pull it down away from her opening mouth, *pleading silently.*

Breaking through the resistance, the edge of the can breached her lips. Several beans glided across her tongue. It was slimy. Recoiling from the mush in her mouth, nausea immediately overcame her as her vision swam.

Her nostrils flared as she took a reluctant inhale. Then her jaw began to move, crushing and grinding each bite beneath her molars. The simple motion made her gag. Goosebumps erupted across her skin, and she minutely shook her head, ridding her urge to spit it out. But Rina was right.

She had to eat.

"Slowly, El." Kai leaned closer, mumbling the order as if he only wanted her to hear.

Her eyes widened as she turned her head and looked at the man next to her. A fire blazed in his eyes. Dull and dim but there nonetheless. The way the words rolled off his tongue made her mouth obediently move on its own, slowly chewing each bite before swallowing the beans. It felt like cardboard grating against her esophagus, yet in this moment, she didn't seem to care.

Dirt was smeared across his top lip and temple. His strong, straight nose stood stark against the shadows of the brightening orange sky above them. The brown of his eyes wasn't a solid shade like Eleri thought. Up close, specks of warm hazel and gold within the rivets and chasms glinted in his irises.

Gods, he's handsome.

Ripping her gaze away from him and willing the blush she knew was staining her cheeks to fade, Eleri tipped the can again and took another bite. It was not easier this time. The beans and sludge glided down her throat despite it closing up and trying to force it away. She stared at the tin wall in front of her, chewing and blatantly avoiding eye contact with Kai.

A slight tingle between her thighs pulled her thoughts back toward his order as she swallowed the last of her latest bite. It was merely a word.

A simple word that held no meaning. A suggestion, really, one for her own well-being. Yet she followed it without hesitation, chewing on the disgusting substance her body wanted to refuse. A warm fire flickered in her core . . .

Shit. Eleri cursed whatever higher being decided to make her weak in the knees when ordered around by a male who was nice to look at. She needed to distance herself. *Maybe I* should *leave . . .*

"I'm going to head back into the market to barter for another canteen. We have a long journey in The Wasteland ahead of us," Jaycen said, chewing on a strip of jerky. His deep voice—although quiet—made her flinch.

"Are you sure it's not because of that handsome man at that booth yesterday?" Rina teased with a glint in her eyes.

"Oh?" Kai raised his eyebrow and smirked. Eleri noticed the deep tint of red running up the side of Jaycen's neck beneath his secured bandana. "You haven't looked at anyone in a long while. Not since that night in The Vale—"

Jaycen huffed and rolled his eyes. Eleri could see him trying to force back his blush. "That guy wasn't even good."

Kai laughed, his eyes squinting and his head tilting back. "Yeah . . . it didn't sound good either."

"Asshole!" Jaycen all but shrieked before burying his face in his hands and chuckling. Gathering his wits, Jaycen secured his hat and turned toward the threshold of the shack. "I'll meet you on the edge of town."

It took Eleri by surprise, seeing this side of him. Right now, Jaycen almost seemed . . . pleasant.

He stepped outside, the flap over the door snapping behind him in the wind. Rina's lingering giggle filled the air around them. It floated like a hovering thread before falling silent as Eleri set her can down. She stood, her knees cracking and spine aching.

Heat seared the side of her face, then trailed its way down to her feet, where the mostly full can sat. Kai rose as well. A quick breath in, and she turned to him.

"That's all I can handle right now."

The words came out softer than she had been hoping, but they pulled his stare away from the can and back to her.

Her heart stuttered, and her gut twisted. Kai softened his gaze, just enough to make Eleri question if she was seeing things. "You did good. A few bites are better than nothing."

"You did good . . ." Fuck. I could be good for him. That tingle returned.

Before she could utter the simple "thank you" that sat on the edge of her tongue, something flashed behind his eyes before his features hardened. Like whiplash, Kai ground his teeth. "Let's get packed up. I want to be out of here within the next hour."

"Are . . . are you going to come with us?" Rina spoke up, bending over her bag and shoving several cans of beans inside before slinging it over her shoulder and standing.

Eleri's shoulders tensed, and she turned her head toward the woman. From the corner of her eye, she could see Kai glance at her with interest. She didn't know what to say. She didn't know whether she wanted to go with them or not. Her head was screaming at her to run as far away as possible from The Pack. From *people* in general.

Clenching her fists and grating her molars, she ignored that insistent scratching against her temple while weighing her options. The memories itched to escape and consume her as they once had . . . as they still did on occasion. She buried the dread burning her esophagus and rising into her throat as she thought about her deadly touch and the sweet soul she damned because of it. Merrin.

And yet . . .

Rina spoke up again after the silence spread thin. "You don't have to—"

"I'm coming," Eleri declared before she could stop the words from falling off her tongue. "My journey is east. Same as yours. When the time comes, we will go our separate ways, but for now . . ."

Squealing and bouncing on the tips of her toes, Rina's face lit up. "Oh, I'm so happy! I must thank The Trinity! I'll be right back."

Neither she nor Kai said anything as Rina barreled out of the shack with a beaming smile pasted onto her face. The sight of her mirth made Eleri's stomach flutter in tandem with the nervousness that made the skin atop her limbs stiffen.

This decision terrified her. She was reckless, giving in to her desperate yearning to be near others, even with its deadly dangers. But there was a part of her—so small it was barely noticeable—that felt like this was where she needed to be.

"Nells asked about you," Jaycen grumbled from the front of The Pack.

Kai sucked in a sharp breath behind Eleri and asked, "What did he say?"

Jaycen glanced at him, a brow arching high beneath the rim of his hat, before he turned back around. "I ran into him in the market. He wanted to know if she was staying in Arkala. I told him I hoped so. Looks like I was unlucky."

"Jaycen . . ." Rina groused.

Eleri didn't say anything. She didn't feel the need to as they crossed over the town's threshold, and the tension released from her body. Her shoulders slumped and jaw unclenched, the tightness unraveling from her limbs with each step they took farther from the settlement and into the barren Upperworld.

She made her decision and had to live with it. It finally began to settle in. She was back with the very people she fled. Back in this world of vigilantes. Back to the distrusting glances and quick jabs.

Never have I felt so vulnerable. Being alone and hiding in the shadows before crossing paths with The Pack felt easy compared to this. Eleri took a sidestep away from them, reinforcing the distance between them. *Never have I felt more dangerous.*

"You doing all right back there, El?" Rina called out just as a sharp gust of wind full of shards of sediment billowed toward them from The East.

The group stumbled back, leaning forward and bracing their weight against the hot dry blast. Losing her footing, Rina teetered to the side, missing Eleri by only a few inches.

Her heart turned icy and lodged itself into the back of her throat.

Another gust followed the first. Then another and another. The piercing wind picked up and shoved Eleri backward. Kai reached out for her; his fingers grasped at the air where she once was. But he was too late.

Thank Gods.

She fell hard, skidding across the sandy ground as her pants tore along the back of the thigh, and her hood flew from her forehead. Curling into a ball with her head down and her gloved fingers digging into her thighs, Eleri braced against the wrathful blasts. She risked a quick glance up before sand could get in her eyes and saw the others doing the same, hunched over and holding onto whatever they could for dear life.

The assault lasted several minutes. A swirling vortex of small debris raged around them violently, whipping at Eleri's cheeks with stinging slashes. With each passing second, Eleri's muscles tired, and it got harder to breathe as dust and grime seeped into her tightly closed lips and coated her tongue and throat.

Finally, it slowed. However, they waited until the strong winds transformed into merely a gentle breeze. A soft caress that ran through Eleri's hair as if it hadn't cut through her very being moments ago.

"Is everyone okay?" Kai called out.

His bandana was lopsided, his face caked in sand. Tan skin nearly completely covered. The same went for the others. He sat up, fixing his hat and securing his bandana, and ran a worried gaze over Rina and Jaycen before they slid to Eleri.

"All good here!" Jaycen called out, adjusting his bag and standing, then grasped Rina's forearm and hauled her up onto her shaky feet.

"Yeah . . ." Rina breathed. "We're good. El?"

Rina's short blonde hair was a tangled mess, with strands sticking to her cheeks and forehead.

Eleri nodded and pulled her hood back over her head before standing up and taking a step away from Kai and the others. Distance. She needed distance. "Yeah . . . I'm all right."

Rina's smile formed as she nodded and turned to Kai. "Onward?"

His gaze lingered on Eleri as the question settled around them before snapping back toward Rina, whose right eyebrow rose. He huffed. "We should be able to make it to the river within four or five days, depending on any breaks."

"I'd rather not stop," Jaycen inserted himself, looking toward the eastern horizon. "The faster we get to the river, the faster I can wipe this shit off my body."

"I need a good scrub," Rina mumbled, nodding her head.

The thought of the river filled Eleri with sudden relief. Her body craved the water's gentle caress she hadn't had the pleasure of feeling since she was in the Western Vale. She couldn't wait.

Kai rolled out his shoulders and cracked his neck, readying himself for the journey to come. He took a few steps onward. Rina and Jaycen fell into line with him. With a silent breath in, Eleri followed The Pack.

22

ELERI

THIS IS FUCKED.

Eleri looked down at the carcasses in front of her. A large black horse lay on its side half-covered in sand. Its coat was mangy, thin, and withered. Beneath it was its rider. His feet were bare; someone snatched up his boots before they got there. Both were covered in patchy rashes, red and crusting.

"I've never seen Sun Death on an animal," she muttered, squinting as she stared at the scene in front of her.

White and green dribble dried across both of their parted lips. The man's skin had begun to crack. A fly landed on his open eyeball. The horse's stomach bulged, swollen as if it had been stuffed full of hay and grass before it perished. Eleri knew that wasn't the case.

"Gods . . ." Rina whispered. She glanced away from the scene before them and looked toward the sky, shielding her eyes and worrying her lip between her teeth. "Is . . . Do you think it's getting worse? The layer between us and the sun, I mean."

Kai circled the scene before kneeling next to the man and searching his pockets for anything useful with a grunt. "Probably. The curse nearly destroyed it. I'd think over time, it would disappear completely."

Eleri watched the three of them study the two bodies. Rina nodded and brought her cowl up toward her face before kneeling next to them.

Kai inspected a small throwing knife he snagged from the man and pocketed it. Jaycen's brows cinched as he poked and prodded at the bloated animal, its skin caving in like mush.

"Food," Jaycen said suddenly, wiping away the pus that dribbled onto his finger. His lips pulled taut. With a grunt, he stood and glanced toward Kai. "We can cut around the infection. Divvy up the edible meat. It wouldn't be a lot, maybe enough to get us through a day or two, but it's something."

Kai grimaced, his nose wrinkling in disgust. A long silent moment passed between them as if he were thinking. With a reluctant sigh, he reached for his knife. "I got it."

"Thanks, Kai. There were some boulders not far back," Rina said with a grateful smile. "It should be hot enough to cook the meat on them. Jaycen, can I get your help?"

Jaycen hummed. The two of them walked past Eleri; only Rina looked back at her.

It was hot. So, so hot.

The last drop of Eleri's saliva evaporated from the very confines of her mouth. Just sitting in the sun, unmoving, exhausted her as if all her energy was being sucked up into the smoggy sky, fueling the fiery orb. The last piece of the horse's dark red meat sizzled against the dusty rocks. There was no hint of grey or green soiled muscle. No sign of the Sun Death that ate away at the creature once cut free.

Eleri stared down at the meat as it browned just as she felt another's gaze roam over her before settling on her cheek. Looking to the side, she was met with Rina's soft smile. A silent question lingered from her. *How are you doing?*

Eleri couldn't wrap her head around someone like her. She was so kind and caring. So selfless in a way that made Eleri envious. She never treated Eleri as if she was *dangerous . . . other* in a negative sense, even though she knew she was.

Eleri wondered if it would stay the same if Rina discovered her other half and the beast that was pent up within. Or what The Darkest Day cursed her to be. She gave Rina her most reassuring smile. She hoped it would be enough. The twinkle in her amber eyes told Eleri it was.

"All done." Kai grinned down at his work.

Eleri followed his gaze; the piece was cooked perfectly. A beautiful brown color that made her mouth water. Kai handed it carefully to Jaycen, who folded it in the cloth he stole from the shack's door before meeting up with them on the outskirts of Arkala with the few other salvageable pieces of meat.

"Let's get going. We can still travel for a few more hours." Jaycen glanced up at the orange sky before slashing his leer down toward Eleri. "If you can keep up. You're looking weak, Fae. I would have thought the magic in you would keep you going far longer than us *measly* Humans."

The fire in her gut swelled, and the air between Eleri and Jaycen hummed, tension seeping around them and surrounding them fully. It took everything—every single lock and chain—to reenforce the cage that held her dark side at bay and keep her from saying what she yearned to.

"What you think you know about me . . . is far from the truth. I don't . . ." She sighed, fatigue overcoming her as she held onto the good within her desperately. "You don't want to know what I can do."

Eleri didn't allow herself to look away from him. She stared into his eyes without flinching.

Jaycen stepped forward, his fists curling at his sides and his chest broadening. "Are you threatening me?"

The bandana around his face swayed outward with the force of each word.

"No." Eleri's voice remained calm despite her persistent beast clawing at its cage, excited by the prospect of a fight. "I'm just telling you the truth."

Kai stepped between them. He eyed Eleri with tightly pressed lips and creased brows before turning his head toward Jaycen. "Let it go, Jayc."

The burly man behind Kai scoffed and stepped away from him, shaking his head. Walking past the horse's remaining carcass and the blood staining the sand, he mumbled, "You're blind, Kai."

23

Eleri

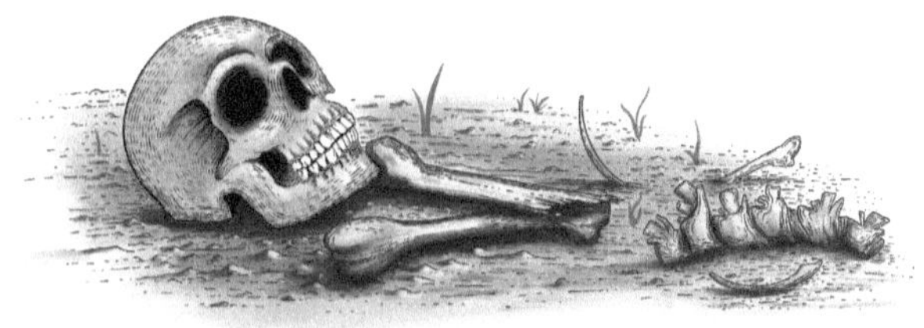

THE ORANGE SKY HAD barely bled into that night's maroon when they got up and began their journey. There wasn't much to pack, having collapsed into the sand dunes hours after cooking the horse the night before. All except Rina. She had been on first watch.

Her lashes drooped as she trudged through the sand weighing down each of their limbs. Kai seemed all right despite the dark circles rimming his eyes. He twisted his back until his spine popped and rolled out his shoulders as he walked. And Jaycen—he was alert. Eyes wide and awake, ready to continue. He must have been up for a while on second watch.

"Ready?" Jaycen had asked before they left their open camp, tightening the strap of his bag and straightening his bandana.

Kai chuckled and shook his head as he secured the hat atop his head. "Someone's in a good mood. Who would have thought you'd be so well rested after sleeping with sand up your ass?"

Jaycen merely shrugged and huffed out a laugh. "I'm just ready to get out of this desert. It's depressing as shit."

That was hours ago. Half the day had now gone by. Each minute was more of the same. Walking. Small talk here and there. Eleri reminded herself to step away when Rina moved too close. Her beast came out every now and then to test if she was in the mood. She wasn't.

The sun was at its highest and hottest point before something breached the horizon and cut the endless golden sand in half. Two figures emerged. The breeze picked up again, sand shredding through the air, making it hard for Eleri to see far.

"Slow . . ." Kai muttered.

His shoulders tightened, and his powerful stance—when faced at a crossroads and needed to step into his leader role—returned. Jaycen and Rina's gaits slowed to match his while still remaining a strong force about to approach an unknown.

Rina fiddled with her hat, securing it onto her head. Jaycen rolled his shoulders back and cracked his knuckles, readying for a fight Eleri hoped wouldn't happen.

Her ears twitched, tuning into what looked like a campsite. The Pack's steady heartbeats faded into the back of her mind as she concentrated. Several others in the distance thudded, vibrating against her eardrums, but it was unclear how many. The howling wind obstructed the path to them. Squinting, she could only see the two figures huddled near each other. From what she could tell, old tires and rusted engines were scattered around what looked like a large piece of cloth propped up in a tentlike structure near a pile of rubble and trash.

A woman's laugh drowned out the heartbeats and pierced Eleri's ears. It was high-pitched and nasally. A deeper chuckle—a man's—echoed and mixed with the woman's. There was something light and airy about their laughs, as if they were finding small happy moments in this deadly land. Like they were holding onto something or someone who made this life worth living.

As if pulled by an unknown force, her eyes landed on Kai. Just in front of her, she narrowed her focus on the nape of his neck. Shadowed by his hat, the tips of his black, choppy hair stood stark against his dirt-and-sweat-covered skin.

Eleri tore her eyes away, letting the crunch of their boots across the gritty, barren landscape distract her. It was mad. It was impossible. No one would want to stay by her side if they knew what a single touch of her finger, her foot . . . her lips . . . would do.

A monster without even trying. A monster just like my beast.

As the wind slowed, she shifted her eyes back toward the approaching campsite. A gasp slipped free at the sight. Her teeth chattered, and her legs stopped working. The Pack halted in response.

"What is it?" Kai growled.

His eyes held a dangerous molten heat, unwavering as he took in Eleri's trembling bottom lip. Fear was stark against her soot-covered face. A look that twisted her features.

She gaped at the sight before her as the wind calmed down even more. The woman and man she had thought were merely laughing and enjoying one another's company were bent over the body of an unconscious man. A man whose heartbeat was so faint she was certain his was not one she had heard before. The deranged man's fingers dug into his eye socket; blood covered his hand and dripped onto the earth. With a sickening pop, the eye snapped free while the woman used the tip of her knife to carve into the man's chest. She was writing something, a single word, but Eleri couldn't make out what it was. It was too far.

Gruesome. Inhuman. Disgusting.

Another brick added.

Eleri collapsed into herself, bending over with her palms bracing against her knees. The scene seared itself behind her eyelids and into her mind.

She heard Kai's breath snag in the back of his throat. Her deep inhale chased the clipped sound before she opened her eyes. Worry knitted Kai's brows together as he stepped closer. "El—"

"Hey!" the man in the distance yelled, noticing their group on the outskirts of their campsite.

A cold chill trickled down Eleri's spine as she slowly straightened her back and stood upright. *We've been spotted. We can't turn around. We can't hide.*

One word—a breathless whisper—broke the threshold of her lips. A warning of what she just witnessed from afar. A warning to tread carefully. "Dangerous."

Jaycen whipped his head around toward the figures in the distance. The man waved at him. It was an eerie sight . . . as if what he was doing to the poor man beneath him was perfectly normal. Their victim's blood splashed onto his shirt from the movement. Jaycen waved back.

"What are we walking into?" the gruff man gritted out. He dropped his arm, and it found purchase on his knife.

Eleri squeezed her eyes shut once more, long enough to banish the sight from her mind. However, it didn't work.

"A man and a woman. They're . . ." Gods, she didn't want to say it. The thought was unbearable. Despite it all, she trod on, just as she'd always done. "They're torturing someone else. He's unconscious, from what I can tell. It's . . . It's bad."

"Shit . . ." Rina mumbled and chewed on her bottom lip, casting a worried gaze in the campsite's direction.

"Anything else?" Kai's stern voice held authority, softly ordering her to give them as much information as possible.

Shaking her head, Eleri swallowed. "That's all I could focus on . . . There're more people, though. I . . . I don't know how many, but I could hear several different heartbeats—"

"You hear heartbeats?" Jaycen asked, perplexed. His eyes narrowed, face contorted with disgust and surprise.

She nodded, paying him no mind as her eyes moved toward the site. "I only saw bits and pieces of their campsite before I saw . . ."

The image of the dislodged eye rolling into the sand flashed across her vision.

"Okay . . ." Kai lifted his hand to her shoulder—an attempt to console her, Eleri thought—then thought better of it. His eyes flashed and fingers flexed as he placed it back at his side. "Okay. We tread carefully.

El, thank you. Your . . . *gifts* may feel burdensome, but it really helps knowing what's ahead before it's too late."

Kai turned back toward the campsite. The man stood with his hands on his hips, watching them. The woman crossed her bloodied arms over her chest.

No one spoke as The Pack began walking again, making their way toward the gruesome scene only Eleri had experienced. She kept her eyes down, though, following the heels of Kai's boots in front of her. A sick, lingering twist tugged at her gut as the scent of blood and dirt wafted just below her nose.

"Oh, fuck . . ." Jaycen muttered.

Eleri refused to look up . . . *couldn't* look up. The desperate groans of the man bleeding on the ground were now deafening. Alongside them, she heard the stirring sand beneath someone's feet. Mumbles—*prayers*—and rattling chains echoed across the empty landscape. And the smell . . .

Snapping her head upward, she saw several other people behind the couple. Chained and bloody and terrified. All forced to wait their turn with the man and woman. Lead filled her stomach; bile burned the back of her throat and her nostrils.

They were the monsters. Not her. Never would she do such a thing.

Eleri took a timid step closer to Kai. She didn't realize she'd done so until the deed was already done.

"You lot all alone?" the man asked, eyeing each of them.

His gaze lingered on Rina before he leaned around Kai and peered at Eleri. A grotesque smile of black teeth and gaping holes twisted his face at the sight.

Eleri purposefully took another step toward Kai, wringing the hem of her tunic and shifting on her feet as the man's eyes raked down her figure. Wickedness gleamed across his ugly features.

"Just us." Kai was curt. A no-nonsense reply that irritated the woman.

She scoffed at them and spat. "Why are you coming this way, then?"

The nasal pitch of her laugh was stronger when she talked. Goosebumps erupted over Eleri's skin with each word as she stared at the bloody knife. It was rusted; several pieces of the blade were chipped and cracked. Eleri could only imagine how excruciating it would be to have it rip into flesh.

To the right, the unconscious man writhed in pain. Even in his sleep, he must have known he was dying. The word on his chest made Eleri's throat bob.

F–R–A–N–C–I—

Her name, Eleri thought. *This sick woman was carving her name into the flesh of an innocent man.*

That flame of anger deep within her belly simmered at the sight, readying itself to explode.

How could anyone do such a thing?

It was repulsive. It was evil.

"Just heading east," Kai said, his eyes never leaving the couple except for a split second as he took in the others chained together like a knot. "We don't want any trouble."

"Then go on now, boy." The man spat mucus onto the ground, barely missing his boot.

"Now, you see . . ." Kai lifted his hands next to his face, each on either side of his head with his palms facing out. A gesture of surrender. But the crinkles at the corners of his eyes told them he was smirking beneath his bandana. "We would have happily minded our business if we hadn't come across *this.*"

He gestured to the man and the people held captive. The couple shifted, eyes hardened.

"We can't just let that slide. You see, we're in the business of helping people. And from what I can tell, these people need help. You've had your fun. This man"—Kai's eyes darted to the unconscious body too still for Eleri's liking—"is on death's door. I don't think there's anything we can do for him. But those over there? Why must they face the same fate?"

The woman barked out a piercing laugh, tilting her head back, revealing more of her bony neck. "What else are we supposed to do in this shithole? It's *fun*. Don't be a pussy, pretty boy."

A huff of a breath on the verge of a laugh and a scoff broke past Kai's gritted teeth. Eleri stole a glance at him. He was a pipe bomb, ready to explode. Rage radiated from his entire being and pulsed in sync with his rapidly racing heart. Ignoring the woman's taunt, he focused on the man. "Release the captured."

"Or else?" the man hissed while reaching for and fiddling with what Eleri suspected was a weapon.

The woman sent a sinister smile as she shifted on her feet behind him in anticipation, excitement glittering in her eyes.

"Or else we'll have to intervene. And"—Kai glanced at Jaycen's looming stature before sending a silent order to Rina and training his leer back on the couple—"I don't think you want us to intervene."

"Hm . . ." the man huffed, glancing at Jaycen, whose hazel eyes flared with the prospect of a fight. Then he slid his eyes toward Rina. "We'll release the others . . . if you hand the blonde over. And this little one hiding in the back."

His ruddy eyes were full of hunger as he shifted them toward Eleri. Something sinister lurked behind those blown-out pupils.

Oh, Gods. A killer . . . and worse.

A growl—so deep and feral—ripped from Kai's throat. He stepped forward. "That's not going to happen."

"Suit yourself." The man let out a gritty chuckle. The woman's echoed his, mixing like a wet, soiled brew. "You didn't think I'd recognize you? With those prissy hats? Your faces—although covered—are all over those wanted posters . . . and that reward will be mine. Immunity from The Wake? I can do whatever the fuck I want with that type of freedom. You gave yourselves away when you said you *help* these pathetic excuses of life who are too weak to survive."

His laugh got louder, more deranged, as he pulled a machete from the back of his waistband and got into a ready stance like a viper gearing to strike.

"Give me a piece of that strange-haired bitch." The woman stalked forward, her eyes solely fixed on Eleri, then whistled.

A handful of others emerged from behind trash, broken carts, and discarded tires. They were covered in shit and blood, some missing fingers and others teeth, emerging to join the fight . . . itching for violence.

Eleri stepped back just as a thickset woman—with buzzed hair and scars across her cheeks—lunged for Rina. The blonde easily dodged the attack, landing a quick jab to her attacker's gut with her knuckles.

Chaos—utter chaos—erupted. Bodies were thrown from one side of the campsite to another. Kai blocked the man's slash of his blade with his own knife. Grunts echoed around them. The smell of blood tinged the air. Jaycen took on three men at once . . . bashing heads in, dragging corpses, and slicing tendons. It was an anarchic brawl between The Pack and these murderers.

And Eleri was stuck in the middle of it.

The growing, incessant need to join in bubbled up in the pit of her stomach. The fire within flared, and her feisty beast tiptoed out of its cage with a feral grin.

No!

She dodged flailing limbs whenever they got too close. Ducking and weaving around The Pack, she tried to stay as far away from everyone as possible. No matter who they were. Eleri didn't want another death on her hands, *couldn't* have another death on her hands. One—Merrin—was one too many. She . . . She didn't know if she could survive knowing she killed another. However, the woman who carved into the unconscious man—the woman with blood on her hands and hate in her eyes—had other ideas.

She rushed toward Eleri with a sharp scrap of metal big enough to cover her chest clutched between her palms and raised above herself. Slamming it to the ground, she released a guttural scream. The flat side rammed into the top of Eleri's head and sent her sprawling.

A sharp pain shot up her temple into the back of her skull; her vision spun. Eleri attempted to focus on her approaching attacker, to no avail. The copper taste of blood filled her mouth and coated her tongue where she had bitten it.

Pounding stomps rang in Eleri's ears.

Thump.

"I'm gonna kill you, bitch."

Thump. Thump.

"And carve my name into your stomach to show the whole world you're mine."

Thump.

Gripping the earth beneath her, she tried to center herself. Tried to force away the constant swaying and spinning obscuring her vision. Tried to run from this sadistic killer who gleamed at the thought of inflicting pain on others.

Eleri scrambled away from the woman. Dust plumed around her tired body as it scooted toward safety.

Faster.

Turning over, she got on all fours and crawled. Forcing away the dizziness that fell upon her, Eleri clawed at the dirt and dragged her knees as fast as she physically could.

Faster. Faster. Faster!

She approached a metal tub near a pile of trash. Frantic, she looked for something. A knife. A shard of iron. Anything to defend herself.

"Please . . ."

The broken word fell off her lips—pathetic and scared.

She inched herself closer and closer to the tub. Each crawl was excruciating as her heart slammed into her rib cage and her vision turned black around the corners. Finally, she gripped its edge, weakly pulling herself up. It was full of murky brown water. Blood splatters stained the metal. Chunks of *something* floated within it. She could barely see her reflection, just a muffled silhouette of sludge.

Ice-cold fear paralyzed her as the clammy grasp of bony fingers wrapped around the back of her neck. She flailed against the woman's grip, ripping herself free just as a scream sliced through the air, and she fell into the tub.

Water gushed into her mouth and down her throat. It tasted vile and burned as she choked. Breaching the water after several painful seconds, Eleri coughed up mouthfuls of the sludge and sucked in a deep breath of the smog-filled air as the woman's howls continued, sending chills down her spine and cementing her gut with iron. Then the fighting came to a halt around them. Shocked gasps and terrified whispers bounced from person to person.

Not again.

She was paralyzed. All she could do was watch.

The woman screeched while gaping at her burning arm. Ashes fluttered into the air as the cursed magic within Eleri's veins worked its way past her shoulder and over her neck. Scrambling to grab Eleri again and haul her out of the tub, the woman lunged toward her with open claws and wild eyes before that hand crumbled into nothing. Consumed only by the numbing panic bursting across her skin, she merely watched. Frozen.

"Witch . . ." one of the people chained to the tree whispered.

Eleri blinked, hearing the word no one else could have.

"Witch!" they screamed this time, pointing at the pile of ash where the woman once was. Ash scattered in the shape of a soul.

Panic exploded around the campsite. Those captured were pulling at their chains as if doing so would free them from her. The man and his followers backed away. Some gripped their weapons tighter than before while staring her down.

"Look! Her ears!" one woman spat out.

Eleri fought the urge to cover them.

"Witches' Marks! Look at them!" another yelled.

Eleri's eyes bulged as drops of water dripped from her face, along her neck and under her sopping clothes. Her hands flew toward her cheeks. Her shaking fingers glided over her wet skin. Terror gripped her heart. The white lines across the bridge of her nose and down her bottom lip were no longer hidden by the dirt. Witches' Marks—marks no Witch had been born with since the Under War.

"Evil is among us!"

Her heart clenched, and her nostrils burned while she fought off the urge to cry. Screams and accusations flew her way, piercing her soul to its very core. They blurred together, becoming a panicked cacophony.

"She probably brought this down on all of us . . ."

"The curse! She must be responsible!"

"She's an abomination. She shouldn't be Above. She shouldn't be *alive!*"

That hungry, fiery beast rushed out at their sneers before Eleri could reel it back in and stop its claws from gripping onto her heart with sheer force. A hefty growl from the creature within vibrated against her chest.

She took one step toward those who had yet to back away. She bared her pointed canines for all to see. A snarl rumbled through the cracks between her teeth. She stared down each murderer, one by one, with deadly intent. A threat lingered in her eyes as she clenched her fists.

They stepped back as she took another step forward. Then they fled.

"Crazy bitch!" one muscular woman spat.

A slimy-looking man joined in as he turned to run. "Fucking freak!"

Freak. The urge to run after them slammed into her. *I could easily get rid of them all. Pathetic beings. Freak . . .*

A commotion at her side snapped her attention as the fire blazed—hungry for a fight, looking for an outlet for its wrath. The people chained together cowered away, bumping into one another and pulling at their restraints desperately. Fear shone in their watery eyes. Their bodies shook as they bowed, praying to their God. The sight alone was like a knife in the chest, branding itself to her soul.

"In through your nose, for fuck's sake," Eleri gritted out, shutting her eyes.

Pushing that darkness to the side, forcing it down, Eleri's mother's voice echoed in her brain. *"You are an Underworld Witch, my little one. Be proud of that. Honor your ancestors while changing its course. Banish the darkness. You are the light. You are Goddess blessed."*

The words lingered, the memory of them swelling around her. Eleri shivered. "Out through your mouth."

Goddess blessed. Her mother would say that as she ran her delicate fingers across the bridge of Eleri's nose and over her bottom lip when tucking her in at night. Eleri couldn't help but clench her jaw at those two insignificant words.

It was bullshit. The fire flared for a split second more before she focused on the rest of what her mother would say to her.

Banish the darkness. You are the light.

Banish the darkness. You are the light.

Banish the darkness . . .

Eleri's breath evened out. Extinguished into the recesses of her mind, that flame—that anger and that animalistic need—went silent once again. Regret and shame took its place, and it left a hole in her chest before spreading across her entire body.

Two people have now perished because of her. *Fuck. Maybe I am the monster.*

Burning—no longer deep within her very being but instead against her skin—pulled her gaze up from the pile of ash before her. Kai, Rina, and Jaycen stared her way. Their peering left a scorching path as they roamed every inch of her body.

Her gaze locked on the horror etched on Jaycen's face, then caught the fear in Kai's, her stomach dropping at the sight. She hated the way they were looking at her. She hated herself for giving them a reason to.

Each whimper from those cowering against their chains was another blade twisting in her heart. Shame swarmed over every inch of her down to her bones. Squeezing her eyes shut once again, she listened. Instead of focusing her efforts on silencing the captured's moans, groans, and whispered prayers, Eleri took it all in. Every single voice, every single word was laced with dread.

"Oh, Great Son!" one man mumbled. "Please spare me from this wicked creature."

A tear-filled wail broke through. "My beloved Trinity. Kill this monster. For the sake of Humankind!"

Every wish for her death, every plea to survive, she embedded it into her memory.

She wanted to remember this. She *had* to remember this. She was the reason for that fear.

Another brick.

Opening her eyes, she noticed Rina. Her jaw hung open, features full of wonder and awe . . . just like when they first met. But this time, tears sat atop her lash line as if she was truly seeing Eleri for the first time.

"El . . ." Rina reached forward, desperately hoping to get through to her. She swallowed around nothing but the dry air. "Eleri."

Eleri's muscles liquified.

Her full name, her real name . . . a name she hadn't heard since that fateful day. Her fingers twitched, and her heart raced. The urge to run away as far as possible prodded at her limbs and settled over her chest. Desperation clawed within, urging a swift exit.

"Eleri . . ." Kai pondered, testing the name on his tongue as if he recognized it, like he had heard it before but couldn't seem to remember where.

Then Jaycen sputtered, stumbling back slightly as recognition hit him. "Good Gods."

Rina released a sudden disbelieving laugh while gripping the rusted pendant around her neck with a watery smile. "You're Eleri Fos, Princess of The Underworld."

As if Eleri's head was on a swivel, she rapidly shook it back and forth and backed away in the tub of water.

I need to get out of here. I need to get away from them. They can't know . . . They can't.

Eleri's eyes darted for the best possible route to flee.

It was already too dangerous for an Under-dweller to be Above, but the princess? A high commodity in a world with no rules.

Another step back. Her body trembled; horror trickled down her spine from the base of her head.

They'll kill me. Or deliver me to the Upper King. And I'll never get home. Instead, chances are, I'll be left to rot like that child on the side of the road.

"Please." Rina's voice cracked as she took a hesitant step forward. "Don't run. I—I have so many questions. So many things I need to tell you."

Eleri's heel rammed into the metal tub after taking one more step back, and her eyebrows knitted together. Kai and Jaycen were also looking at Rina, seemingly trying to understand what their friend meant.

What could she mean?

Rina's lower lip wobbled, and her knuckles turned white around her necklace. She begged once more, choking on the word. "Please."

24

RINA

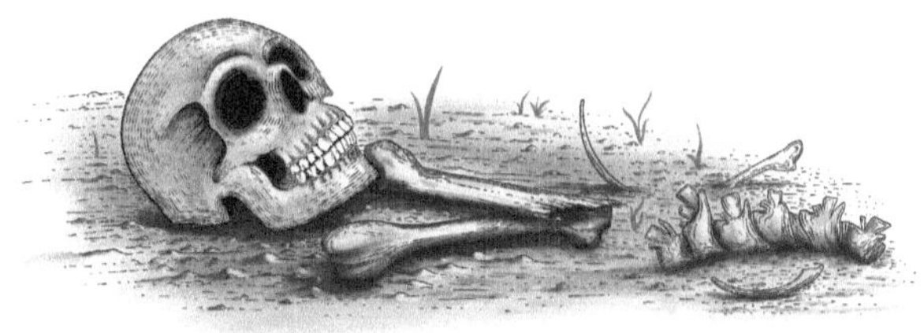

THE PRINCESS OF THE Underworld. Holy Trinity. The fucking *princess.*

Rina kept stealing glances at the Fae-Witch standing off to the side. She looked shell-shocked. Her eyes were wide. Her arms were crossed. Her feet fidgeted, and she flinched at every little sound.

A twinge of guilt prodded at Rina's chest as she gazed at the terrified woman. El—*Eleri*—didn't want her identity to be revealed, that much was clear. Rina could've kept her mouth shut, admired the royal from afar if she had any brains. But when the realization processed through the adrenaline of the fight, nothing could stop the words.

Emotions—so many emotions—rammed into her, from the tips of her toes to the base of her skull. She . . . She just couldn't hold it in. And she couldn't help but feel as if she'd struck down—*destroyed*—the wall that had given El any sort of safety.

"Rina!"

Her attention snapped back toward the task—to her friends and the people in chains. Jaycen was staring at her, his hands moving to lift his hat slightly and wipe the sweat from his forehead. "C'mon! We need your help if we want to get this done before nightfall!"

She nodded before stealing one last look at the princess, then made her way toward the gruesome scene left behind by those monsters. About a dozen people—men, women, even a child shielded behind what looked to be her mother—were chained. Shackles wrapped around their wrists and ankles. Rusted bindings tied each of them together.

Bloodied and bruised, their bodies told their stories. Malnourished, their bones protruded against leathery, exposed skin. Terrified, their eyes shifted from The Pack to El.

Slowly approaching, Rina took careful steps until she was shoulder-to-shoulder with Jaycen and Kai. They locked eyes with one another—faces solemn, shoulders tensed. No one spoke. Then, after a handful of breaths, they got to work.

They'd done this before and knew how to do it efficiently. They knew to offer the food they carried in their packs, bypassing their own hunger in hopes those who needed help could gain some strength.

They were a well-oiled machine.

Rina slung her bag off her shoulder and crouched before rummaging through it. Pulling out the cans of beans she's taken from Arkala, Rina placed them next to the small, roughly cut pieces of horse meat Jaycen retrieved and turned her head. "El, would you like to help?"

She wanted to break through the horror-filled fog she could tell was consuming the Fae-Witch. She wanted to help her and these people. El's eyes widened, and her body tensed as she gaped at The Pack. Rina gave her time to answer, tipping back her hat and trying to send reassurance through her own gleaming gaze.

The moment was shattered when a woman wailed in protest. "Don't let her come near us. She's a monster. Evil runs through her veins!"

Rina's heart broke, her gut sinking as if it were weighed down by the very chains she was planning on breaking. El looked away, but Rina saw it. A few tears fell from her bottom lashes and rolled along her reddened cheeks. Under her breath, El whispered, "I should stay back."

"Don't you think about running." Jaycen shot a glare as sharp as a knife over his shoulder as he walked toward a pile of rubble made of large tin sheets and rusted metal shards.

"Where do I have to go?" Eleri sat near the grimy tub of water and pulled her knees to her chest.

Kai quietly sighed as he spared Eleri a quick glance before joining his friend. Rina tried to send her a warm smile—anything to stop the self-deprecating cloud swirling around her. She didn't look up.

Resigned, Rina exhaled. Reaching behind her, she found a spare piece of metal partially buried in the sand and slammed it into a can's top, wrenching it open. The smell wafted around her as she peeled the lid back. It made her nauseated, her body revolting from being so full. Rina breathed through her mouth, opened each can, and stacked them together as loud clangs and ear-splitting cracks filled the air—Jaycen and Kai working on the chains.

The prisoners cowered, flinching with each hit to their bindings. Grunts and hisses filled the campsite as the men swung down on the restraints, and one after another, they were freed. Several fled without a single glance back.

"Don't trust them. Don't thank them," one man muttered as he backed away from Kai and Jaycen, then turned once his chains were removed. "They travel with the Witch."

Others, however, stayed at the promise of food. They gathered in a huddle and watched Jaycen and Kai work. As Rina approached, they recoiled; her heart shattered, and she tried to calm her pulse despite the smells and sights swarming her.

Be with me, Rina silently prayed. *Be with me and these poor souls, oh Great Trinity.*

A cool caress fluttered across the inside of her wrist. The Daughter.

A neutral presence settled across the nape of her neck. The Mother.

A hot pulse thumped the air around her. The Son.

"We are here, child."

Slowly setting the items piled in her arms down, she sent the malnourished people a gentle smile. "We have some beans here for you to eat. Horse meat as well."

The child standing behind a woman stepped forward, but her mother pulled her back against her leg and whispered, "The Witch could have tainted the food."

Fear filled her eyes, but behind it burned hunger—desperation.

An urge to defend El surged through Rina. She may not have known her for long—and truth be told, she didn't know her well—but Rina had seen the softness in her. She'd seen how The Underworld's princess was just as scared as these people. But something told her not to. A warmth in her chest seemed to know that if she defended the Fae-Witch, these people would run far and fast. And they wouldn't make it without some kind of sustenance.

"You need to eat." Rina kept her voice steady. "Please, all we want to do is help. That's all. These cans were sealed. No one has tampered with them. I just ate one this morning. Please . . ."

The last word caught in the back of her throat. She wanted to admonish herself for the slip in the shield she tried to bear, but she couldn't seem to do it. She felt for these people, felt for El. Rina . . . just wanted to help. To save them.

The child with one brown eye and one milky white slipped through her mother's grasp and slowly inched her way toward Rina. "I . . . I don't think I can eat. It hurts too much."

The little girl's voice was rough—dry from the dust, burdened by all she'd seen at such a young age. Too young to even understand the world they'd lost.

A familiar burn rose into the back of Rina's eyes, goosebumps rising as she tried to stop her emotions from boiling over. "I know. I know, little one. Just one bite. It will help you—"

"Don't do it," another woman hissed.

Aiming all her sincerity and hope toward the child, Rina nudged the can forward. A whisper. "Please."

With eyes full of naïve hope—full of a wariness a child should never have—the girl slowly reached for the can like a scared animal trying not to be detected. Her small, nimble fingers gripped the lip of the can and dragged it toward her. Both of her hands wrapped around the tin, and she wearily brought it to her trembling lips. A split second passed before she dumped a mouthful of beans into her waiting mouth and chewed gingerly.

Her face lighting up, she took in another mouthful before handing the can to her mother. Soon, curious stares and apprehensive leers transformed into the needy hunger Rina had seen countless times. She handed the other cans and meat out as she watched the food slowly disappear with each bite shared among the group.

As she looked at the prisoners of those vile, sorry excuses for Humans, her heart swelled. They were doing good in this world—even when it didn't seem like it at times. They truly were.

Rina stole a glance at Eleri Fos and vowed to help her, too.

25

Kai

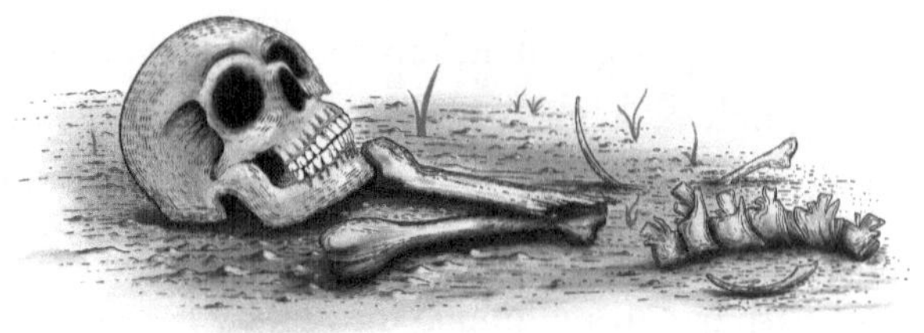

Scraps of wood cracked and popped under the fire's blazing heat. Kai blankly stared at the flames as they danced in the subtle, arid breeze. The movement was peaceful—hypnotizing—as the three of them finally digested what they had learned about the being sitting opposite him. His mind, however, was anything but.

He drifted from his body as if watching from above, navigating the truth before him while dodging rampant, hurling thoughts. After Rina convinced El—*Eleri*—not to run and they released the survivors, they decided the murderers' campsite was the best place to settle in for the night.

A Witch. And a Fae.

A princess.

Kai's breath stuttered, flitting out of his lungs as he wrapped his mind around it all.

So much confusion ate away at him. Fear settled inside his chest. His heartbeat raced erratically. *She could hear it, couldn't she? Oh Gods.*

And her *magic*. That woman had burned from the inside out. It was a sort of power that sent dread through his entire body. A sort of power that could obliterate his entire world.

Deadly. Dangerous.

Something scratched against Kai's skull. A thought or a memory of some kind burrowed into his subconscious like a spider in a pile of sand. *Eleri Fos . . .*

Kai remembered learning about The Underworld's royal family in his lessons as a child. For diplomatic reasons, his tutors had said. But for the life of him, he couldn't recall much of what had been taught—his mind always wandering. But that insistent feeling gnawed at him.

Those Beneath were always said to be dark and deadly by Upper-dwellers, but he didn't think his lessons had mentioned anything about it running through their veins—running through the princess's.

Hesitantly, he slid his gaze to her. She was hunched over, her arms wrapped around her knees, pulling them to her chest. Her stare was unwavering, nearly vacant, as she watched the flames.

Her hood was off. The orange of her hair looked even more vibrant under the shifting fire's light. Her pointed ears peeked out through those soft-looking locks. Her canines dug into her bottom lip. Her pale skin—now on full display—was absent of dirt and muck, and those white lines stood stark against her flesh now that he knew they were there.

An overwhelming sense of tranquility washed over him, frightening him just enough to make his blood sing. It tried to stomp out the negative thoughts and speculations whirling around in his head. He couldn't shake the sense that this calmness stemmed from the very force that had led him to Arkala . . . and El.

Her duality intrigued him.

But her power . . . it was something he couldn't seem to comprehend. *I want to run for the hills far away from her. And I want to stay right here and learn everything I can about her.*

He was splitting in two.

"You lied to us," Jaycen growled, breaking the silence.

Kai's muscles twitched at the harshness of his friend's voice. All eyes turned to Jaycen with his hardened hazel gaze and feathering jaw. Jaycen had always been rough around the edges ever since him and Kai were teenagers, but the hatred he shot toward Eleri was in-tense—raw and unconfined. Kai's fingernails dug into his palms.

Eleri's lips pursed together, a small frown tugging at her mouth. "Why must I tell you everything about me when I don't know anything about you?"

She was met with silence. None spoke as a heaviness filled the campsite and turned the air thick. How could they when they knew that, deep down, she was right?

A dejected huff came from Eleri, and she shook her head. "It doesn't matter anyway. I'm . . . not that princess anymore. Would it have made a difference if I had told you?"

"Yes," Jaycen said.

"No," Rina answered at the same time.

She whipped her head toward the former. They stared each other down—a standoff of wills. The shadows from the fire danced along their narrowed eyes and twitching lips.

"Now's not the time," Kai interrupted, authority lacing the words. He leered at Jaycen before turning his dagger-like gaze toward Rina. He pulled his bandana down and ran his palm across his face. "Knock it off."

Irritated, Jaycen addressed him. "What do you think, Kai?"

Kai opened his mouth despite not knowing what he thought or how he felt.

Rina said, "It doesn't matter what he thinks." Her voice was firm, unwavering. "Eleri is right. We haven't told her anything about us—where we come from, who we were before The Darkest Day. Do not fault her for protecting herself."

She stared pointedly at Kai, and he hated that he inwardly cow-ered away from her glare. He didn't say anything—could barely look at his friend of nearly five years defend this being she hardly knew.

Turning to Eleri, Rina's eyes softened, and she smiled timidly. "My name is Rina, as you know. Rina Yarrow. I was born in what used to be Mountmend."

Eleri's eyes widened at that. It was a small piece of information that shared so much more about the blonde. And Kai couldn't help but balk at her. Rina was so open with her past, so trusting with it. It was admirable, really. And yet he couldn't bring himself to be the same. Too much shame was attached to his.

Rina continued, "I had a loving mother and father who used to work in the produce fields on the outskirts of town. They were older, so when The Darkest Day happened . . . I wasn't surprised they didn't make it. They were taking an afternoon nap together when the curse barreled into our town after it had raced toward the Western Vale, then shot back toward us. I was outside writing in my journal while my sister played with some of her school friends—"

Rina's voice cracked, a watery smile betraying her carefully placed façade.

Kai's heart shuddered at the broken sound that left his friend. Jaycen sighed, his brows pinched together. And Eleri . . . Kai noticed her hand flex atop her knee. It was a small movement—minuscule, really—and he watched her with an intensity he wasn't used to. It looked as if she wanted to reach out and console Rina.

"I'm . . . sorry, Rina. What"—Eleri cleared her throat uncomfortably—"was your sister's name?"

Rina beamed at the Fae-Witch for simply asking. "Brynn. She . . . she was only sixteen when the curse hit. She survived the initial impact. We were all we had after Ma and Pa. But not long after, she began to decline and developed this . . . horrid cough. It would wreak havoc on her body—spitting up blood, shards of glass and debris from the smoke cutting her throat as she gagged. Brynn passed just before her seventeenth birthday."

Kai removed his gaze from Eleri and settled it on his friend. His chest constricted as he watched her battle a fight he couldn't help her win. Emotions—several emotions all wrestling to be at the forefront—etched over her features.

He remembered the day they had found her. It wasn't long after Brynn had died. Rina was alone in front of her house, kneeling at three long piles of dirt. Graves. She had been crying before Kai and Jaycen approached on their horses, dried tear tracks staining her cheeks. They had seen horrors on their journey, yet something tugged at him and told him she needed them more than he would ever know. He had offered to let her join them, and after a day of thinking it over, she accepted.

Tracing her features, he took her in now. Kai knew how much she had changed. Rina was now a force to be reckoned with. She was strong and quick-witted and a fighter . . . a *survivor*.

"She would have loved you, Eleri. She *did* love you." Rina wiped a wayward tear with the back of her hand before clutching that necklace once more. "Brynn had a . . . fascination with Beneath. She . . . when she was in school, she learned of The Trinity. The Mother and The Son and The Daughter. The Daughter was always her favorite. She gave me this necklace. A sketch of The Daughter is etched onto it. And with that love for The Daughter came a love for The Underworld. She learned as much as she could about its inhabitants with what few resources we had up here.

"But out of everything she learned from stories told by merchants and fairytales she found at the library, the Fae were always her favorite." A sad laugh slipped free. Rina cast her sight toward the shadows dancing along the ground. "During her final days, she told me she'd get through it and visit The Underworld one day to meet the half-Fae, half-Witch princess who was a symbol of unity."

Kai's heart seemed to have stopped beating. He thought he knew everything about Rina. He studied her with a small frown. *I guess I didn't.*

Eleri took in a shaky breath at the confession that hung in the air. The barely audible sound pulled at Kai. Her bottom lip trembled. "She sounds . . . incredible, Rina. I—it would have been an honor to have met her in another life."

Wiping another stray tear from her cheek, Rina sent Eleri smile. It was full of gratitude. Kai could do nothing but observe these two women—from completely different worlds—share a moment together. Jaycen was frozen as well, and Kai knew he was thinking the same, even if he disagreed with Eleri's presence here. After a few breaths, Rina opened her mouth before closing it again, unsure whether she should say anything.

Should I say something?

Eleri must have caught on. She nodded. "Go on. I can see the question on the tip of your tongue. Ask what you'd like."

A chuckle breached Rina's lips, airy and light, a tinge of embarrassment twining around the tune and a faint rouge painting the apples of her cheeks.

"Your . . . markings. I don't think Brynn ever mentioned them. She had talked about Witches' Marks hundreds of years ago, before the war between the Witches and the Fae. But I remember she had said they were black." Eleri hesitantly nodded again. *Bracing herself for the inevitable question*, Kai thought. "Why are yours different? And why did no one mention them to Brynn when she was alive?"

Eleri was silent for a long moment, her lips pressed tightly together as her head swiveled slightly. Kai could see her trying to gather her thoughts. With a deep breath, she said, "I don't know why no one mentioned them. My only guess is that the stories and books your sister poured herself into might not have been entirely accurate. Kind of like how many Above believe *Vampires* come from our realm."

Eleri shifted slightly, releasing her knees from her chest and sitting straighter. Kai's gaze zeroed in on the ripped fabric on the back of her thigh and the ivory skin peeking through as she continued. "They were correct, however, when it came to the other Witches' Marks. They were a deep, inky color and came in many shapes and sizes. No Witch had been born with the marks since The Under War. I . . . also don't know why that is. Some believe it was The Daughter's doing . . . to punish the Witches for starting the war in the first place. I don't truly know. And I don't know why I was born with them and why they're different. I was just born with them, just as you were born with the one under your eye. Beautiful and so unique, Rina. But that's it—just markings. Nothing more, nothing less."

Rina hummed, taking in this new information. "The Daughter . . . The Trinity works in mysterious ways. There's a reason, Eleri, even if you don't understand it yet."

Unbidden, a scoff ripped from Eleri's throat. It shocked Kai. It seemed to have shocked Eleri as well. Her eyes widened, and a ferocious blush tinted her neck all the way up her cheeks as she sputtered out an apology to Rina. "I-I am so sorry. I didn't mean to react like that. I just"—her voice turned quieter, timid with a hint of resentment—"don't believe in all that stuff."

This time, Rina's eyes bulged as Jaycen huffed off to the side. Kai studied the Fae carefully as Rina murmured slightly. "You don't believe in The Trinity? Not The Mother or The Son? Not even your own Goddess?"

Eleri's piercing blue eyes slid away from Rina and quickly swept over Kai and Jaycen before landing back on the woman. "No."

"You . . . you have to believe in *something*." Rina's grip on her necklace tightened. Sorrow flared in her eyes. "Something to get you through each day in this fucked-up world."

Hesitation gripped Eleri, her demeanor turning skittish and unsure. "I . . . don't. I'm sorry. If The Trinity were real, then The Darkest Day would have never happened. And I wouldn't have been cursed with this deadly touch."

A silence blanketed them. *Cursed?*

Rina cleared her throat. "I . . . I was going to ask about that, too." She looked down sheepishly. "I have only ever heard of Fae with light magic. Nothing so . . ."

"Deadly?" Eleri bit out, the word sounding like acid on her tongue.

Rina looked at her with round eyes and parted lips. She merely nodded.

Eleri's teeth ground so roughly Kai felt as if he could hear the bones screeching. "I wasn't always like this. I had . . . the gift I was born with gave life. It didn't take it."

Kai blinked, wrapping his head around her confession. Eleri was once able to brush her fingers over another without turning them to ash. His gut tightened, and his chest constricted.

He dug his fingers into the flesh above his knees; he flexed his jaw muscles sharply. Watching her, Kai studied the way her hands balled into fists. She had to be itching for contact, itching to no longer be a source of such destruction.

I wonder what her skin feels like. Soft, probably.

Kai blinked, forcing that thought of Eleri and her forbidden touch away, and peered at Rina once the words sank in. He could see the disappointment on her face. Eleri must have seen it, too, because she leaned closer.

"For me, being in a world this desolate and hostile and not being able to touch any living thing—animals, grass . . . *people*—as I was once able to . . . it's hard to hold on to the faith I had before. But . . . maybe your faith, Rina, can be enough for the both of us."

Light returned to Rina's dim, disappointed eyes. They sparkled against the firelight as she nodded vigorously toward Eleri and clasped her hands together. The princess smiled at her before shifting to Jaycen, who watched the exchange without a hint of emotion. Then her eyes landed on Kai.

They were piercing—enrapturing—as she lingered on him. He hardened his eyes once more, forcing his wide stare into narrowed slits. He couldn't push away those thoughts fast enough. "Why exactly are you heading east?"

Eleri sat there with fidgeting fingers. For a split second, a moment that gripped at his chest, Kai thought maybe she *was* working with The Wake or traveling to join them or perhaps with the man responsible for it all.

"You know our reasons for our journey. Why would you leave The Vale and travel to the most desolate, unsavory part of The Upperworld?"

Suspicion punctured each syllable as Kai's spine straightened and his jaw tightened.

Perhaps that was the feeling he was following before Arkala. An instinct to intercept her before it was too la—

"I'm heading home," Eleri all but whispered.

"But," Rina softly said, "the entrance is west of here. We passed it after we parted ways in the forest."

"Yeah, I know." Eleri sighed. "Nothing can get through The Pathway. I've tried."

So, those were *her scratch marks.*

She continued. "But . . . I heard rumors, mutterings from a couple out West who said there was another way. I didn't hear it all. I was hiding in an alleyway, but what I heard . . . I don't know. I just went with it. I just . . . want to go back home."

Eleri's voice cracked, and Kai's toughened façade did just the same.

She cleared her throat. "They said deep beneath the mountain range, past The Wasteland and the Upper Palace, were tunnels. Catacombs. I . . . don't know where they got that information, or if it's even real, but . . . I have to try."

Holding his breath, Kai's eyes softened even more. That strange feeling was back, pulsing around him and straining toward her. It wasn't to intercept the Fae. It was as if the force yearned to be near her, reaching for her.

After a long, taut silence that hung above them, Eleri muttered, "I'm turning in for the night. Today was . . . a lot."

As she stood, she slightly twisted her spine to stretch the stiffness that had gathered from the exhausting fight and high emotions and turned from the fire.

"No running off this time?" Kai couldn't help but ask this. He tried to hide the way his voice shook, unsure if he even wanted an answer.

Eleri turned and looked at him. Something flitted across her eyes as they shifted down toward his chest. His heart rammed rapidly around his rib cage; it felt as if she understood what he was feeling.

She didn't say anything, merely shaking her head no, then found a spot beside a rusted sheet of metal—near the broken shackles—and lay down.

26

KAI

THE ONCE-ROARING CAMPFIRE WAS nothing more than burning embers with the occasional snap from the wood.

Kai couldn't sleep. His mind wouldn't stop moving—racing, *thinking.* About the fight earlier. About Eleri. His world was swaying, readying itself to be tipped completely over its edge. Not only because El was truly Eleri, Princess of The Underworld, cursed with powers beyond his grasp, but because the world was changing. He had just started feeling as if he was beginning to understand these lands after The Darkest Day.

It was simple.

Fight. Survive. Help others when they could.

Now, new towns were popping up. Factions were forming full of killers. The Wake was expanding its territories. So much was happening at a rate that he didn't think he could stay at pace with . . . on top of trying to do what was right for his friends, *his family.*

Jaycen—awake on first watch—shifted, stretching his legs out closer toward the dwindling fire and popping his back. Silence surrounded them as they sat, but Kai could feel Jaycen looking at him. Looking for guidance. Looking to simply talk. Kai didn't know.

Turning to face his friend, Kai was met with unease. Concern in his eyes.

"What?" Kai asked.

Jaycen snapped his gaze back toward the embers. "Nothing."

Kai sighed. "Jaycen . . . talk to me. I know this life isn't ideal—shit, it's worse than ideal—but at least we have each other. You're my best friend, my *brother*. Nothing you say will change that."

Something was off. Recently, Jaycen wasn't just gruff. He was *angry*. If Kai knew why, perhaps he could help him through it.

Jaycen gave Kai a moment to study him. In waves—pulsing and scorching hot—trepidation seeped out of his pores and rolled off him. He could tell his friend was mulling over what to say . . . if he decided to say anything at all. It felt like he kept so much from him.

When had he started doing that?

Biting his bottom lip and trying to will away the water Kai noticed pooling at the corner of his eyes, Jaycen shook his head. He didn't want to talk. Not tonight . . . or any night, Kai saw right then. He wouldn't push him. He just . . . He wanted him to be all right. He wanted him to return to the boy he grew up with.

With a deep sigh, Kai changed the subject. "You beat the shit out of those fuckers today."

An easy conversation between them.

Jaycen's lip lifted in a small smirk. At least he was listening. At least he had yet to dive into that silence so deep he couldn't come out of it. That was all Kai could do. "And Rina . . . Shit, she's fast. She came out with barely even a lick. I wish I could say the same. I wish *you* could say the same."

Kai gestured toward the cut down his eyebrow and Jaycen's swollen cheekbone.

"Gods . . . and Eleri? I don't even know—"

With a sudden scoff, Jaycen rose from his spot on the old tire and began to walk away. With a quick turn over his shoulder, he mumbled, "I'm going to do a lap around the perimeter. Make sure no one is still lingering around."

"Jaycen?" Kai's brows lifted and his mouth parted.

A deep, long sigh blew out of Jaycen's nostrils, and he rubbed his hand down his face. Looking back at Kai over his shoulder, Jaycen stated, "You want me to talk to you? Fine. There's a lot I *won't* say. Not because I don't trust you but because I . . . it's hard to speak the words out loud. But that's neither here nor there. You've been acting off lately. Ever since that Fae left us while we slept in the trees. I . . . worry about it. Don't get too close to her. She's a danger to all of us. Today was proof of that. Just . . . Just keep your head on, Kai. I—*We* need you sharp. We need you to be the leader we've confidently followed since day one."

"I am," Kai muttered.

His voice was low—so low it rumbled against his rib cage.

"Are you?" Jaycen's brows furrowed.

A hint of sadness lurked behind his expression . . . *pity*.

Kai kept his face neutral, and silence loomed between them. It thickened as the seconds passed. Growing . . . Accumulating into a mass so dense Kai wanted to scream. Opening his mouth to end this tension, Kai was cut off.

Jaycen huffed. "I—I can't just watch you be reckless for a . . . *being* we barely know. I don't trust her."

Jaycen's cracked lips stretched into a tight smile that didn't meet his eyes before he turned his back on Kai who stared after his best friend, watching as he strode away with a rigid spine and clenched fists. His head swiveled, always looking out for their safety. Kai's eyebrows creased together, and he curled his mouth into a deep, worried frown.

Resting his elbows on his knees, Kai let his head hang low. He didn't know how to fix something he had no idea was broken. If it even was.

Jaycen didn't trust Eleri. Kai hadn't trusted her either. He . . . still didn't. Not fully. He felt it in his very bones, but another, more content feeling blanketed over him. It was as if something was pushing him toward her, telling him it was okay to get close.

Not that he complained. Not really. He couldn't deny her beauty. It was enrapturing. Even when they first met, her blue eyes reeled him in, as if he was a bass hooked on her line. Heat traveled up his neck and settled beneath his bandana.

And it wasn't as if Eleri was *there* for the end of the world. She had no direct part in the cesspool they now lived in. But somehow that *vile excuse* of a man had gotten hold of The Underworld magic she inherently owned and brewed it into a deadly potion.

Kai didn't know how, for sure. He truly didn't wish to know.

The facts were there, though—laid bare for him to sift through on his own. The memory of that day—of hiding behind that slightly ajar door and watching the end of the world happen before his very eyes—made Kai sick.

He wished he could voice his worries. But no one he knew grasped the truth behind the barreling black cloud that hit that day. And he couldn't bear to say it. For if he did, that guilt he tucked deep into the darkest parts of his soul—that guilt of knowing who was to blame, that guilt of truly acknowledging his cowardice—would eat him alive.

His arms hung limp at his sides; tremors ran up his fingers.

What would Jaycen and Rina think of me? What would Eleri? They'd hate me. Shun me.

On his path for atonement, he needed to work through this quietly. He never wanted to put that burden of the truth on them. He was too ashamed to anyway.

"Fuck, I don't even know what's up from down right now, do I?" he muttered.

Kai sucked in a deep breath before letting it out slowly, then squeezed his eyes shut and tried to ground himself, to no avail. His past and his best friend joined the endless loop of thoughts bouncing off Kai's skull.

The Siren.

The Wake.

The curse.

Jaycen.

Eleri.

He glanced to his left at the Fae-Witch princess sleeping soundly under the red sky. Kai's instincts gripped tight and told him to put his guard up, too—to be wary in the face of this new unknown . . . to listen to the one person he was closest with. His oldest, dearest friend. And yet a conflicting feeling pulled at him. A need to make the decision for himself. A carnal want for them to be wrong.

"Fuck me," Kai sighed.

27

Jaycen

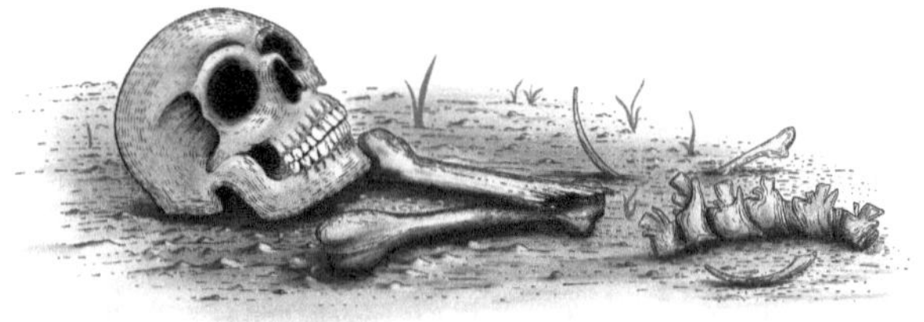

THE RIVER AND ITS cool caress were the only things getting Jaycen through the journey. The desolate lands surrounding them made the trek even more excruciating because he knew there was an end in sight—a small paradise tucked in the middle of this cesspit of a world—even if it didn't feel like it.

He couldn't wait for the rush of the water against his skin. He was desperate to get the weeks-old grime off him.

I need this.

Perhaps once he was clean and rested, he could fight the frustrated storm roiling within his skull and chest. Jaycen spiraled, control slipping as it seeped down his spine and settled in his stomach. And there it sat, festering.

A near-silent growl vibrated in his chest as he tried to shake free his mind from the thoughts that began to trickle into his subconscious.

Get to the river. Get clean. Clear your head. And you'll be okay, Jaycen.

That trickle's stream grew heavier until Jaycen found himself looking up from his scuffed-up boots and at the back of Kai's head. It had been two days since the night around the fire with Kai. A failed conversation that sat heavy on his heart.

The sour trace of inadequacy bled into his chest. The feeling was ridiculous, a projection of his own fucked-up feelings and insecurities.

Yet a part of him—a small, minuscule part he tried to push down into the darkest depths of his being—leaned into it.

You're not watching over Kai well enough.

He's slipping further away from you.

You're not even good enough to fulfill your so-called purpose.

"It would have been easier if things had gone as planned on The Darkest Day . . ." he whispered.

The words barely held any sound. It was as if he merely mouthed them.

Biting the inside of his cheek, Jaycen banished those thoughts. It was ugly. It was pathetic. But it was a deep-rooted part of him that formed years ago and had grown into something he couldn't ignore, no matter how hard he shoved it into a corner.

Jaycen's eyes slid from the base of Kai's neck to the Fae trailing him and Rina. Her orange hair flowed down her back and tangled in the wind. She was a full head shorter than Kai, a head and a half shorter than Jaycen, but that small frame packed a punch. To Jaycen, she was upending everything he strived to do with those big doe eyes and that soft voice.

Why couldn't Kai see that? Why couldn't he see she had her claws in him?

It was better when it was just the three of them. Rina was less . . . sappy. She'd always been a steady light for their group, but her emotions seemed volatile after one glance at the Fae. And Kai . . . if Jaycen thought Rina's emotions were all over the place, Kai's were tempestuous. And all Jaycen could do was helplessly watch.

I feel like I just got into a nice groove with them after five whole years. I know how they will react to certain things. I know when they're feeling a particularly strong emotion and how to navigate that. Jaycen chewed on his bottom lip, the edge of the fabric covering his face catching in his teeth's assault. *But now . . . I feel lost. I feel as if the dynamic between us is changing, and I'm being left behind. It'd be better if I weren't—*

No.

Jaycen shook his head. He refused to think such a thing. He couldn't fall into that deep, dark pit he was so familiar with—at least not until his goal was accomplished.

Not until I'm confident he doesn't need me anymore. Then . . . then maybe.

All those late nights pleading with The Son—tears soaking trough pillows—and the desperation of each prayer jammed into his chest, burrowing into his bones and stealing his breath. The insecurity strangled him. The distress clawed at his throat. Things were changing, and he could do nothing about it.

Please . . . How many times had he let that word hang from his lips?

Please . . . Just as it had when Eleri begged him to stay away from her when he tried to tie her wrists together.

He had faltered when she said that. The raw emotion sitting in that one syllable pierced through him for a single second, transporting him to his life before The Darkest Day. And right now, he felt that same fear and defeat once more—

"Hey, Jayc. You okay?" Rina was watching him carefully while walking beside him. Tilting her hat up slightly, she wiped sand away from her cheeks and sent him a soft smile. "Looked like you were deep in thought."

Looking down at her, Jaycen's heart clenched. He couldn't tell Kai, but maybe he could tell her. All his worries . . . his deepest thoughts. It'd be easier, not having fully opened up to her in the years they had traveled together. He always kept his distance. She wasn't his main priority, so he didn't let her in. But . . . maybe he could now.

"O-Oh. Yeah, sorry. Was just thinking about what we're going to do once we finally catch The Siren." He didn't.

Fucking coward . . . like you've always been. Why can't you ever just man up for once?

Rina squealed and beamed at Jaycen. "I can't wait for that time to come! We might even be able to relax. I can see it now . . . you, me,

Kai, and even Eleri if she wants, in a tavern out West—or maybe in a cabin we build by the river! I'm sure there will still be bad people we'll have to take care of, but the main threat will be gone. Doesn't that sound so nice?"

Jaycen's chest shuddered as he gazed down at her. She was so hopeful, so optimistic. He was envious of her in that regard. "Yeah"—he mustered up his most convincing smile—"that sounds great, Rina. We'll all be happy then."

Winding her arm through Jaycen's, Rina leaned into him and rested her head atop his bicep. His muscles tensed as they followed Kai and El. "We deserve it, Jaycen. We deserve to be happy, and I have faith that we will be one day."

28

Eleri

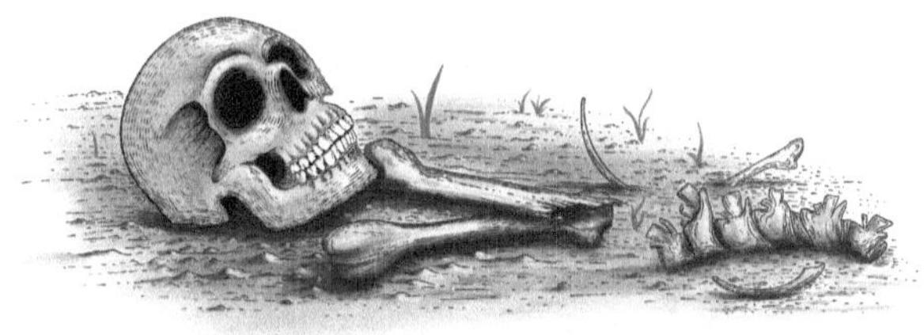

Jaycen twisted his head over his shoulder and called out to Eleri, who trailed The Pack. Another day had passed. She'd never been this far east in The Upperworld, and The Wasteland was nothing but a desert of death and decay. It rattled her to the bone.

"Don't call me that," Eleri grumbled, hardening her eyes as best as she could at the burly man leading the group.

After learning the truth she kept closest to her heart, Jaycen had become even gruffer than normal. As if that was possible. The tension between her and The Pack the morning after the brawl closed Eleri's throat, a sour unease coating her tongue.

Jaycen didn't say much that morning, but she saw the apprehension etched across every line of his face. Kai kept glancing her way, a deep crease between his brows and a slight frown tugging at his mouth. She still wasn't sure what thoughts or emotions lay behind those glances. And Rina was . . . hesitant. Eleri could tell she didn't know how to approach her now that the adrenaline from the fight had faded and the blazing sun was up. Rina had opened herself up for Eleri's sake. A friendly, timid hand reaching out toward her even if she felt as if she couldn't reach back.

However, that nervous ringing in the air between the two of them dissipated soon after, once Eleri sent the woman a smile and asked how she slept. Even if Eleri didn't think she could reach her hand fully out toward Rina, she could offer at least that.

Now, as they trekked through the sandy, never-ending vastness around them, Rina slowed her gait and began to walk beside Eleri, leaving enough room between her and . . . her friend.

Her friend. Eleri liked the way that sounded.

It was something . . . new. Something she had longed for even before The Darkest Day. Beneath, she'd had those who were always around, never truly being lonely. But they had served her parents. Doing their duty and caring for her in the only way they knew how, while still keeping their distance. And the Fae Lords she frequented in the Moon Flower Fields . . . She didn't think she'd held a meaningful conversation with any of them before they secretly fucked, then went their own way. She could see their weariness toward her other heritage. Ultimately, they pushed it away for their own release.

A wave of being seen—*understood*—for the first time in a long time filled Eleri's soul. She felt at ease—comfortable in this new companionship with Rina. And with that, Eleri found the courage to let down her barriers if only just a little. The Pack now knew everything about her. It felt like she'd been stripped bare, her entire being—her true self and soul—on display for them to see.

It was terrifying. In a way, it was *refreshing*.

"So you're telling me you skipped out on balls with sparkling gowns and never-ending dances just to sneak up *here*?" Rina asked, eyes wide and brows raised.

For a split second, Eleri thought they were twinkling with mischief. It must've been the sand hitting her lashes. Eleri simply nodded with a smirk.

"All the pleasantries were *excruciating*. I could only take hundreds-of-years-old Fae women bragging about their sons and entitled courtiers for so long," Eleri chuckled.

Kai, walking a few paces in front of them, snorted under his breath. Eleri's gaze slid to his broad back; the muscles straining against his tunic shifted with every step as he observed their surroundings.

"I would love to experience a ball! It sounds magical—bragging and entitlement included," Rina laughed while tucking an unruly strand of hair behind her ear. "The closest I ever got to something like that was when we were at this rundown tavern in The Vale soon after I had joined these two. I danced under broken lights with someone who smelled like onions and grime. It was fun at first, until he wouldn't leave me alone. Kai—" Another chuckle bubbled up. "Kai beat the living daylights out of him when he didn't get the hint. My knight in shining armor!"

Kai laughed and winked at a giggling Rina before facing forward again. "I beat the shit out of him, and I'd do it again in a heartbeat for you, Rin."

It was a heartwarming sight—two friends laughing together as they recalled a shared memory. A scene Eleri wished she could have one day. A small flame—that fire—flared slightly. Eleri studied them as her stomach twisted and her chest ached.

I want companionship like that. I want him to look at me like that. I want . . . a friend. A new friend. Hopefully, a true friend.

The whispering breeze running through her hair and the lapping water in the distance tugged at her attention. The sounds were tranquil, quieting her thoughts and easing her wary bones . . .

The lapping water! They were nearing the river. Finally.

Eleri focused on the rushing current just as the sand beneath her feet began to turn into the dried soil of the forest out West, and a few leafless, charred trees came into view.

Oh, how I've missed the sight of dead trees and the protection they provide.

The laughter between Kai and Rina died down, fluttering in the wind as they, too, realized they were approaching their destination. Eleri sneaked one more small glance at Kai. His shoulders were relaxed, although she could tell his muscles slightly tensed with each sound in the distance.

Kai . . .

Four days ago, Eleri had witnessed him free those people chained together without a second thought. He hadn't asked for anything in return. He'd simply smiled warmly at each and every one of them with trauma-infused stares and wished them well. It was commendable, really.

Eleri was in awe of them . . . all of them—even Jaycen.

Seeing Kai do that . . . the way he looked, sweat dripping along his temple as he swung down on those shackles with any piece of scrap metal he could find. Eleri's heart stuttered and swelled, pumping harder—the blood in her veins rushing to her fingers and making them twitch as they yearned to run through his black locks. It was a strange feeling, one she wasn't quite used to. Not since before The Darkest Day. And it battled against those self-deprecating thoughts and the memory of his suspicious leer to be at the forefront.

Her taut, clenched knuckles rubbed against her leather gloves. She resisted that incessant urge, silently admonishing herself.

Gods. Get a fucking grip.

"Finally," Jaycen huffed.

As they crossed the threshold of the first few trees surrounding the river, Eleri could see the tension leave The Pack's bodies almost immediately. No longer were their heads on swivels. No longer were their movements rigid.

The trees became less sparse. Twisting roots and sharp branches created an eerie canopy. Not even that could diminish their obvious excitement.

Jaycen pulled down his bandana and took a deep breath. "No more sand," he sighed.

It was odd—seeing this rip in The Wasteland. The river ran through the middle of the sandy dunes, but she had expected it to be just as desolate as the rest—not for the sand to disappear or for dead, bare, upright trees to sprout from the ground.

Kai pulled his own bandana down and exhaled, his breath shuddering as his body loosened. Rina couldn't help the small claps and soft giggle bursting past her lips. Jaycen's mouth twitched into a faint smile. An expression foreign to Eleri. That same relief she could tell they were feeling ran through her veins, too. It was as if her body—her instincts—knew they were safer than they had been. Like they had stumbled upon an oasis.

A muffled thump echoed between them as Jaycen dropped his bag and cracked his neck with a deep sigh. "I'm going to check the perimeter. Make sure no stragglers are hanging close by."

Kai nodded in approval, and Rina smiled at the man.

Before Eleri could think better of it, she asked, "Can I join?"

This grabbed everyone's attention. Kai's eyebrows lifted in surprise. Rina's smile widened. She must've thought it was a good idea. And Jaycen . . . Jaycen stared at her, his lips twisting into an upside-down crescent moon.

She quickly added, "I don't know what to look for when scouting. I'd like to learn a bit. And I want to pull my weight within the group before we part. I can help out if I just . . . knew how to."

What had started as a strong explanation ended in uncertainty within those quiet and timid words. Jaycen wasn't fond of her. It was easy to see, and she understood. A being—unlike any in this realm—with deadly magic tagging along like a stowaway . . .

And, to be frank, she wasn't fond of him either. But if she joined him, Eleri could feel as if she belonged with people before she left and headed home. And when she did, she'd hopefully learned a skill or two to help her survive on her own.

Jaycen shifted his gaping stare past her to where Kai stood. He was looking for approval, advice . . . Eleri wasn't sure. No words were spoken. No gestures. Nothing. Just silence as Jaycen stared past her. A soundless conversation not meant for her or Rina.

Finally, a long sigh escaped him. Jaycen closed his eyes briefly. "C'mon, Princess."

He turned his back on the group and walked toward the thicket of trees. Eleri didn't know what Kai did or conveyed, but whatever it was had Jaycen relenting. Scrambling, she went after him, following his long strides with earnestness until she was near enough for him to acknowledge her presence.

"I told you not to call me that." Eleri swiped a strand of hair from between her dry lips and ducked under a particularly sharp branch.

"That's what you are, aren't you?" Jaycen voiced, his head twisting from side to side.

His eyes were sharp, alert.

"No . . ." Eleri said. Jaycen stopped, planting his boots into the hard ground and turning toward her with an expectant stare. "Well . . . *yes*. But I feel as if that part of my life is over. Like it died the day the world did. I'm just . . . Eleri. I'm just trying to survive."

A grunt broke through the barrier of Jaycen's tightly sealed lips. A man of few words.

They began to walk once again.

Weaving through dead trees on the way back to the others, Eleri stepped carefully over the rare patches of new grass rising from the desolation. A clear indication the river was close. She strained her ears, willing to hear the plant life's whispers she used to listen to before The Darkest Day.

Silence.

"Why do you do that?" Jaycen muttered, raising a thick eyebrow at her.

It was the most he had said this entire time. Jaycen didn't talk as they worked their way through the branches and roots, didn't teach her a single thing, but she watched him carefully.

He picked at leaves he suspected had been walked over or moved. Sniffing the soil—the air—he stopped in his tracks and gazed into the surrounding brush. The cogs turning in his head were on full display. It was intriguing, watching him listen and observe his surroundings as if he could read the very air that brushed alongside them. Eleri hoped she could remember all that she saw for the future if she needed it.

"Do what?" She stepped over another patch of grass.

Eleri knew what. She just didn't want to acknowledge it if she didn't have to. Avoidance. It was easier, she had learned.

"That. Step over the grass." Jaycen gestured at her boots. "Don't tell me even your boots can't stop the death that comes with you."

The death that comes with me. Eleri's heart sank because that was exactly what it was. Death surrounding her. Death because of her. Death within her.

She turned away. She didn't have to say anything to confirm what he was thinking. Not wanting to see his reaction to the silent truth, she focused on the path ahead.

From the corner of her eye, she saw Jaycen open his mouth once more, perhaps to ask again, to taunt her.

"Why aren't there more people by the river? If I was east, I would've stayed here the entire time," Eleri rushed out.

She didn't want to hear whatever he was about to say . . . she *couldn't*.

Jaycen huffed. "Not going to talk about your life now?"

It was like he was provoking her . . . *pushing her* . . . waiting for her to snap. The fire in the deepest part of her gut flared again—just enough for her to feel its singe. Her little beast smacked its lips together.

Eleri sent Jaycen a scathing glare that made him huff, his eyes rolling. "Whatever. Most people fled the river and headed toward the Southern Coast. Didn't think it was worth being so close to Wake territory."

Humming, Eleri nodded and stepped around a boulder. That was understandable. No one in their right mind would want to be close to the cannibals. "What was your life like before The Darkest Day?"

As the words hovered in the space between them, she realized Jaycen wasn't wrong. She talked so much, peeling away layers and layers of safety and secrets after the fight and revealing who she truly was. She told Rina about the royal balls she went to and her garden she adored. Rina did the same, telling stories of her sister and the life she used to live. Yet Jaycen and Kai offered no insight into who they were. A small part of Eleri no longer wanted to feel like a stowaway, and because of that, she needed to know *something*.

Jaycen ignored her question.

She tried again. "How long have you known Kai?"

A reaction. It was small enough no one would've noticed except her, her senses picking it up even without needing to look at him as his heartbeat skipped and the muscles along his neck stiffened.

"Rina said you both found her," Eleri prodded softly. "Did he also find you shortly after the curse was cast? Or did you find him?"

Jaycen halted his steps and turned, fully facing her, his large frame looming over her. His eyes narrowed into small slits. "What's with the questions?"

Eleri peered at him, eyes unwavering. "I'm just trying to understand you better."

"There's nothing for you to understand."

He was curt.

The way he's looking at me, Eleri thought. *It's like he's piercing my soul, judging me . . . resenting me. Sure, he knows my past now, but he doesn't know me. Not really.*

Eleri almost gave up. She almost turned back toward their path and began walking away. But something stopped her. It wasn't the echoing growl from her dark side as it bounced around in her skull. It was a small tug in her gut. She didn't know why she felt this way or what it was exactly. Instinct, perhaps?

There was something about him, something inside him that was yearning to open up despite the impenetrable walls he built around him.

Please. Eleri wanted to say.

She didn't.

Finally, after what felt like a standoff that lasted an eternity, Jaycen exhaled long and loud.

"I'm answering your stupid question so you stop asking and stop bothering me, okay? Kai and I met thirteen years before The Darkest Day." Eleri's lips popped open, and her jaw slackened. Jaycen ignored the reaction and continued. "We were only eleven. And we've been best friends ever since."

That little tidbit shocked Eleri. *Best friends?* She could tell they cared for one another. The worried glances Jaycen always sent Kai. They took care of each other. They had a strong bond, but there was a crack between them. Some type of emotional block prevented them from being as close as they once were. As she studied the man before her, something inside her screamed that the barrier was coming from him and his walls. And Eleri could tell it was hurting him, eating him alive.

"You're lucky you have each other." Eleri merely offered him a brief smile and continued walking.

At least they each have someone. What else is there to say?

Jaycen merely huffed and followed.

"You're back!" Rina gazed up at them.

She was hunched over a hole in the ground, fingernails black from soot and forearms smeared with dirt. Kai was next to her in a similar position. He was fiddling with something inside the hole. His brows were furrowed, and his eyes squinted in concentration, refusing to take his gaze off his task.

"Yup."

The end of the word popped against Jaycen's lips as he sat across from them.

Eleri decided to follow suit. After a hesitant breath, she sat beside Jaycen—far enough to avoid closeness yet near enough to draw his suspicious glance. As if her presence distracted him, Kai finally peeked up at them just as a small flame caught on a pile of dead moss.

"Did you learn anything while you were out, Eleri?" Rina asked, leaning back on her palms.

Shifting her gaze toward Jaycen, Eleri waited for him to say something—*anything*. Like how he barely said a single word to her until she poked and prodded him, he didn't.

Eleri faced Rina with a small smile. "I observed a lot of things I had never thought of."

It was true. He hadn't taught her how to scout or check perimeters, but she had watched him, and if that was all she could get, she'd take it.

"That's good." Rina smiled at them both. So much light lay within those eyes. So much good. So much *hope*. It was truly commendable. "Learning something new that could save your life out here is always beneficial."

Jaycen changed the subject. "The river's clear. I saw remnants of old campsites, but they seem abandoned. Probably headed south like the others."

Rina squealed, clapping her palms as her cheeks flushed and her eyes cleared. As if those words rejuvenated her after the long trek here. Kai's brows raised at the news as well. It had piqued his interest, and the small tug at the corners of his lips made it seem as if he was as delighted as Rina.

"No sign of *anyone* in these parts?" Kai asked Jaycen.

"None. I'd say that campsite was left a month or two ago. The place is ours." Jaycen grinned.

With a nod, Kai added another handful of moss and leaves to the hole. "The fire should be fine unattended for the next hour or so. I say we wash up now before it gets dark."

"Gods, finally!" Rina quickly stood and stretched her back. "I can't wait to get clean and wash my clothes. They're disgusting."

Eleri stood as well just as Jaycen got his footing and stepped away toward the tree line. "You're washing your clothes?"

"Of course I am." Rina tilted her head to the side, observing Eleri after such a question. "When you were in The West and bathed in the lake . . . you never did?"

Gods, I feel dirty. And them staring isn't helping. Eleri felt the blush run up her neck and settle at the tips of her ears.

"I . . . I always bathed at night. After everyone went to sleep. I never had more than the clothes on my back, so getting them wet didn't seem like a good idea."

"Well"—Rina smiled—"I have a bar of soap in my bag I traded for a few months ago. I figured we'd all share to wash off our bodies and scrub our clothes a bit."

Makes sense. I just . . . I don't have . . .

"I have an extra long sleeve you can wear until your clothes dry. No pants or anything but something to cover yourself with," Rina offered as if she could read Eleri's swarming thoughts.

"Are you coming or not?" Jaycen called over his shoulder, ducking beneath a branch as he stepped into the deadwood toward the river.

"I'll catch up," Kai called back, adjusting the edge of the hole. "Need to make sure this doesn't catch wind and spread."

"C'mon, El!" Rina stuck out her hand, an invitation for Eleri to grab it. As if a sudden realization hit her, she snatched her hand away and brought it to her side as her eyes widened. "I am so sorry. That was insensitive of me."

A small twist in Eleri's stomach pained her. Sharp and fast and mind-bending. She wished she could've grabbed Rina's hand and taken off into the trees together. Just as normal friends would. Another reminder of what she really was, spearing her in two. Even as those thoughts burdened her, she tried to smile. "It's okay."

"Oh Gods!" Rina gasped. The hand that was once reaching out to Eleri came up to cover her gaping mouth. "I also called you El. Is that all right? Or do you want to be called Eleri?"

This time, Eleri's smile was more genuine. A laugh bubbled up her throat. "It's fine, Rina. I promise. Call me whatever you want."

"Okay . . ." Rina nodded to herself as if she was calming down her racing, anxiety-stricken heart. Eleri could hear it pattering against her chest. "Okay. Good to know. I'm still sorry, though. I'll be better."

Just as Eleri was about to wave it off again, Rina's smile was back. "If you want, we can head to the river now. Or I can wait with you if you aren't ready. Whatever you want to do."

She was giving her a chance to make her own choice. For some reason unknown to Eleri, a lump formed in the back of her throat.

A good friend, indeed.

Nodding, Eleri stepped toward Rina, and the two made their way after Jaycen into the small thicket of dead trees between them and the river.

Kai

Brushing past several leafless branches, Kai breached the tree line and arrived at the river soon after Eleri and Rina did. He had set the last rock around the hole's edge to keep the fire from spreading through the dry woods when he heard Jaycen splash into the rushing water nearby.

The river was breathtaking to Kai, in a way only something as rare as running water in a barren desert could be. On the few occasions they came across it—no matter how long it had been—he seemed to lose his breath at the sight. It was a navy, nearly black color, a blanket as dark as night that rushed by in a never-ending stream. Grime and sludge covered the boulders along the far bank. Where the water met the earth, a sickly green film sat atop it. The occasional scrap of metal wedged itself between nooks along the river's edge. Small reminders of the curse and death and rubble that littered the lands beyond this slice of paradise.

As the waves flowed by, Kai noticed the current was slower than the last time he was here. The glaciers in the Northern Icecap melted after The Darkest Day, fueling the tide of the river until it met the sea in the Southern Coast. But it looked like the frigid water from the ice was beginning to run low. And with no rain in sight . . .

Shit, that's concerning.

Still, there was a safety here no other place Above had offered since the curse swept through. Each rapid felt as if it was able to cleanse him of the burdens the world suffocated him with.

Jaycen splashed through the water, treading against the current in the deepest section as he vigorously scrubbed his body with Rina's small bar of soap. Rina herself leaned back and wet her hair, letting it flow around her as her eyes fluttered closed in a moment of serenity.

Kai's eyes slid to Eleri. She was standing at the edge of the grassy riverbank just before the earth slanted down into the blue water. She scanned the length of the river as if searching for something. Her spine straightened, her body going rigid—motionless—when she found nothing. Then her head dipped, eyes fixed on the green ground.

Holding his breath, Kai didn't move. He didn't take a single step toward the river, not wanting to alarm her. He could tell she was working through something.

A visible shiver trembled across her body, and her shoulders rose and fell as she took a deep breath. Then, slowly—oh so slowly—Eleri began to undress. Kai couldn't help but notice how each movement was meticulous, like it was something she had rehearsed in her head. One shoulder shrugged off her cloak before the other followed suit. Her wrists flexed as her fingers plucked off her gloves. One leg lifted to free herself of—

Kai looked away, although he didn't want to. Gods, did he not want to. But he also didn't want to pry. He didn't want to break her trust before it even had a chance to form.

Clinks of buckles rang against his eardrums. Shuffling feet moved with the rustling of her clothes as they hit the ground. A quivering breath—nearly a hiss, full of dread—left her lips. Before long, all sounds ceased. Only then did Kai glance back up.

Sandpaper. That was what his mouth had become, tongue shriveling and saliva evaporating.

Pale, smooth skin, once covered under layers and layers of cloth, was bare. Skin that—despite the sweat dripping down each crevice and the dirt smudging between creases—somehow glowed. A slender back. Slightly wider hips. Long legs. A small, plump ass. *Fuck.*

Otherworldly was the best way to describe her. To him—in that very moment—there was no one who came close. Not the busty women he fucked in taverns before The Darkest Day. Not the wenches and barmaids. No one. He could only compare her beauty to what he would believe a Goddess looked like. He thought she could even rival The Daughter.

Kai's eyes were greedy despite his head yelling at them to close. They raked over every inch, every petite curve as if hungry. Starved. Then they snagged on something. Her ribs were showing, the dips between each bone prominent beneath her tight skin. He was used to the sight of thinness since the curse. It wasn't shocking or appalling, yet a wave of anger rushed through him, barreling into him like a ton of bricks. Because it was her.

That strange force he started feeling before Arkala built within his gut and hovered over him like a cloud heavy with rain. It pulsed reassuringly as if he was meant to be right here with them, all of them . . . Like their paths had been carved by the Gods, and they were living it now.

Rolling out her wrists, Eleri readied herself to take a step. Then she strode toward the water onto the new patch of grass. Kai's throat instantly dried, becoming as barren as The Wasteland around the river, and his breath snagged against his vocal cords. Blazing footprints trailed her with every step across the riverbank. Each fiery stride began to spread. Each blade sizzled under the heat of the embers she left behind, curling in on itself before crumbling into nothing but ash.

"Whoa!" Jaycen yelled, eyes widening as he glanced at the quickly diminishing grass, leaving nothing but a charred patch in the blaze's wake.

At his reaction, Eleri quickened her steps, submerging herself into the water and leaving only her head above the ripples. Rina peeked out of the waves due to the sudden noise and saw the rapidly growing destruction left behind.

"Oh!" she exclaimed. "Oh, shit!"

Quickly wading through the water, Rina reached the bank and thrust her arm forward. A grunt fell from her lips as she exerted all her energy into the movement. She sent a swell onto the last patch of green nearby. A black cloud shimmering under the daylight erupted from the ground just as the water connected with the encroaching blaze. Smoke exactly like the cloud that barreled across the land and destroyed The Upperworld. It was a disturbing resemblance.

Eleri truly was cursed, and it was all because of . . . Kai's stomach clenched, a knot forming full of lead.

With bulging eyes, Eleri whispered, "I never knew you could stop it."

Despite each quiet syllable, the words floated toward Kai, sticking to his eardrums. Whipping his head down, he couldn't help but gasp. She was right. As the smoke cleared, the visible line between the charred ash and the green grass was stark. The water had stopped its spread.

"You've never even tried?" Jaycen interjected.

Curiosity hung within each word. It was laced with a touch of accusation.

Kai's shoulders tensed, and Eleri squeezed her eyes shut for a moment. Pain. Shame. It was all there etched onto her face for everyone to see. Then, turning toward the man, she gritted out, "I—I never thought there was a chance. And even if I had . . . I never had enough water to test the theory."

Jaycen paused before shrugging and turning away from her dismissively. "Fair enough, Princess."

Leaning her head to get into Eleri's line of sight, Rina spoke slowly and softly. "This is a good thing, no? We know how to stop it."

Rina beamed at Eleri, who shrugged, mirroring Jaycen's previous gesture and waded farther from her. "I guess . . . I'd rather not have to stop it in the first place."

"Hey!" Jaycen called out to Kai as he swam to Rina, handing her the bar of soap. Kai snapped his head toward his friend. "Are you going to get in or just keep gaping?"

Kai glared at Jaycen, who shot a faint smirk edged with irritation. Averting his gaze from the river, he felt the way the skin under his eyes and neck warmed up. Embarrassment rushed through his chest and down his body. Desire trailed it like a dirty satin ribbon dancing on the wind. Now would be a great time to crawl into a hole and never appear again.

Asshole.

Quickly, he undressed. He unbuckled the holster strapped across his chest before shucking off his shirt. The sweat pooling against his skin immediately cooled once released from the confines of his clothes, despite the hot air. He didn't dwell on the refreshing feeling as he removed his pants and briefs next.

As he approached the now dead, bare riverbank, Kai glimpsed Eleri. A wave of gratitude clashed with the disappointment washing through him. She was underwater, completely submerged beneath the waves.

A part of him was hoping she'd ogle at his body just as he had done to her. It seemed wrong, but just the thought made his skin flush even more and his stomach constrict. But then she'd see his scars. The scars covering his back in wrinkled, puckered flesh. The scars slashed across his torso. He didn't want her to see that.

Setting his dirty clothes next to the pile Jaycen had left on the edge, Kai then stepped into the water. It was frigid. Icy to the point of pain. Yet refreshing against the heat of the air around him. Fighting a shiver, he walked down the sandy slope until everything below his torso was underwater. Chills made the hair on his arms stand up and bumps erupt across the skin of his chest.

With a deep exhale, he waited for his body to get used to the chill. *Just a few more minutes.*

Shaking each limb under the water and kicking his feet as he went deeper, Kai found his gaze drifting toward Eleri. And he forced it away each time. She was still underneath—nothing but a pale blob floating below the opaque water.

A quick thought infiltrated his senses. Unwanted, yet it lingered like a welcoming embrace. *Would it be possible to touch her here? The water acting as a barrier between me and the curse. How would it fee—*

With a deep inhale, Eleri suddenly breached the water. As she opened her eyes—more unbearably blue than before against the light reflecting off the droplets along her cheeks—Kai averted his gaze once more.

Never had he been so unsure of himself as he was when she was around. Never had a woman had him in such a fierce, unrelenting grip without her even knowing.

"Gods, El! You look like a Mermaid," Rina gasped.

The sound floated into the beginning notes of a giggle. Light and airy and full of awe.

She's not a Mermaid, Kai silently said. He dipped his head back and wet his hair, running his fingers through each lock to get the dirt caked along his roots out. *She's a Siren who's luring me in each passing second I'm near her.*

Kai flinched. The chill wrapping around his bones from the water turned frigid. No. How could he think such a thing when the real Siren was out there, doing unspeakable things?

"Wait!" Rina added, wringing out her own hair and carefully handing Eleri the bar of soap. "Are there Mermaids in The Underworld?"

A melodic tune carried in the wind toward Kai. Eleri's laugh. She didn't hold back this time. A tendril of mirth flowed out of her pores like an early morning sunrise before The Darkest Day. "No, Mermaids don't exist, Rina. Just another storybook creature."

Rina pouted, causing Eleri to laugh even louder.

Kai never wanted to go another day without hearing that sound again.

THE HIGH SUN DIPPED, casting shadows across the boulders along the river and turning the icy water even colder. Kai rubbed his arms, willing the goosebumps to disappear. Despite the bitter touch of the water, warmth flushed him as he watched his friends freely breathe and relax for the first time in months.

"What do you mean you wouldn't go back to your life before The Darkest Day?" Rina gaped at Jaycen as he shrugged and ran his palm down his chest, wiping away sediment from the riverbed.

"I *mean*, I wouldn't go back. What do you not understand?" he bit out, rolling his eyes before a bark of laughter ripped from his throat at Rina's twisted expression. "Rina, for the love of The Trinity, don't pout at me."

His laugh floated over the three and made its way toward Eleri. Several feet away, she sat in a shallower area, her bare back to them as she finished scrubbing her clothes clean.

Turning her head slightly, she called out over her shoulder, "Why wouldn't you want to go back before all this? The Darkest Day corrupted our world and drained it of anything good. People were happy before."

She dunked her clothes, rinsing the soap residue off before using the pile to shield the front of her body while she waded to deeper water once again, where she was concealed.

"Well, I wasn't." Jaycen stared off downstream, watching the waves ripple together in a dance so fluid it was mesmerizing.

Kai's eyes grew larger and his brows pulled together, creating a deep rivet between them.

He wasn't? I was with him nearly every day. Kai stared at his friend. The friend he would die for. The friend he thought he knew better than himself. *I would've known if he was unhappy. Wouldn't I have?*

"We all didn't live lives as luxurious as yours, Princess." Jaycen ran his palm down his face, clearing his skin of the lingering droplets.

Eleri scoffed and rolled her eyes, treading to a large boulder off to the side and placed the soaked clothing next to Rina's. "You don't know anything about me."

"I don't? Didn't take long for you to spill every little detail about your life. And all because you finally got caught."

A triumphant smirk pulled at Jaycen's lips when a flinch rippled through her body and made Eleri's movements stutter.

"*Jaycen,*" Kai warned.

Jaycen's hazel eyes locked onto Kai's brown. Tension wafted between them; Kai could practically see the disruption in the air if he concentrated enough. A huff broke through Jaycen's grinding teeth. "I'm going to go check on the fire and get the rest of camp set up for the night."

He swam to the edge of the river and began to stride away . . . from his drying clothes, from his friends. His long, steady steps stomped against the dead ground. Each hit to the earth felt like a slab of concrete piling on top of Kai's gut.

Kai could've gotten out, too. He could've checked on Jaycen and finally get to the bottom of what was bothering him and firmly refuse the deflecting he was bound to do. Turning back toward the river, Kai glanced at Rina and Eleri. Eleri was facing away from the shore, giving Kai and Jaycen whatever privacy they needed. Gratefulness rushed over him. Rina's feet kicked at the surface as she dove, before breaching the water.

Yes, he should get out. The wrinkles on his fingers rubbed against his palms. His toes were in the same state. He had been in long enough. And leaving would give Rina and Eleri more time to spend together. To deepen their friendship. Rina was the one who brought a smile to Eleri's face the most. The Fae-Witch was comfortable with her. He should let them get to know each other more.

As Kai turned to the shore, ready to make his exit, he was stopped by Rina's voice piercing the area. "I'm going to get out, too. I should try to track down some food for the night."

The blood in Kai's veins turned icy. His heart sped up, pumping that frigid feeling through the rest of his body. And his skin tightened over his bones as the pulsing within his gut intensified. All he could do was watch as the blonde swam past him toward the shore, wide eyes begging for her to stay . . . to not leave him alone with the woman he increasingly thought about.

Turn around, Rina. Gods, please.

Rina ascended out of the water, and only then did he avert his eyes and turn around, inhaling deeply, trying to calm his pounding heart. Nerves bounced against his bones.

"Find something extra good for us, Rina!" Eleri called out, waving at her friend with a soft smile before leaning her head back in the water with a content sigh.

Silence grew between them, but, to Kai's surprise, it wasn't uncomfortable. It was easy, despite the minute trembles dancing up his spine. However, a deep yearning to break the silence washed over him, overtaking him. Kai wanted to hear Eleri's voice. When they were traveling. When they were eating. Even when her words weren't aimed toward him.

"It feels good to be clean for once." Kai winced slightly at his words.

That's all you could come up with? It's not like she was the first woman he had ever talked to. He was good at this before she came along.

Eleri lifted her head and turned toward him, watching him tread in the water. Her deep blue eyes shone as a hesitant laugh bubbled up her throat. It was music to his ears.

"Yeah, it does."

Gods, you're such a fucking idiot, Kai silently admonished himself. A flush crept up the expanse of his neck. Clearing his throat, he tried again. "I can clearly see your Witches' Marks now."

A soft, nearly silent inhale caught Kai's ear as her eyes widened just a smidge before she dipped down into the water once more, until it was covering everything but those blue irises. She turned to the side away from him.

Hiding. She was hiding her marks, hiding her true self. A rush ran through him as he realized he never wanted her to hide again, after doing so for so long. Not with them . . . not with *him.*

"They're pretty."

In an instant, faster than any Human could move, Eleri lifted her head out of the water and whipped it back around toward him. Her mouth hung open, like a fish blowing bubbles in the waves. A blush engulfed her cheeks. Red mixing with her ivory-smooth skin. She was trying not to smile. With a bashful twitch to her lips, her canines dug into the plump, pink skin.

Softly—barely a whisper—she said, "You're the first person to ever say that to me. Besides my parents," Eleri chuckled, though her eyes had gone from mirthful to melancholy.

It was as if the blue within darkened.

"What? Why's that?"

His mouth moved on its own. He felt as if he was prying.

Eleri hesitated, the breath catching on the tip of her tongue as a breeze brushed through them. Goosebumps rose along his flesh. Kai couldn't help but think it was because of what Jaycen said.

"Didn't take long for you to spill every little detail about your life."

Gods. Kai could smack the living shit out of Jaycen for saying that. Meaningless words meant to hurt her, to knock her down.

A few breaths lingered between them, then a hint of resolve sparked across her face.

"Most beings . . ." Eleri began, "still had animosity toward the Witches of The Underworld. They said they didn't, but it was a lie. There was no letting go of The Under War. The Witches tore apart our realm and left trails and trails of blood when they revolted against the Fae Crown. I guess I could understand that, though. The Witches ruled for tens of thousands of years before the Fae took over when the last Witch Queen was stripped of her title and found guilty of conspiring to eliminate the Fae population altogether. The animosity—in all beings—festered deep down toward every Witch . . . except my mother. Everyone loved her."

Eleri's fingers knotted together below the waves. The movement was a blurry smudge beneath the opaque water. Her eyes darted from side to side, avoiding him with all her might. But like an invisible pull, they landed back on his.

She continued, "And these . . . marks . . . They were a reminder that I was *other* in a land that's supposed to embrace otherness. A *halfling* they would say. I think people tried to pretend my marks didn't exist, imagining me without them—imagining my face was bare, *clean* from that darker side of me—when they spoke or approached or even looked in my direction. I guess it was easier for them to do that."

The last several words forcefully pushed between Eleri's teeth. A hiss with each breath, a bite on each consonant, venom lacing each vowel.

Kai saw that *darker* side she had mentioned. Her Witch side. It was the same side he saw when that gang of scum spat insult after insult at her after she had burned that woman alive. But this time, he got the feeling that anger was inward facing.

"Don't be ashamed of where you come from."

Kai's soft words washed over them, dancing atop the ripples of water. Those words settled within his chest. If only he could take his own advice.

Eleri didn't say anything. Her widening eyes and half-open pout were the only indication that those words were settling within her as well.

Kai added, "Truly. Your marks are what make you unique. They're beautiful."

You're beautiful.

KAI

SWEAT PEBBLED ALONG THE top of Kai's upper lip. Leaves and dead brush rustled around him, the breeze cooling his skin despite the warm night air . . . despite the heat simmering deep within his gut.

Silence.

He yearned for his mind to match the peacefulness of his surroundings. A light breeze glided through the spear-like branches. Soft deep breaths from the others as they slept. Occasional pops of embers within the dwindling campfire.

It was tranquil. *Still*—unlike his thoughts. They had been running rampant a lot more lately, ever since Eleri came into his life.

Sleep would fix his problem. Falling into that cocoon of deep slumber would stop the rattled mess within his skull. It would stop the unwanted images flashing across his vision as he leaned against a dead tree and stared at the eerie, smog-stained sky between the black, charred trees overhead.

Pale skin reflecting in the hazy daylight . . .

Orange hair falling down her naked back . . .

Plump flesh curving down her ass and bouncing with every step . . .

White Witches' Marks reeling him in . . .

Squeezing his eyes shut, Kai attempted to banish the memories from earlier at the river. Yes, sleep would do him well. But sleep would not and could not come for him tonight. On watch, he had a duty. And no matter how much his veins tingled with want and how distracted the Fae-Witch made him, he would not put the others at risk. He refused to do so.

But . . . Kai's eyes locked onto Eleri's sleeping form. She was facing the opposite direction, curled on her side with her hair sprawled around her. Gods, help him.

I want her. More than I've ever wanted anyone in my entire life.

The tips of his fingers snagged on the burnt bark at his back. Each rivet and chasm rubbed roughly against his skin as he shifted slightly on his feet.

I wonder what her skin feels like. Kai silently pondered. He ran his gaze across her small curves, snagging on her bare thighs just beneath Rina's oversized spare shirt. *It's probably soft, so silky smooth. Enough to get lost in the feeling.*

Eleri shifted in her sleep. The movement pulled Kai out of the haze he was beginning to fall into.

Turning his head sharply away and adjusting his stance so only his left shoulder was leaning against the tree, he refused to get lost in it. The lust-filled spell she had on him. The one ruminating since he had stared at her in the trees before she fled.

A waft of her scent now uncovered after her time in the river—baby's breath and lemon—floated on the breeze and filled his nostrils. Then another flash crossed his vision. Another image from earlier.

A glimpse of the side of her breasts as she scrubbed her clothes clean . . . the way they swayed with each swipe . . .

Fuck.

Kai shut his eyes, squeezing tightly until the memories, the images, were no longer there. With a deep breath, he opened his eyes, stealing a glance at the others and taking in their sleeping forms. They were fast asleep. Before he could think better of it, he swept his gaze across the surrounding woods. No movement. No one lurking nearby. Utterly still except for the breeze.

Fuck. Okay.

Kai turned to face the tree, his back to the others. His throat bobbed, swallowing around nothing as he hastily unbuttoned his spare pants and shoved his hand beneath the cloth of his briefs. Pulling out his slowly growing length, relief sagged his shoulders; the uncomfortable pressure in his gut was slightly alleviated as he sprang free.

With a shattered breath, Kai braced his left palm atop the rough bark above his head while slowly—so slowly, it was agonizing—bringing the pad of his thumb to the tip of his cock. A hiss pushed past his teeth.

"Fuck," Kai whimpered, so quiet the word lost its sound, nothing but a breath of air in its wake.

Pressing down a touch harder against his slit, he threw his head back with furrowed brows and dug his teeth into his dry bottom lip until the copper taste of blood spread along his tongue as he grew harder. Harder and needier.

Eleri again flashed across his mind, now forever burned into the back of his eyelids. She looked so pretty—bare and naked—as she approached the water. She was so obedient when he ordered her to eat slowly in Arkala. She was fucking perfect. He wanted to *feel* her. He wanted *her* to feel *him* . . .

Trailing his touch farther, Kai wrapped his fingers around his shaft and squeezed. Frustration moved his hand slowly—up and down in a steady rhythm that turned his knees slightly weak. More pressure, and a grunt slipped through.

Frustration and yearning. He wanted so badly to touch her, to massage her breasts and twist her nipples until she was writhing under him. He wanted so badly for her to touch him, to experience the light caress of her fingers as they trailed down his neck, nails scratching his skin every once in a while.

Kai's hand sped up. His gut tightened, veins thrumming with antici-pation. Squeezing his cock hard enough to pull a strangled whine from the back of his throat, he imagined it was her hand around him. Petite. So much smaller than his.

"Gods," he whispered.

She would look so good on her knees before me, hand wrapped around my length . . . with her big blue eyes looking up at me through her lashes.

His hips bucked, thrusting into his fist fast and hard as his head fell forward. It hung limply between his shoulders. The sound of his balls slapping against his wrist filled the quiet air around him.

Concentration pulled his brows together, his mouth hanging open pathetically, while heat seared his skin. Sweat trickled down his temples, and his breaths became ragged, hissing through his heaving lungs.

Eleri. Her name was a chant within his subconscious.

Eleri. Eleri. Eleri. Eleri.

The memory of one of his more recent lays came to mind, but instead of the busty brunette, it was her. He imagined peppering her neck with kisses and bites, tasting her sweet baby's breath and lemon skin with every swipe of his tongue. Sucking her rosy nipples into his mouth and getting a taste between her legs.

She would taste immaculate. I'd be able to survive in this shithole of a world off her alone.

Faster and faster he pumped his hand. His other hand dug into the bark above his head harshly, fingers tearing into each individual strip, causing several pieces to fall. Pleasure built, winding tightly in his gut and blinding his vision.

Eleri.

Kai imagined how it would feel to finally glide inside of her. Wet . . . *warm.* It would be a paradise he'd never known before. The sounds he imagined she'd make as he spread her legs and pistoned his length into her deep enough it had him seeing stars.

Gods, she'd look so good. Sound so good. Feel so good. *Be so good.*

"So good for me . . ."

The words were a lazy mumble, falling from his lips unbeknownst to Kai. Dazed with gut-churning pleasure.

Eleri. Eleri. Eleri.

"E—*shit.* Oh, fuck. Just like that." Kai's body tensed, his muscles going taut.

With several more pumps, Kai squeezed his shaft as his thrusts turned sloppy. Tears lined his lashes, and his mouth hung open while he choked on a breath before going silent. A rush of ecstasy flowed through him. That tightness in his gut released in a wave that made his body shake.

His cock twitched in his hand, and white spurts of his release coated his palm as he continued his ministrations, spreading it over his shaft slowly until his hips came to a stop and his stomach shuddered.

Silence surrounded him once again, interrupted only by his panting breaths.

"Fuck," he rasped while running his left hand through his hair.

He shouldn't have done that. A moment of weakness. A perverted moment of weakness. *Fuck.*

Kai merely stood there, staring down at the mess he made. He blinked. Then, as quickly as he could, he shoved himself back into his pants with trembling hands. He attempted to ignore the stickiness trapped below his briefs before hastily surveying his surroundings to see if the coast was clear.

31

ELERI

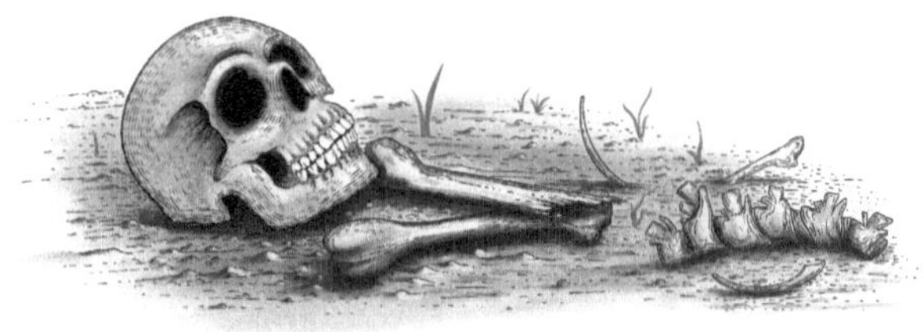

"DON'T, ELERI."

Thin fingers clenched at her side as she sat near the new roaring fire. Eleri's words were lost in the sizzling branches, enough for the others to not notice. A piece of the leftover rabbit Rina had caught the night before hung limply from her other hand. The bite turned sour as she chewed, like a vinegar-soaked piece of cardboard. Staring straight ahead into the yellow flame, she forced the heat of the smoke to sizzle her skin.

That's why my skin is flushed. She tried to convince herself.

It was of no use.

She knew the truth . . . A truth that was eating her alive. A truth gnawing at her skull—insistent and desperate—since she woke up. Her gaze slid to the left . . . tracing the dead wood floor, bouncing over the pile of sticks that lay neatly aligned for the fire . . . approaching large brown leather boots. *His* boots—

"Don't," she gritted out, forcing her eyes back to the fire, where they would rest for the remainder of their stay . . . at least until she could come to terms with her shame.

She had heard him last night. She . . . didn't mean to, didn't mean to pry during such a private moment. Something had pulled her from her sleep, and just as she was about to fall back into its deep, dark depths, she heard it. With a sweep of his hand unbuttoning his pants came a shattered breath followed by a hiss and then a *whimper.*

Sleep evaded her when she realized what was happening, and when she quietly glimpsed Kai leaning against that tree as he pleasured himself, her blood sang, and her heart tumbled. His broad back muscles tensed and shifted with each movement. Narrowing in on his heartbeat, she relished the erratic tune as it tickled her eardrums in the most delicious way. The saliva in her mouth evaporated. And a carnal need to taste him overtook her. She wanted to lick each crevice along his toned back, wanted to run her fingers along his muscles before dropping to her knees.

By then, she was fully awake, ears twitching with each quiet grunt and slip of a curse under his breath. A subtle, heavy need wrapped itself around her gut as if it were a tightly coiled rope and settled even lower.

Turning back around, away from the man who had been consuming her thoughts ever since Arkala, she squeezed her eyes closed. She had tried to tune him out, knowing that what she was doing—*eavesdropping*—was wrong. And yet, she couldn't stop wondering what . . . *who* he was thinking about.

A part of her—a vain little sliver of her being—wanted it to be her. The way his eyes occasionally lingered on her gave her hope that he was imagining her hand . . . perhaps, her mouth . . . around him instead of his fingers. Maybe he had imagined running them through her hair and gripping tight, wrapping each strand around his knuckles and forcing her mouth down on him.

Her fingers traced the dip in her neck before she even realized what she was doing. A gentle glide over her collarbones and down the cotton top Rina had lent her. Her thighs squeezed together, looking for friction as the sound of slapping filled the air.

Gods. The pressure between her legs grew with every passing second, until finally she slipped her hand under the hem hanging over her body and brushed against her pussy.

Slick immediately coated her fingers as she trailed them up and down, dipping inside teasingly before rubbing her clit in agonizing circles. Her other hand flew to her mouth to keep the mewl threatening to push through at bay.

"So good for me . . ." Kai had mumbled, and Eleri nearly came right then and there.

The pressure she applied atop her clit made her throb; her hips moved on their own, jolting forward in a desperate attempt to chase that feeling of ecstasy she hadn't yearned for in years.

She was so close, a whine lodging into the back of her throat as she imagined his lips wrapped around the spot her fingers continuously rubbed.

"Shit. Oh, fuck. Just like that."

Desperation had laced itself around Kai's voice as his ragged breaths became more frantic. And those words . . . they'd stick with Eleri until the end of her days. Haunting her. *Pleasing* her.

She didn't last long after that, his strained noises sending her over the edge easily. The adrenaline of her quiet touches spurred her on. Unbeknownst to him, she finished at the same time he did, her body tensing as his choked breaths made his heartbeat slam against his rib cage. The two, coming together in secret, left Eleri feeling guilty, *dirty*. A moment of insanity. But Gods, did it feel good . . .

"Are you okay, Eleri?" Rina asked, leaning closer and running her gaze over Eleri's face. "You look a bit flushed."

"Yeah, I'm fine. I . . . just didn't sleep well last night."

The words rushed out of Eleri's mouth a little too quickly, as if they were trying to hide something. They *were* trying to hide something.

A quick rush of movement in the corner of her eye pulled her attention toward it. Kai's mouth hung open slightly, a bite of half-chewed rabbit sitting on his tongue as he stared at Eleri with enlarged eyes. When their gazes connected, he coughed and looked toward the ground, vigorously gnawing on the meat in his mouth.

Heat spread up Eleri's neck and settled against her cheeks, then shot south, sitting in her gut, churning idly. As she forced herself to swallow her bite, the feeling grating down her esophagus, Eleri stood and wiped her palms across her bare legs.

"I'm going to go for a walk," she muttered, keeping the breathiness between each word under control.

Kai started, "El—"

"Don't worry. I won't run off." She halfheartedly smiled at him.

She needed to get away, needed some space from him . . . and Rina and Jaycen, space to be by herself and get her thoughts in order.

Without hesitation, Kai seared her with a stare that shook Eleri down to her core. So much was said in that single look. So much hidden meaning that it scared her. Because for a split second, she felt like he also felt this strange power over them.

"I'm not worried," he simply said, a corner of his mouth ticking upward slightly. "I was just going to see if you could grab our clothes by the river while you're out. I think we should stay another day. We need the rest, so take your time."

Oh. Gods, she felt foolish. *I really do need some space.*

"Y-yeah . . ." Nodding, Eleri swiftly turned on her heel and walked to the edge of the forest. The tension in her shoulders released when she stepped foot in the thicket.

Inhaling deeply, Eleri focused on the lingering smell of burnt bark mixed with the fresh cool water. It was a calming scent, a scent grounding her as she strolled between trunks and low-hanging branches.

The rushing river grew louder as Eleri approached its banks. A light fog waltzed along the ripples like a wave of Pixies showing up in the early morning just before they curled atop floating leaves and allowed slumber to pull them under.

Eleri's heart clenched and stomach dropped at the thought of her home. She stopped and stared into the dark water. She always imagined going on early morning strolls along the springs of The Underworld with a Fae Lord wrapped around her arms. But now, the blurry figure next to her in that fantasy cleared, transforming their reddish-brownish-blondish hair into choppy black. Pale skin that matched hers darkened into a light tan. Pointed ears rounded out.

Kai.

She could see it clear as day. Him by her side, walking around the glittering water, under the never-ending night sky. He would rest his hand on her lower back, leading her in a promenade full of laughter and carefree conversation. They would playfully splash one another until their clothes were damp, sticking to their skin. He would lie her down against the plush green grass and slowly undress her, worshipping her body with feather-light touches and sweet kisses. They would make love.

Eleri shook her head, ridding those unrealistic thoughts from circulating. She forcefully halted them from banging against her skull and tiptoed toward a boulder sitting on the edge of the water before sitting down.

I . . . I can't help but feel attracted to him. But it's nothing more than that. We're two completely different beings, from different worlds. Pulling her knees to her chest, she shook her head again. *He doesn't trust me either. But . . . when I'm near him . . . things just feel* right.

Bumps erupted along her bare legs from the steady breeze. Its cool caress brought her thoughts back from her fantasy to what hurt more than anything.

The Underworld was no more. Nothing remained in what was once her lush home. She'd live out the rest of her days alone in the ruins of Beneath. Kai could come. He wouldn't, but he could. Even then, she could never touch him like she desperately yearned to.

A rustle in a tree nearby spooked Eleri, her head snapping in its direction. Focusing on the swaying branch, she heard a small squeak and little claws digging into the rough bark. A mouse or perhaps a squirrel.

The spike in her heart rate calmed, and the adrenaline coursing through her muscles dissipated.

The creature skittered and jumped to another tree. Dinner was getting away, yet Eleri didn't move. She'd eaten too much lately; she couldn't even stomach the thought of eating for a few days. With a long, loud sigh, she lay back until her body was stretched across the expanse of the cool stone and her hair cascaded its side like a fiery waterfall plunging into a deep brown lagoon.

Eleri turned her head to the side, her cheek rubbing against the boulder, and stared down at the burnt grass along the bank that she herself destroyed the day before. Her eyes locked onto the small green patch Rina had saved, still intact farthest from her.

Unblinking, she didn't move. Her gaze stayed on the anomaly, refusing to budge as if it would turn to ash if she glanced away.

"Don't."

The word was barely a whisper upon her tongue.

She didn't listen. Hinging at her hips, Eleri sat up and swung her legs around the stone below her—feet touching the crunchy, charred ground, toes digging until it reached the cool soil beneath.

One step. Eleri paused. Then another.

It was a slow process. Her head was in an internal battle with her heart.

Avoid it. Her head. *Don't destroy just to destroy. Stop, Eleri.*

Do it. Her heart. *You must try—to ensure that it works. Just try it once and be done.*

Eleri's toes stopped at the line of life and death. Green and brown.

"Just once," Eleri rasped out. "Just once . . ."

She knelt, resting atop her shins. The rushing river was to her left, awaiting the dip of her hands. Reaching out, Eleri's fingers trembled. Her movement was met with resistance. Her head yearned to snatch her hand away from the grass as her heart clung to any hope that her eyes didn't deceive her the day before.

"Just once . . ."

A tall blade of grass brushed the tip of her middle finger. It was smooth against her skin as it bent under the pressure. But in the blink of an eye, the blade of grass crumbled, ash floating toward the ground as the surrounding ones were consumed by red-and-orange embers.

Quickly, Eleri plunged her hands into the frigid water, cupping as much as she could and flinging it atop the fast-spreading burn. Opaque, glittering smoke erupted from the ground as the water sizzled against the curse. Eleri splashed more water, just to be sure. Hisses and crackles filled the air. The black smoke churned.

Finally, the smoke cleared, catching on the breeze and floating away as if it had never existed. A ring of plush green grass now surrounded the black ashy spot in its center.

It worked . . .

A breathy laugh bubbled up and out of Eleri's throat. Disbelief that had convinced her it was all a dream exited her body and left something she hadn't had in five years . . .

Hope.

32

ELERI

"ELERI!" RINA CALLED OUT, standing from her spot around the burning campfire.

Eleri smiled at her friend—arms full of their clean clothes and Rina's shirt she'd changed into the day before—as she stumbled back into their clearing while the hazy sun set. She hadn't realized she'd been gone so long. The majority of the day had passed in the blink of an eye as she sat by the riverbed. Rina stepped forward to help her but stopped when she couldn't grab the clothes without the risk of touching Eleri.

Instead, she cleared her pack from a log. "Here, you can set all that down here."

"Thanks," Eleri muttered, placing the pile atop the log and brushing her palms across her pants.

Jaycen strode forward and rummaged through the pile, pulling his pants and top free and stuffing them into his bag. Kai spotted his tunic and quickly swapped it with the one he was wearing before Eleri could get a glimpse of his body, also throwing his pants into his leather sack.

"Thanks, Eleri," Kai said.

Her name on his lips felt forbidden, a burning stroke along her soul. It ignited something—something deep rooted—within her. As the last syllable of her name fell from his plush lips, he sent her a kind smile that held the power to make her weak in the knees.

Eleri's breath caught in her throat as she stared at him. While she was the one from a land of magic, never had someone seemed so ethereal. No Fae Lord who tried to woo her for a night in the field, nor flirtatious Pixie dancing under the moon.

There's something truly rugged about Kai, something unkempt and unruly. He's a conundrum in so many ways—

But that softness in his eyes she occasionally saw shone bright despite it all. It didn't disappear behind his hardened mask this time. It stayed—lingering, penetrating. Something changed. Why it had, she had no idea. It was . . . unnerving. But a quiet thrill rang through her all the same.

This . . . This is new.

"Y-You're welcome," Eleri softly replied, brushing a wayward piece of hair behind her pointed ear.

"You'll never guess what we found!" Rina shrugged her vest on and fastened her cotton gloves.

Excitement gleamed across her features.

Eleri shrugged, forcing her gaze to stay on the blonde and not the handsome man currently strapping his holster across his chest.

"C'mon! Guess!" Rina shifted in her boots.

She couldn't stand still, eager to explain.

"Rina, I don't know. Um, perhaps—"

"Okay, I'll tell you!" Rina paused, attempting to build the anticipation that Eleri could tell seized her bones and quivered beneath her muscles.

Eleri laughed. Rina was . . . *something.* A good something. Eleri was happy to have met her.

"Liquor!" she squealed.

Eleri's brows flew to her hairline just as Rina skipped toward the other logs around the fire and retrieved a rusted metal bottle stained with grime. Its label was halfway peeled, and the words were beginning to fade. Much of it was unreadable. Except for a single word: "*Whiskey.*"

"Huh . . ." Eleri huffed with wide eyes. "Where'd you find it?"

Rina placed the bottle back down and walked toward Eleri. "Kai and I went on a walk to find some food. He found it jammed into the trunk of a tree."

"If only," Kai muttered, prodding a stick into the flames, "I had actually found something of substance. No dinner tonight, unfortunately."

Guilt sent a pang into Eleri's gut. She should've gone after whatever was in that tree. For the sake of the others, at least. Realistically, though, even if she had, it wouldn't have been possible to seize the animal. She had no weapons on her, never needing to carry one with the threat of her touch.

"It's okay," she said, trying to reassure him. "I'm not hungry anyway."

He looked up at her, and a sad smile pulled his lips upward. "You should eat."

The words were so low Eleri was positive he only wanted her to hear them. A blush stained her cheeks in response.

"Well, I'm starving." Jaycen was now slumped against a nearby tree, arms resting behind his head. His eyes were closed. He appeared content for once, despite the whine in his words. "Let's get to drinking. That'll take my mind off my empty stomach."

RINA TOOK A SWIG from the bottle, careful not to cut herself on the rusted bits along the edge. A small burp bubbling up her throat was quickly followed by a giggle. A light chuckle escaped Eleri's glistening lips. The whiskey relaxed her muscles with every sip. It seemed to be doing the same to Rina. Kai and Jaycen appeared to be holding their liquor much better, but she could see the sheen in their eyes and their crooked smiles loosening as the night went on.

It felt . . . different. A sense of normalcy seeped into the air that Eleri was learning she craved despite how unfamiliar it felt. This was the most normal Eleri had felt since she last stepped into The Underworld.

She couldn't put her finger on what it was. Being around them the last several days seemed to chip away at everything she had ever known. It was enough to make her want to stay. And that thought alone was disarming, terrifying even. But at this very moment as she glanced between the others—while they laughed and told stories and no longer seemed to have the weight of the world sitting on their shoulders—she didn't care why she felt that way. It was . . .

"Incredible."

Seated next to her, Kai turned. "What is?"

Eleri's mouth opened as she faced Kai. He was much closer than she remembered. But still, there was room. *Safe* room. He appeared celestial, fuzzy from the alcohol . . . lit up by the dancing fire before them under the darker-than-normal maroon sky.

She hadn't realized she uttered that out loud.

"Just . . . *this.*" Her arm swung open, gesturing to the campfire and the people around it. Jaycen playfully snatched the bottle out of Rina's hands and swallowed a large gulp. Rina pouted and got up, swaying toward him to take it back. "I don't know. It's just . . . I feel like, right now, in this moment, we're truly living. Not surviving. *Living.*"

Kai smiled down at her, his lids heavy and his skin flushed from the booze.

Celestial, indeed. I wish I could read his mind, to know exactly what he's thinking . . . Eleri glanced at his lips so quickly he wouldn't even register it. *I wish he could read mine, so he would know what I'm thinking. What I'm wanting despite everything.*

"Hey, Jayc!" Rina sang out with a slurring, lilting voice. As Eleri turned toward the blonde, she hiccupped. "I wish you smiled more."

Jaycen huffed out, exasperation whirling around the breath that escaped his parted teeth.

Rina didn't let him reply. "You have a nice smile. You shouldn't try to hide it as often as you do. Like the last time we were here, when you accidentally hit your head on a branch and fell on your ass. You couldn't stop laughing! I loved that moment."

Jaycen shook his head, one corner of his mouth ticking up so slightly it was barely noticeable. "I think you're cut off, Rina."

Shaking her head, Rina giggled and swayed before Jaycen as he looked up at her. "Noooo, I'm not. You are, Mr. I Have a Perpetual Scowl on My Face."

Kai chuckled under his breath, pulling Eleri's gaze away from the others and back to him. His eyes twinkled as he watched his friends. So much love lay behind his brown irises.

Beautiful . . .

Emboldened by the traces of whiskey in her system, Eleri scooted the hand resting at her side, bracing against the log beneath her, closer to Kai. The movement was slow, cautious. The callouses on her palms snagged against the brittle bark. Sweat gathered between her knuckles. Every fiber in her being was telling her, *screaming at her*, to stop.

She shouldn't move another inch. It was dangerous. She was dangerous. But . . . that yearning was ever-present, insistent . . . tenacious.

One touch. Just one quick glide of my finger over his skin. Just a brush . . . barely a brush. I need to know what he feels like—

The fire within her flared. Not because of anger or rage, like it normally did, but passion. Passion and want spread through her veins and settled against her bones.

That's never happened before . . .

Just a little closer. A little closer, and then she would stop before their dangerous reality set in and snatched her hand away. Her fingers flexed, inching toward his until they couldn't continue. Only a sliver of air separated their skin. A thin line of recklessness and desperation between their pinkies.

And Kai stayed silent as he watched it all happen. She watched as his enlarged eyes never left her slow-moving hand, and his teeth bit into his bottom lip. His spine straightened, and his throat bobbed, his heartbeat increasing—*pounding*—so hard it banged against her skull.

When Eleri could no longer creep closer, he peered into her wanting eyes. And that look he gave her was devastating. His brows were downturned. His lip trembled. He choked out, "El—"

"Whoa!" Rina gasped.

The sound pulled them out of the disastrous trance. Eleri quickly snatched her hand away; she physically moved her body completely, scooting farther until she was at the edge of the log.

Careless, Eleri. So fucking careless.

She didn't glance at Kai to see his reaction. She couldn't bear to see if dejection twisted his face, or if relief let him breathe easily. Instead, she stared at Rina, who was standing over Jaycen. The bottle of whiskey was forgotten by them both, dangling from the man's fingers. Both of their eyes were glued to the sky.

Just as Eleri and Kai followed suit and peered up, a flash of light in the sky raced by, obscured by the sickly smog swirling above. Bright enough, however, to still see. Another streak of white. Then, another.

Eleri turned toward Kai just as a breathy laugh floated out of his arresting smirk. "A meteor shower."

Awe laced each word. Tears lined his eyes.

A boisterous bark echoed around them. Jaycen's features were lit like a glimmer of hope. "Gods damn. An actual meteor shower."

A meteor shower.

She glanced at the sky. Meteor showers were rare in The Underworld. The last one Eleri saw was on her sixteenth birthday, after she'd been presented with her first crown. A stunning piece with lively white opal stones, a representation of the Fae, and branches of dark obsidian twining around each one for the Witches.

As Eleri and her parents stood on a private balcony while the celebratory ball happened behind them, her father had whispered into her hair, *"The Mother is watching you, little one. You will do great things."*

The night sky lit up as a sour taste lingered across Eleri's gums, those words her father spoke long ago ringing against her conscience.

A breathy, awe-laced chuckle came from Rina. "It's her! The Mother. We haven't had a meteor shower in ages. She's here with us, watching us. I just know it. I can't help but think the tides are changing."

Eleri bit the inside of her cheek until a small amount of blood smeared across her tongue. She didn't say anything, *wouldn't* say anything that could tear the hope brightening Rina's entire being. The hope that had left Kai in silent awe. The hope that made Jaycen clench his jaw and wipe his eyes. She couldn't crush them and bring them down with her, despite how lonely—how sad and *other*—she felt at this moment.

Because, as the last few meteors struck the dark sky, she was certain, no one was watching.

33

Rina

The buzz from the whiskey continued to rush through Rina's veins as she leaned against the wooden log near the dwindling fire, her head resting atop Jaycen's shoulder. She was in a daze as she stared at the flames, her vision going fuzzy . . . her limbs turning heavy.

Tonight was incredible.

Warmth flooded her—not only from the liquor—and she smiled to herself, biting her bottom lip to stop the laugh yearning to flutter free.

The Trinity has blessed us. They truly are watching over us on our travels.

The meteor shower was the most beautiful thing Rina's witnessed in a long while. The bright white streaks, painting across the deep red sky like a gentle stroke of a brush, were like strikes into her very heart. Each flash of light represented the hope that filled her soul.

She whispered, "Jaycen, wasn't tonight—"

A soft snore interrupted her. Gently she lifted her gaze and was met with a sleeping Jaycen. His head lulled to the side, lashes fluttering against his cheekbones. His lips were parted; his rugged features softened, no deep crevice between his brows.

Sleeping was one of the few times Rina didn't see the unknown burdens he silently carried, nor was she met with that impenetrable wall he hid behind. If it weren't for the alcohol in his system, he'd never willingly let her this close.

Out of her two companions, she worried about him the most. Sure, she tried to nestle her way into his life, bickering with him. A familial type of bickering. A type that warmed her heart, hoping that warmth would spread to him. It never did. But despite that, a small dash of concern lingered through it all. She didn't know what ran through his mind. Not truly. She didn't understand his hardened demeanor, only softening towards Kai while keeping her at arm's length. But as she traced her gaze across his face, she realized she didn't have to understand.

All she needed to do—all she *could* do—was be there for him if he ever decided to open up. She trusted him enough to do so one day. And he trusted her on a certain, miniscule level. She'd just have to wait for him to make that final leap.

"You big brute," she mumbled, and smiled at Jaycen's large sleeping form before sliding away from him and leaving him be.

Finding her footing, Rina inhaled deeply, willing the earth below her to stop spinning, and took a few steps until she was at a different log. Plopping down in the dirt, she closed her eyes once more, and a grunt broke through the barrier of her lips.

Thank you, Great Trinity, for the gifts of friendship in times when friendship is sparse.

And as her hazy consciousness dipped into a sea of black, she swore she felt their presence once again. The Mother. The Daughter. The Son, however, did not show this time.

RINA DIDN'T KNOW HOW much time passed when she opened her eyes again. It was still dark out, the maroon sky looming over her, so she was certain it hadn't been long. But the grogginess encroaching around her vision made it difficult to tell.

She was on her side now; her back faced the fire she assumed had long been out. There was no more warmth. Only a cool breeze running along the fabric of her top. Shutting her eyes, she tried to force sleep down upon her. Rina needed it. She could already tell the morning was going to be rough as her head pounded and her eyes swam in a daze.

Every time she closed her eyes, however, the earth beneath her spun, making her sick.

Gods, how much did I actually drink?

It was of no use. She couldn't sleep like this. If she did, she'd surely vomit all over herself. Turning onto her other side, Rina adjusted herself until she found a somewhat comfortable position on the hard ground. Then she simply stared and stared into the darkness, focusing on the waning smoke in the fire's hole and listening to the silence surrounding them.

A quiet grunt sounded off to her left. Sliding her stare toward it, she glimpsed Kai sitting up and running his palm down his face. The fact that they were all sleeping should have worried Rina, should have sobered her up enough to reprimand Kai and Jaycen . . . and herself.

We're idiots for getting so fucked up. We're vulnerable. No one on watch. Intoxicated beyond belief. Fuck . . .

But as the slowness of her body caught up with her mind, she couldn't seem to put in the effort to wake the others. The liquor held her hostage as it took over her bloodstream.

She thought Kai felt it, too. He swayed a bit, squeezing his eyes closed and running his fingers through his hair. When he opened them once more, they looked even more glazed over.

Gods, they were a mess.

Rina watched as Kai's eyes lingered on Jaycen, his brows pulling together as if they were controlled by an invisible string. Then they glided to her with heavy eyelids. She didn't think he noticed she was awake . . . didn't have the energy to tell him either. All she could muster was enough energy to keep her eyes trained on him and will her stomach to calm down enough to get some sleep.

Kai removed his hold on Rina and slid his gaze down toward Eleri. His brown eyes softened, and a small grin tugged at the corners of his lips. Rina stayed as still as she could, observing her leader look at someone in a way she had never seen from him before. It startled her before the intoxicating lull of the whiskey pulled back at her.

Then a rogue thought brushed past her foggy mind. Brynn would have loved to witness this, conjuring up in that creative brain of hers a love story of the century. Because as Rina observed them—a man from one world looking down upon a being from another—she couldn't help but think her sister would have predicted this long ago. She had an eye for things like that. Star-crossed lovers in a grand tale.

Happiness, full and content, filled her chest. The sight nearly made her sigh longingly. Her chest constricted with the memory of her sister and how enraptured she would have been at the sight.

"Right where I'm meant to be . . ."

34

Kai

A DULL PAIN PULSED behind Kai's right eye socket. He rolled over, the dirt and dust of the ground sticking to his sweat-soaked neck as he sat up. A pathetic groan rumbled deep within his chest.

"Please keep it down," Rina whined.

It was too bright; Kai squinted and glanced around. The once maroon sky, filled with beautiful white streaks of light, was back to its sickly orange. The burnt bark of the trees surrounding him was stark against the dull grounds. It was as if it was all a dream. But it wasn't.

Rina groaned again as a cooling breeze rustled through the branches. Kai could only imagine the sound it would make if leaves were still perched atop them. She was sitting on the opposite side of the clearing. Her elbows rested atop her knees, and her head was buried in her palms. Jaycen was lying closest to him. His back was pressed against one of the logs and his right arm was draped over his head, pressing down into his ears to tune out his surroundings.

"Oh!" Eleri squeaked out quietly. "You're all awake."

"Not all," groaned Jaycen.

Kai couldn't help but chuckle. It was raspy and deep, laced with lack of slumber and his raging hangover. Turning his attention to the right just as feather-light steps bounded toward them from the edge of the clearing, he was lost for words. Eleri seemed fine . . . more than fine, actually. No dark circles sat below her eyes. No groans of pain left her lips. Her skin was flushed. The soft smile tracing her lips and pulling her cheekbones up wasn't twisted in a grimace, attempting to hide the hangover she was nursing. No, none of that. She looked lovely.

Did she not drink at all last night?

Gracefully, she came to a stop near Jaycen first. Handing him his condensation-covered canteen, she sent him a smile when he carefully grabbed the farthest part of the bottle and took it from her. His brows were furrowed, with a deep line running between them. Then she made her way to Rina. Reaching toward the bent-over woman, she whispered, "Rina. I filled your canteen at the river. Drink up. You'll feel better once you do."

No . . . she did *drink last night.*

Kai remembered the way her lips wrapped around the whiskey bottle's edge as she swayed and watched with rapt attention as Rina told animated stories of what they got up to before Eleri had joined them. Kai remembered the way she looked up at him with hooded eyes, the deep blue pools glossy from the alcohol. He remembered how she lowered her inhibitions, inching closer toward him . . .

Was that just the alcohol? Oh Gods, he hoped not. *Let it be real.*

Watching Rina reach toward Eleri without looking, their fingers nearly brushing, he gawked at how Eleri reacted. Quickly—so quickly it startled him—she stepped away from Rina's flailing hand with just enough time to avoid disaster. The movement was so fluid. Magic—and not that dreaded curse—ran through her indeed.

Kai couldn't help but think that the way she recovered from the blurry night before had something to do with her Fae heritage . . . or Witch roots, whichever side of her was responsible for faster recovery. It was entrancing.

"Rina!" Eleri shrieked.

The terror sharpening the name on her tongue ripped those unimportant thoughts out of Kai's head and replaced them with panic.

It snapped Rina out of her drowsy, muddled state. "Shit!"

Amber eyes nearly bulged out of her head. Her lower lip wobbled.

"Oh Gods. El—Eleri, I'm so sorry. Fuck. I wasn't thinking." Frightened, wheezing breaths squeezed out of her lungs. Her words were choked. "Are you okay, El?"

Disbelief contorted Eleri's features. She huffed and shook her head fiercely as she knelt down to get eye level with Rina. "Why are you asking me that? You . . . could have *died*."

Rina's eyes held conviction. She cared not about that whatsoever, Kai realized. "And you would have spiraled if that had happened, blaming yourself for my mistake."

Rina . . . He silently admired as he watched the two. Glancing at Jaycen, Kai saw he too was watching with his lips pressed into a thin white line. *Rina, the best of us all.*

Eleri gaped at her. Her large eyes misted over. Opening and closing her mouth, she couldn't seem to put any words together. Rina offered a watery smile and leaned down to make sure Eleri's gaze stayed on her. "So yes, Eleri. I am sorry. I will be careful next time."

Eleri choked out, "I really wish I could hug you right now."

"One day." Rina took her canteen from Eleri's trembling fingers and beamed at the Fae-Witch. "One day, Eleri. I have faith. Thank you for the water."

A silent, tense moment passed over the clearing. The breeze stopped blowing, and the hazy sky dulled as if it were waiting in anticipation to see what happened next.

Then, hesitantly, Jaycen cleared his throat. "We should, uh, really come up with a game plan. We can't stay here forever."

The tension dissipated almost immediately.

Rina sent one more smile to Eleri and moved to sit next to Jaycen, who was perched on a log gulping down the water he was given. "I wish we could . . ." Rina pouted and leaned her head against Jaycen's broad shoulder.

The man's body tensed at the contact between them. *I wish he would open up. If not to me, to Rina . . . anyone.*

Eleri didn't say anything, standing on her wobbly legs and making her way toward Kai. She stared at the ground, watching each footstep, as if she couldn't even look at him.

Maybe it was *just the alcohol . . .* Kai's heart clenched at the sight; his stomach knotted. *She must regret everything.*

Without lifting her gaze, Eleri held his canteen out and quietly said, "Here, Kai. I got you some water, too."

Look at me. Please Gods, look at me.

She didn't. And his heart crumbled, stuttering to a stop until he felt it seizing beneath his ribs.

"Thank you, Eleri."

Kai tried to put every emotion he was feeling into those three words. Confusion. Desperation. Compassion. Desire.

He thought she sensed it. Eleri's eyes snapped toward him, and a pink blush painted her cheeks and nose. It softly ran down the expanse of her neck into the cowl of her cloak. Kai traced it meticulously with his gaze before slowly making his way back to her darkening eyes.

The corner of his lips tugged upward, sending her a crooked smile that warmed her pink-dusted skin into a dark rose.

"What do you think, Kai?" Jaycen called across the ashy hole their campfire was in.

Kai blinked. "What?"

Jaycen rolled his eyes and sent a dagger-like glare toward Kai and the woman now sitting next to him. "I was saying . . . once we get to Mountmend, we need to stay low, out of sight from anyone. Every single person we see is either a part of The Wake or an accomplice."

"Agreed." Kai nodded once, sipping the icy river water from his canteen. It tasted divine. "We can't trust anyone. Let's stay on the outskirts of Mountmend—hidden—until we can confirm The Siren is there. Then we'll make our move."

Jaycen nodded at Kai.

Rina chewed on her bottom lip. "Okay, then. Let's say we scout, and we see the bitch with our own eyes. What then? We can't just barge in. It's a town full of cannibals and murderers. Likely armed and ready to kill at a moment's notice."

Kai hummed before sucking on a tooth in thought. A quiet hush blew through the four of them as he tried to conjure up a plan. They could disguise themselves, rubbing soot on their faces and blending in with The Wake. Or they could wait until nightfall and ambush The Siren as she slept. *If* she didn't decide to journey somewhere else.

No. We need something better, something smarter. We could . . .

His chest seized. "We'll need to lure her in. Pique her interest."

Even though he hated the conclusion he came to, it was their best bet.

"Bait," Jaycen growled out, hazel eyes hardening and nostrils flaring. "It's reckless, Kai—"

"I'll do it."

Eleri's voice carried conviction despite the quiet lilt in her tone.

"No—" Kai snapped his head in her direction. "No. I'll do it. They don't know what I look like. I'll simply take off my hat and bandana. They will be none the wiser."

His heart stalled when he realized Eleri's hands were clenched as she tried to hide the way they quivered. Over his dead body.

"Kai," Eleri's lips pursed as she turned to him with so much determination within her features. "I-I'll do it. They don't know me; they've never seen me. I can do it. Let me help. Besides, if we're being realistic, others are in more danger from me than I am from them. Think of it as a parting gift for letting me travel with you before I leave . . ."

Those last words were nearly silent, getting stuck in the back of her throat. Each syllable was like a claw to Kai's heart.

I . . . I don't want you to leave.

Her big blue eyes sliced into him, crushing his ribs and puncturing his arteries until his resolve seeped out of his pores and disappeared.

Slowly—as if moving on its own—Kai's head nodded, which betrayed his very soul as it screamed for him to deny her.

Why am I agreeing to this? It's reckless, idiotic.

"Kai. . ." Rina muttered.

His head continued to nod, eyes refusing to avert from the orange hair falling over her forehead and her wide, thankful eyes. How could he deny her such a thing when she was right? Her touch alone was like Death beckoning one home. She could do it. She would bravely endure, and he would watch with pride in his chest.

"Okay," Kai whispered. "Okay."

Eleri mouthed a sincere "thank you" before she turned back toward the others. With a sigh, Kai did the same and met Jaycen's eyes. They were guarded, unsure of the plan. Kai's molars ground together.

Rina broke the stare-off. "She'll be there. What you just agreed to . . . You'll need to prepare, El."

"How do you know she'll be there?" Eleri chewed on her inner cheek.

"I don't. Not truly. She could be long gone by now. But . . . I have this gut feeling. All our hard work *will* pay off. That meteor shower? It must be a sign. The Mother was telling us we're on the right path. We were meant to find you, El, and reunite once again. We *will* find The Siren."

Eleri grew silent. Kai stole a glimpse at her. Her lips were pressed into a thin line, but she tried to smile. For Rina's sake.

What is she thinking?

"And what of the leader?" Jaycen chimed in. "The former royal guard . . . If that's true, he must be strong—powerful—to have kept his rule of The Wake all this time. Maybe still has connections to the palace."

Kai sighed. So much was happening all at once. He was itching to get to Mountmend . . . to put an end to that vile woman. He was dwelling on the decision to put Eleri in harm's way and use her as bait despite her cursed touch.

"One step at a time. Our priority is The Siren. This *guard* may be leading these people, but The Siren is providing The Wake with large amounts of their food. She's the biggest threat right now. Then, we'll deal with the rest of the scum."

Rina and Eleri nodded. The airy atmosphere from the night before was nothing more than a memory. Kai could see the weight on their shoulders, burdened by what was to come. Jaycen simply clapped his hands together and stood. "Let's try to get some food to fuel the rest of this journey then."

He strode toward the tree line. Rina hopped up and followed him as Eleri picked at the ground near her feet, throwing twigs and dried leaves into the ashy hole. He smiled softly as he realized she was preparing a fire if they didn't come back empty-handed.

She's so good.

As if it were a train barreling into a brick wall—colliding with the thought that crossed his mind—shame bloomed across his chest. For the first time, Kai hoped—prayed to The Trinity—that The Siren was not in Mountmend.

35

Kai

The journey to Mountmend wouldn't take too long. They had crossed the river at its shallowest depth, the frigid water reaching Kai's knees while his pants got soaked. The water in his boots sloshed with every step and was now coated in The Wasteland's golden sand after entering the dunes separating the oasis behind them and the den of debauchery they were heading toward.

As the day passed, trekking through this stretch of the dreadful desert, the skin around Kai's bones grew clammy and his fingers fidgeted around the hilt of the blade strapped at his side. Anxiety coursed along his muscles. He shouldn't have been feeling such trepidation. He should've been grinning like Jaycen and rolling his shoulders back like Rina. He should've been readying for a fight they've been preparing for far too long. But that anticipation was clouded by a fog of fear and uncertainty.

Eleri never asked to be a part of this fight. In fact, he was the reason she was here in the first place. Unable to decide what to do with her when they first crossed paths, he forced her to stay with them until he could deal with her later. Now, she was putting herself right in the middle of it. The gemstone in his pocket suddenly became noticeable—too heavy against the fabric—after days of not even realizing it was there. Like it was meant to be there.

If The Siren was truly in Mountmend and Rina, Jaycen, and he moved on to eradicate The Wake as a whole while Eleri parted ways and headed toward the mountains, what then?

I-I don't know if I want to go on without having her nearby. A heaviness in his gut pulsed. *But . . . I can't ask her to stay when her home is waiting for her.*

Stealing a quick glance at the woman just ahead of him beneath the rapidly setting sun, his fingers tingled; his heart pounded. She was truly one of a kind, a being that would have never normally crossed his path . . . a sweet blessing now that he had gotten a taste of having her in his life.

Eleri . . . *His Eleri.*

The air in his lungs vanished at the hopeful thought. He tried to get it back, tried to get a grip on even a fragment of breath as he cleared his throat. His steps stuttered against the sandy terrain. There was this undeniable feeling of *knowing*, knowing that Eleri was supposed to be with him, walking the same path, that she belonged at his side. Yet he couldn't be certain that she wanted the same.

My Eleri . . . I'd like that very much.

"Up ahead!" Jaycen called back.

Kai blinked, shaken out of his daydream that wouldn't matter if their plan went awry. He quickened his gait, hopping into the hardened leader position once more. Striding past Eleri's petite form, lemon and baby's breath invaded his senses. Nostrils flaring, Kai's hand flexed as it glided across the air that separated hers from his.

A violent crush of his teeth. *Focus, Kai.*

Jaycen squinted toward the horizon just as Kai neared. "Looks like some rubble."

Kai craned his head forward. He couldn't see shit besides a rough outline of the pile. "Nice spot. Eleri, can you see anything?"

Without a word, she jogged toward him and Jaycen, and gazed into the distance, her lashes fluttering as sand hit her eyes. "I . . . can't tell.

There's too much sand in the air from the wind, and with the sun setting . . . It does look to be abandoned, though. I don't hear anyone, but this wind is drowning out anything useful, so I'm not completely sure."

Kai sent her a thankful smile before he turned back toward his friend and clapped him on the back. "We'll stay cautious. Keep your guard up. Rina, take the back."

Her normally soft features hardened, solely focused on their mission. With a nod, she slowed her steps and trailed the rest, only abandoning the mask when she passed Eleri and sent her a friendly grin.

No one spoke. Not a single word or sigh was uttered until they reached the pile of rubble.

"Eyes up," Kai muttered.

A large steam car wheel stuck out of the thick sand dune. Pieces of splintered lumber ripped apart by others, no doubt, surrounded it. An abandoned shoe lay just behind it; its colors were faded from the sun's heat. Shreds of cloth were knotted together. A broken beer bottle was discarded. A door, ripped from its hinges, was half buried. Along it, scratched in jagged letters, were the words, "The end is here." Thrown about across the area, piles of trash swayed in the wind, and a small heap of bones was concealed under a sheet of metal.

Eleri was right. This area was completely deserted, a place for passersby to dump and take. It was their lucky day.

Jaycen and Kai looked around more closely while Rina stayed back with Eleri, keeping watch. Rummaging through a stack of discarded items, Jaycen grunted when he found nothing of use.

Kai hummed, sidestepping a dried-out tree root carved into a jagged spoon. "I don't think there's anything here—"

Like a beacon, his gaze snagged on a corner of deep purple. Bending down, his fingers ran along its velvety surface, and his breath hitched. Perhaps The Mother *was* watching over him.

"What is it?" Jaycen called out, craning his head around to see what caught Kai's eye.

Quickly, Kai shoved it into his bag and stood up, wiping his sandy hands across his thighs and stepping toward the others. "Nothing. I thought it was an unopened can of corn. It was empty, though."

DARKNESS FELL UPON THE desert like a blanket of blood-red velvet. The sun was long gone, and in its place were clouds of smog and soot swirling overhead.

"We should stop for the night," Kai mumbled. "We need as much rest as we can get if there's a chance of a fight once we arrive."

A strong blast of wind ripped through them. Sand flew into Kai's eyes and mouth. He coughed, choking on the gritty minerals. To his right, Eleri whimpered, crouching low to the ground and burying her head into her knees. Rina did the same, her knees cracking from the sudden movement.

"Fuck," Jaycen jumped up, his body teetering from the wind, "this shit."

He stomped back in the direction they had come from just as the gust slowed into merely a blow. Eleri lifted her head to watch him, her hood falling. Her once whipping orange hair fell across her shoulders.

"Where are you going?" Kai's gaze followed his friend.

"That sheet of copper we saw back at the rubble?" Jaycen called over his shoulder. "We can set it up as a barrier from the wind for the night. I'm going to go grab it."

Kai stepped forward to follow.

"Wait up!" he called out. "I'll go with you."

"I got it, man." Jaycen waved him off. "Don't worry. Stay with them. I'll be thirty minutes max."

A tear split down Kai's chest, pulling him in two different directions. He wanted to run after his friend and help. That was what he should've done. That was what any good leader—any good best friend—would do. But a part of him rooted him to the spot, digging past the sandy dunes and latching onto the deep earth below, and the reasoning had pointed ears.

No. I won't be that selfish.

Looking back around, his eyes met Rina's.

"Go." She graced him with one of her kind smiles and sent him a wink.

With a small huff and chuckle, he grinned at her and then chased after his brother.

"You didn't have to come," Jaycen said, glancing to the side as Kai caught up and sucked in a deep inhale.

Kai grinned. "I know."

With each step they took away from Rina and Eleri, that strange feeling that propelled him toward Arkala pulsed. Desperately, it banged against his rib cage and slammed into his skull. It tugged at him, telling him to turn around.

Jaycen . . . he needs me. He gritted against the need to run back. *I can tell. I won't abandon him.*

A long moment of silence filled the air around them. The breeze brushed between them, running up Kai's tunic. Goosebumps erupted across his skin. As neither spoke, something Jaycen had said at the river gnawed at him.

"Jayc?" Kai mumbled. Sending him a quick glance, Jaycen raised his eyebrow and hummed. "What you said at the river, about how you weren't happy before The Darkest Day, why didn't you tell me?"

Jaycen's strong and sure gait faltered. A wave of sand was kicked into the air as he stumbled slightly. For a long while, he didn't say anything. Kai didn't think he would, despite wishing desperately for him to.

Finally, after an eternity, Jaycen said, "It wasn't your burden to bear."

At that, Kai stopped altogether. He stared after Jaycen, who took a few more steps before halting as well and turning back around toward Kai. "I would have happily helped you carry it though."

Kai's words were nothing more than a broken mutter. His heart constricted under the reality that perhaps he didn't know Jaycen as well as he thought. His chest caved, thinking of Jaycen not coming to him.

Jaycen said with a sad smile that barely reached his eyes, "I know you would've, Kai, and that's why I didn't tell you."

Swallowing around nothing, Kai closed his eyes as if he were in pain. When he opened them, he asked, "And what about now? Are you happy now?"

"It's . . . complicated." Jaycen let out a long exhale, lifting his hat and rubbing his palm across his short, buzzed hair. "But I've found something that pushes me forward."

Kai nodded. "Helping people."

Jaycen didn't say anything. He simply sent Kai that sad smile once more and turned back toward the direction they were heading. "C'mon. We still have a ways to go."

36

ELERI

ELERI'S HEAD WAS BURIED deep into her knees as she pulled her hood over her ears. She tried not to breathe too deeply, lest she wanted sand to wedge itself into every crevice of her nose, mouth, and throat.

The journey from the river to here was excruciating. Not only because of the elements—never-ending shifting sand dunes and whipping violent winds—but because of the building anticipation and dread with each step east.

She was so close, closer than she'd ever been to reaching her home—if the rumors were true. She hadn't felt as if it was within arm's reach since she sprinted toward The Pathway and slashed into the rubble that trapped her in this land. A phantom pain burned from her fingertips to the base of her throat and nestled there as it seeped into the very marrow of her bones.

The memory dug its claws into her, pulling her under into a flashback that would no doubt consume her. It felt as if a huge hole had been punched through her chest, leaving ragged, unsealed gashes around the edges that continued to throb and bleed despite the passage of time. Biting the inside of her cheek, she tried to stop the black from inching its way into her vision.

In through your nose. Out through your mouth.

For a moment, she sat with that feeling. Of sadness and regret. But then, she channeled it back into the hope that sat idle deep below. She was going *home*.

But a twining tendril of dread slithered up her gut and into her chest, where it sat and simmered. Being alone again—with no one to talk to . . . no one to even smile at—gnawed at her as it left a stinging feeling behind her eyes. Five years ago, she banished all desire to be around others, and now that she got a taste of it with the curse in her body, she didn't think she could go back.

Because once she parted ways and arrived Beneath, she would be alone once more.

I . . . I don't want to be alone again.

The heat of Rina's gaze seared into her. It was dark out. No fire sat between them and, yet she could feel the woman's stare travel up and down her body as if she were seeing it under the bright sun.

"Can I ask you something, El?" Rina broke the charged silence between them.

Turning to the side, Eleri glanced at her. Despite the darkened sky and lack of light, her amber eyes still shone. Eleri didn't know what Rina wanted to ask, and it was a pleasant surprise when she realized she didn't care. "Sure."

"The Pathway . . ." Rina began. Eleri's body straightened, and her muscles stiffened. "I-I know it must be a hard subject . . . so please don't answer if you don't want to. But I heard one must feed it the thing closest to their heart. Something valuable—irreplaceable—for the being wanting to cross. Is that true?"

Eleri's heart stuttered before increasing in speed. It slammed against her chest as if it wanted to flee, escape this conversation and the direction it was heading.

This is what you wanted, she reassured herself. *A friend to talk with, to share things with that might be hard. Now's your chance, Eleri.*

Still, that didn't make it easy.

"Mhm," Eleri hummed and faintly nodded.

Rina beamed at her as if she knew that answer alone took more courage than she'd like to admit. She was so . . . intuitive. "You must have sacrificed so many precious things to come up here as often as you did, tending to your garden."

"Oh," Eleri couldn't help the chuckle that accompanied the word. "You only need to feed The Pathway once. Once you do, it's free rein, and you can cross over as many times as you'd like. With just the risk of getting caught looming over you, of course."

"That's a relief, then. You only had to give up one thing. I'm curious, though . . . what was it?" Rina scooted just a smidge closer.

Eleri swore she felt her heart stop completely. Her jaw ticked, and her canines dug into her inner cheek. As Rina took in the sight of her, she must have realized she'd crossed a line.

"Oh! Oh Gods, El. I'm so sorry! It's none of my business. I don't even know why I asked. I just—"

"A secret. I shared a secret."

Those first two words felt like acid on Eleri's tongue. But she pushed through. She wanted a friend, a true friend, and that didn't come without opening up, even if it sent terrifying tremors along her skin.

Besides her mother's crystal she kept before Kai snatched it up, this was the one thing she kept closest to her heart.

"I figured it had to be something physical. That's interesting. Don't worry, though, I won't ask what your secret is. It isn't my place. Sometimes I wish I weren't so nosey." Rina blew a short strand of hair away from her face before securing it behind her ear with an understanding smile.

"I . . . trust you, Rina. You're my friend." Eleri breathed out to steady her quivering lungs and knotted gut. The way Rina lit up at the word "friend" made it a little easier. "I . . . I just have never even uttered the words out loud. When I was about to journey up here for the first time,

The Pathway seemed to know what my secret was before it could even be spoken. I just had to think it, so just . . . give me a minute."

Rina nodded and pressed her lips into a thin line. Her brows were slightly raised; anticipation radiated off her as if she were trying to hide how much this meant to her. And to Eleri . . . this meant even more.

A step in the right direction. Toward what she hoped would be a life that wasn't so lonely.

After several moments of silence, Eleri exhaled. "I wish I weren't half Witch. That's my secret."

Rina didn't speak for a long while. Her eyes merely traced over Eleri's features as if trying to find something. Perhaps understanding. It made Eleri's skin itch, made her want to cave in on herself and hide away from the blonde.

Finally, she spoke. "Why would you wish that?"

The words barely penetrated the air around them, a soft whisper lingering on the sandy breeze.

"Why wouldn't I?" Eleri bit out, the words sharper than intended. "Witches were bloodthirsty. Rage fueled them. The magic they brewed wasn't of light or life, like the magic the Fae had in their veins. They concocted curses and diseases. Anything to one-up their enemies. There was a reason others avoided them, avoided *me* . . ."

Rina's brow furrowed, with a deep, worrisome crevice separating the two. "Who told you that?"

"My history." Eleri studied her as she removed her gloves and wiped the sweat along her pants—the callouses snagging on the fabric—before putting them back on swiftly. "The Witches of The Underworld started The Under War. They killed thousands of beings all because they couldn't admit they weren't fit to rule."

"I guess," Rina slowly stated, "what I heard looked past that. I was told Witches were powerful beings who stepped into their true selves, never apologizing for who they were. I heard they used to dance under the moon and around bonfires—naked, fierce, beautiful. I was told

Witches were formidable, that I should strive to be like one because they steadfastly believed in themselves no matter what."

"I've only been to the covens once in my life, and I was too young to truly remember it. So how would *you* know, Rina?" Eleri asked, the gruffness in her voice apparent as she tried to ignore her beast as it peeked its head around the steel bars of its cage.

She hadn't thought the conversation would go this way.

Rina chuckled. "I guess I don't, not truly. But isn't it better to see the good in the people you come from? I don't know. Perhaps that's just me. But I'm going to take Brynn's word for it. Her books were unreliable, as we've learned, but this . . . ? I guess I have faith that she was right."

Eleri thought she should speak, but what was there to say? It didn't change how she felt. She hated her Witch side. Hated the way it made people treat her. Why . . . Why couldn't she have been loved? Why couldn't *all of her* be loved? Like her mother. It felt as if she were a mistake. And for that, she could never welcome that part of herself with open arms.

After they sat in their thoughts, Rina said, "I know you don't believe in Fate or the Gods, but I truly think I was meant to cross paths with you, Eleri. I think we all were for one reason or another. Myself, Jaycen . . . Kai. It probably sounds crazy to you, but I can't help but believe it. We're right where we're meant to be."

Eleri hummed, sending a hesitant smile toward the woman. And despite her head and heart disagreeing with Rina's thoughts on Witches and Gods, something inside stirred as if it agreed with her on that. And that was hard for Eleri to comprehend.

37

KAI

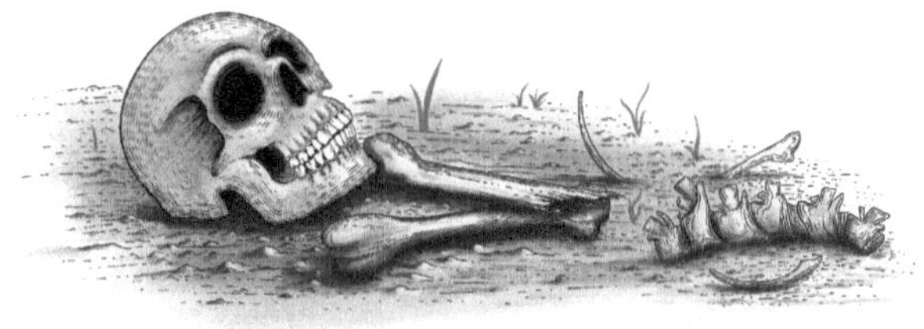

A GRUNT SOUNDED off in front of Kai as he noticed Rina was beginning to drag. Two days had passed in this endless sandy hell. Heat beat down on them; Kai's sweat clung to his clothes and made his skin itch. Rina's feet stumbled over one another. Her spot at the head of the group was quickly overtaken by Jaycen.

Alarmed, Kai rushed forward and steadied her. "Stop, Rin. Sit. Rest."

"I-I'm fine." Rina tried to shrug him off, but his grip was firm atop her biceps.

He reached for her canteen, the lightness concerning. Opening the cap, he saw it was empty. Bone dry.

Shit.

Reaching for his hip, Kai grabbed his, but before he could unclip it, another canteen blocked his vision.

"Here." Eleri's outstretched hand presented her own canteen.

Lips parted narrowly, Kai looked up at the woman. "Thanks, El."

Gingerly taking the canteen from her, he opened it and held it up to Rina's trembling white lips. One small sip glided over her tongue and dribbled down her chin. Once she swallowed it, Kai repeated the process.

Jaycen knelt next to them, his eyes roaming over her body before quietly apologizing as he lifted the fabric of her clothes to inspect Rina more closely. "No Sun Death. At least no rashes that I can see."

That didn't stop the distress curling around Kai's gut. "She needs more than her hat. This long in The Wasteland . . ."

Damn it. We should have taken that sheet of metal we used to block the wind with us. It could have protected her if we had taken turns holding it above our heads.

A sudden rustling sound pulled his gaze. Eleri lifted her cloak from her body and over her head before holding it out carefully for Kai to take. A thin, nearly sheer long-sleeve hung over her frame. Kai's mouth went dry at the plunging neckline that gave him a little peek of her cleavage over her breast band.

"I . . . can't put it on her, but hopefully this will help. At least until we get to Mountmend."

Eleri's voice cut through him viciously despite her soft, worried tone. *Get your head out of your ass, dipshit.*

Her voice continued to pierce through him. "Are there trees around the town she can rest at before we start the plan?"

"No . . ." Rina rasped out, shaking her head weakly. "They're all gone."

Kai glanced back at Rina while handing her the cloak and watched as she slowly slipped it on. "But we might be able to find a cloak of her own there once The Siren is taken care of."

Jaycen grunted. "We'll need to be stealthy. Stealing will most likely be the safest route. Maybe we can find a body."

"I'm sure we'll be able to find plenty of bodies where The Wake is," Kai muttered, never taking his eyes off the blonde.

Eleri knelt next to him. Her eyes, full of worry, roamed across Rina's body. Something inside Kai pulsed. His heartbeat quickened as he looked at her, and his cheeks flushed beneath the bandana. Each second, that strange force got stronger like a steady drum within his gut.

Gulping, Kai didn't say a word, not knowing how to navigate what he was feeling.

But something inside told him to trust it. *"Stay with her . . . Protect her . . ."*

Suddenly, the Fae-Witch turned her head as if she heard that voice within his own. That same heat he felt from the sun sparked within his blood. He smiled softly, wincing as his dry lips split open.

Rina handed Eleri her canteen back, and Jaycen nodded, standing up and readying himself to continue the journey. "Let's get going."

"No," Kai stated. "Let's stop for the night. Rina needs to rest more."

"We're almost there, guys," Jaycen gritted out.

Eleri hooked her canteen back at her hip. "She'll be there in the morning, Jaycen. We should stop for the day."

Jaycen narrowed his eyes at Eleri like her input was nothing more than something to be brushed aside. "Kai," he gritted out.

"Jayc." Kai laced his name with seriousness. "We will catch her. Just . . . resting will do us good."

A long sigh rushed out of Jaycen's nostrils as he plopped onto the ground opposite Rina. "We leave before the sun rises. We're . . . we're *so* close. We can't let her slip away."

ELERI WAS ON fIRST watch tonight, but Kai couldn't sleep. Not because he didn't trust her looking out for them but because he didn't know how to shut his brain off when she was *right there.*

There was so much he felt he needed to say to her. But he didn't know where to start, *if* he should start. Firstly, he felt as if he needed to tell her the truth of his past, to show her his true self—past, present, and hopefully future. Share with her the burden and shame he felt every day. That terrified him to no end. He didn't—*couldn't*—even share that with Jaycen and Rina.

I-I'm not ready . . .

He could tell her how he felt about her, though. His heart pounded at the prospect of sharing that small bit of information. Everything—this journey with her, his feelings—seemed to be moving faster than he thought imaginable. It felt unstable, as if he were teetering on a rotting plank above shark-infested waters. Yet it came with a certainty. Like he knew he was being pushed toward her in a way. That might be even more terrifying than sharing his past.

With a groan, he sat up and rolled out his neck. Kai immediately felt the heat of her stare on him as he opened his eyes and let them adjust to the darkness. She didn't say anything, though he knew she could hear the way his heart stuttered.

Leaning toward the princess—his body automatically wanting to be nearby—Kai risked a glance at her. Eleri quickly swiveled her head away from him with darting eyes filled with embarrassment. In the dark, he watched a deep blush spring up to the tips of her ears. Hope bloomed across Kai's chest. Actual hope that felt tangible this time. Not just wishful thinking and his overactive imagination. Something changed within her after they drank around the fire . . . the way she moved as close as she'd ever gotten to him . . .

"Eleri," he whispered, not wanting to wake the others.

She turned to him, and the sight of her, head on, took his breath away. Her hair was like fire, wrapping itself around her pale skin. Her Witches' Marks were like beacons that drew his eyes in. Thin white lines across her nose and down her bottom lip called him in like a moth to a flame. Her round, blue eyes were large as she stared into what felt like his soul. And the tips of her pointed ears, still tinged with pink, poked out in a way that made him bite his inner cheek.

He was so intrigued by all of her—Fae and Witch and every other side that didn't have a label.

"About . . ." Kai cleared his throat, gathering all the saliva his mouth had to offer and swallowing it down his dry esophagus. "About that night . . . at the river . . ."

Eleri's eyes shuddered—now guarded—as the words died on his tongue. The air around them shifted. It became heavy, stifling in a way that suffocated Kai. Her throat bobbed. Then, she opened her mouth. Nothing came out.

Silence. His words died in the wind; the air between them was now consumed with her silence. Silence swallowed him whole into a deep, dark pit of distress. Fuck. He did this. Ruined it by putting whatever was between them into words, making it real in an instant when it should have stayed hidden beneath his pathetic longing and stolen glances.

"Let's go for a walk." Eleri's unsure voice pierced deep into the worry settling over Kai's chest. Her eyes ran over Rina and Jaycen's sleeping forms before landing back on him. "I need to do a round of checking the perimeter anyway."

Without waiting for his answer, she stood and stepped away from their makeshift camp. When he didn't follow, she turned back around, arching her brow. Sucking in a breath and scrambling to his feet, he made his way after her.

Walking now, shoulder-to-shoulder, they let the silence blanket them. Her breathing picked up, and her hand trembled as she said, "That night . . ." *Finally. I felt like I was going to keel over and die if she didn't speak.* She continued, "That night was a mistake."

His heart dropped. It wasn't a mistake. It couldn't be.

Kai's voice cracked. "Was it?"

Something shifted in Eleri. He saw it in an instant. Her distant gaze and hardened jaw softened as Kai's wavering voice left his lips. Something was buried in her eyes he couldn't be sure of . . . and it scared him.

This was a brand-new fear that wrapped around him in her presence. No longer was it because of what she was and where she was from. Now that fear stemmed from not knowing if he'd ever have her in his life once all was said and done.

Swallowing around nothing and biting her bottom lip as she stared at the seemingly never-ending abyss of the desert they were in, Eleri gently shook her head. "No, it wasn't a mistake," she whispered.

She turned back around and locked eyes with Kai, vulnerability shining through her deep blue irises. And that look shook Kai down to his bones. "But it was dangerous, Kai. I . . . I was foolish to get as close to you as I did. I don't know what I was thinking."

"Can I be honest with you?" Kai asked, sweat pooling in his palms.

He was just going to go ahead and say it. He *had* to say it. A need pulsed in his gut to get the words out. When Eleri didn't say anything, he began again.

"I don't care." A nervous laugh flew out of his lungs. "I don't care how dangerous it was . . . *is* to be around you. I. Don't. Care."

There it is. My secret—my heart—out in the open for her to see. Vulnerable and waiting.

Waiting . . .

Waiting . . .

His words finally hit Eleri. Her eyes got bigger as her mouth opened. Then, her features twisted together. She backed away from him, no more than a single step, but it was enough to punch Kai in the gut. "Don't say that," Eleri practically growled, her canines glinting in the darkness. "I could have killed you."

Surprisingly, Kai didn't find himself retreating. He didn't even flinch at the sharpness of her voice. Instead, that persistent need grew stronger, pulsing through every inch of his being. His ligaments creaked with the pressure. His bones trembled, and his muscles flexed.

"Yes." He was matter-of-fact, absolute in his words. "I know. But I feel this force urging me to stay put. Growing toward you, expanding until it almost engulfs us. It's this deep feeling of . . . *knowing*. Deep in my gut, I know it wants you near."

His truth hung in the air between them. It was so tangible he thought he could reach out and touch the very words he spoke as they stood there. After several breaths Kai held firmly in his lungs, Eleri seemed to truly register what he said. A shaky inhale in, and then a stray tear fell from her lashes and hit the apple of her cheek.

"I feel it, too," she whispered.

"What . . ." Kai cleared his throat. "What is it?"

Shaking her head with downturned lips, Eleri replied, "I have no idea."

Kai leaned forward toward her, making sure his gaze lined up with hers. "I meant what I said. I don't care, Eleri. I, honest to Gods, don't."

Eleri's eyes fluttered shut as she took another deep breath in. When she opened them once more, she seemed grateful and cherished for the first time.

She told me others avoided her, all of her. I will do no such thing. Kai vowed. *Not anymore. I will make up for the judgment and fear I held onto when we first met.*

Then, she smiled shyly, her canines sticking out ever so slightly in the cutest of ways. It made Kai's stomach lurch forward. As her lips trembled, her nose scrunched together.

"Don't you see?" he whispered.

Don't you see that this *Eleri, right here with that curse running through her veins, is who I want. And that want will never go away.*

Eleri sniffled and nodded. She whispered back, "Yes."

Like music to Kai's ears, her voice was. That one simple word rang into the back of his skull and nestled into his very soul. A huff of disbelief pushed past the barrier of his lips. "I think you've bewitched me, Eleri Fos. Y-you must have. That's the only explanation I can come up with as to why I feel about you the way I do."

She laughed, with her head tilted back and mirth within her eyes. The sound was arresting. "So, you're saying it wasn't my gleaming personality?"

Kai's deep chuckle joined in and wrapped around hers as it floated away. "Every scowl and distrustful leer really sold me."

They laughed again. Eleri wiped a gleeful tear from her lash line and clutched her stomach. Kai's chuckle faded out as his jaw went slack. Mesmerized by the sight of her. He tried to sear it behind his eyelids and into his memory forever.

"Eleri . . ." Kai shifted on his feet and dug into his pocket. "I want to give this back to you."

In his hand sat the purple rock, which appeared a deeper, richer shade under the night sky. However, she didn't grab it. She merely . . . stared. "My crystal?"

He fidgeted, curling his fingers around it and gently caressing its edges with his thumb.

"I'm sorry it took so long to return it. When you left, I felt . . . guilty for taking something so precious from you. I've been meaning to give it back to you since the river, but it never felt like the right time. But, after everything we said tonight, I don't want to keep it—*you*—hostage anymore. I know it's important to you but—"

"Kai, after I was reunited with you all in Arkala, I didn't stay because you had my mother's crystal. I left it once; I could leave it again. I . . . felt safe with you . . . and Rina and even Jaycen. I chose to stay. You didn't hold me hostage." He brought his gaze back toward her, and they locked eyes. "Please don't think you did."

Kai nodded and rubbed his eyes in an attempt to stop the burning settling on the edge of his lashes. Swallowing around nothing, he muttered, "It's your mother's crystal?"

Eleri nodded with a fond smile.

"What is it, exactly?"

Her smile widened. He was out of his element, and from the look she sent him, he couldn't help but think she thought it was endearing. A soft chuckle slipped free. "It's an amethyst. My mother said it's for protection."

Kai nodded with furrowed brows, trying to understand. "Does it work?"

She stepped an inch closer to him. "Crystals are the one thing from my Witch heritage that has stuck with me. They're powerful tools, Kai. And I like to think it provided some type of protection over the past five years. Even up here where there is no magic."

"That's . . . good," Kai stumbled over his words. He was trying to understand how something so small could hold so much power. "I'm glad it will be back in your hands again, then."

"Actually . . ." her voice glided freely out of her mouth, a glint shining in her eyes. "You should keep it. I'm not one to believe in much these days, but after spending time with you all, I believe in your mission to help people. You helped me . . . You showed me that good still exists. And for that, I'm thankful. So please, keep it. I want you to be protected as you continue to show that to others as well."

38

ELERI

BEFORE SHE HAD AWAKENED with sand stuck between her teeth, gums coated in grit, Eleri and Kai stared into one another's eyes before she finally succumbed to slumber. She didn't have words for her feelings as she lost herself completely in the depths of his deep brown eyes . . . the feelings she still felt as he now walked beside her through The Wasteland toward Mountmend with Jaycen leading The Pack and Rina flanking the rear.

Uncertainty. Anxiety. Excitement. Fear. Hope. They churned and bubbled in her knotted gut, seeping into the depths of her soul and imprinting into the very fabric of her being.

Biting her bottom lip to keep from smiling, she dipped her head to hide the blush heating her cheeks.

"Gods. Finally," Jaycen exhaled deeply, just as a hot blast of wind barreled into them.

Eleri braced her body against the force of it, digging her boots deeper into the dune, and saw the outskirts of Mountmend on the horizon. Squinting through the churning sandy wind, Eleri peered toward the town. It was far and hard to see well, but from what she could tell, dozens of structures stood tall. Plank roads wove between them and met at small intersections lined with tall, broken lamps. A single steam car chugged along its path, stalling every few feet. From here, it looked like any old town. No nefarious sightings whatsoever.

The fear and hope Eleri was feeling from the night before were pushed aside by her other wavering emotions. They sat at the forefront of her mind.

Mountmend. We're . . . here.

Chills ran from the crown of her head to the back of her heels. That confident determination she held onto as she offered to sit on a platter for The Siren wavered as the town neared.

Now more than ever, she wished she could default to her old ways and hide behind her cloak, a small protective shield she relied on. That one weak moment of yearning to belong, to be a part of something bigger than herself, took over, and now she was uncertain of her decision. And her little beast was oddly quiet.

No going back now.

And Rina still wore her cloak, so there was no hiding. In that moment, when Eleri saw her sitting in the sand, exhausted and unable to move, her only thought was to help. It was strange. Even though the gesture was small, this was the first time she didn't retreat from helping someone else.

Thankfully, Rina was feeling better today. Physically, at least. She was at the back of the group, walking slower than normal. With one look back at her, Eleri saw pure unadulterated heartbreak. Lowering her head, Rina avoided her gaze for the first time since they met. It looked as if she couldn't stand the thought of looking at her old home. Near silent whispers fell from her trembling lips.

"My Trinity, give me strength," she repeated over and over again.

"We're getting to the point of no return," Jaycen mumbled. "No one make a sound. Don't even breathe too heavily. We have one shot at this."

Kai nodded, Eleri followed suit, and from the corner of her eye, Eleri saw Rina meekly do the same.

Gods, I wish I could hide.

Clenching her fists, Eleri followed as they wove around eroded corners of buildings and pressed themselves into the shadows before arriving at a denser section on the outskirts of town. More structures. More heartbeats.

They lowered themselves close to the ground. Lying on their stomachs and crawling toward a deteriorating building on top of a hill, they inched their way closer and closer.

Eleri could see Jaycen restraining himself, stopping his brawn from barging in to fight through the hordes of cannibals and murderers in town. Rina was the slowest. Eleri thought she was prolonging the time before she had to see her old home. She couldn't even imagine what must be going through her head.

"Okay," Kai whispered just as they reached the rotted side of what looked like an old antique shop. "Slowly, we'll make our way around this building. There's an alley off to the side with a view of the town's center below. We'll stay there until we're sure we can proceed."

Eleri, Rina, and Jaycen all nodded.

"Let's move," was all he said.

Gone was the vulnerable man who showed himself the night before, and in his place was the hardened fearless leader clad in his menacing hat and tattered bandana—the intimidating shadow that loomed over her when they first met.

Following Kai and Jaycen, Eleri made her way down the alley's path until she reached the hill's peak. Below her, she saw the town of Mountmend's center . . . or what was left of it. The smell hit her first. Death and decay wafted through the entire town. Buildings that Rina told her once held life and love were crumbling. Large holes where doors should be. Cracked wood and disintegrating bricks fell from the subtlest breezes.

Gods.

Eleri could tell this was once a beautiful town but now . . . She felt sick just looking at it.

A shrine of strips of bloody scalps—some with hair still stuck to them—was sitting in the center of the town's square. One scrawny man with streaks of black running down his neck walked up to it and nailed a new prize to the large wooden post. The skin was still dripping with blood, dyeing the short white hair as it fell to the ground. It was fresh.

Off to the side men and women covered in necklaces made of tiny bones stood around a fire pit. On a spit above the flame was a leg. The skin was bubbling and the muscles beneath were browning. And next to that was . . .

"Gods . . ." Eleri said.

Bile rose into the back of her throat. Decaying torsos, limbs, heads, hands, and feet were all mounted onto the outside of a log building. Some were green, some completely withered from the heat of the sun like jerky.

Fuck, were they making jerky?

Eleri yearned to look away—to rid herself of the way her mind wandered to the jerky they ate in Arkala—but her eyes betrayed her. They took in every inch of the vulgar sight and burned it into the back of her skull. For this, several bricks replaced the holes left by Rina and Kai.

As her stare raked over each appendage, her eyes stalled on the centermost piece. A torso eerily similar to the one she tripped over on the side of the road before she met The Pack. No legs or arms were attached yet the head still was. Instead of a young child, however, it was an older man with craters where his eyes should be and graying hair.

And there, carved across his yellowing torso, were two words: *"Arkala, beware."*

A man who had pursued The Wake left as a warning for anyone else brave enough to do the same.

That bile sitting in the back of Eleri's throat now pushed its way upwards. It sat on her tongue, waiting to be spit out onto the ground. Instead, she swallowed it down, forcing it away. Now was not the time to be weak. She was part of The Pack, in this moment at least. She needed to act like it.

Finally, Rina slid next to her.

"Sorry," she whispered, looking at the ground. "Just needed a minute."

Kai and Jaycen didn't say anything. They simply nodded with their sights still set on the town. Eleri unlatched her gaze from the horrors below her and turned toward her friend. A few silent breaths passed, and Rina's amber eyes rose from the sand and landed on her old home.

It was the first time Rina was seeing Mountmend since leaving with Kai and Jaycen all those years ago. The anxiety pulsing from her had been near suffocating since she woke up. And now . . . Eleri could see the emotions swirling around in her heaving chest and flitting across her entire body.

Anger hardened Rina's eyes. Sadness furrowed her brows. Guilt made her throat bob. Disgust curled her fingers into fists.

Eleri wanted so badly to squeeze her friend's hand. A show of support during a soul-crushing realization: the home she loved would never be again. Eleri knew that feeling all too well. She felt it the day Merrin burned, and she realized she couldn't get through The Pathway back to her parents.

It was a feeling that she could have drowned in . . . *wanted* to drown in. And, Gods be damned, Eleri refused to let Rina fall into that crippling pit.

"Rina," Eleri whispered. Rina didn't look away, her molars grinding together so roughly Eleri could hear the creak of bones within her mouth. She tried again. Still a whisper, but this time, with more force. "Rina. Look at me."

A breath snagged in the back of Rina's throat, and she snapped her attention toward Eleri. Her eyes were rimmed in deep red, where water sat at the corners.

"Do not fall into the darkness trying to consume you, Rina. Don't let what you're seeing now destroy what you love about it. Your good memories will live on if you allow them to. Do not fall."

A sniffle. Rina tilted her hat up and harshly rubbed her eyes. Nodding, she sent Eleri a teary smile before taking a deep breath and turning back toward the town.

"Fuck . . ." Jaycen murmured just as Eleri turned back toward the barbarity. "There she is."

A tall, slender woman stood in front of the wall of bodies. Her muddy brown hair hung down her back as she looked up at it. And a thin arm plucked a dried finger as if it were an apple hanging off a branch and free for the taking.

Eleri couldn't see her face, but she zeroed in on the large, raised scar that took up much of her bicep. Her signature "*S*" in all its glory was branded onto her skin. The sight pulled at Eleri's gut, her nose wrinkling.

Just as the woman turned, popping the finger into her mouth and chewing, Eleri froze. Just as quickly as they came, the courage and wisdom she lent Rina vanished in the blink of an eye.

Eleri's throat constricted and snapped closed, rendering her breathless as she choked on the realization threatening to pull her under. The Siren was striking. Not quite beautiful but alluring in the same way a predator hides its true self to lure in its prey. And Eleri had seen her before.

As Eleri stared at the woman, disgust, guilt, and anger tore through her calm exterior. As silently as she could, she sat in sorrow. And she cried. Tears fell in streams, like a river cascading down her cheeks.

"Okay, Eleri . . . I'll keep my eyes on you the entire—What's wrong?" Kai's voice turned panicked as soon as he noticed the glistening streaks stain her face.

Rina whipped her head back around and took her in with wide eyes. Even Jaycen pulled his gaze away from the town's center to see what had Kai so alarmed.

"I—" She choked on her words, refusing to look at them. With a shaky exhale, she tried again. "I've seen her before. It was just a few months ago. I-I didn't know who she was. She was wearing long sleeves."

The others didn't speak, giving Eleri the time she needed in a moment where time was futile.

"I had come across this woman—*that woman*—in the Western Vale. She looked like she was sauntering toward an unsuspecting couple sitting around a small fire. I-I remember how she moved. It terrified me how swift and agile and seductive she was. She wasn't donning the marks of The Wake then either. I-I remember I took a step back, hoping to conceal myself further in an alley, but a twig broke beneath my boot.

"It . . . it was like time had stopped when that sound echoed against the surrounding trees. She snapped her head in my direction. The couple did as well before taking off, sprinting without even checking to see what made the sound. That woman turned and watched them go before looking back at me. Her eyes roamed my entire body before she sent me a sickly grin as she took in my terrified eyes. Then, with a smile that turned into a contortion of teeth, she strutted off into the thicket and continued to stalk her prey. And . . ." Eleri's voice quavered, inhaling a shaky panicked breath. The tears flowed harder now, reddening her cheeks and nose. "And all I did was turn around. I-I knew she was up to no good. I knew she wanted to harm them. I knew that and left anyway . . . just like that. I didn't want any trouble."

Eleri squeezed her eyes shut and attempted to clear her blurry vision before looking up at Kai. His eyes went wide, then softened as he stared back at her as if he understood the guilt she felt.

He couldn't understand. No one could.

Tearing her broken stare away from the man who consumed her, it landed on Jaycen. "You were right. I just stand by and watch the horrors of the world happen. I was just too consumed in my fear—and shame—to realize."

Jaycen's brows jumped to his hairline before he turned his features back to neutral. Just as he opened his mouth to—no doubt—make a snide remark, Rina whispered and pulled Eleri's eyes toward her.

"Do not fall, Eleri," she repeated the words Eleri had said moments ago. The blonde's eyes watered once more, and a thoughtful expression relaxed her face. *Sympathy.* "Do not fall."

A lump formed at the base of Eleri's throat. All she could do was nod as a silent understanding developed between them. A sisterhood that went beyond basic survival. Eleri and Rina. Two halves that should never have come together. Two halves that did.

"Shit!" Jaycen barked, pulling the two women away from their new tender bond.

Whipping her head back around, Eleri frantically searched for what Jaycen saw through her blurry, tear-filled vision.

"Shit!" Eleri exhaled.

The Siren was gone. Eleri had fucked up. She should have been more thoughtful. She should have had more control over her emotions. They would've never been distracted if she had.

"I-I'm sorry. I'm so fucking sorry."

"Cannibals be damned." Jaycen readied himself to barge into the square to find her. Gaining his footing, he slung his bag over his shoulder and unsheathed the knife strapped to his hilt.

Before he could take a single step, a voice rang out behind them. "Looks like dinner came to us tonight."

39

ELERI

THE SKIN AROUND ELERI'S muscles tightened as terror rushed over her. The blood in her veins turned cold; her stomach knotted and filled with dread. A rugged, bulky man smiled down at them. He was missing several teeth, and the few that were left were brown and rotten—gums bloodied and inflamed. His thinning hair was greasy with sweat and grime that ran down his neck beneath what looked like a collar made of fingers. And his smell . . . soiled flesh.

Eleri's stinging nostrils flared as she exhaled, trying to rid the stench from invading her already muddled senses and trembling limbs.

Kai moved faster than she had ever seen him. One minute he was crouched, watching as she broke down. Then, in a flash, he was standing tall next to Jaycen and staring danger in the eye.

Rina scrambled to her feet as well and tightened her spine until she was the formidable female in The Pack. Eleri couldn't help but feel a twinge in her chest as she slowly stood, the three of them a menacing wall of force between her and the threat.

Insignificant. A silent, self-deprecating voice prodded its way through her fear. *Unworthy. A liability.*

"I think"—the man sucked on a tooth and twisted his face into a grin as he roamed his eyes over Rina's lean body—"I'm going to taste you first. I have a feeling your meat is gamey."

Jaycen and Kai growled, the cadences of each twining together in a low harmony that would make others run for the hills.

"Get fucked, freak." Jaycen's words were all teeth, sharp and precise in the anger that roiled through his body.

The man barked out a laugh. It was a disgusting sound that rang against Eleri's eardrums. "This is going to be fun now, ain't it?"

He lunged for Jaycen, who met him with a glint in his eyes. As they tackled each other, sand flew and fists barreled through the air, landing skull-rattling blows. A few of the people with the man closed in. Whoops and hollers rang in the air as they watched the fight. The commotion made others nearby stop what they were doing and gather around. What was once five turned into a group of ten. Then fifteen. Then at least twenty.

Eleri gaped as realization ripped her in two. It was a spectacle for them. Predators playing with their prey before the dinner bell rang.

Jaycen gained the upper hand, leaving the man breathless as his back slammed into the ground before Jaycen straddled his torso and rammed his fist into the face below him.

One punch. Bones cracked and caved. Another. Blood gushed and leaked.

"Hey, blonde bitch!"

Eleri ripped her eyes away from Jaycen and saw a woman with long braided hair and a thick line of black over her eyelids sprinting toward them from the gathered crowd. The craze in her eyes was the same look the woman Eleri turned to ash had. Murderous. Revolting. A chill spread over Eleri's skin and her muscles involuntarily clenched as dread seeped down into her bones. Excitement and bloodlust were all this woman knew.

Several more men and women began racing toward them, wanting a bite of the bloodlust.

True Vampires. Eleri thought as her eyes grew large, and she took a step back. *Savages, monsters . . . willing to do anything for a taste.*

"Fuck this," Rina hissed. Venom dripped from her tongue. Her upper lip rose in a snarl. "This is for destroying my home."

Her blonde hair whipped behind her as she flung her body forward, bending at her hips and striking the woman in the gut with her shoulder. Four others encircled Rina. A single breath passed between them, and they pounced, a pack in their own right, bloodying their outlier. Rina's hat flew off after a harsh punch to the jaw.

"Stay by me, Eleri," Kai growled, never taking his eyes off the fight before them.

Rina took blows that made the fire in Eleri's gut flare with rage. Jaycen yelled out in pain as a different man bit into the exposed skin of his forearm, ripping a chunk of flesh free. His hat was also gone, exposing his face twisted in pain.

"You protecting this pretty little thing, huh?" A man twice the size of Kai stalked toward them, dodging a flurry of fists and kicks along the way. "Don't be greedy, boy. Bet she feels real good wrapped 'round your cock."

A deadly snarl ripped from Kai's throat; Eleri's beast echoed it, snapping its teeth. He crouched lower, readying himself.

"How does she taste?" The man laughed, his markings stark above his quickly reddening skin. He was almost upon them now. Eleri took a step back just as her fiery side stepped forward. "Better yet, don't tell me. I'll get myself a taste before we roast her alive."

"I'll kill you," Kai whispered as he took his knife out, the words slicing through the air despite barely having any sound.

Kai dove toward the man just as he got within range. The man easily outmaneuvered him, sidestepping his advance and jabbing his fist into Kai's throat. Kai's knife flew out of his hand and skidded across the sand while he reached for his neck. Gritty coughs wracked through his body, rendering him useless for just a split second.

At the last moment, he dodged his attacker's boot aiming right for his gut and swiped his leg out, tripping the man. Before his body could even touch the ground, Kai was upon him, straddling his waist. He pummeled his fists into the man's face, throat, chest, anything he could get beneath his knuckles.

The man beneath him rammed his head upward and slammed into Kai's. Blood spewed down both their faces. Kai fell back and rolled off the man with a groan before chubby fingers wove into his short hair, tightened its grip, and dragged him deeper into the brawl.

"Kai!" Eleri screamed, taking a step toward him and the encroaching cannibals blocking him from her sight.

"Well, well, well . . ." A familiar voice broke through the groans and grunts. A voice that Eleri would have given anything—another molar, all of her hair, her gloves—to not hear again. "The Witch."

Hopping over an unconscious woman sprawled across the ground, a group of dirtied Humans practically skipped toward her, buzzing with dangerous excitement in their gazes. And leading them was the man they ran into while his partner carved into the chest of an innocent . . . the man who ran away while his partner was nothing but ash in the wind.

His gritty voice rang clear as he continued, "The reward is real nice . . . not having to worry about The Wake and all. Sure, we didn't bring you lot in, but we did tip them off that you were heading east. So, they decided to stay put and wait to see if you were stupid or arrogant enough to waltz right into their town. Looks like they were right."

Oh Gods . . . The fire igniting within her gut faltered. It took every last drop of Eleri's will to not fall to her knees. *We walked right into a trap.*

"They were really interested when we told them about you, Witch."

Another voice bellowed over the fighting. Kai. He was yelling her name. Over and over again. Her gaze quickly swiped past the group slowly encroaching upon her and saw him struggling . . . struggling to get to *her*.

His elbows swung as he attempted to fight off the man twice his size and three of his friends. His eyebrow was bleeding and red covered his teeth. A woman took advantage of his immobility and bit into his shoulder, ripping the fabric away and exposing raw red skin beneath.

A gunshot shattered the air, and Eleri flinched. A single breath of silence fell upon the brawl before a raspy voice yelled out, "No guns, fresh meat! We like to play before we eat!"

Then the roaring fight continued.

A slow chuckle rumbled from the approaching man, pulling Eleri's attention back toward him. The group accompanying him stepped closer as well, surrounding her from all sides. She had nowhere to go. Her body trembled; her chest rapidly heaved, struggling to breathe in the sandy air around her.

Shit. Shit. Shit . . .

She held out her hands—covered palms on display—and turned in a circle, making eye contact with each of them. A threat to what she could do, what she knew they knew she could do. Despite this, Eleri hated the way they shook. "Stop."

Like cackling grackles, they laughed. Their spit flung into the air and landed in droplets across her cheeks. "Now, now, sweetheart . . . You didn't think we'd be stupid enough to let you touch us now, did you?"

Suddenly, the earth beneath Eleri's feet was pulled away from her, a frayed rope wrapping around her ankles and yanking her down. Her back slammed onto the ground a second before her head followed. A cutting pain sliced up her skull. A sharp ring penetrated her eardrums. Her vision blurred, and her head spun. She thought she could hear someone yell "back up," but she wasn't quite sure.

Time slowed and sped up at the same moment. In her muddied state, she thought it skipped completely at one point. As Eleri's vision came to—the black fading from its edges—she saw brown hair whip in the wind.

A rough, quick tug at her ankles caused Eleri to lift her heavy head. It felt as if it was chained to the floor, gravity trying to pull it back down with each second it was up. The Siren sat atop a horse looming over

Eleri's limp body. It was thin, emaciated with its rib bones protruding and its skin wrapping around each one tightly. The fighting continued in the background, but Eleri couldn't seem to focus on anything but the monster before her.

Striking. Alluring. Sinister.

The rope lassoed around her was connected to the saddle The Siren sat on. Just before the woman jabbed her heels into the horse's side and it took off, her lips contorted into a sickening sneer. Eleri was jolted back once more, her head slamming into the ground again as she got dragged by the galloping horse.

Through unconscious bodies and standing legs, Eleri was hauled over. Her body bumped into unsuspecting brawlers, leaving them to burn as she sped by. Ash filled the air. Panicked screams as they died punctured her soul.

A boot connected with her collarbone. A knee collided with her temple. Her thin top ripped, gaping at her back and leaving it bare to drag against the ground. Her skin split.

The black around her vision seeped its way back in. She could smell her blood. Blood that trickled out of each cut on her body. In and out, her consciousness went. She tried to scream as the unbearable pain ricocheted across every bone and tendon.

Nothing came out. Dirt and soot got trapped in her throat when she opened it again, hoping this time sound would fall free. Any sound. *Please Gods . . .*

Again, nothing.

Her body stayed together by sheer force of will and the power of her heritage. However, her energy was quickly depleting. Eleri tried to lift her hands.

Untie the rope, Eleri. Gods damn it. Untie it! Do not die like this. Do not die before you can tell them just how much they mean to you.

Through the dust and sand pluming around her behind the speeding horse, her hands reached her face, and she saw them.

A strangled, silent cry split her in two at the sight.

Her right wrist was broken, with bone protruding from her skin. The fingers on her left—now bare where her glove once was—were shattered and bent in several directions.

She thought she had vomited. Through her horror-stricken daze, she couldn't tell. She could only feel a cool breeze on her cheek as a streak of wetness rolled out of her slack mouth. Then she blacked out.

40

KAI

HORROR WASHED OVER KAI as he beheld Eleri getting dragged from the back of the horse. Her mangled body rammed into anyone unlucky enough to get in her way, like ricocheting shrapnel in a battle of heroes. The sight turned his blood cold as it pounded in his ears and warped his vision.

The aching force within intensified and pulled toward her as if it were straining, needing to be near her. Fury blasted from his gut up into his skull and down into his toes. His feet tingled. His heart thudded against his rib cage. And that blanketing power that yearned for her went taut. He needed to go after her.

Kai ran, his feet pounding against the sand dunes—

Jaycen and Rina. No.

He needed to stay with them. Help them through this mess. But El—

Fuck!

A rogue hand snatched away his bandana. Strong arms scratched at him and pulled him back into the throng of people. With a scream fit for a savage, Kai slammed his skull into the woman and ripped his arms free from the man holding them. An ear-splitting, sharp, slicing pain traveled from the center of his head to the base of his neck. His vision turned black for several seconds, and nausea rumbled in the pit of his stomach.

Two hits in a row. Shit . . .

The woman shrieked, piercing the chaos surrounding them, and dropped her tiny switchblade she had meant to carve into his skin. Blood gushed down her face and neck after the skin near her hairline split in two like a melon. The man yelled with a ferocity that would pause any sane individual.

Good thing Kai wasn't sane. Not when it came to the people he cared about . . . Not when it came to her.

Crouching low and dodging a flying fist wrapped in metal, Kai snatched the switchblade from the shifting sands beneath them. Then he rammed it into the bottom of the woman's chin, skewering her tongue in the process. He shoved her to the side, leaving the small blade embedded in her head and retrieved a jagged shard of tin near a body off to the left.

A wiry man with a bloody nose barged through others encroaching on their area.

I can't let him get too close, Kai thought. *He'll overpower me.*

He felt off balance the further Eleri went. Channeling the frantic feeling bubbling within into the fight, he allowed it to spur him on. Kai hurled the metal above his head. It sliced through the air around them, and with a stomach-churning squelch, lodged itself into the side of the man's neck.

He sputtered, blood gurgling out of his mouth and down his chin, then fell over with a loud thud.

Looking around, Kai saw the crowd swarming him. Rina was fighting off several at once, her knife slicing up the spine of a spindly man. Jaycen dislocated a muscular arm, nearly ripping it out of its socket completely. And Eleri . . . Eleri was gone.

"C'mon!" A war cry left his panting lips.

Kai raced past bloodied bodies and retrieved his own knife now buried in the sand except for the hilt. Then, he was slashing his blade through the air—dismembering limbs and cutting through bone—as he cleared a gruesome path toward his companions.

Blood sprayed. Screams echoed. Several cowered. Others fought.

It was a brutal scene. Yet his vision was zeroed in on the foul excuse for a Human who ran straight for The Wake after his encounter with them not too long ago. He was trembling, frozen in fear as Kai stomped toward him like he was Death himself. His face was splattered with blood. His knife dangled from his shuddering hand.

The man wanted to run. Kai could see it in the way his muscles tensed—yearning to move, yet his feet stayed planted in their place. A smirk lifted Kai's lips as he reached his target.

"Fuck you," he growled when he jabbed his knife through the man's chest, bones crunching under the force of the steel. Holding him up by the handle of his buried blade, Kai leaned closer and stared into those dead dark eyes. "You deserve a slow death for all the evil you spewed out into this world, but lucky for you, I have somewhere to be."

Kai twisted the knife, and the man screamed out in agony. The others around him backed away.

No louder than a whisper, Kai muttered, "I just hope the souls you so brutally took are waiting for you on the other side."

Then, he ripped his blade out, blood sputtering in sync with the man's dying breaths and turned away.

"Kai."

A muffled voice broke the ringing in his ears, pushing against his spinning vision and throbbing head. It was disorienting. He felt drained, like his body couldn't physically move, yet the adrenaline pumping every fiber of his being screamed to run. To find her.

Kai tried to stand, struggling to take a few steps in the direction the horse ran. But as he did, his eyes finally saw the reality they were in. The edge of Mountmend, where the brawl began, was long gone. Now, they were tucked between large boulders and the unrelenting wind of The Wasteland.

Kai vaguely remembered Jaycen pulling him out of a swarm of people and throwing him over his shoulder as if he were a kid in trouble. Rina had yelled over the screams and groans, ordering them to hurry up. They escaped the mob of cannibals—bloodied and broken—but escaped nonetheless.

He didn't know where he was exactly. But he knew where he needed to go. He felt it in his very bones. Eleri was south, left in the hands of a woman known to kill and maim and rape.

He tried to run after her but like a war happening inside him, his body didn't listen. It gave out under its weight. Stumbling, he fell onto the barren ground. His palms and knees—covered in blood, his and those monsters—hit the sand. Each grain stuck and grated against his sticky skin.

"Get to her. Protect her." That woman's voice again rang within his mind and the force around him, connecting him and Eleri, swelled.

He tried again, gaining his footing and swinging his arms at his sides as he forced his feet to move. However, a sudden strong pull stopped him. It jerked him back, unable to take another step. Jaycen's large hand was wrapped around Kai's right shoulder, holding him in place. Kai struggled against him, writhing within his grip.

I need to find her.

"Kai! Kai, look at me, man!" Jaycen yelled, his nails digging deeper into Kai's shoulder. Shooting pain traveled down toward the tips of his fingers from the pressure.

Fuck . . . no.

Another harsh squeeze from Jaycen, his nails jabbing into Kai's flesh. The world spun beneath Kai's feet as he glared at the muscular man stopping him. He was covered in blood. Cuts and bruises littered his skin, and his clothes were tattered. Kai thought he probably looked the same. A wave of nausea overcame him. His body was still weak. Keeling over, he vomited.

"You're hurt," Jaycen grumbled, keeping his hand placed atop Kai's shoulder. "Sit down."

Kai shook his head. While his body heaved around nothing, he tried to get back on his feet. *I need to find her.*

"Kai, Gods damn it, sit!" Jaycen's large palm pushed down on his crouched body, forcing him into a sitting position, the side of his boot dipping in his own bile. "You're going to hurt yourself even more."

Kai's voice sounded dead, void of life as he muttered, "They took her . . . They *took* her. We need to get her back. I-I *need* to get her back."

Looking up at his looming friend, Kai pleaded with his eyes, all of his pain and panic shining through his brown irises. Jaycen's brow furrowed.

Jaycen slowly turned his head toward Rina, who was tending to a bloody red gash in her arm that looked as if it were grazed by a bullet. "She couldn't have survived getting dragged like that, could she?"

"She's alive." Kai's words gritted against his tongue.

Raising a brow, Jaycen asked a silent question. Kai didn't answer.

"From what I know, Fae can heal faster than most. And Witches have superior strength and grit." Rina said softly as she sat on the other side of Kai, their bags in tow.

Jaycen reluctantly nodded. "We'll find her, Kai. But you're badly hurt. You need to rest."

That panic seeped into him once more. Swift and burning, it plowed through his entire being, leaving him breathless as he shook his head and squeezed his eyes shut.

Rina's hands engulfed Kai's face, turning it to her. "Listen to me, Kai. You're no good to Eleri in this state. Give me a few hours to patch you up, okay? Just lay back, and once I'm done, we will go. I promise."

Frustration quelled that panic, but after a breath he nodded. Kai felt his lips moving, the words falling off them were nearly silent. But the chant was loud and clear in his mind. His voice mixed with the unknown woman's over and over again until darkness took over.

"Stay with her. Get to her. Protect her."

41

ELERI

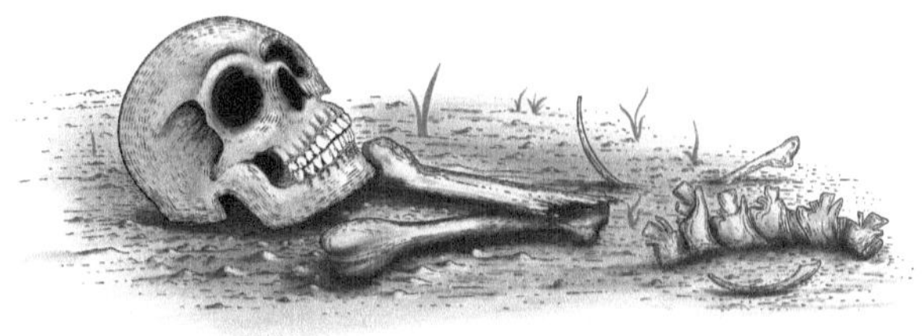

Splitting pain shot down Eleri's skull and settled against her temples. Her tongue was dry, making it hard for her to swallow. Deep throbs reverberated behind her eyes. Blinking them open, Eleri stared into nothing but darkness. It was nearly *too* dark, her usually keen vision having trouble adjusting.

Her back was pressed against something cold and hard. Lolling her head to the side, she let out a blood-curdling scream. Sharp, burning pain spread across her entire body. She felt it over her skin and down into the marrow of her bones. Everything throbbed. Everything ached.

Fuck. That's not good.

"You're finally awake," a raspy melodic voice rang out behind her. "You've kept us waiting."

Eleri's body stiffened, and the movement made another wave of pain rush over her. Light seeped into the darkness in the distance, glinting off the damp stone walls. It looked like an entrance to wherever she was . . . a cave, perhaps, or a dungeon.

I can run. It would hurt . . . Fuck, would it hurt. I don't even know the condition I'm in, but I need to get away from—

"I remember you, you know. You almost ruined my meal. Good thing sometimes I like the chase."

The Siren.

Eleri's stomach hardened under the weight of ice-cold dread. The pounding in her chest stopped completely. She didn't move, couldn't move. Fear gripped her, paralyzing in its embrace.

A long sigh bounced against the walls around them. "Get up. You're boring me," The Siren ordered.

Eleri didn't want to get up, didn't know if she even could. But what would happen to her if she didn't?

Rolling onto her side, Eleri levered herself up onto her elbows slowly until she was upright. She bit her tongue until blood burst across her gums, stifling the scream that threatened to rip free once more. Nausea roiled in her gut and shot up her throat. Even though she had nothing in her stomach to release, her body didn't seem to care, heaving and convulsing.

Her constricting muscles felt as if acid was injected into her. Burning agony all over her body as her vision went white against the darkness around her. She allowed herself a few moments, closing her eyes and ignoring the threat before her. Deep inhales and long exhales were the only sounds disrupting the humid, sticky setting.

Eleri slowly opened her eyes again and took in her surroundings as she filled her lungs to the brim with more air than she could handle, coughs tearing through her throat. Rock walls glistened with condensation. They were bare and blended into the floor made from the same mineral.

Definitely a cave, she thought.

She glanced down at the cave floor she sat atop, and time seemed to suspend by a cruel thread as she saw it. Rusted and heavy, an iron chain was wrapped tightly around her ankles and bolted into the rock beneath her. And next to it . . . Eleri's breath stuttered, lodging itself in the base of her throat. Multiple piles of ash.

"That one's Edmund," The Siren mused, her voice a melodic lilt. "He accidentally brushed his finger over your leg when securing the shackle. That one over there is Lily. She was just a stupid bitch. Forgot what you were for a moment and kicked your stomach while you were unconscious. Oh, and that one? That's Leo. He happily volunteered to hold you down when you started writhing in your sleep as Edmund tried to bind you. For the cause, of course."

Excruciatingly, Eleri finally lifted her head. It was heavy at its hinges. Almost unbearable. For the first time, since they crossed paths not long ago, Eleri locked eyes with the monster The Pack had been hunting.

She was uncanny up close. Like a gruesome monster wearing a woman's skin that didn't quite fit correctly. Her features were sunken in, her cheekbones standing out as a result. Her eyes were dark brown. But unlike Kai's—rich and warm—hers were muddy like a marsh full of shit. And yet that alluring pull tugged Eleri closer, drawing her into the uniqueness of her curving grin.

A Siren, indeed.

Blinking, Eleri peeled her gaze away from the woman. Behind her loomed a menacing sight. A seat carved into the stone wall. It was rugged and rough, with no intricate designs. No one sat upon it, yet Eleri knew exactly what it was supposed to be: a throne, a symbol for The Wake.

A pile of red-stained bones lay to the left of the throne. A few dozen skulls were scattered about. Tossed without care after skin and muscle rotted away.

Trophies for their leader. Reminders for their enemies.

"Why?" Eleri slid her gaze back toward the woman. "Why do this?"

The Siren chortled and swung her hips as she approached the throne and sat atop it. "Power. That's why I do what I do. It's a rush of power knowing I hold my prey's life between my fingers."

Eleri pressed her lips into a thin white line. She pinned the woman down with narrowed eyes. The Siren continued with a glint of intrigue. "Have you ever felt powerless, pet? Because I have. Every day, I felt it. Before The Darkest Day, when those men used me and those women berated me, I was nothing. Now . . . Now I am *something*."

"You're sick," Eleri hissed out. Peeking through the bars of her cage, the fiery beast spat at The Siren. "You rape and kill and eat innocent people because you had a bad life before this?"

The brunette leaned forward and bared her teeth at Eleri. "Shut the fuck up, you pathetic bitch. If it were up to me, I would have chopped you up, bit by bit, in front of your little friends after I had my way with you. But when that slimy little man ran to us with news of an Under-dweller who turned people to ash, our leader wanted to see you for himself."

Lead filled Eleri's stomach. The words got stuck in her throat, but she pushed them through, choking on the syllables. "W-Why? The *cause* you mentioned earlier?"

The Siren hummed while examining her pointed nails.

Curling her fists, Eleri bit back the cry of agony as her broken fingers popped and cracked. "What cause does The Wake have? Y-you are nothing but vile, wicked beings praising a God that doesn't even exist."

The Siren's cracked lips twist into a sickening grin. It looked like she was having fun, watching Eleri grapple at understanding. "To rule, of course. It's The Son's will. I think that's why Aeric wants to see you for himself. You could be a great asset to The Wake, Princess Eleri Fos."

The Siren paused. Her grin widened, and her eyes glinted as she stared at the horror seeping across Eleri's features and into her pores. Her laugh was screeching, grating against Eleri's eardrums.

"It's a win-win for me. You see, because if Aeric doesn't see your worth—and why would he—I get to do with you what I please. I wonder if your touch is still destructive when you're dead." She giggled and bit her lip while roaming her eyes across the expanse of Eleri's broken body. "But if he does want to keep you around, I'll still get to have fun. Because The Pack will inevitably come to rescue you with their tiresome hero complexes, and we will rip their spines through their chests and gut them clean before eating their entrails and leaving a pile of skin in their place. And then, we'll have true power over these lands. No pesky Pack ruining our fun."

Eleri's heart rammed against her chest, nearly breaking through completely. Her gut knotted even more, and a wave of goosebumps overwhelmed every inch of her skin.

Gods—The Trinity—now's the time to prove me wrong. She silently pleaded as she stared Death in her face. *If you truly exist, don't let them come for me. Stop them. Please.*

But deep down, she knew it was useless. The Gods wouldn't help. They haven't helped all those suffering. They wouldn't help her now.

The Gods aren't real.

Kai would come for her just as she would have come for him if he was the one chained to the cold, hard ground. Something deep inside her felt empty, pulsing around nothing, now that they were separated. That cloud of energy loomed over them both.

Staring into those muddy, sunken eyes, Eleri stole away her nerves—snuffing them out before they ate her alive—and slightly lifted her chin, hiding a tremble.

Be brave for them, Eleri. Be brave for yourself.

"You really do like to hear the sound of your own voice, don't you?" she asked, tilting her head. The pain made her wince slightly. But The Siren's amused grin twisted with rage. A long vein protruded down her forehead as she sprang up out of the throne and stomped toward her. "All you said doesn't matter anyways. No matter how infamous you may be, the Upper King still rules these lands—"

A deep chuckle rumbled behind The Siren.

A man in his late thirties appeared, with taut shoulders and a tall spine, followed by a handful of loyal, greasy subjects in ripped clothing. Their eyes were alight, and their rotted teeth pressed into their grins. The cannibal with the bone muzzle she saw in the woods—Hamish, if she remembered correctly—was one of them.

The man—their leader, Aeric, she assumed—walked past The Siren toward Eleri, crouching to her eye level. He cocked his head and raked his eyes over her face and down to her shredded clothes, observing her. He was rugged, and she'd even go as far as to say he was attractive if she didn't know what a horrible being he truly was. His markings were simple compared to his followers'. A single thick line of black soot ran across his forehead like a crown. Wavy auburn hair hung down past his chin, the tips brushing against his shoulders. The color complimented his bronze skin. His eyes were green, with small wrinkles at the corners from laughing long ago, long before The Darkest Day . . . long before he indulged in this new foul life.

He hummed, dragging his gaze back up her body before standing. His hips creaked as he straightened. Then he turned and strode toward the throne.

Another man—one keeping to the back, flanking the throne—sniffed the air. "That's what I smelled in the woods that day. Fear . . . with a hint of lemon." His eyes locked onto Eleri's form, hunger dilating his pupils. The round man took a step forward. "You evaded me, little girl."

"Luther, stand down." An order from his leader. "We're not getting a taste. Not yet, anyway."

With a quiet snarl, the man fell back in line. His eyes, however, never lost that fierce craving for her flesh. "Yes, Aeric."

With a tall spine and hardened eyes, Aeric took his seat, his glare locking onto Eleri once more. "The king is a lazy piece of shit. No new direction after The Darkest Day. No changes." His lips curled over his teeth, a silent snarl. "He just sat in his castle and did absolutely nothing. That's why I left his guard. That's why I'm here. Someone has to bring in the new age. So, I stepped up, and I am doing just that."

A smug smile pulled at his lips, and his chest puffed out. Aeric had a chip on his shoulder. It was glaring, and Eleri was staring down the barrel. It left a bad taste in her mouth.

"What you're doing is wrong." Eleri tried to hide the way her voice pleaded for him to listen. "It's inhumane . . . *disgusting*. You must know that."

The Wake's leader barked out a laugh—a booming sound that reverberated across the damp walls. Resting his elbows on his knees, Aeric leaned forward . . . eyes staying trained on his target. "What I'm doing, Princess, is *surviving*. And this is how we do that. The Son told me himself."

"You're delusional," Eleri breathed out, her chest tightening.

Aeric shot a grin at her. "He came to me in a dream."

He was a fanatic who listened to the hallucinations in his very mind. She shallowly shook her head. Disgust rumbled in her stomach and pity . . . Pity for a man who believed in something so absurd. "Soon enough, there won't be anyone left to eat—"

"And when that time comes, the world will have adapted," Aeric declared. Eleri could tell he could see the pity wafting off her. A growl rumbled in the back of his throat. "Just as The Son foretold when I was merely a walking ghost with nothing to do in the palace. He came to me then. It wasn't long after I noticed the skin on my forearms shriveling up and a dark rash forming atop it from the heat of the sun after The Darkest Day. The beginning stages of Sun Death before the delirium begins. You've seen it. People shriveled up, baking in the sun. The foam dribbling down their chins. That could've been me, but The Son saved me."

Eleri didn't move an inch. Revulsion wound its way around her gut. But she *had* seen it. And she had stolen off those very corpses to cover her body and protect it from the thing that killed them.

"He told me to leave behind the palace and lead The Upperworld's people into a new era," Aeric continued. "He told me to bring people I deemed worthy to survive. And he told me to eliminate all who were not by consumption."

"The Son sounds like a real psychopath, if that's the case. Or perhaps he's merely a figment of your imagination. Crazy conjures crazy," Eleri spat out. The words were laced with a biting venom fueled by her little beast who watched from the edges of the darkest parts of her.

"Do not"—Aeric slammed his fist down upon his throne—"say such blasphemous words to me. The Son will make sure you regret it. You will perish just as all those not in The Wake will perish from the sun's wrath, for digesting the meat of our own and drinking their blood protects us."

Splotches of red, rash-covered skin stained some of his followers, blinded by their faith in Aeric and The Son. Only he was covered head to toe, protected from the heat of the sun. Yet that look in his eyes—crazed and unhinged—told her he believed in this story he was spewing.

Aeric laughed—manic and mirthful—before it dissipated. In its place lay stubborn corruption. "This world will grow again. Animals and plants will prod through the death underground and sprout life once more. And when that happens, us—The Wake . . . *my* loyal followers—will be all that's left, and we will start again. We will rule the new world. Just as The Son said. And you could be a part of that."

"You know . . ." Eleri began, a defiant taunt twining around her vocal cords as she ignored his heinous offer. "Others could come together, rally against you. New towns, communities, are popping up all the time. Soon, you won't be the only one with the power of numbers."

Sheriff Nells came to mind.

"I know, and we've been taking care of them," he paused with a sickening grin, "by plucking out their eyes and adding them to our stews. And at the top of our list of meals is that irritating, backstabbing Arkala scum."

Aeric wet his bottom lip and flicked a stray pebble on the throne's armrest to the ground. "He's been a thorn in my side since long before that pathetic cluster of shacks they call a town popped up. He was a follower until he decided to be weak and leave. When our scouts found him building a new town—a so-called new beginning for his pathetic life—I sent my Siren after them. A warning, a promise for payback. And his people came after us in a sorry excuse of retaliation. Nells can rot but not before I suck the marrow right out of his betraying bones."

Eleri startled, heart shuddering and mouth drying.

Sheriff Nells was once a Wake member. He used to pillage and plunder, eat the meat from Human corpses.

She was going to be sick.

Reaching into the opening of his boot, Aeric chortled just as Eleri's eyes shifted. Nerves buzzed while she watched his every move. As if he were reveling in the anticipation, the leader of The Wake slowly sat back up and slid his hand out, revealing what was gripped between his fingers. Small, sharp throwing knives glinted against the scarce light. His follower, Luther, handed him a whip, the leather cracking. And Eleri's gaze snagged on the revolver attached to his belt.

Oh, Gods. Eleri paled.

"Now, enough about me and my grand plans." Aeric's smile turned into a sinister grin. "While we wait, let's have some fun with you."

42

KAI

FIVE DAYS.

Five days of trudging through The Wasteland. Five days of tracking any hints that might lead to Eleri. Five days of the excruciating pain of waiting and not sprinting toward the pull he felt that connected them.

Five fucking days.

Kai's muscles twitched. His fingers flexed as he stared at the entrance of a cave system hidden in a nook of several boulders between Mountmend and the Upper Palace.

A short gust whipped around them. The sand below their feet, slicing into the exposed skin beneath their tattered clothes, funneled into the mouth of the cave. The pitch-black void sucked in a whirlwind of air harshly with an eerie whoosh and cut through the pale, sun-bleached rock.

She's in there. Kai shallowly swallowed and pursed his lips. *Show that fiery side of you, Eleri. Don't let them dim it.*

Tensing his body, readying to barge into the cave, he took a single step forward before being pulled back toward his companions. A firm hand gripped his elbow. Whipping his head around, Kai opened his mouth to say something, but the sight of Rina and Jaycen stopped him in his tracks.

No longer did they don their protective coverings. No longer did they have that barrier of safety from the sun and others. Their identities were out in the open, bare for all to see, as all three of them lost their hats and bandanas in the fight. Their faces were dirty, caked in dried sand and blood. Dark circles stained the skin under their eyes. Fear furrowed Rina's brow. Fatigue weighed the corners of Jaycen's lips.

"We need to come up with a plan, Kai." Rina removed her hand from his elbow and lifted her cracked lips into a tight smile. Several cuts were beginning to scab over across her cheeks and neck.

He was *right there*. And Eleri was *so close*.

How he could wait another second was beyond him. But the looks in their eyes pulled at his heart and, with it, his resolve. They were right. Kai nodded. Any words he might have said wedged themselves into the back of his throat.

For them. For Eleri.

One hesitant, feather-light step at a time, Kai slipped through the cave entrance. Damp, musty air assaulted his lungs when he breached the threshold. Holding down a fit of coughs and forcing them to vanish, Kai exhaled deeply through his nose.

One step at a time.

He had struggled to tell Rina and Jaycen how he knew Eleri was inside this cave system. How could he explain something he didn't understand? But he *felt* her.

Despite his broken words and his uncertain rambling, he was glad at least Rina seemed to believe something tied him and Eleri together.

Something only they could feel. After several minutes, trying—and somewhat failing—to explain, they came up with a plan that seemed simple enough.

Kai would enter through the mouth of the cave. He'd stay hidden, assess the scene, and then wait. *Wait.* It was a task he didn't know he could fulfill, but he'd try.

For them. For Eleri.

Jaycen and Rina would sneak around the perimeter of the system and find any side or back entrance. Rina said she had known of these caves prior to The Darkest Day. She said her friends would explore them when they traveled to the Southern Coast with their families during the summers.

"All entrances lead to the middle," she had said. He hoped they were faring well.

The hilt of his knife creaked under the pressure of his tightening knuckles. The sound halted his careful steps, and he forced himself to loosen his grip. After a few seconds of hushed breaths, he began again, toeing his way deeper into the darkness.

The quickly dying light glinted off the damp cave walls. They were covered in gruesome sketches of killings and feasts. Stones of various sizes with sharp edges littered the ground, discarded without thought once the drawings depicting The Wake were complete. Beneath Kai's feet, line after line of white scratch marks tainted the ground. Scratch marks that reminded him of the ones at The Pathway's entrance . . . *Eleri's scratch marks.* Desperation and fear etched into each one.

As he ventured farther down the tunnel, the light dimmed, and a bend curved to the left just ahead. Kai pressed his back against the cold stone wall, gliding with one slow step after the next until piercing, manic laughter halted his progress. Several people were here. High-pitched, nasal chortles mixed with deep baritone chuckles.

One sound—drowned out by the loud whoops and hollers echoing against the cave walls—burrowed deep into his heart and filled his gut with cement-like dread. Soft whimpers like a wilting flower floated toward him. Heavy inhales punctured the space in between. *Eleri.*

Kai clenched his fists, his blunt nails carving crescent moons into his palms.

One step at a time, Kai . . .

Another step. Another whimper. Another inhale.

Suddenly, Eleri released a shrill scream. Kai's world stopped, tilting on its axis as that horrid sound banged against his skull and embedded itself into his mind. His heart seized, shooting an ache so painful into the rest of his body, the very cells within throbbed. It was a crippling thing, a sensation that tore into the very fabric of his soul, bleeding him dry.

It took everything in Kai to not sprint toward the sound. Grinding his molars together, he continued slinking down the tunnel as the salty scent of iron—*blood*—wafted through the air.

One step at a time.

Rounding the corner, Kai's back never detached from the slick wall as the dense shadows of the cave concealed him. But the scent. Fuck, it left him breathless. The muscles in his legs suddenly gave out. He pressed his back into the wall. A sturdy anchor rooting him to this earth and holding his now limp body upright.

Chained to the ground by her ankles, Eleri's head was bowed, and her body was hunched over, folded like a limp piece of parchment. Her orange hair looked duller—matted and mangled with sand and dirt. It fell over her face like a doleful, threadbare curtain forgotten throughout the passage of time.

Underneath the cave's gloom, Kai could make out her tattered clothes and shredded skin. Each slash was beginning to knit itself together once more. Eleri's fingers—no longer hidden beneath gloves—were mangled, swollen and crooked and bruised, yet healing just the same. They pressed against the ground in what looked like an effort to keep her body from collapsing.

Fresh wounds also littered her skin. Streaks of blood pooled in the dip of her collarbone, and just below that was a throwing knife's hilt. Its blade was wedged deep within her flesh, barely missing the bone above. Slashes covered her thighs, the fabric of her pants ripped, and the skin below torn open. Blood pooled around her, drying on the rock below.

Wrath. That was the best word to describe what purred beneath his skin. Wrath so terrifying and raw, it bubbled and threatened to boil over from a place within he had no idea existed. Wrath so real, he didn't know if he could contain such a dangerous instinct. His lips curled back and revealed his gritted teeth, and his muscles strained against his skin.

A biting whistle whined past him. Another blade cut through the air with keen accuracy and embedded itself under Eleri's other collarbone. She screamed again, ripping Kai in two—a deep chasm now scarring his heart.

That frail curtain of orange whipped up in an arc as Eleri shot her head back. Dried blood marred the side of her face, leaving a crusted track down her neck. Bruises littered her cheekbones, jaw, and eyes, yellowing as if she'd had them for weeks.

As she sat there, face contorted in a grimace, her chest heaved. Silence invaded Kai's mind. The foreign energy swelled around him and reached out for her.

"Protect her . . ."

The woman's words echoed against his skull. Louder this time—an order. Tensing her shoulders and slightly tilting her head, Eleri acknowledged him in silence, as if she sensed it. Relief sang through Kai as he refused to take his eyes off her weakened form.

She knows I'm here for her—

"Ah, he's finally arrived," a man somewhere within the room cooed. Eleri's reaction to the force between them and the words spoken by the unknown voice—though subtle—must have tipped him off. It was time to face the threat. It took everything in Kai to tear his gaze away from Eleri. He didn't want to, but he didn't have a choice.

In front of her stood The Siren and three others, looking around with slacked expressions. And sitting atop a sorry excuse for a throne was a man Kai never thought he'd see again. "Welcome, Your Highness. We've been waiting for you."

43

KAI

FROM THE CORNER OF his eye, Kai saw Eleri's body stiffen and her head turn toward him. A frown tugged at her lips, and her jaw feathered.

Fuck. She knows. I didn't—No. Now's not the time.

Kai hardened his glare as the leader of The Wake finally pulled his attention away from his prisoner. Following Eleri's gaze, Aeric's eyes locked onto Kai. Tension thrummed between them, waves pulsing off their bodies and colliding in an explosion of dominance.

The others around Aeric seemed to stiffen. Some gaped in Kai's general direction, following their leader's line of sight. Others, like The Siren, gaped at Aeric himself.

"Your Highness?" The Siren whispered, her mouth twisting in confusion.

Interesting . . .

It seemed the guard kept Kai's identity to himself, most likely wanting to use it against him in the perfect moment. Eleri's bloody body flashed across his vision, blocking the man before him. And now, Kai understood, was that moment.

Aeric barked out a loud cackle before leaning forward toward Kai's still shadowed body. The weight of his gaze pressed down on his lungs. This was not part of the plan.

"Come on out, Prince. I'm sure your little princess is dying to see you."

A deep breath in—Kai's heart pummeling against his rib cage—and he steeled himself away. He focused on the hand he'd been dealt. He would overcome, would *win*. Taking a slow step away from the wall and out of the shadows, Kai's gaze turned back toward the only person in this musty cave who mattered.

Nothing could have prepared him for the ache in his chest at the sight he was met with. Hurt flared in Eleri's eyes as they locked onto him. That look . . . It was as if he wasn't the Kai she knew, the Kai she'd gotten to know over the past month.

Another laugh trickled out of Aeric's amused grin.

"You haven't told her yet, have you?" He was gleeful. Deranged giddiness pulsed off him at the silent conflict between the princess and what was supposed to be her knight in shining armor. "The Under-dwellers, and their vague names for the Upper Royals. You all aren't so superior now, are you, Princess? If you had only called us by our names instead of looking down on us—only using titles—you wouldn't be in this mess."

Resentment buckled under Aeric's hardened façade. It was only a flicker but quick enough for Kai to notice. As if nothing of the sort happened, though, Aeric's crazed features returned to the forefront. A twisted grin pulled at his cheekbones. His nostrils flared. His eyes twitched.

Before him was a man who was unrecognizable to Kai. Aeric had always been hateful—leering at his subordinates, the villagers who petitioned the king for an audience, and Kai himself. But now that hate was corrupted, distorted and warped by a mad, fervent energy that thrummed nonstop.

"Where's the broody one? Jaycen, was it?" Aeric tilted his head and scanned the tunnel's bend in the distance. "I know he's around here somewhere. Never far from Kai Eogeum—"

Grunts rang in the distance, echoing down a smaller hidden tunnel behind the throne. "Oh!" Aeric exclaimed. "Right on time!"

Six more people breached the shadowed entrance, dragging Rina and Jaycen alongside them and constraining them beneath their brute strength. "We found them posted up on each side of the stronghold, sir," one of the women with her arms wrapped tightly around Rina's torso stated.

Aeric turned to face the newcomers and revealed his teeth in a disturbing smile that knotted Kai's gut. "Ah . . . we were just talking about you, boy. Nice to see you again."

Jaycen growled and pulled at the muscular arms holding him back.

Ignoring Jaycen's struggle, Aeric slid his gaze toward Rina. "You . . . I don't know you. But you're a pretty little thing, aren't you? I might just have to keep you for myself, hm?"

Rina lunged forward, spitting in his direction with a deadly look that would send most men running. Aeric was not most men. He simply chuckled.

"I like it when they struggle." Aeric's words were acid disguised as a seductive purr. His eyes lingered on the blonde before he turned his attention back toward Kai. "Now, where were we? Oh yes! How does it feel"—Aeric's green eyes flicked toward Eleri—"to know you've been parading around with the son of the man who's the reason for The Darkest Day, Princess Eleri?"

No. Oh, Gods, no. No, no, no, no.

"What?" Jaycen turned slack in the arms of his captors. Rina's eyes held so much pain within them as she, too, stopped fighting to free herself and stared at Kai.

No. Fuck. They weren't supposed to know.

No one was supposed to know that his piece of shit father unleashed the very thing that destroyed their world.

Aeric barked out a laugh. "Don't tell me you kept that from them, too. Gods, Kai. This is why you'll never be able to stop us. You hold on to too much."

Nausea rumbled within Kai's gut as he felt his entire world crumble. One look at Jaycen and Rina broke him wholly. He opened his mouth to say something—*anything*—but nothing came out. The words were wrenched away and strangled beneath his guilt.

Aeric turned his attention back toward Eleri, a triumphant grin pulling at his cheeks.

"Devastating, isn't it? The Upper King, as your kind call him, forced that Witch he holds captive to help cast the curse and—"

"What?" Eleri whispered.

It was the first word she'd spoken aloud since Kai arrived. It was a relief to hear her soft voice even in such circumstances.

One man standing off to the side growled. A man with a gruesome muzzle. "Don't interrupt our lead—"

"Wha—a Witch?" Her entire body language shifted; her eyes stayed glued to the man reveling in his reveal. A sadness surged around her.

Aeric lounged back against the stone seat and watched her with keen eyes. He merely smirked. "Yes, a Witch. An Under-dweller just like you. She's been a prisoner of King Eogeum for fifteen years now."

"What?" This time, it was Kai's whisper that bounced between the standoff within the cave's depths.

That woman . . . the one he saw from behind his father's study door on The Darkest Day chained to the wall . . . the one he saw before he ran, like the coward he was.

Eleri's voice rose. "And—and none of you in that damned palace thought to help her?"

"Why would we help a creature that's beneath us? She barely moved, her eyes empty as if no soul occupied her vessel. Filthy, barbaric Under-dweller." Aeric sucked on a tooth and shrugged. "At the time, none of us knew why the king had kept her or brought her there in the first place. Several of us thought he was simply fucking her. A sack of flesh with no life to keep the king's cock warm. But then that blast broke through the palace's roof, and it all made sense. He used her to create a world so desolate and desperate that it was easy for him to rule. No opposition. He didn't even have to try. Thinking back on it, it makes sense, after The Purge. I guess he didn't account for the possibility of the Gods stepping in."

Kai always thought his father stole a spell book or made a deal to cast the curse. He wasn't capable of conjuring up such a thing himself. But he naively thought that woman was merely Human. He thought his father just needed her blood, any Human's blood, for it to work. Now, he knew the truth. Human and Witch blood—mixing to make the horror that fell upon the land.

The king must've tortured her—drugged her, even—and forced her to offer her blood on a platter. If Eleri had only half the strength of a Witch, this Witch must've been a force to be reckoned with. His father must have compromised her strength. The way he dug his teeth into her arm and ripped her skin open . . . Kai saw it happen, and yet . . .

His heart pumped blood into his pounding ears. *Fifteen years?*

Kai couldn't look at Eleri. He couldn't look at Jaycen or Rina either. A sudden desire to fade into the shadows once more sprung to mind. Shame, so much shame seeped through his entire being.

Aeric laughed. "Gods, Kai, you're pathetic. If you were a competent prince, you would have known. She was chained up in the palace's dungeons while you were off doing Gods knows what, ignoring your duties."

He . . . he was only fourteen when the king imprisoned her. He was just a kid—

No. No excuses. Aeric is right. I should have known.

Shrill clanks scraped against the ground, chains sliding against the stone floor and leaving scratches in their wake. Eleri's twisted fingers gripped the rivets beneath her and dragged her limp body one labored breath at a time. A collective gasp rose as some of Aeric's followers took a step back, no doubt knowing what she could do if she got too close. The piles of ash around her were proof of that.

"I'm going to kill you." A small purr layered itself over the dangerous timbre of Eleri's voice as if another joined in. It was low and deadly, nothing like the woman Kai had gotten to know. The hair on Kai's arms rose—alarmed . . . intrigued—as a darkening fire blazed in her eyes. "And then I'm going to kill your king for what he did."

Aeric's slow chuckle gained momentum, transforming into an exhilarating cackle. "How delightful! The Witch in you has finally decided to come out." Just as quickly as The Wake's leader lit up, his smile dropped. Waving a hand toward a woman and a man off to the side, he muttered, "Shut her up now. I'm tired of her."

They jerked, the man blinking between Aeric and Eleri. "But, sir—"

"Do not defy me," Aeric growled, shooting his dagger-like leer at them before sitting back against the stone throne with a baleful smile.

He handed his whip to one man and trailed his fingers over the barrel of his gun as his eyes lingered on Kai before shifting toward Jaycen and Rina. It was a threat in and of itself. Kai could practically hear the scrape of his nails over the metal.

"You know, I could kill each and every one of you now. It would be so, so easy. But I enjoy a show. Good entertainment is the prefect pre-meal treat." Aeric then sliced his gaze toward the two followers he had ordered. "Now, go. Do as I say."

The woman visibly gulped. The man inhaled deeply. Then, they took a slow, cautious step forward as Eleri stared them down. Her big, blue eyes were nearly black. Only a thin ring was left around her blown-out pupils. Her lips lifted in a snarl. She continued her crawl until the chain pulled taut and stopped her from going any farther.

Kai stepped closer to her, raising his knife. "If you touch her . . ."

He'd rip them limb from limb if their weapons so much as grazed his Eleri.

The two approaching figures didn't pay him any mind, never taking their eyes off the bigger threat. They dug their boots into the stone, halting their steps far enough away so Eleri couldn't reach. Without warning—without a deep breath in or a change in his gaze—the man prodded her violently with a meat skewer, digging its pointed tip next to the newest throwing blade jammed into her skin.

This time no agonizing scream ripped from Eleri's throat and before Kai could pounce into action, she moved. At lightning speed, her hand snatched the skewer just above its point of entry and pulled it deeper into her skin, yanking the man with it. He lost his balance, stumbling forward, fear spreading across his face, as she sent him a menacing grin.

Broken fingers and swollen knuckles reached for him. A feral look gleamed in her eyes. Then, he screamed. Her grip wrapped tightly onto his arm fell to the floor as the skin and muscle and bone beneath it turned to ash.

Frozen from shock, Kai watched the horror before him and the woman in the middle of it. She was a true predator on the hunt for blood. Terrifying. Ethereal.

One collective breath in, and chaos ensued. Kai blinked, then jumped into action as the remaining members of The Wake charged forward. Many stayed clear of Eleri and the piles of ash around her, rushing toward Rina and Jaycen off to the side. Their frozen shock from Kai's secret faded as they struggled to free themselves against the firm grip of their captors.

Jaycen rammed his head back into one man's nose. Blood trailed down the man's face, and his grip loosened enough for Jaycen to grab his knife. Rina clawed at the pale forearms around her chest. Deep cuts sliced the skin, and a shriek tore out of the woman's throat. Kai took a step toward them, readying himself to fight his way through and kill the fuckers who surrounded his friends. Before he could, another bloodcurdling scream ripped through the cave.

Kai flinched. Another victim of Eleri's deadly touch.

"A prince, huh?"

Kai's head swiveled toward the voice, trying to push his worry for the others away and zero in on the lilt of it . . . on the current threat in front of him. The Siren swayed her hips as she approached with a wicked grin, encroaching toward Kai's adrenaline-fueled body. "Maybe you can be my new plaything."

She giggled. The sound grated against his skull. It was wrong. Nothing like the soft laugh of Eleri or the slightly raspy chuckle of Rina. The mirth that filled The Siren's eyes vanished in a second. Her smile dropped, and her jaw tightened. Then, she lunged toward him.

With nails on display as if they were claws, The Siren swiped at him. Kai rotated his knife, tightened his knuckles around the new grip, and plunged it down. He aimed for the top of her shoulder. She easily dodged it, swiftly spinning around with grace while slicing her fingernails down his neck.

Sharp stinging radiated from the cuts and blood pebbled just above his heated skin. Steeling himself, he used the split second before her next attack to study her, study the way she moved and thought. She attacked. He watched. Attacked. And watched.

Then he saw it. Before each attack, her eyes shifted slightly, widening a hair. A tell Kai could use against her.

He dodged her quick jab and nicked her forearm with the tip of his knife.

She struck with her boot, aiming at his chest. Kai blocked the blow and shoved her against the nearby wall.

She struck. He blocked. She charged. He hit.

Back and forth, they continued this dance. At one point, her fist collided with his jaw. He felt his brain rattle under the force of it. He retaliated and rammed her nose in, the crunch of cartilage caving under his palm.

Stumbling back, The Siren yelled out. A battle roar full of frustration. She quickly shook her head, her blood flinging to the side, and she stalked toward him once again. Bright red blood poured out of her nose and coated her teeth as she smiled viciously at him.

She enjoyed this. He could see it. She wanted her victims to try to fight her off. She reveled in it. It was a game of cat and mouse for her—foreplay.

This bitch is sick.

Kai stared her down as she closed in. His chest heaved, nostrils flaring.

Nearly upon him now, she giggled again. "It was fun playing with you, Prince. But I'm getting bored now."

Just as she readied herself to pounce—muscles tensing under her skin and her eyes acutely widening like the predator she was—Kai was yanked back. A heavy hand gripped his hair and pulled him down.

"Can't let her have all the fun." A large man growled excitedly. "You were there in the woods that day, weren't you, boy?"

Eyes alight, he rammed his boot into Kai's stomach. Crushing pressure collapsed his organs, and a burning sensation traveled up his esophagus. He couldn't catch his breath. All air within him vanished.

The man cackled loudly and straddled Kai's much smaller frame as a woman's name was yelled in the distance. A muffled name he didn't know, bouncing across the cave walls. Before he could comprehend whose voice it was, knuckles slammed into his cheek.

The cackles above him increased in volume as the man punched him once more. He was too large to remove. Kai was too dazed to even try. Blinks turned into seconds. Seconds turned into minutes. Minutes—

Suddenly, the man stopped in his tracks. His body became rigid atop Kai. His joints locked up, and his jaw hung open.

"No! No, no, no, no, no!" he screamed.

Clawing at his chest, the man stumbled forward until he was nose-to-nose with Kai. His eyes bulged, and salty tears fell down his cheeks, dripping onto Kai's bloodied face. Pungent, burnt flesh and bones assaulted Kai's senses. His nostrils flared, and he exhaled sharply, pushing the scent away. Ash fluttered from the man's backside, around his shoulders, until it wrapped itself over his torso and devoured his chest.

And Kai merely lay there beneath this doomed man, watching as he screamed and cried and begged for mercy before he crumbled into a pile of dust that covered Kai's chest. Empty boots and discarded clothes lay around him.

He strained his head, looking forward. Frozen before him were another pair of boots covered in gray ash. The shackles locked onto her ankles remained, but the rusted chain was shattered, leaving a short train of links behind. His eyes flicked up and locked onto deep blue pools consumed by fire.

Eleri.

Her chest heaved, and her left hand stayed motionless in front of her, hanging onto the moment she touched the man's back. Slowly, she blinked. That once raging fire dissipated. Her eyes dimmed and softened before her features twisted into what looked like shame. A few silent tears breached Eleri's reddened eyes and fell down her cheeks, leaving paths of gleaming tracks.

The look in her eyes . . .

Devastation clawed at Kai's gut as he sat up like a bear ripping open his stomach and leaving him to bleed out after taking a bite. Eleri swayed, the guilt in her eyes dimming. Then she collapsed. Kai lunged for her, but she collided with the ground before his sluggish body could catch her. He *couldn't* catch her, even if he wanted to. So instead, he stayed kneeling next to her, her body sprawled across the rocky floor, tears in his eyes.

"Shit!" Jaycen hollered. The sharp curse split Kai's eardrums in two, and he winced, pulling his eyes away from Eleri's limp body. "Where are they?"

Looking around, dread filled Kai's muscles as if they were weighed down by iron chains and cement.

Fuck. Aeric and The Siren were nowhere to be seen. All that was left behind were two throwing knives crusted in dried blood—Eleri's blood, Kai assumed—sitting on the stone throne.

44

ELERI

ELERI GAZED ACROSS THE sand dunes surrounding her, catching the sun's heat waves in the distance. She was out here, more often than not, since the fight in the cave three days ago. After days—five days, according to Rina—of nothing but damp darkness while she was held captive, Eleri craved the heat. So, here she sat, not far from the very cave that held the lingering scent of her own blood, where the stone transformed into the gritty sands of The Wasteland.

The wind blew around her, and she tried to focus on that, on the mundane breeze caressing her healing body and endless dunes shifting like a hypnotizing dance. She tried to focus on the unchanging outside instead of the raging storm inside.

Confusion. Hurt. Anger.

Conflicting thoughts roiled around her in a whirlwind of uncertainty.

Too much . . . it's all too much.

Absentmindedly, her mending fingers traced the shackles still wrapped around her ankles. The skin beneath was raw from the friction. The chain dangled freely, its chime catching in the vortex of wind that swirled between the stones. She couldn't bring herself to take them off. Not yet.

So much death. And it's all because of me. Eleri couldn't help but mull over. *So much . . .*

She had killed several people—several not-so-innocent lives, but lives nevertheless—while lost in the burning flame of her rage. Her little beast was a wild animal she was unable to control when the leader of The Wake mentioned another Witch held captive. It was as if the creature dug its claws into Eleri's very mind and steered her movements.

She had bashed the chains connecting her shackles with the steel gauntlet welded together in various shades of scraps the man who stabbed her wore. Not to free herself but to relinquish herself to revenge. And as she did so, a part of her—Eleri *and* beast—relished in the feeling, the thrill, of it.

Eleri despised her dark side—the side she tried to conceal with every choice she made—despite her mother trying time and time again to teach her that her kind's past didn't define them . . . that there was good in it. But, right now, she didn't feel good at all. She felt like a monster.

Eleri bit into her bottom lip to stop the burn in the back of her eyes from spreading down into her nose. So much shame swarmed within her. And the memory of when she woke from her brief blackout made her want to sob. Kai had reached for her; he stepped forward despite having seen the horrors she could truly inflict on anyone close to her, with a look in his eyes that told her she was still the most beautiful being in the world to him.

How could he when she was no better than the people who wreaked havoc on these lands? How could he when she was tainted? How could he when she didn't truly know who he was? She couldn't wrap her mind around it. She couldn't be around him. She just . . . couldn't.

"Don't talk to me," Eleri had said in a voice so quiet she wasn't sure he heard after coming to. *"Just . . . give me a moment. Please."*

But Kai heard. The hurt in his demeanor was palpable. His eyes dimmed, and his chest deflated. Yet understanding peeked through. She needed time. And he'd given her three days so far. For that, she was thankful.

But the time away from the others hadn't helped her sift through everything. Eleri was hurt, of course, by his withholding the truth from her after having opened up to them, even if it was because she'd been caught red-handed.

It shouldn't matter, anyway, whether he told her or not. She didn't know him like that. Not truly. And he didn't know her either.

Fuck this heavy weight surrounding us. Fuck the way it pulsed when he was near. It means nothing . . .

A rip in her chest inched lower into her gut, the chasm of hurt expanding only slightly. Every small moment they shared, every time she cautiously rid her wall of a brick or two, slammed into her. Because that secret of who he was and what he knew—a secret that felt detrimental like the first piece of a game falling and knocking over the others—made her feel more vulnerable than when she dug through people's trash in the Western Vale and stayed in the trees for days on end.

The Upper Prince. The son of a king who destroyed his land and his people . . . a king who destroyed her land and her people.

He knew. The little beast growled from behind its cage where Eleri banished it once she woke up. *Everything you know and love is gone because of his kin, and he* knew.

Hesitant footsteps slowly approached her perch near the cave's opening. Thudding boot soles against the stone turned into a soft crunch as the terrain grew sandy. Without looking, Eleri knew it was him. She recognized his gait even if, right now, she wished she didn't.

Kai sat down beside her. She didn't look at him—keeping her eyes trained on the rolling desert—but she *felt* him. The energy thrummed as if it were glad he was finally nearby. Leaving plenty of space between them, Kai didn't talk, and he barely breathed. Simply being there for her, *with* her, he didn't insert himself, nor did he explain himself. A part of Eleri thought it'd be better if he did.

If anything, hearing his voice—hearing his reasoning—would give her a glimpse into what he was thinking. It'd help her figure out what to say herself. Because they were a mess, her thoughts. A tempestuous maelstrom of contradictions, as she glanced at him before snapping her gaze back toward the sandy stretch.

Between the echoing screams of those she ended and the doubt prodding at the barriers of her consciousness urging her to run, one word penetrated it all.

"Why?" Eleri's voice was raw, not having used it in days.

Kai swiveled his head harshly at the sound. She kept her eyes trained ahead of her, but she felt his intense, regretful gaze on her cheek. It burned through her skin, right to her bones.

That word again, pushing through the distracting pull his stare had on her thoughts . . . *Why?*

"You didn't tell me . . . Even when I told you so much about me, you still didn't tell me."

He didn't even tell his closest friends, that self-deprecating voice hissed in the back of her mind. *Why would he ever trust you enough with the truth?*

Her bottom lip wobbled. Eleri didn't want to show that weakness, but her emotions took over. She dug her canines into the plump flesh of her lip, forcing the movement to yield. She spoke again, the sound cracking. "Why?"

Finally, Eleri peered at Kai. She slowly turned her head, and their eyes met for half a breath before he shifted his gaze. Now, he looked into the distance. He simply stared and stared at the sunlit horizon. After several long moments of silence radiating around them, thickly, she didn't think he would.

Say something . . . anything.

Taking in his features, Eleri shifted her gaze from his foggy, distant eyes to his battered profile. She scanned his bruised cheekbone, down the swollen, strong bridge of his nose, to the chasms of dried blood across his split lips. A hardened façade of The Pack's leader slid into place once again.

Before she could stop herself, the words slipped out. "You're wearing that mask again."

Kai's shoulders tightened. His spine straightened, and a sharp breath inflated his chest a second before he turned to look at her again with furrowed brows and parted lips. "What mask?"

His eyes locked onto hers, and this time neither broke it. She gazed into the deep brown depths of his irises. The sounds around them—the whoosh of the wind, the sand sliding by their feet—dulled to nothing. It was just them and the weight of her words.

A silent exhale to steady herself. "You know what mask, Kai. The one you used to wear when we first met."

Kai's features warped. His eyes widened. His jaw loosened. His nostrils flared, steady heartbeat surging.

Vulnerability slipped through the cracks as his eyes shifted and his breaths turned shaky. Then, he sighed. "I . . . I never wanted who I truly am to be known. T-That's one of the reasons Jaycen and I started wearing bandanas." His voice was gruff like he was forcing each word out, each syllable gritting against his teeth. "I didn't even know if the public—my . . . *people*—remembered what I looked like, anyway, but it was still good to be careful. I only made public appearances until I was fourteen when . . ."

His pupils grew as if he were remembering something he wished not to.

Finally, after a few silent moments, he continued.

"I—I *refused* to make any appearances after that. I revealed my identity to Rina after several months, when I knew I could trust her. Jaycen had always known. And he still stuck beside me despite what type of person I was before The Darkest Day."

"And what type of person was that?" Eleri whispered, careful not to jolt him out of his train of thought.

Kai huffed and shook his head. "A person I don't wish for you to know. I-I'm ashamed of the prince I was. Gods, thinking back on it brings me so much shame . . ." Another sigh. "I was selfish. I didn't want to be a prince. I didn't care about my duties or my people. How—how could I when they supported the monster that is my father?"

Eleri examined him as he shifted. His fingers flexed before running through his black locks. A dejected laugh escaped his tightly pressed lips. "Fuck, I don't want to relive this . . ."

"You don't have to," Eleri immediately said.

She knew what it was like having to reveal her past when deep down she didn't want to. She knew all too well.

"No," Kai interjected. "No, I need to. For you—*us*. For Jaycen and Rina, too. No more hiding behind the shame and guilt that still, to this day, eats me alive."

Kai silently worked his jaw for several long moments before he opened his mouth to speak again.

"He was good at it—my father—hiding his true self. I-It showed its ugly head not long after my mother died when I was thirteen. Just over a year had passed, and a switch flipped inside him. He—uh—he turned cold and hard . . . *violent*."

The way that single word fell from Kai's lips sent alarms ringing through Eleri. She clenched her jaw as she watched his gaze turn distant, and he lost himself in the past.

"He beat me for arriving to dinner only minutes late, once. On several occasions he berated me in front of his guards—in front of Aeric—and his court. When I was eighteen, he threw a shovel of embers from the grand fireplace onto my back while I was sleeping next to it after a revel. After that and a torturous healing process, I petitioned to do a tour around the kingdom. I made it sound as if I wanted to meet our people and hear their concerns. In truth, I just wanted to get away from him. But he denied it. He . . . he savored inflicting pain upon his own son. That's why I pulled away from my duties, my people. That's why

I didn't publicly show my face and turned cold. The king fooled all but those of us in the palace . . . and those in the palace turned their backs on me as if I were *nothing*."

Hollow venom laced his words. "How could they see the vile acts that man bestowed upon me and turn a blind eye? How could they abandon me like that?"

He was asking himself questions he likely had thousands of times. As if realizing he was beginning to lose himself in the what-ifs, he was jolted back into the present and finally turned to face Eleri's unwavering eyes once more.

"I hated him. I hated my kingdom and my responsibility . . . even my own people. All except Jaycen. He tended to my wounds after my father's lashings. He even got a few of his own after confronting him about it. On the morning of The Darkest Day, I went to my father's study to pick up a book on ancient Upperworld art that was collecting dust for him. But then I saw the king, and that woman—*Witch*—and as the curse was cast, I fled. I was a coward, a selfish coward who abandoned her without so much of a thought. As if I was no better than those that knew the truth about me, I used that billowing black smoke as a distraction to run. When I saw Jaycen staring at the barreling cloud, I hauled him onto the empty horse I grabbed from the stable, saving the only person I cared for—the only person who cared for me through all the blood and broken bones and tears—and took off."

Shaking his head, Kai squeezed his eyes shut as she watched the memories take hold. Shame weighed heavily on his shoulders. The corners of his mouth dipped into a deep frown. But he continued, "One woman . . . ran in front of our horses and begged us to take her baby. She wasn't even a year old. But her mother willingly handed her over with pleading eyes and faith that we would keep her safe. With her arms stretched toward us, she asked us to deliver the child to her family in Mountmend. I-I remember staring down at her. Speechless. Scared.

I felt paralyzed. How could this woman hand over her entire world to a horrid prince, just for a chance at a future?

"Jaycen"—Kai exhaled—"Jaycen was the one who met the woman's trembling hands and took the child. He's the one who persevered in a time where hesitation would get us killed. He's the hero. And because of him, we found the baby's family. It took about a week. Only one had survived the initial blast. A cousin. He couldn't have been older than nineteen, but he gladly took on the responsibility . . ."

Turning his watery gaze back toward Eleri, he pressed his lips tightly together, attempting to stop the tears before they fell.

"For two months after that, I was a husk. I sat and remembered Jaycen's sharp gaze on me after returning the baby to his family. I remembered the way he never took his eyes off me as I rotted away and let myself spiral in my disgrace." Tears finally breached his lash line. He harshly wiped at them as Eleri's chest clenched. "My people were scared and suffering. Truly suffering. I had abandoned them, was abandoning them as parents handed their children off to strangers who had the means to flee . . . as lovers embraced one another with tears in their eyes one final time. Th-They screamed for their lives as I simply galloped on by. And that sight—*their fear*—sat with me. Over time, it changed me. I wished all the resentment I held toward those who didn't know the truth never spawned in the first place. So, now I'm trying to make up for that. I need to make my surviving The Darkest Day worth it."

Kai shook his head roughly and released a strangled breath.

"I don't know why I'm telling you all of this. It doesn't excuse the fact that I wasn't honest with you when you were honest with me . . . I—It doesn't matter anyway. There are no excuses. But I'm not that prince anymore. I'm happy I'm not him. He was a coward. He was filled with so much anger, holding deep resentment in his gut like a vice. It was the only thing keeping him afloat. I . . . *Fuck.* I'm rambling."

Kai's gaze locked onto hers once more, and his eyes cleared, filling with resolution. "Eleri," he whispered. "*My* Eleri . . ."

His. Fear ricocheted around her chest. Warmth spread over her skin.

Kai continued, "I'm sorry I couldn't trust myself to open up to you. You are an enigma to me. Someone I'm still getting to know. Gods, it's only been a month or so . . . And yet, I feel like I'm supposed to be here in this fucked up realm with you."

A crease formed between Eleri's brows as she studied him, the movement pulling at her slightly swollen eyes. Kai told his truth. He finally opened himself up to her. That was what she wanted, wasn't it?

And in that moment, she realized something.

I see myself in him . . . in the way his eyes turn haunted and his shame eats away at his very soul. Because I was—am—also a coward, refusing to help those who might need it. Why would I hold that against him, when that very feeling sits within me still?

Neither Eleri nor Kai looked away from the other. Neither Eleri nor Kai said a word. And as she lost herself in the rich browns of his eyes, she felt it. A shift distorted the air—in their very existence—where their relationship ceased to balance as it once had on the sharp tip of a knife.

There was nothing to forgive, she realized.

What she wanted to say seemed stuck, gripping onto the back of her tongue, holding the muscle hostage. No words came, no matter how hard she tried to conjure them. Words, however, weren't a necessity.

It was a strange sensation, being alone for years and then suddenly here came someone who saw straight into her soul . . . or at least made it feel that way. He made her feel safe and seen. And although there had been a day when she wished she didn't, now she embraced that.

Eleri slowly inched her hand closer to his. Careful not to touch. Just as she had done under the falling stars by the river. Kai's eyes shifted toward the movement, and his breath hitched before a trembling, relief-filled sigh released through his nostrils.

Eleri smiled. For the first time in what felt like an eternity, her lips tugged upward toward the orange sky. That symbolic knife, teetering and tottering as it tried to regain its balance, fell over. Then, a wave swallowed her whole.

Acceptance. Utter acceptance.

They would persevere.

Eleri couldn't help but think Kai felt it too. A watery smile and a huff of a laugh slipped through his grinning teeth before he lightly shook his head. "I, um . . . I have something for you."

He twisted around and dug through his leather bag. She ducked her head, trying to peer around his broad shoulders. Minutes passed before he turned back toward her, and her heart stopped.

Clutched in his hand was a book. It was deep purple, its cloth binding adorned with dull gold script and faded white flowers along the spine. She couldn't make out the title, or even the genre. Splotches of black soot stained the corners of the burnt pages. Biting her bottom lip, Eleri traced her gaze across the book's cover before landing back on Kai. He was looking down now, avoiding eye contact with her. But she saw the way the curves of his ears turned a deep red and his cheeks flushed. She bit her lip even harder.

So handsome.

"I . . ." he began, still looking down at his lap. "I remember you found a book in the rubble after we ran from those two Wake members in the woods. It was so old and disintegrated, it crumbled in your hands. Gods, you were so sad. I . . . found this one on the trek between the river and Mountmend. I wanted to give it to you when I tried to give you your crystal back, but for some reason something told me it wasn't time. Like . . . my very being knew it wasn't right to gift it to you until you knew everything. I-I don't know if you've read it before—"

"It's perfect."

The last syllable hitched in pitch as those stagnant tears cascaded down Eleri's flushed cheeks. She felt seen—truly seen, indeed. *He's perfect.*

"Thank you, Kai," she whispered.

Eleri

The Pack decided to venture into The Wasteland to camp for the night. Jaycen raised the point that if they spent another night near the cave system, they were risking The Wake or Aeric or The Siren coming back. Rina and Kai had no qualms with that.

So here they were, sitting in silence as sand crept into their boots and piled atop their legs. There was nothing to build a fire with—no flames to keep them warm. They wrapped themselves in any spare cloth they plucked from bodies and piles of ash in the cave as the evening cooled.

Her new book sat open in her lap beneath her crossed legs. The slowly setting sun lit each inked word. For ten minutes now, she'd been staring at the same page, same paragraph, same sentence.

Lost in her thoughts.

Every few words, her mind wandered to one thing . . .

Focus, Eleri, she chastised, biting her inner cheek. *Focus.*

Her lashes fluttered closed in a slow blink while she inhaled deeply. When they opened after a few held breaths, she read once more.

A dark-brown finger reached toward hers. Delicate. Dangerous. The woman's body moved of its own accord. She was in a trance, unable to control the pull she felt. The curly hair of the woman before her was a beacon calling upon the very soul that sat within her chest. A temptress siren that lured her in . . .

"Gods," Eleri muttered as her mind drifted.

She tried again.

The curly hair of the woman before her was a beacon calling upon the very soul that sat within her chest. A temptress siren that lured her in . . .

A temptress siren that lured her in . . .

Eleri shook her head before leaning down to rest her cheek against her palm. It was of no use. Her mind wandered yet again. To the same thing. To *her.* To the Witch held captive by the Upper King.

Fifteen years . . . the king had held this woman for fifteen fucking years.

A fiery flare swelled where Eleri kept her beast hidden. Through the flames, it took a step out. It didn't slink around with swaying hips, nor have its claws on display. Never had Eleri seen the creature like this.

We need to help her. No purr or hiss followed its words this time. *She's one of us.*

Eleri shook her head. *No. You controlled me back in the cave. You made me kill. And I never would have if I wasn't . . . I don't claim that part of m—*

You should! White-hot flames erupted around the witchy thing before they subdued slightly. *Why—*its voice cracked—*why do you keep me locked away?*

Eleri didn't answer for a long while. A silent void surrounded her mind until the words hesitantly broke free. *You . . . scare me.*

Her little beast took another step forward. Its eyes hardened into slits. *I am the way I am because I am in a cage. I am what you made me. This is of your own doing, Princess.*

Eleri felt her very being pulled in two different directions. One of safety and happiness. One of danger and hardship. Biting her tongue and squeezing her eyes shut, Eleri tried to quiet the whirlwind within her mind.

Focus. Focus. Focus.

The beast stood firm. Its claws were out now, digging into Eleri's soul and refusing to be put in its cage again. It said, *You should feel honored to save a being from our world when the rest of our Under-kin are gone. You locked me away because this side of you made you feel other? This Witch must feel that way, too, up here as a prisoner.*

Trying to ignore the way her heart clenched, Eleri homed in on the voices around her instead. Kai and Rina were discussing what their next move should be. Their tones conveyed urgency and seriousness. A search for Aeric and The Siren was in the works.

"Say we do kill The Siren next time we see her. What about him? Ridding The Wake of its leader could potentially rid this world of the faction completely," Rina said, voice penetrating the fog consuming Eleri.

"Or . . ." Kai countered, the mesmerizing timbre of his voice sending chills down her scalp and relaxing her muscles. "He would become a martyr, pushing The Wake to rise in protest of his death. They could easily pick a new leader all while avenging their former."

A deep, usually insistent voice—one that always spoke up when it came to their enemies—was noticeably absent, Eleri realized. Opening her eyes, Eleri lifted her chin. Her gaze attached to Jaycen's instantly. He was staring at her. His eyes were hardened with a hint of something else. Something vulnerable he was trying to push away. His leer shifted lower, locking onto the book in her lap, and Jaycen's eyes shuddered.

Eleri's brows creased as his previous words echoed against her skull, haunting her like an ancient phantom: *"We can't all just hide—standing by and watching it happen."*

Before she could think better of it, before she could stop the words from falling from her lips, she spoke. Her voice pierced their hushed campsite. "I'm going to the palace."

She spoke to no one in particular. Her darker side rejoiced, retracting its claws from Eleri and jumping in glee. For the first time, Eleri didn't lock it back in its cage. But Kai and Rina whipped their heads around, gaping at her with horrified looks that twisted their faces. Jaycen's eyes enlarged, bulging at the seams. It was as if she sprouted another head. Unrecognizable to The Pack.

"Why would you want to go there?" Jaycen asked, suspicion coating each word like poison.

The silent accusation hurt, burrowed deep down into her chest. He would never stop scrutinizing her. But still, she tried to explain herself. "I can't sit back and watch like I have always done. That Witch is a part of me, and she needs my help."

With a pointed look, Eleri's gaze seared into him. His lips parted, a cut from the fight splitting from the movement and a sharp inhale hitched his breath, his previous words now haunting the both of them.

"Eleri," Rina began. Eleri turned to her friend with pleading eyes. Rina stood slowly and stepped toward her. "I don't think that's a good idea."

"I think . . . I want to start seeing the beauty of the Witches you mentioned, Rina." Eleri mumbled, the back of her eyes burning with unshed tears. "This . . . this could be my first step. She is a Witch, and so am I. I need to do this. I—I have to try."

Rina opened her mouth as her brows rose. But she didn't say anything as Eleri moved her attention to Kai. He sat next to Rina. His eyes were wary, wavering. Skepticism oozed from his rigid shoulders. Eleri whispered, "I couldn't live with myself if I didn't try."

An incessant tug in her chest nearly pulled her forward. It was urgent. And Kai's large eyes told her he felt it, too. It was as if this were the path they needed to go on. He stood and stepped toward her before squatting to her level. He studied her, his regard shifting across the expanse of her face, down toward her chest, then back up again.

The wind stilled, and after a moment of tense silence—Eleri holding her breath as he looked deep into her soul—he whispered back, "Okay."

"Kai!" Jaycen shouted. He stomped toward Kai and Eleri. Gripping Kai from the tattered collar of his tunic, Jaycen hauled him onto his feet and spun him around. Eye to eye now with his best friend. "What the fuck? We can't go back there! If he gets his hands on you, he'll . . . It'll be far worse than anything he ever did to you in the past. He'll *kill* you!"

"Jaycen—" Eleri said, standing as well with her palms raised.

Rina was monitoring the situation with sharp precision. She worried her lip between her teeth.

"You,"—Jaycen sliced his hardened stare toward Eleri—"shut your mouth."

"Hey!" Kai roared. He roughly shoved his friend away from him. Jaycen's grip slipped free as he stumbled back with rage-filled eyes. "Don't you dare talk to her like that."

Jaycen shoved his friend back. "She's dangerous, Kai! Open your eyes, Gods damn it. You've been nothing but reckless ever since she showed up. If your father doesn't kill you first, someone else will."

"Stop!" Rina bit out, stepping between the two. She shoved Jaycen to one side and pulled Kai to the other. Her outstretched arms trembled as she stood with a heaving chest and fire-filled eyes aimed at them. "Stop acting like fucking idiots! I know we're tense. Secrets were kept"—she looked at Kai—"and emotions are high." Rina turned her gaze toward Jaycen. "So, just . . . *stop*!"

Jaycen's dagger-like stare penetrated through Kai. His lips curled. "Why? Huh, Kai? Why didn't you tell me? Why would you keep the fact that your father is the cause of all of this from me? Why—"

"Because I was ashamed!" Kai yelled.

His skin transformed into a deep shade of red, and his veins bulged against his neck.

Jaycen scoffed and rolled his eyes. Eleri could see the anger pulsating within him. Pure rage.

Kai growled, then raised his voice again. "I feel like I don't even know who you are anymore, man. What the fuck happened to you? You're unrecognizable."

Something crumbled within Jaycen as Kai's words registered. Eleri saw him fall apart before her very eyes. The sight he was trying so hard to conceal shone for her as she studied him. A sight she could tell Kai didn't notice as he ground his teeth and shook his head.

"Everything I've ever done was for you," Jaycen whispered, stepping away from the man he'd known for most of his life.

Jaycen erected that hardened wall once more and concealed himself behind the mask Eleri was so used to seeing.

Rina opened her mouth to say something else, but Jaycen turned his back on them and stormed away. Kai did the same in the opposite direction. Eleri . . . Eleri merely stood there. Her arms were slack at her sides. Her mouth was agape.

What . . . What do I do?

She wanted to go after Kai to see if he was okay. She wanted to be that pillar for him, something to lean on when times got tough.

But perhaps she could talk to Jaycen. It felt like there was more to the hostility between the two men, but Eleri felt—no, she *knew*—she caused the widened chasm between them. She never wanted to get between their friendship. It ran deep . . . deeper than The Underworld springs.

Shifting her feet beneath her, Eleri itched to go in either direction.

But Rina spoke before she could and said, "Let them be. They just need to cool off."

"Has"—Eleri inhaled—"this happened before?"

Rina—with kind eyes shattered by pieces of worry—glanced at her, then shook her head. "No." Her voice faltered slightly. "Never in the years I've known them."

Something deflated in Eleri's chest. Guilt. Worry. Uncertainty.

It really was her fault, then.

KAI AND JAYCEN HADN'T spoken in two days. In fact, no one spoke—afraid to slice between the tension that engulfed the group completely, like a suffocating fog. As they trudged south through The Wasteland, it pulled taut at the air and weighed down upon their shoulders.

Eleri's lower lip trembled when she replayed their fight over and over on a loop inside her mind. So much guilt; it was practically consuming her. She didn't mean to cause such a rift so deep and wide she didn't know if it would ever mend again.

Even offering to go to the palace on her own so The Pack could finish their mission to eradicate the world of The Siren and The Wake didn't seem to help. She may not have been the most skilled when it came to fighting. But now that she had left her beast free to roam, she could channel her deep burning fire. However, Kai wouldn't have it.

"No," he had ground out, vehemently refusing with a firm shake of his head as the words barely left her mouth. *"I'm not leaving you."*

So now here they were . . . step after gruesome step through the tough terrain. Sand flicked toward the sky and settled beneath the lips of her boots. Biting wind lashed at her cheeks. The red sun beat down upon her tired body.

Together physically as a group. Emotionally, not so much.

Rina broke the silence as Eleri's steps slowed. "The palace sits on a tall hill in the distance. Small villages and neighborhoods sit below it. We should set up camp for the night to get some rest. By tomorrow morning, we'll reach the outer towns. And in the afternoon, the palace grounds."

Kai huffed and came to a halt. Eleri and Rina stopped their steps and stood at each of his sides. Jaycen stayed behind them. Eleri risked a glance at him. His gaze lingered on the large expanse of Kai's back. His nostrils flared, and his eyes shuddered.

"Cheers to our last night alive, I guess," he muttered before removing his bag from his shoulder and plopping down into the sand.

46

Kai

Kai was the perfect depiction of a marble statue as the others settled in for the night. Solid and still, looming powerfully over their makeshift campsite. His hands rested atop his hips; his gaze was locked in on the direction of their destination. Small beads of sweat rested in the divot just above his top lip, his heart pounding uncontrollably against his rib cage.

Tomorrow, they would be back at the palace. Tomorrow, he would step foot in his home . . . a home that stopped feeling like one as soon as his mother passed. Never had he wanted to be back in that shithole again. It was a place shrouded in darkness, tainted by his worst memories because of *him*. It was a place where his father beat and berated him. Where he lost a part of himself, where the once confident boy deteriorated into a man who felt useless and undeserving of love.

Kai's limbs trembled, insistent tingles running down his arms and settling into the tips of his fingers. His skin heated up, and his chest caved in under the weight of the suffocating heat radiating off his form.

The pace of his heartbeat ticked up. His muscles began to twitch uncontrollably. Panic.

Shit. I can't breathe . . . I can't—

Biting down harshly onto the inside of his cheek—forcing the feeling away as best as he could—Kai swayed slightly on his heels.

Get it together . . . Gods, Kai. Get a grip.

They couldn't see him like this . . . He couldn't be weak.

Hide it, for fuck's sake—

"Hey."

Her voice broke the debilitating panic like a smooth silk cloth gliding through his muddy thoughts. A beacon parting the cold haze surrounding him.

Eleri stepped up next to him, their shoulders in line. Those big blue pools saw right through him, worry swirling around the different hues as if she were staring into his soul entirely and penetrating his very being.

"In through your nose. Out through your mouth," she whispered only loud enough for him to hear.

She was so sure of herself, certainty rooting itself in each of her words. She'd done this before, recited those words to herself, he thought.

In through my nose . . . Out through my mouth.

Kai followed her instructions, his eyes never leaving her.

In and out, in and out he breathed until his heart slowed and the tingling sensation crawling under his skin disappeared. In and out, until his chest stopped caving in above his frantic breaths.

Something changed in him.

"Better?" she asked softly.

Nodding slowly, he took her in. Awe bloomed across his chest. She was beautiful. Inside and out, he learned over the time they had together.

Eleri flashed Kai a warm smile, and his heart swelled triple the size. In this moment, he knew he'd do anything for her. He'd face his father . . . He'd face more. Kai's lungs burned and heart pounded violently. This time for a different reason. It was as if it craved to get out from the confines of his chest. Because his heart no longer beat for him. It was hers completely, to do with it as she wished. "Thank you."

"For what?" Eleri's mouth pulled into a frown.

"For . . . being you."

A sharp inhalation filled Eleri's lungs. Her lower lip quivered, and a crease formed between her brows as she shook her head ever so slightly. "You haven't seen the rotten bits yet."

"I look forward to the day you show them to me." Kai leaned closer. "Because rotten or not, you are still you, and you are *everything*."

The air between them turned heavy. He wanted so badly to trace her bottom lip against her Witches' Mark and finally learn what she felt like. He needed to experience that once in his lifetime.

"We'll find the Witch." His voice was certain. "We will save her and maybe . . . Maybe she can rid you of your curse."

Kai would do anything for Eleri. *Anything.*

47

ELERI

THE SUN HAD LONG since set, and Eleri sat on watch quietly with her knees pulled up to her chest while the others slept. It was a nice way to clear her head. Her fingers dug into her shins, a dull pain striking through her still slightly swollen knuckles.

So much was changing . . . So much was happening.

Eleri couldn't help but get lost in the whirlwind spinning around her. Tomorrow she'd be storming into the palace, facing the Upper King, and hopefully freeing the Witch who had been held captive for so long.

Was she scared? Had she lost hope? Was . . . she even still alive?

With furrowed brows, questions swarmed her. So many unknowns about this woman and the situation she must have been forced into.

Did the Council of Priestesses know? Surely someone would've noticed one of their own was missing. They must've been distraught as they searched for her . . . right?

But Eleri didn't know as much as she should about her Witch relatives on the eastern side of The Underworld. Every fifteen years, the rare Shadowed Lunar Eclipse was celebrated across the covens. Her mother told her that, in her long life, she had never missed a celebration. Eleri went to one long ago with her mother. She was only five and didn't remember a thing.

The year of The Darkest Day was supposed to be the next time she got to go again. She hadn't been looking forward to it. By then, her disdain for the Witches was already rooted deep into her being, starting with the wary looks other kids sent her way when she was growing up.

Right now, she wished she paid more attention to her mother's stories about their kind. Eleri's little beast purred and rubbed against her mind as if it was trying to soothe her.

The covens and priestesses must've searched for this lost Witch. They *must've.*

Of its own accord, Eleri's gaze slid toward Kai and his sleeping form. He seemed so confident that the Witch could help them, help *her.*

Eleri felt the corner of her mouth lift toward the sky as if the smog-hidden moon held a string connected to it, tugging it upward. Warmth and . . . happiness—*actual happiness*—spread across her chest and down to the tips of her toes.

Happi—

A shift broke the quiet solitude of the night. Jaycen rolled over onto his back and let out a long sigh, opening his eyes and staring up into the darkened sky.

With bated breath, Eleri watched the man who despised her, unsure whether to acknowledge him as awake or ignore him as he'd ignored her since they met.

Always second-guessing herself . . . always walking on eggshells when he was around.

She had long since accepted that she'd never know why. Yet her mouth betrayed her. Still, she extended that olive branch he'd rejected time and time again.

"Can't sleep?" Eleri mumbled.

Turning his head toward her and pressing his cheek against his leather bag, he simply stared at her. Unblinking. Unresponsive.

He wouldn't say anything. Despite her best efforts. *Why can't I just let it go?*

Removing her gaze from his, Eleri stared into the vast darkness before her. The heat of his stare remained on her skin. But soon enough, he would twist his head back around and pretend she didn't exist, just as it'd been for the majority of their time together.

"Just a lot on my mind," Jaycen muttered.

Eleri flinched from the sound of his voice, whipping her head back around to face him just as he sat up. He hastily brushed the sand off his body before bending his knees and resting his forearms atop them.

He answered. He actually answered.

Rolling out his neck and twisting his back until they cracked, Jaycen adjusted himself before settling back into a more comfortable position.

"What's on your mind?"

Eleri was timid when she asked. She didn't want to pry, didn't want to push him into silence once more. But the way he was looking at Kai with so much hidden emotion, she couldn't help but be curious.

A few breaths passed, nothing but the rushing breeze between them. It caressed the tips of her ears and ran through her knotted strands of hair. Then, he exhaled and answered. "You. Us." A humorless laugh rolled off his tongue, singeing the space around them. "I was—*we* were fine before you came along."

Although not surprising in the least, the words hurt. It felt as if a small throwing knife, like those Aeric used, wedged itself between the crevices of her heart. It hurt more than she'd like to admit. "I know—"

"Don't," Jaycen huffed. He shook his head ever so slightly and sucked on a tooth as his stare turned from his best friend to her. "Don't just agree with me now that you seem to have infiltrated our family. I see right through you."

His leer pinned Eleri in place.

Eleri's jaw flexed. "And what is it that you see?"

"A creature who's using us for her own gain . . . using our protection to get what she wants before she disappears forever."

She was at a complete loss. That *had* been what she was doing, but not anymore.

"Why are you so cold?" she asked. "You have what I've always wanted. People around you who accept you for who you are, no matter how cruel you may be. I—I just don't get it."

The tension in Jaycen's shoulders deflated slightly; his head bowed low. In a hushed voice, he whispered, "I . . . didn't used to be like this."

Eleri raised her eyebrows, shock morphing her face into stark lines. As he took in her expression, Jaycen chuckled. "Believe it or not, I used to be pleasant."

"You're still plea—"

"There you go again, agreeing even if it isn't true." Jaycen's features hardened minutely, barely noticeable . . . but still present. "You're not one to lie, I've learned, so don't start now."

Eleri shut her mouth tightly and nodded. Jaycen averted his gaze, his eyes falling back on Kai's sleeping form. A heavy silence fell upon them. Eleri's heart trembled under the weight of this conversation. Never had she spoken with Jaycen to this extent. Never had she had the opportunity to.

"Can I . . ." She shouldn't. But the need to know pushed the question out before she could swallow down the words. "Can I ask what changed?"

Silence shrouded them once more.

Jaycen chewed on the inside of his cheek, most likely weighing whether he should open up. Then a sharp sigh escaped him. "Fuck it. We're all going to die tomorrow anyway."

Eleri opened her mouth to say something, to encourage Jaycen—and herself—that what he said wasn't true. But he didn't give her the chance. "Before The Darkest Day, I was just the son of a palace groundskeeper. I used to go with my father to work sometimes when his savings ran out, and we could no longer afford my tutor. That was when I met Kai. And over the years, we became inseparable."

Jaycen straightened his spine as he remained looking at his friend. "Those years were the best of my life. I'd get to play with him in the forest and explore the palace. It even got to the point where I was with him so much, his tutors started teaching me. My father never had to worry about money or my education again thanks to Kai. Then I turned seventeen." Sadness tinted the words. "And I . . . fuck, okay."

Jaycen's fingers flexed against his shins, and a shaky breath fumbled past his chapped lips. "Kai means everything to me . . . when I was seventeen, I began seeing him in a new light. I . . . thought I loved him. I *did* love him, and I still do. But not how I used to. Back then, this realization felt monumental. I think the feelings came on gradually. I'm not sure. But I vividly remember watching him sitting near a small pond as the sun illuminated him one day while my father waited for his duties and thinking I was going to marry him."

A small, sorrowful chortle brushed through Jaycen's lips. "About six months into this infatuation, I realized he would never love me the way I loved him. I knew I had liked men for most of my life but knowing the man I wanted more than anything, didn't want me back, hurt. It was my first taste of rejection. Naïvely, I thought that if I could push my feelings down and stay his best friend, everything would be fine."

Jaycen's voice rose, and Rina shifted, mumbling in her sleep and cutting off his story. Eleri's eyes sliced to her. Jaycen sat silently, frozen in place. They waited until she settled back into slumber once again. A collective breath hung between Eleri and Jaycen, and as if in sync, their regard slid to the very man they were discussing. Kai slept soundly, lips smacking twice before resting into a peaceful smile.

He really is beautiful.

Jaycen softly chuckled. He must have had the same thought.

Looking around to make sure the others were truly sound asleep, Jaycen turned toward her. Clearing his throat, he rubbed his neck. "Right . . . where was I?"

Perhaps it was a hypothetical question.

"You thought it would be fine . . ."

Jaycen raised his brow before rolling his eyes. A look that told her it was, in fact, hypothetical. He wasn't looking for an answer. After a beat, he exhaled and quickly nodded. "Right. And it was fine . . . until it wasn't. I, uh, I had trouble dealing with the feeling of not being wanted. As if I didn't *deserve* to be wanted. I started to spiral a little. Everything started to feel like it was . . . too much. Too much effort. Too much pain. Just . . . *too much.* That one little seed burrowed itself into my mind and sprouted into an uncontrollable, thorny vine that poked and prodded me."

Absentmindedly, Jaycen traced a finger across the shifting sand they were sitting in. He was doodling a person.

"I started closing myself off to those around me. Not on purpose . . . it just kind of happened. But soon, those malicious feelings made me feel hopeless, *helpless.* It wasn't even about Kai anymore either. Not really. After a little while, I couldn't even see myself with him. Even if he *did* like men. But still, I felt undeserving of anything good. It got to a point where it was so bad that I . . . *Gods,*" Jaycen breathed out, "I've never said this out loud. And why I'm telling you, I have no idea."

Another deep breath in. He held it for a few seconds, then he blew it out. Eleri let him get his bearings. This was hard for him. That much was evident. She would give Jaycen the time he needed to speak his truth. And if he decided he didn't want to share any more, then that was okay, too. He bore so much for her.

"I—" Jaycen forced a dry swallow down to clear the airway of his throat. Another minute passed before he looked as if he was ready again. "I had planned on taking my own life. I . . . woke up the morning of The Darkest Day with this new feeling. A feeling I had never felt before. I was resolute. I was confident. I decided I was going to journey to the river, tie rocks around my ankles, and jump in."

A ragged inhale.

Eleri's eyes watered, and her fingers flexed, itching to comfort the very man who wished they had never met. *Oh, Jaycen . . .*

"I—I was just on my way to say goodbye to Kai when the curse came." Jaycen's eyes were squeezed shut tightly, small wrinkles sprouting out the corners. "And that sight . . . I felt like that was the answer to my prayers, like The Son had been listening. I stopped in my tracks and gladly welcomed the black cloud of smoke with open arms. And then . . . Kai came in and saved the day. Saved me when I hadn't asked to be. He grabbed me by the collar and practically hauled me onto that horse and dragged me to safety.

"For a long time, I resented him for that. I was *ready* . . . and he took that choice away from me. I . . . I—I don't want to be here anymore." Jaycen's voice cracked as he grabbed a handful of sand, ruining his drawing. The skin of his knuckles stretched over the bones. "I don't want to be in this world . . . *alive*. But I am. Kai made sure that happened."

A cold weight fell from Eleri's heart into her gut. She had no words. Nothing would come close to what he needed, or even wanted.

"Jaycen . . . I'm so—"

"Don't pity me." He growled out, releasing his fistful of sand, and turned to look at her with heated eyes.

"I don't." Eleri didn't hesitate. And Jaycen's hardened gaze crumbled. "You'll be all right, Jaycen. Maybe you'll find a reason to happily live again. I hope you do. But that darkness you feel, it's okay to actually *feel* it, you know."

A gentle caress from her inner beast, as if it were proud of the words Eleri spoke. With a contented sigh, it nestled against the darkness of her being.

Eleri continued, "Despite it all, you still wake up every day and help those who need it. You're making a positive difference in this world. I hope one day you can be proud of that."

Eleri sent her best smile to Jaycen, which was all she could offer him.

Jaycen shook his head. "I could never be proud of that."

"Why not?" Eleri asked with raised eyebrows.

"I . . . don't truly care about anyone in this world besides Kai. I would do anything for him. He wanted to save people. So, I followed, making sure he was okay. That's why I'm going to that Gods-forsaken palace that should've been the first to crumble after the blast. Everything I do is for him. I'd happily die, if it meant he was safe."

As Eleri stared deeply into Jaycen's eyes, she realized she cared for him—for his well-being—even if he'd never given her a reason to.

Jaycen huffed out a hollow laugh. "Who would have thought you'd be the one I shared my deepest secrets with? But sitting here, talking to you, Eleri, properly for the first time since we found you . . . No wonder Kai's head over heels for you. If things were different—if I was different—I probably would be, too."

Eleri shook her head vehemently. "Jaycen, you don't need to be different. You just need to be you."

48

JAYCEN

A SLIVER OF HEAT trickled across Jaycen's skin as the sun rose. It barely breached the horizon, yet its rays brutally battered down against him and his sleeping companions. Envy pushed at his gut as he watched them.

He didn't sleep a wink last night. Too much was on his mind. Too much he had to sift through after confessing everything to Eleri and offering to take over watch. For him, it was easier to say those things to someone he didn't necessarily like. It was terrifying and yet, a small, barely there part of him celebrated, knowing he no longer had to carry that burden alone.

"Hmmm." Eleri stirred, rolling onto her side facing away from him toward Kai.

Kai's eyes fluttered behind his eyelids and his mouth ticked up into a slight smile as if he felt her very soul calling to him even in their sleep.

Jaycen stared at them. And as their chests rose and fell in sync with one another, resolution engulfed him. His purpose after The Darkest Day had always been to watch over Kai. And now, after speaking with Eleri last night, he thought she could carry that torch for him.

Jaycen would ensure Kai was safe as they entered the palace and faced the man responsible for killing so many of his own people. He would put himself in harm's way, to make sure Kai . . . and Rina and Eleri came out of it alive. And he, too, would come out of it alive. Only then would he journey to the river to finish what he couldn't start and take his final breath, feeling like he was finally enough.

"Hey . . ." Rina grumbled to his left.

She slowly sat up, rubbing the back of her hand against her eyes.

"Hey," he muttered.

"How are you feeling, Jaycen?" She trained her puffy, sleep-filled eyes on him. "You seem different this morning."

Jaycen's heart stuttered, increasing in speed. "Oh?"

"Yeah, I don't know. You just seem different, lighter. There's a sheen to your eyes I've never seen before."

Resolution.

"Huh." He feigned confusion. "Not sure why. Nothing's changed since you went to bed, Rina."

But everything had changed. She didn't need to know, didn't need to worry about him. Soon, he would be released from the inadequacy he felt for so long.

"Good morning."

A tired voice pulled at him.

His eyes landed on Eleri, whose hair was knotted and stuck to her cheek. She was looking at him. Clarity shone through her and radiated toward him and him only.

Understanding.

She sent him a soft smile as Kai sat up with a groan, stretching his arms over his head and twisting his spine before settling back toward him. Kai studied Jaycen, the two staring into what seemed to be the deepest parts of each other without truly *seeing*. A rigid strain pulled between them; the air turned taut.

Say something. Say anything. Fix what's been broken before you leave for good.

Jaycen opened his mouth. All words rammed themselves into the back of his throat, refusing to spill free. What was he to say anyway? *I'm seething. I'm scared. I'm sorry.*

All of it and none of it seemed right.

Perhaps he shouldn't say anything. Perhaps he should stay quiet and let Kai believe what he wanted about him. That would be better than knowing the truth.

"We should get going," Jaycen mumbled, tearing his gaze away from Kai and letting it fall.

The sand swayed around his legs as the wind picked up.

Fucking coward.

Kai cleared his throat. "Yeah . . . let's pack up camp and leave in ten."

Kai and Rina stood to rummage through their packs. Tears burned Jaycen's nostrils as he flexed his jaw, crushing down upon his teeth.

One long breath in. Then, another.

Jaycen's lungs constricted, but he pushed it away. Pushed the sorrow prodding against his chest and the anxiety weighing down his gut.

"Jaycen." A soft whisper. Snapping his eyes up toward the sound, he was met with Eleri. Her lips lifted into a smile. "You can do this. Things will get better, and in time, you will heal. Be happy, even. I hope I get to see that version of you one day."

Jaycen gulped and glanced away from the princess.

49

Kai

Kai's heart stuttered as they approached the first village on the outskirts of the palace grounds. It was rundown. Crumbling brick homes lined the dust-covered walkways. Soot-stained fences leaned sideways, warped from either the curse itself or the lashing winds of The Wasteland.

Anxiety pumped through his veins; his palms were sticky with sweat. Dread and fatigue weighed down on his eyelids as he struggled to keep them open. He barely slept last night. Only a few hours while Eleri was still keeping watch. His mind wouldn't slow enough to reach that deep slumber for more than that before he was wrenched back into consciousness.

Keeping to the shadows, Kai and the others stayed hidden from prying eyes. No villagers would look their way anyway, all too focused on simply surviving their own fucked up lives. However, palace guards patrolled the area, protecting their king . . . protecting him from starving and dying people. But protecting, nonetheless.

A coward. That was what his father was. And Kai was a product of that coward inside those jade walls.

"Worthless. Inferior. Flawed. Better off dead."

Kai clenched his jaw and curled his fingers until his nails dug into his palms. He tried to banish the voice of his father prodding into his mind, obstructing his focus on what needed to be done.

"Worthless. Inferior. Flawed. Better off dead."

But it was too loud. His father's voice pierced through everything else. Harsh names, belittling comments, raging screams that nearly busted his eardrums.

"You don't have to do this, Kai." Rina stepped up next to him and stilled. She placed her hand on his shoulder blade in an attempt to ground him and his subtle harsh breaths.

Eleri and Jaycen rounded the corner into the alley he and Rina had entered moments ago. Jaycen's head was on a swivel, making sure an incident like Mountmend didn't happen again. Kai would trust him with his life despite everything going on between them.

He needed to speak with him. Clear the air so things could get back to normal. He vowed that would be the first thing he did once they rescued the Witch and left the Upper Palace behind them once and for all.

Kai couldn't help but notice the subtlest of changes within Jaycen as he and Eleri approached them. A lightness in each step that Kai hadn't seen in years, as if whatever was weighing him down had lessened if only just a little. The spark in his eyes was like a beacon, a breath of fresh air Kai hadn't had in five years.

His eyes trailed from his friend toward Eleri, whose gaze was already locked onto his. Intense and unwavering, before they softened from underneath her hood and she sent him the most devastating smile. It was like she knew what he was thinking . . . like she could feel the anxiety coursing through his entire being. Just knowing that eased him slightly.

Kai turned back to Rina. "I'm fine. Truly. I want to do this. For her." He paused. "And for me. I'm going to have to face him sooner or later."

Rina watched him closely, looking for any signs he was lying for the sake of the team. She chewed on her bottom lip, and her eyebrows pulled together. There was conflict beneath her features, but he saw her steadfast belief in him push it away. Trusting him just as he trusted her, Rina simply nodded. And Kai was grateful she didn't prod.

"Why'd we stop?" Jaycen asked, alertness lacing his question as his eyes darted from side to side.

"Just needed to take a second." Kai gave him a small reassuring smile before he found himself gazing at Eleri once more. And the look she sent him . . . it shook him to his very soul. Gods, she was everything to him. "Let's keep moving."

They weaved through the first surrounding village, which had once been a quaint little town full of straw roofs and sparse structures. To Kai's surprise, it held up better than he imagined. Traveling through it, however, was a slow process. They stopped and started, taking breaks for breathers as they steadily climbed the hill that led to the palace.

Once they entered the second village, the ruins were more prominent. Crumbled structures loomed over piles of rubble, and trash was strewn about. They hid from passersby when they came too close and even stopped to drink a few handfuls of water from a stream between two decrepit buildings.

Then, they got to the third village, the one closest to the palace grounds. Jaycen's old home. Slowly, they gained ground as they stuck to the alleyways and shadows, until they could finally see the gates to the palace.

What used to gleam a bright, angelic gold glow was now dull and rusted. Two guards stood tall on either side. They were thin, their armor hanging off their limbs and swallowing them whole. With sunken, bruised eyes, they stared ahead. No emotion behind their stance. Walking corpses. Why they had yet to defect, Kai had no idea.

"What are you doing?" A small voice squeaked out near his hip.

Kai's heart leaped out of his chest. Jaycen whipped his body toward the sound. Rina jumped and whispered a curse. And Eleri took a giant step back, her brows furrowed as she shook her head as if ridding herself of whatever thoughts were distracting her enough not to hear their intruder.

Looking down, he was met with one light blue, nearly teal eye and another white, foggy eye that drooped. A boy with sandy brown hair and freckles across his dark tan cheeks stared back at them. Part of his lips were missing, revealing rows of yellow teeth.

Deformed from the curse.

This little boy appeared no older than four. His mother, whoever she was, must have been hit hard on The Darkest Day. Kai's heart clenched.

"Hm?" the child prodded again, leaning forward and swaying on his heels. "What are you doing?"

Opening his mouth to say anything to get the child to turn away from them, Kai was cut off just as Rina's kind lilting voice pulled at the boy's short attention.

"Kid, want a bar of soap?"

THE COOL COVER OF shadows concealed Kai and the others as the little boy—Hendery—approached the looming gate and tired guards. Kai leaned forward slightly and observed with keen eyes. A square lump protruded from Hendery's tattered pocket—Rina's prized soap bar.

With confidence only a child who grew up in such a world could have, he sauntered right up to one of the guards. His head was held high; not even a glimmer of fear or hesitation flickered across his features as he somehow looked down upon the two men.

Kai couldn't hear what the guard said, but one look at Eleri's concentrated face—no alarm or panic setting in—and he knew it was pleasant so far. The little boy was the face of innocence, swaying back and forth on his toes and heels. His hands were behind his back.

"He's good," Eleri whispered, eyes trained on the child as well.

Rina quickly turned her gaze toward Eleri before watching the guards once more. "What's he saying?"

"He's asking about a piece of their armor . . . wants to know if he can try it on," she muttered.

However, the guards' initial smiles sank into annoyance. Their wrinkles became deeper, and their eyes rolled. What was once a nice brief encounter that distracted them from their mundane post was turning into a nuisance. One of the guards snarled. Kai thought a gruff "beat it" was said.

But the kid didn't flinch. He simply continued to speak, pointing at things behind them and sending them innocent smiles. Then, just as one of the guards took a step toward Hendery, he struck.

Small hands lunged forward and snatched a ring of keys hooked onto the man's waist before bolting down the cracked cobblestone pathway and disappearing between the partially erect buildings.

"Hey!" the guard on the left shouted while barreling after Hendery.

The other guard sighed, fatigue slumping his shoulders. Closing his eyes briefly, he exhaled loudly before racing after his companion. "Kids are assholes . . ."

Several seconds passed. Waiting in the shadows, they didn't move, fixed to their spots as they listened intently until they no longer heard the shouts of the first guard. Then, Kai, Rina, and Jaycen all turned their attention to Eleri.

Concentrating, her lips puckered before pressing into a line, and a crease formed between her brows. She shut her eyes, exhaling with bated breath. She looked adorable. Small face surrounded by unruly orange hair. With a quick and determined nod, Eleri opened her eyes.

"Hendery is safe, and the guards are far enough away now," she muttered, swiftly looking at them.

Jaycen nodded. He glanced at Eleri, then Rina, before landing on Kai. "Okay, let's go then."

Sticking to the sparse shade, they slunk their way through a gaping crack in the stone wall near the gate and wound their way across the grounds and toward the looming palace. Kai's heart began to pick up speed again as they closed in on what was once his home.

It was rundown now. The white-tiled roof was missing in several parts. Grime coated each tile, black and green slime hardened and crusted over from the sun. Several slates of jade that made up what were once the elaborately carved walls were missing. And dusty piles of broken, crumbling debris sat nearby.

It was so different from the last time he was here. Yet it felt the same. The heaviness in the air surrounding the palace crept in on him. Kai felt as if he was back to being the fourteen-year-old boy who was hit for the first time, and his steps faltered.

Thinking of Eleri, he repeated her words back to himself silently. *In through your nose. Out through your mouth.*

A deep inhale in. Kai held it for three long seconds before blowing it out. Once more, he sucked in a large breath. Once he released it, he continued on his path. *Okay, Kai. You can do this.*

They passed the shell of a large bush. Nothing but bleak twigs and stems protruded from the ground. Kai and Jaycen used to use it as a hiding place when they were small enough. Glancing at his friend, he was surprised to see Jaycen looking back at him as if they both remembered this insignificant bush and mourned what was left.

Silently clearing his throat, Kai led the others toward a hole in the wall of what used to be a parlor. Peeking his head through the crumbling structure, he looked around inside and made sure the coast was clear. Then he turned to his companions and nodded before stepping through the hole into what had once been his own personal hell.

Winding the others through the curving hallways, Kai channeled Jaycen's elite focus and level-headedness he saw when they came in contact with a threat. Picturesque art that used to give the large walls life was gone. Shards of golden frames were broken and scattered across the ground. The once pristine jade floors were hidden by sand and soot. He couldn't help but think the black streaks and scuffs were symbolic. A picture of what lay inside his father's heart.

No one uttered a word . . . too afraid to now that they were here. On occasion, handfuls of guards turned the corner, and Kai watched them pass from hidden nooks in the hallways. With each corner turned, fear gradually twisted Kai's features until he came to a stop at the foot of the dark wooden stairs.

His father's study positioned high above them cast a threatening impression upon them. It was where the king used to spend the majority of his days before. It was where Kai saw him cast that wretched curse from behind the slightly ajar door. It was where the Witch had been chained up.

This was where his father would be. Kai was confident of that.

But that confidence waxed and waned like the moon he missed so much. He knew his father was up there. He could feel it as if some old, deep-rooted connection to the man who he once looked up to was present.

He didn't move. He didn't think he could.

How he wished he could clasp Eleri's hand in his to calm himself. While his bravery faltered, he knew her touch—the feel of her skin pressed against his—would solve nearly everything.

"He's not alone," Eleri whispered to no one in particular. Her eyes were trained on the door atop the stairs. "Several people are up there."

A frustrated groan echoed down the stairwell before something shattered.

"What *was* it?" the king roared.

Kai froze at the sound just as he set one boot atop the first stair.

The king. His father. His abuser.

Hesitation and terror wrapped around him in a smothering embrace. Kai's joints locked, and his muscles trembled. The others lingered behind him, unwilling to say anything . . . not wanting to spook him. They gave him time, and he had never felt so thankful.

Dear Great Son, Kai silently prayed to himself. It was the first time he'd done so in a long time. *Please give me the strength to do this. Please guide me as I face him.*

Kai waited, searching for any sign The Son was with him . . . yearning for the bravery he needed to fill him up. But nothing happened. He still felt like the terrified teenager he once was. His prayer went unanswered.

Maybe Eleri is right. Perhaps The Trinity doesn't exist.

With a ragged breath in, Kai tried to muster the courage The Son denied him. He tried to take that next step, a step that would change everything. But he couldn't seem to do it. He tried and tried, silently screaming at himself to stop being a pussy and just *do it*. His body just wouldn't listen.

Move . . . Gods damn it, move!

Suddenly, he felt her presence . . . like a calm wave blanketing over him and extinguishing every minute drop of anxiety coursing through his body in the blink of an eye. A feeling The Son was supposed to provide him.

"Thank you for getting me this far, Kai." Her soft voice penetrated his stupor.

Turning his head away from the frightening entrance toward her, he took her in. Eleri's eyes were glossy as she stared straight ahead. After a few breaths, she then turned to meet his gaze. Admiration wove through the crystal blue chasms that made up her irises.

"You don't need to go in," she whispered. Eleri's serene smile was kind and understanding. "You shouldn't have to face your past just for me."

Kai's chest heaved, and his heart beat rapidly. Barely moving, he attempted to shake his head, ridding her words from hanging in the air. "I would do anything for you, Eleri."

"But—"

"No." Kai was firm this time, causing her gaze to falter. "No buts. Nothing will change that. It is fact, absolute. Do not ever doubt that."

The world stilled around them. Rina and Jaycen long forgotten as Kai stared into her overwhelmed state of knotted hair and dirty cheeks. Only she existed in this moment. It was then that he realized he could conquer any obstacle that came his way . . . As long as she was by his side.

50

Eleri

Brown eyes seared into Eleri. The way Kai gazed at her . . . Goose-bumps covered her skin, and her stomach flipped like never before. He had this ability that made it feel like it was just the two of them—

Jaycen cleared his throat softly. The sound was like a vacuum, sucking her out of the hypnotizing trance she so easily fell into when it came to Kai. Slowly blinking, she found her bearings once again.

"Okay, then," she breathed.

She tried to sound like a leader—the one who declared she go on this mission in the first place—but her words wavered.

You can do this, Eleri, she told herself, her little beast nodding. *Do not sit back any longer. Be brave. Fight for what's right. Be like Rina . . . and Jaycen. Be like Kai.*

With a single nod to herself, Eleri straightened her spine before releasing a shaky breath and taking the first step. She tiptoed around Kai's frozen form and ascended the stairs.

Steps creaked beneath her boots. Each one was louder than the next, the broken shackles still secured around her ankles, clinking with the movement.

"One step at a time," she mumbled. "For *her.*"

Each step was like a beat to her pattering heart. Each stair brought her closer to, perhaps, a new chapter in her life, one of learning how to accept who she was. She would bring this Witch home and start anew. And she dreamed, just like Kai hopefully declared, that new life would be one of soft caresses and stolen kisses.

Once face-to-face with the door, Eleri noticed the rotted wood that split the ornate carvings in two and the rusted, warped hinges. She couldn't help but wonder what this door—the entire palace, really—would have appeared like as it was intended. She was sure it was once beautiful, just as her home had been.

"I've got it," Jaycen said, stepping around her motionless frame. He stood, fists clenched and back straight, and took a deep centering breath in before kicking the fragile door open.

One guard was stationed near the door. He jumped at their arrival, immediately reaching for the baton at his hip. Two other guards were posted in the middle near the swaying Upper King.

The older man's back was hunched, and he was breathing heavily as he stood beneath the gaping hole in the ceiling. His eyes were trained on the toppled iron cauldron, similar to the one her mother had. Disdain curled his lips as he stared at the empty pot. He looked thin and sickly. Tan skin that Eleri imagined was once just like Kai's was ashen and gray.

Just behind him, another guard stood tall within arm's reach of the Witch Eleri so desperately wanted to save. The pale woman sat against the wall. She looked better than Eleri had been expecting.

But she still looked weak. Her frail wrists were chained above her head, and her eyes were closed. Her black hair hung limply over her shoulders. Her brows knotted together; her small frame rose and fell as steady breaths whooshed out.

Eleri felt her creature erupt into an inferno at the sight, whipping around as the flames licked her soul. And unlike so many other instances, Eleri welcomed it.

The guard stationed closest to the door bellowed out a war cry so loud it stabbed Eleri's eardrums before he charged toward them. She ducked, dodging the attack. His swinging fist missed her head and barreled into

Jaycen's chest, causing him to fall to his knees with a grunt. Then, all hell broke loose. Kai didn't miss a beat. He wrenched the guard's fist free from Jaycen's tunic and twisted it around until the man collapsed, mirroring what had just happened to Jaycen.

The others jumped into action. Rina weaved around Eleri and met another guard one-on-one. Jaycen got back on his feet and placed himself between the first guard and Kai. Fists flew; boots kicked. Grunts and hits filled the air.

Eleri's eyes, however, were trained on the king, who was standing unnervingly still in the background with a vacant gaze and on the Witch, whose head whipped around just as her beast roared within. Large dark eyes widened for a split second when she spotted Eleri. Then, the king turned his head and sent her a nasty grin. Yellow teeth jutted behind paper-thin, crusted lips.

Eleri's flesh tightened, and her hearing warped. Only one word echoed through the chasm in her mind: *burn*. For what he did to their realms. For what he did to the innocent woman chained to the wall like a display. For what he did to Kai.

The chaos in the room was nothing but a dull drum, like a gnat buzzing in her ear. People were thrown into walls, vases shattered . . . it was nothing compared to the beat of her heart. A heavy *thump, thump, thump* like a gong leading an army of soldiers to battle, in sync with each step she took toward the back of the room.

The guard keeping a watchful eye on the Witch noted her calm approach and charged toward her. Focusing on the unleashed fire in her gut—her fearless heritage she never let herself experience—Eleri gripped it until the blaze tripled in size.

She would not cower. She could not.

Burn.

Close enough to feel the guard's heady breath caress her face, Eleri saw him grip his blade.

Burn.

She reached out, nails on display like she donned the very claws her beast sharpened within.

Burn.

Then, her palm touched the bend in his elbow. His skin disintegrated beneath it, crumbling away into a scorching blanket of ash.

Burn.

He screamed, falling and writhing in pain. And through his piercing yelps, Eleri barely registered the quiet. The fighting paused before quickly starting up again. Through it all, her eyes and resolve never wavered.

The king stood as still as stone as she approached. His eyes remained cold and empty as he stared at her. Not a single hint of terror traced over the thin lines in his skin.

For them. For her. For him.

Eleri's arm felt laden as it floated forward. Time slowed. Brushing her fingers against the king's chest before firmly placing her palm against it with more force, she waited for the fire within her veins to scorch him alive.

Nothing happened.

Eleri pushed against his chest with more force—harder and desperate—urging her curse to take him as it had taken others before. Just as it had with Merrin.

The Upper King didn't burn.

"Gods . . ." someone behind Eleri murmured, muffled beneath the pounding in her ears.

Acutely aware that the fighting had stopped once more, Eleri stared into the king's eyes. It was like they were pulling her in, ensnaring her, as if he'd been waiting for this moment from the beginning.

Like calls to like, her beast gasped.

"Eleri . . ."

It was Kai's voice behind her—soft and hesitant—as he took a step toward her.

But the tail end of her name faded as black smoke—inky like spilled oil in a river—filled her vision. It was a welcoming feeling. A cold rush enveloped her. She felt as if she were suspended in the air, thick darkness holding her consciousness aloft.

There was a sense of safety in the void she was in. But after a moment, as the darkness dissipated at the edges of her vision, that serenity shattered into sharp shards. *He's here.* The Upper King was sitting down in the middle of what looked to be a completely white room, cross-legged with his eyes closed. Surrounded by light, he rested his palms atop his knees and breathed out a soft sigh. He looked young here, unmarred from the last five years as if he were decades younger than he should be.

"What's happening?" She didn't mean to make her presence known. The words simply slid out before she could swallow them whole. "Where am I?"

The king opened his eyes. Brown—the same brown, almond-shaped eyes as Kai's—met blue. "Ah . . ." He sighed with a small smile. "A child of The Underworld. Sit. Tell me, what is your name?"

Eleri was rooted to the pristine white floor, rippling like a shallow puddle with every shift of her feet. This place . . . wherever she was . . . calmed her despite the grip she had on her anger. The Upper King simply smiled at her, waiting for her to decide. She didn't sit, but she did answer.

"E-Eleri. Eleri Fos." Subtly cringing away from the hesitancy in her voice, Eleri tried to straighten her spine.

The king's smile widened now, rows of nearly perfect teeth glinting under the natural brightness surrounding them. His heartbeat thrummed strongly around her, so different from the beat she heard in the study. "The princess . . . here in The Upperworld. Have you come to do what I failed to do all those years ago?"

Eleri had yet to move. Her spine was tall, and her jaw was clenched. But curiosity gripped her, pulling her next question free. "What . . . what did you fail to do?"

The Upper King smiled again and stood. A gesture to meet her halfway. His knees cracked as they straightened out, and a groan spilled through his plush lips. It sounded so Human, she faltered. So unlike what a monster should sound like. He stepped toward her. Eleri stepped back. His smile turned sad, wilting like a dehydrated flower. "Unite the realms, just as the Fae and Witches had done Beneath. I . . . had hoped to bring the two lands together to live in prosperity. It was my love's dying wish."

Her beast roared and its fire flared once more, pushing through the tranquility this place blanketed over her. The audacity of this man—this *bastard*—to hide behind a martyred façade. Eleri couldn't contain the fury that burned within her veins. "So, you—*what?* Capture a Witch? Chain her up? Hold her captive to do your bidding? You abuse your son and leave your people out to die? You didn't want to unite us. You wanted to destroy us. All of us. You're *sick*."

The king's shoulders slumped as if a weight pulled them down. "It must look that way to you, doesn't it?" He shared another sad smile, the corners of his lips barely lifting now. "I love my people. I just wanted the best for them—"

A flash momentarily blinded Eleri, like the crack of a whip within her skull. She saw the room she was once in, the king's study. Bodies lay unconscious on the ground. The Pack and the Witch were frozen, staring at her and the king, motionless.

"My . . . my son . . ." The king whispered as if he saw the same thing she did.

Eleri stumbled back. The black smoke once held at bay leaked into her vision, slowly creeping closer and closer until the weight of it closed in. A strangled sound escaped her quickly closing throat, ripping through her esophagus.

I-I'm choking!

"You must go, Eleri Fos!" The Upper King took another step toward her, his palms gripping her shoulders as his head swiveled from side to side. Panic twisted his face. "Something has shifted. Her sight is set on you now. *You* are the catalyst in what's to come. *Go!*"

His frightened yell terrified Eleri, shaking her down to her core. His grip on her released, and she stumbled backward again. The smoke . . . It was suffocating now, wafting around her and slithering down her throat agonizingly slow.

What's happening? What does he mean? I-I'm . . . I'm scared.

The Upper King's voice prodded through the darkness creeping in. It was faint now as he called out one last time. "Even if you don't believe me . . . when all of this is over, tell my son that I love him. And I will atone for all the pain I caused . . ."

Then, like a cobra—fast and sudden and *deadly*—the swirling smoke struck. Like a snake's fangs, it sank into her skin. And she screamed.

51

Kai

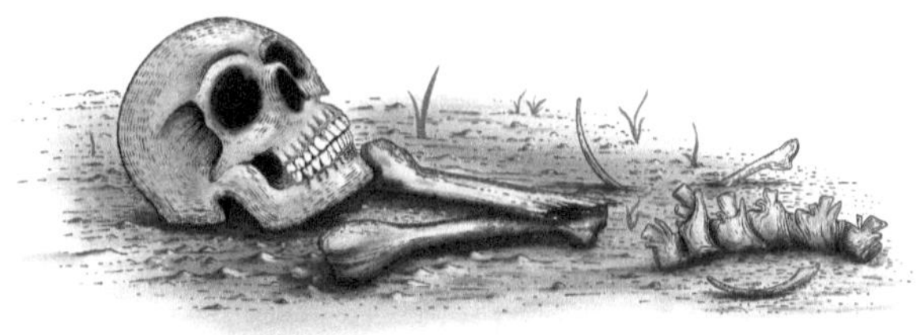

Like talons ripping and shredding his very soul, Eleri's guttural shriek was the worst Kai had ever heard.

Something's wrong. Something's entirely wrong.

He stepped over one of the unconscious guards on the floor. He needed to be near her, needed to see if she was all right.

"Get to her, Kai! Now!" The voice in his head made him stumble. It wasn't the woman he'd come to expect. It sounded like . . .

Father?

A split second passed as he waited for that deep timbre to return. It didn't, and Eleri screamed again.

"Fuck!" he growled.

You're wasting time, you idiot, he said to himself.

Another frantic step in her direction. Kai hopped over a discarded sword and lunged toward his princess. Then, a sound that chilled him to his bones rang out and stopped him in his tracks.

Kai turned to face the Witch as she cackled from her spot at the wall. Her eyes were alight, madness shining through. Tilting her head back, the Witch's mouth hung open as the shrill laugh trailed into a quiet giggle. "You won't get her back . . ."

Her voice was sultry in a sickening way. Raspy. Alluring. A chill crept along the back of Kai's skull at the sound. Changing course, he strode toward the chained Witch and bent down, now face-to-face with her.

"What are you talking about?" he growled, looking down his nose at her as ragged breaths heaved out of his lungs.

She ignored his snarling question as she lazily slid her eyes away from Eleri's unmoving form—frozen in agony with a silent shout hanging off her open mouth—to him. "You look well, Prince. Something's changed within you since I saw you last."

Kai started. "You've never seen me—"

The Witch cackled again, her eyes lighting up with menacing mirth. "Oh, Kai. I know you better than you know yourself. I know what moves you. I know what breaks you. The sweet sounds of anguish I used to elicit from you were some of the best I've ever heard."

What . . . What the hell is she talking about?

Kai studied her pale face and mad features. She looked amused as she watched him watch her. A knowing glint in her eyes chilled his blood.

Then, it hit him one second too late. *No.*

Kai stumbled backward, falling onto his ass. *No, it can't be.*

His world spun, tilting around him, until bile rolled up his throat from the deepest part of his stomach. That uncontrollable panic, like scattering little bugs crawling under his skin, returned in waves. Hordes of bugs this time.

"Gods . . ." Jaycen breathed out, understanding noticeable in the way his voice broke.

Kai could hear him take a few, rigid steps in their direction.

Finally, as if she was waiting for him to realize what she meant, the Witch continued. "You were my favorite toy, you know? Sure, your father was fun at first, but I quickly became bored. There's only so much you can do in one's mind." She glanced past Eleri now and settled her gaze on the king, also unmoving where he stood. Then, she turned back toward Kai. "But you? The possibilities were endless. I loved tormenting you. And in my own little way, I tormented the king as well. You know, he always begged me to stop. Praise The Daughter. He had the sweetest tears."

Lead filled Kai's stomach to the brim, weighing it down. This woman—this Witch—somehow, some way, infiltrated his father's being. Controlled him. Used him. Just as he thought the king used her.

His limbs trembled, shaking uncontrollably as he looked at this woman who forced his father's hand. Breathing became harder for him. He couldn't seem to get a full breath in. Sweat pebbled at his temples, and his heart felt like it was shattering into millions of pieces.

Kai scooted away from her even more until he was met with Rina's hand gripping onto his shoulder.

More space . . . I need more space. I need to get away from her.

The Witch, however, followed. She leaned forward until the chains at her wrists snagged tightly. A sensual smile replaced the madness. "Daddy issues look good on you—"

"Evil bitch!" Jaycen roared. He charged at the vile being before them. "You! You caused him all that pain over the years!"

The Witch's sharp gaze sliced through Jaycen, and that sensual smile twisted into wickedness. A closer look at her true self. Then, she slipped her hands out of the shackles around her wrists easily, that wicked sneer morphing into crazed enthusiasm.

I-It was all a ruse. It was all . . . fuck.

Kai whipped his head around toward his charging friend. He was a barreling behemoth. Crazed and unconfined. Fear wrapped around Kai's heart. And when Jaycen finally noticed her free wrists, he faltered.

Fuck!

But Jaycen didn't stop. He couldn't with the brisk momentum of his body, fueled by pure rage and loyalty for Kai. As he dove toward the Witch, she easily sidestepped him and gripped the top of his skull with her bony fingers, ramming his head into the stone wall behind her.

It cracked. Deep rivets in the stone spiderwebbing out from the point of contact. The pure strength of an Underworld Witch.

Blood poured out from Jaycen's hairline as he slumped to the ground, unconscious.

"Jaycen!" Kai dashed, shaking off Rina's trembling hands and fumbling for his holster. He lunged for the Witch who merely stood there and stared at his best friend's limp body with a slight tilt to her head.

Gripping her skeletal shoulder, Kai whipped the woman around and plunged his knife into her chest. He twisted and ripped it out, then, for good measure, stabbed her three more times. Thick blood poured out of the gaping slashes in her chest, oozing down her body and puddling on the floor by her bare feet. The Witch didn't scream just as he silently was. She didn't move, merely smiling at him. A knowing glint in her quickly dimming gaze.

Gray ash floated in the corner of his eyes. Turning, he saw it. His father burned, finally feeling the effects of Eleri's touch. Like the Witch, he didn't scream. He even appeared serene, as if he had accepted his fate.

This time, however, Kai's silent screams breached his lips and sliced across the room. That scream . . . laced with agony and anger, conflict boiled deep in his gut. The man he hated for fifteen Gods damned years, wasn't that man whatsoever. But the damage he did . . . that would remain forever ingrained in him. He mourned the father he could have been, the father who was forcefully taken from him.

The Witch laughed again, a wheeze slipping through the grating sound as she slumped down the wall and slid toward the ground. "This . . ." Another wheeze. "This is just the beginning. An accidental meeting turned into the perfect moment I've been waiting for."

The ash of Kai's father swirled around Eleri's body as it rose into the air. She floated, her head tilting back and arms hanging limply below her. Tendrils of opaque black smoke oozed out of the dying king and intertwined with the Witch's, like onyx ropes dancing toward each other.

The king and the Witch's smoke writhed around one another for a single breath more before they stilled, hanging in the air motionless. Waiting . . .

Like a whip, the tendrils shot toward Eleri, striking her levitating form as if it was called to her . . . as if it couldn't help but race to be with her. Her body sucked it in as another scream ripped from her raw throat. Back arching and orange hair floating around her pale skin, Eleri convulsed from the intrusion. Her face twisted in agony. And . . .

Kai's heart plummeted; his stomach knotted.

Black veins spiderwebbed from her eyes to her cheekbones. Her Witches' Marks turned an inky black, just as Witches once donned centuries ago. Her ivory skin paled even more. And then she stilled. No more screams ruptured from her lungs. Her body floated toward the ground. Her feet gracefully landed, and she opened her eyes.

Kai's breathing stopped completely as if his entire world was crashing down above him.

The rich blue pools of her eyes—irises he was mesmerized by from the moment he saw them in the charred forest—were now black voids.

"Hm . . ." Eleri said. Kai couldn't wrap his head around her voice. His Eleri's sweet, beautiful voice, yet it was not. It sounded off as if another was mixed in. "I like this body better."

52

ELERI

Darkness surrounded Eleri. A biting cold seeped down into her bones. Her muscles constricted under the constant shivers wracking her body. She blinked, trying to determine what happened.

"Where am I?" The words barely held any sound, merely breaths slipping through her chattering teeth.

Laughter—manic and crazed and distant—echoed from all directions. Looking around, she searched for the source. Nothing. Nothing but the void of black surrounded her, weighing down on her very being. Stifling.

An eerie familiarity settled into this place. It reminded her of where she had been mere minutes ago . . . At least she thought it had only been minutes. The place where the king resided. But where he sat was full of light, white surrounding his peaceful form. This . . . was anything but.

In both places lay a sense of loneliness without truly being alone. No one was here with her, yet something lurked in the background, watching her . . . observing her.

The Witch.

She was here. She must be. Turning around, searching for the woman she had come to save, Eleri was met with nothing.

"Hello?" she yelled out.

Nothing but her voice echoed back.

A whine—high pitched and anguished—resonated around her, and her stomach sank.

W-where is my beast? I hear it. I feel it. B-but I don't see it.

Suddenly, pale white eyes flashed in the distance, piercing her soul.

Eleri gasped, stumbling back with a racing heart. A sudden realization slammed into her. Two beasts were in here. One was hers who she needed—*wanted*—now more than ever. And the second was the Witch's, who somehow invaded her mind. It held a different aura. Nothing like her own creature. More sinister. More conniving. A remnant of who this Witch truly was, no longer hidden behind a weak woman's frail body.

That feeling—that realization—hurt even worse. It churned Eleri's stomach until she felt as if acid bubbled across her entire body. Feeling the Witch's venom-covered claws run down the back of her mind, Eleri sensed a hateful poison—*her* hateful poison—leaking through the cracks.

The Witch's desires and motivations seeped in like a slow trickle. Her loathing and anger beat at the corners of Eleri's vision. So much anger. Surrounding her. Taunting her.

I have to get out of here. Eleri spun, looking for a way out of this dark prison . . . for a way back to her friends, back to *Kai*.

One sharp turn stopped Eleri in her tracks. Peeking through the wall of darkness, light shone through. It was just a small dot in the vast nothingness surrounding her but light, nonetheless.

One step forward, her bare feet trudged through inky goo, pulling her deeper into this pit of despair. With another step, Eleri swore she saw a black, warped hand reach out from the ground toward her.

One more step, then another, and then another until she approached the light. It blinded her momentarily, blinking away the spots in her vision. When her eyes could focus again on the stark difference from where she was now, her heart stopped.

Kai struggled against Rina's firm grip as she held him back, practically dragging him away from her.

Why is she taking him away? Why are they leaving her? Where is Jaycen? Where is the Upper King?

Questions bombarded her—bringing her to her knees—as she observed, looking through what she assumed were her own eyes.

Trapped.

She sucked in a stuttering breath that burned her lungs. Her lips trembled. Her heart raced.

Trapped inside her mind.

"We have to go, Kai!" Rina screamed. She was red in the face as she pulled him from the broken door and dragged him down the stairs. "W-we have to regroup. We can't help them like this!"

"Eleri!" Kai shouted, clawing at anything he could to keep him there. "Jaycen!"

Repeatedly, he screamed their names, tears flowing out of his wide, panic-stricken eyes, and blood pouring from his ripped fingernails that dug into the wooden walls.

"Kai!" Eleri screamed back.

She tried to run toward him, gaining her footing again and stumbling forward before the sticky ground confined her. Falling to her hands and knees, she curled her fingers and pushed off once more. Using all the momentum her tired being could muster, she forced her limbs to move. "Kai!"

That piercing laugh was back. It rang through Eleri's head and brought her to her knees once again. It belonged to her. It sounded just as though it had when Rina last made her laugh on their trek here, but there was a raspy tone that mingled with it. Just a pitch higher, twining with her soft voice and creating something new, something *other*.

The Witch.

"Kai!" Eleri screamed again, head hanging below her shoulders as she collapsed in defeat.

Tears rolled down her nose and dropped into the inky depths beneath her, creating ripples with each soft splat.

"He cannot hear you, Princess." The Witch's voice slithered up Eleri's spine, protruding through every unseen corner. Echoing. Taunting. "Do not bother. You're mine now."

END OF BOOK ONE

Survivors of the Smoke will continue in Book 2
Beneath the Ruin

Acknowledgements

For the second time in my life, I'm staring at my computer and reflecting on the journey that got me here. My second published book. I don't even know where to start.

Above the Ashes picked me apart, taking chunks of me in the process. Writing and rewriting and editing and revising, it was one of the hardest things I've done. I think there was a fear within me—one so deep and terrifying it was hard to acknowledge—because after The Shackled Serpent, I felt pressure. It was as if there were expectations from readers and the weight of it was overwhelming. What if I didn't live up to it? What if I disappointed them?

But in truth, I think that's what makes this book so special. There were a lot of firsts this time when it came to my writing and my process in getting published, and a lot of scary unknowns that made it such a stressful and uncertain journey. But in the long run, I believe it was for the best. My writing improved. My outlining and plotting skills also improved. I'm finally learning that while I hope my readers love the story I've crafted, I'm proud of the end result and nothing can take that away from me. I'm so thankful for this story and the growth I've felt as an author while writing it.

I wasn't alone in this journey either. So many people supported me.

First, my incredible developmental editor and writing coach, Cianne. You are truly a godsend. You read my very messy early draft and helped guide me as I rewrote the entire book, changed the tense, and added more in-depth world building and character motivation. You pointed out things I never thought of or quickly brushed over and taught me to refine my writing. Thank you for allowing me to bounce ideas off you and for talking me through this epic journey! I'm so grateful for you.

Samantha, my line editor and proofreader. You keep me concise. Helping me sift through my writing to make sure it's the best it can be is no easy feat with my constant questions and changes. I appreciate everything you do!

Susan, my blurb writer, proofreader, and dear friend. You came into my life through my writing, and I'm so thankful for all your love and support while you talk me through plot holes and road bumps. You have such a gift for taking my words and crafting them into the perfect blurb and being my final set of eyes before I publish. I'm so grateful for your hard work and friendship!

My amazing cover designer and illustrator, Rena. Thank you for your flexibility when I want to change the simplest things. You craft the worlds I create and bring them to life in the most stunning ways. I will never not be in awe of your talent. Thank you, thank you, thank you!

Amarin, you took my somewhat vague and messy character descriptions and created the most perfect character art pieces. It felt like you were able to read my mind, plucking out what I had envisioned and putting it on paper. My characters have come to life because of you. Thank you for that!

My sensitivity reader, Nev. I cover some heavy topics in this story, and because of you and your advice, I feel like I've represented those who have gone through this correctly. I'm incredibly thankful for your notes and guidance!

To my friends whose support never wavered, thank you. I don't know what I would do without you. You know who you are. I love y'all so much.

And lastly, my family. Your unconditional love fuels me in the best ways possible. You may not understand everything that goes into writing and publishing, but that never stops you from asking questions and engaging in my process. I'm always so grateful for your support. I wouldn't be here without you!

MORE FROM K.M. LISTER

**"KNOW THE TRUTH, MAEVE.
EMBRACE THE TRUTH.
SPEAK THE TRUTH."**

THE SHACKLED SERPENT AVAILABLE
ON AMAZON, KINDLE UNLIMITED,
BARNESANDNOBLE.COM, AND MORE!

About the Author

K.M. Lister is a native Texan who spent her childhood imagining stories and scenarios any chance she got—on the playground, in the shower, under the covers when she was supposed to be sleeping…you name it. She studied Communications and Media Studies at Texas A&M University—Corpus Christi and went into the journalism field soon after graduation. While she has a passion for news, her mind always drifts to her true love: the endless amounts of stories that fill her heart. As a lover of angst, K.M. hopes her stories speak to her readers while bringing out emotions that might be hard to swallow.

Be sure to follow K.M. on her social media for any writing news.

@earthtokace

kmlister.com